"You go without me," she said.

Owen looked at her as if she'd lost her mind. "I am not leaving you," he growled.

The sudden urge to wrap her arms around his neck and kiss him caught her off guard. She'd set aside those nascent feelings of attraction to Owen a long time ago, valuing his loyal friendship far more than she valued any sort of sexual attraction she might feel toward him. To have it come back now, in this awful situation, was confounding.

"Now!" Owen growled, and he tugged her with him through the underbrush to their next bit of cover.

So far, she and Owen seemed to be staying ahead of the danger rustling around in the woods behind them.

But what would happen if they ran out of woods?

FUGITIVE BRIDE

BY
PAULA GRAVES

MILLS & BOON

First Published in Great Britain 2017
By Mills & Boon, an imprint of HarperCollins*Publishers*
1 London Bridge Street, London, SE1 9GF

© 2017 Paula Graves

ISBN: 978-0-263-92867-9

46-0317

Our policy is to use papers that are natural, renewable and recyclable products and made from wood grown in sustainable forests. The logging and manufacturing processes conform to the legal environmental regulations of the country of origin.

Printed and bound in Spain
by CPI, Barcelona

Paula Graves, an Alabama native, wrote her first book at the age of six. A voracious reader, Paula loves books that pair tantalizing mystery with compelling romance. When she's not reading or writing, she works as a creative director for a Birmingham advertising agency and spends time with her family and friends. Paula invites readers to visit her website, www.paulagraves.com.

For Melissa, whose cheerleading got me
to the end of this book.

Chapter One

The afternoon was perfect for a wedding, currently sunny and mild, with no hint of rain in the forecast until after the ceremony. Staring out the bride's room window at the blooming dogwood trees that lined the church lawn, Tara Bentley had the urge to check her to-do list to see if "achieve a perfect day" was somewhere on the page.

Everything she had so meticulously planned had fallen into place with ease. Her dress fit perfectly. The white tulip bouquet brought out the delicate floral pattern of the lace in her veil. Her wavy hair had, for once, cooperated when the hairdresser straightened it and twisted it into a sleek chignon low at the back of her head, where the snowy veil provided a striking contrast. And she was ten minutes ahead of schedule, which gave Tara a few moments to simply breathe and think about what came next.

Robert. He came next. Robert James Mallory III, successful lawyer and all-around Mr. Perfect. Literally.

Two years ago, as her midtwenties suddenly became her almost-thirties, Tara had written out her list of perfect traits for a potential mate. It hadn't been a particularly long list—she might be hyperorganized and prone to overpreparing, but she wasn't a robot. People weren't ever really perfect, so her list included only things that would be deal breakers.

Things like honesty. Hard work. Respect for her mind. Ambition. And, okay, a few bonus wishes, like a man who was good-looking, fit and amusing.

Three dates with Robert Mallory, and Tara knew she'd met the man who ticked off every item on her checklist. Now she was less than an hour from marrying him.

"I'm so happy," she told the green-eyed woman who stared back at her in the full-length mirror by the vanity table.

Her reflection looked skeptical.

Dang it.

She turned away from the mirror and sat on the small vanity bench, taking care not to wrinkle her wedding dress. Without planning it, she snaked out her hand and snagged the cell phone lying next to her makeup bag. She gave the lock screen a quick swipe and hit the first number on her speed dial.

A familiar, growly voice answered on the second ring, his soft drawl as warm as a fuzzy blanket on a cold Kentucky night. "Shouldn't you be practicing your vows?"

"Owen, am I making a mistake?"

Owen Stiles was quiet for a second. When he spoke again, the lightness of his earlier tone had disappeared. "What's happened?"

The serious tone of his voice made her stomach hurt. What was she doing, dragging poor Owen into her self-doubts? As if he hadn't already suffered half a lifetime of being her sounding board and shoulder to cry on.

"Nothing. Forget I said anything. See you soon." She ended the call and set the phone on the vanity table again.

A few seconds later, the phone trilled, sliding sideways on the table with the vibration. Tara didn't even look at the display. She knew who it was. She picked up the phone. "Owen, I told you it's nothing."

"If you're wondering if you made a mistake, it's not nothing. Are you in the bride's room?"

"Owen—"

His rumbly voice deepened. "I'll be there in two minutes."

"Owen, don't." Her voice rose in frustration. "Please. Just stay where you are. Everything is fine."

There was a long pause before he spoke again. "Are you sure?"

"Positive. Today is absolutely perfect. Beautiful weather, the sanctuary is gorgeous, my dress fits perfectly and I'm marrying the most perfect man in the world. Nothing can possibly be wrong on a day like this." She stared at the bride in the vanity-table mirror, defiance glaring from her green eyes.

"If you're sure." Owen didn't sound convinced.

"I'll see you at the altar." She hung up the phone again and set it in front of her, her hand flattened against the display.

"Nothing will go wrong," she said to the woman in the mirror.

The bride stared back at her, unconvinced.

It was just cold feet. Everybody got cold feet, right?

This was where having a mom around would have come in handy. Orphanhood sucked. Her mom had died when she was small, and her father had never remarried before his death three years ago. Not that Dale Bentley would have been much help on a day like today. "Suck it up, soldier," she muttered aloud, mimicking her father's gravelly growl. "Make a decision and stick to it."

Man, she missed the old sergeant. He'd have known what to make of Robert. He'd have known whether or not Tara really loved the man or if she loved the idea of him instead.

That was the sticking point, wasn't it? She just wasn't sure she loved the man she was less than an hour away from marrying.

She pushed to her feet. What in the world was she doing getting married if she wasn't sure she loved the man? Had she lost her mind? Was she so addicted to her stupid lists that she trusted them over her own heart?

She had to tell Robert what she was feeling. Talk to him, let him try to talk her out of it. Then she'd know, wouldn't she?

You already know, Tara. Listen to your gut.

Maybe she already knew, but either way, she had to tell Robert. And now, before it was too late.

She was halfway to the door when a knock sounded from the other side. She crossed to the door and leaned her ear close. "Yes?"

The voice from the other side was male and unfamiliar. "Ms. Bentley? There's a package outside we need you to sign for."

"A package?" Sent here, to the church? That was strange. "I'm not expecting anything."

"I don't know, ma'am. It's just for you and it requires a signature. You want me to tell them to send it back?"

"No," she said quickly, curiosity overcoming her impatience. Maybe a distraction was just what she needed to get her head out of her navel for a few minutes. Robert would still be on the other end of the church with his groomsmen, so it wasn't like he'd accidentally get a peek at her dress before the wedding, right?

Assuming there was even going to be a wedding…

Stop it. Just go see what the package is. One thing at a time.

She opened the door to a tall, broad-shouldered man wearing a blue polo shirt and khaki pants. "Hi," she said, feeling a little sheepish as he took in her seed pearl–studded dress and tulle veil. "It's my wedding day."

"I see that." He nodded toward the door down the hall that led to the church's parking lot. "Out here."

She followed him down the hall and out the door, taking care as she crossed the threshold not to let the skirt of her dress get caught in the door closing behind her. Once her dress cleared the door, she started to turn her attention back to the deliveryman, but something dropped over her face suddenly, obscuring her view.

Instinctively sucking in a quick breath, she got a lungful of something sweet and cloying. Her lungs seemed to seize up in response, making it hard to take another breath. Fighting panic, she tried to lift her hands to push the offending material off her face. But thick, strong arms roped around her body, holding her arms in place. Her head began to swim, her throat closing off as she struggled for oxygen. She seemed to float into the air, which was impossible. Wasn't it? She wasn't floating. People didn't float.

Somewhere close by, she thought she heard a voice shouting her name. It sounded familiar, but her suddenly fuzzy brain couldn't make sense of what she was hearing. Then she heard a swift thump and the voice went silent.

There was a metallic clank and suddenly she wasn't floating anymore. She landed with a painful thud onto a hard, cold surface, unable to make sense of what was happening to her. The sweet, slightly medicinal smell permeated everything, seeping into her brain as if it were a sponge soaking up all those heady fumes.

Another thud shook the floor beneath her, and something solid and warm settled against her back. She struggled against the encroaching darkness, one lingering part of her acutely aware that something terribly wrong was happening to her. Today was supposed to be her wedding day, even if she'd decided it was a wedding she didn't want.

She should be looking for Robert to tell him what she'd decided. She had to let people know the wedding was off. She had to call the florists to take away the beautiful roses and tulips that festooned the sanctuary. She supposed she could let the reception go on as planned, feed everyone as an apology for her attack of cold feet.

She had too much to do to be sinking deeper and deeper into the darkness now spreading through her fuzzy brain. But within seconds, she could no longer remember what those things were.

Slowly, inexorably, darkness fell.

OWEN STILES WOKE to darkness and movement. He tried to lift his hands to the hard ache at the back of his head, but his arms wouldn't move. He was bound, he realized, animal panic rising in his throat. He forced it down, trying to remember what he'd learned at Campbell Cove Academy.

First, ascertain where you are and what the danger is.

The where was easy enough. He was in the white van that had been parked outside the church when he went looking for Tara.

He hadn't liked the way she'd sounded on the phone. And if he was brutally honest with himself, there was a part of him that had been nearly giddy with hope that she was going to call off the wedding.

He wasn't proud of feeling that way. His love for Tara was unconditional. Her happiness meant everything to him.

But he couldn't deny that he wanted her to be happy with him, not some blow-dried, Armani-wearing Harvard Law graduate with a chiseled jaw and a cushy job with a top Louisville law firm.

Ignoring her command to stay put, he'd turned the corner of the hallway that led to the bride's room just in time to see a wedge of tulle and lace disappear through the exit door about twenty yards away.

Hurrying out after her, he'd been just in time to see a large man throw a pillowcase over Tara's head and haul her into a white panel van parked in front of the door. He'd called her name, shock overcoming good sense, and earned a punch that had knocked him into the side of the van. At least, that was the last thing he could remember.

Okay, so he'd ascertained where he was. And the fact that he was trussed up inside the moving van made the danger fairly clear, although he couldn't see anyone lurking around, ready to knock him out again, so he supposed that was a plus.

The back of the van seemed to be closed off from the driver's cab area by a metal panel. That fact posed a problem—he couldn't see how many people were in the front of the van, so he couldn't be sure exactly what he was up against. However, he had seen only two men wrestling with Tara, and they'd both been big guys. He wasn't sure there was room in the van's cab to accommodate more people.

So there were probably two bad guys to deal with. And thanks to the closed-off cab, he could move around unobserved, which would give him a better chance of working out a way to escape.

He felt warmth behind him. Tara?

With a grimace of pain, he rolled over and peered through the gloom. A bundle of silk, lace and tulle lay on the floor of the van beside him. The pillowcase over her head was still there, and he caught a whiff of a faintly sweet, medicinal odor coming from where she lay.

He wriggled closer, ignoring the pounding ache in his head, until his face lay close to the pillowcase. The odor was much stronger suddenly, giving off fumes that made him feel light-headed.

Ether, he thought. The pillowcase was soaked with ether.

Those idiots! Ether could be deadly if used without care, and they weren't even monitoring her condition.

He jerked at the bindings that held his arms behind his back to no avail. They'd apparently duct-taped his hands together. They weren't going to come apart easily. But he had to get the pillowcase off Tara's head.

Wriggling closer, he gripped the top of the pillowcase with his teeth. The smell of ether nearly overwhelmed him, but he held his breath and tugged upward. Inch by harrowing inch, he dragged the ether-soaked pillowcase from Tara's head until he finally pulled it free.

He spat the taste of ether out of his mouth. Then, his heart in his throat, he leaned over to make sure Tara was still breathing. A few terrifying seconds passed before he felt her breath on his cheek. Shaking with relief, he pressed a kiss to her forehead. "That's my girl. Stay with me, sweetheart."

As he waited for her to come around, Owen started working on the tape that bound his wrists together. His eyes had finally adjusted to the darkness inside the van, giving him a better look at their immediate surroundings.

The interior of the cargo van was empty except for Owen and Tara. Also, what he'd mistaken for a closed panel between them and the front cab wasn't technically closed. There was a large mesh window in the panel that should have given him a look at the occupants of the cab. But their captors had covered the mesh opening with what looked like cardboard, not only blocking out any light coming through the front windows but also keeping them from hearing whatever conversation might be going on between their captors.

The upside to that, Owen thought, was that their captors probably couldn't hear much of what was going on in the back of the van, either.

He looked around for any sharp edges he could use to tear the tape around his wrists. The covering over the wheel well was bolted to the floor of the van, but the bolts were old and worn, not providing much of a cutting edge. Still, he scooted over to the nearest bolt and gave it a try.

The van must have left Mercerville Highway, he realized a few minutes later when the swaying of the vehicle increased, forcing him to plant his feet on the cargo hold's ridged floor to keep from toppling over with each turn. But he couldn't stop Tara from rolling across the floor. A moment later, her head knocked into his hip with a soft thud.

"Ow," she muttered, her voice thick and slurred.

"Oh, sweetheart, there you are," he said softly, twisting so that his bound hands could reach the side of her face. He brushed away the grit on her cheek with his fingers. "Tara, can you hear me?"

Her head lifted, her hair and the torn remains of her tulle veil obscuring part of her face. "Owen?"

"Yeah, it's me. Careful," he added when she tried to sit up and nearly fell over.

She managed to steady herself in a sitting position and shoved her hair and the veil away from her face with clumsy hands. They, too, were secured by duct tape, he saw, though her captors had bound her hands in front of her rather than behind her. She seemed to belatedly notice the bindings and stared at her wrists. "What's happening?"

"We've been abducted," he said, though he wasn't sure *abduction* was the right term. Neither of them was exactly rolling in dough, so he didn't imagine they'd been taken for ransom purposes. Tara's fiancé was successful but not what anyone would term wealthy. Not yet, anyway.

So why *had* the men grabbed her?

"That's insane," she muttered, still pawing at her veil, which sat askew on her head. "Why am I so woozy?"

"They put a pillowcase over your head." He waved his hand at the offending piece of material lying against the front of the cargo hold. "I think it was soaked with ether."

"Ether?" Tara finally pulled her veil free and threw it on the floor beside her. The van took another turn, forcing Owen to brace himself against the side of the cargo hold. Tara was unprepared, however, and went sprawling against his side, her nose bumping into his shoulder.

"Ow." She righted herself, rubbing her nose. She finally noticed Owen's bound hands, her eyes widening. "You're tied up, too."

"Think you can get the tape off me? Then I'll return the favor." He twisted around until his back was facing her.

"My fingers aren't working so well," she warned him as she started fumbling with the tape. She wasn't lying; it took a full minute before she was able to find the end of the tape on his bindings and start to slowly unwrap his wrists. But she finally ripped away the last of the tape, making the flesh on his wrists sting.

He stretched his aching arms, grimacing at the pain.

"What time is it?" Tara asked.

He pressed the button on his watch that lit up the dial. "Just a little after four."

"Oh."

He turned to look at Tara. "You were supposed to get married at four."

She nodded. "I was supposed to."

He reached for her, taking her bound hands in his. "We'll get you back there, Tara. We'll get out of this and get to a phone so you can call Robert and tell him what happened. And then we'll get you back to the church and you'll get married just the way you planned—"

"I was going to call it off."

He went still. "What?"

In the low light he couldn't make out much about her features, but the tone of her voice was somewhere between sad and embarrassed. "I was going to call it off. Right before that guy knocked on the door and told me there was a package outside."

"That's how they got you outside to the van?"

"Yeah." She wriggled her bound hands at him. "Get this off me, please?"

He pulled the tape from her wrists, taking care with the last few inches to spare her as much of the sting as possible. When she was free, he rolled up the tape from both of their bindings and shoved it in his pocket. It might come in handy if they could get themselves out of this van alive.

Freed from her restraints, Tara curled into a knot beside him, wrapping her arms around her knees. The puffy skirt of her wedding dress ballooned around her, almost glowing in the low light, making her look like a piece of popcorn.

Owen had the clarity of mind not to speak that thought aloud.

He put his arm around her, trying not to read too much into the way she snuggled closer to him. They were in the middle of an abduction. Of course she was seeking a little comfort from the guy who'd been her best friend since middle school.

"What do they want?"

"I don't know," he admitted. "I don't suppose Robert is secretly a multimillionaire with a hefty trust fund?"

"Not that he's ever told me." She made a soft mewling noise. "I am so woozy. They used ether?"

"That's what it smelled like to me."

She cocked her head toward him. "Exactly how do you know what ether smells like?"

"I took a history of medicine course in college, when I was still considering a medical degree."

"And they let you sniff ether?"

Tara's skeptical tone made him smile. She was sounding more like her old self, which meant the effects of the ether were wearing off. "Not on purpose."

He glanced to the far side of the van's cargo hold, where he'd thrown the ether-soaked pillowcase. In this confined area, the fumes it emitted might still be affecting them, he realized.

"We need to find a way to wrap up that pillowcase so that we limit the fumes it's putting out in this van," he told Tara. "I wish I had a garbage bag or something."

"Don't suppose you carry one of those around in your back pocket?"

"Not in a rented tux, no," he answered with a grin, feeling a little less grim about their chances of survival now that his smart-ass Tara was back. He shrugged off his jacket. "I can wrap it in this."

"The rental place isn't going to like that," Tara warned.

"Not sure it's enough, though."

"Well, I have about twenty yards of silk, lace and tulle you can use." Holding his shoulder, she levered herself to her feet and started to tug at the seams of her skirt until the fabric tore free. In the darkness of the van's enclosed interior, Owen couldn't make out much besides a cloud of faint brightness in the gloom floating away from her body. Tara gathered the fabric into a ball and presented it to him. "Will this do?"

He crossed carefully to the corner of the cargo hold, feeling a distinct unsteadiness he attributed to the moving van, although he should be a lot more worried about the blow he'd taken to the head. He'd been unconscious long enough for their captors to shove him inside the van and tie him up. He might have a concussion. Or worse.

But for now, he was conscious. His head didn't hurt too badly. And he had a job to do.

He wrapped up the pillowcase inside the layers of silk, tulle and lace, and pushed it back into the corner. Already, the distinctively sweet scent of the ether was almost gone.

Gingerly, he edged his way back to where Tara perched on the wheel well cover. "That should take care of—"

The van gave a hard lurch, sending him toppling over. He landed hard on his side, pain shooting through his rib cage and hip.

"Owen!" Tara grabbed his arms and helped him to a sitting position. "Are you all right?"

He rubbed his side, reassuring himself that nothing was broken. "I'm okay—" He broke off, aware that something had changed suddenly.

The engine. He no longer heard the engine noise, or felt the vibration beneath them.

The van had come to a stop.

Chapter Two

Most of the haziness left in her brain from the ether disappeared in a snap when Tara heard the van's engine shut off.

"We've stopped." She looked up at Owen, wishing he wasn't just a shadowy silhouette in the gloom. Sometimes just the sight of him, so controlled and serious, could make her feel as if everything in the world would be okay. At least she could hear his voice, that low Kentucky drawl that had always steadied her like a rock, even in the midst of the craziness life had a habit of throwing her way. "What are they going to do to us now?"

"I don't know. Maybe nothing." He didn't sound confident.

She reached across the narrow space between them and grabbed his hands. "We need a plan."

"We don't have anything to fight with, Tara."

"Yes, we do." She squeezed his hands and pushed to her feet, heading for the corner where he'd buried the pillowcase inside the remains of her skirt. She grabbed the whole bundle and brought it to where Owen waited.

She saw the faintest glimmer in his eyes when he looked at her, just a hint of light in the darkness. "You are brilliant, sweetheart."

"There were two of them. One who came to get me, telling me there was a package waiting for me, and one standing by the van. I think he was the one who put the pillowcase over my head." She kept her voice low, in case their voices carried outside the van. "They think we're still tied up. At least, we'd better hope they do."

"It'll still take two of them to get us out, so we won't have an advantage. Except surprise."

She grabbed his hand and gave it a squeeze. "Surprise can go a long way. So, first one through the door gets the ether pillowcase over his head."

"And we shove him back onto the second guy while he's off guard."

She looked at Owen, wishing she could see him more clearly. "Think this has a chance of working?"

"No clue, but it's all we've got. So let's make it work." He reached across and gripped her hands briefly. Then he unwrapped the pillowcase from the dress skirt.

The sickly sweet odor of the ether made Tara's stomach twist, but with a little effort she controlled her nerves. She had one job—to fight with every ounce of strength and will she had to get out of this dangerous spot.

At least she wasn't alone. Owen was with her, and if there was one thing in her life she knew completely, it was that Owen would do everything he could to keep her safe. He'd been doing that for her since high school.

The back door of the van rattled, and Tara's heart skipped a beat. She sneaked a quick look at Owen and found him staring at the door, his focus complete.

He'd undergone training at Campbell Cove Academy, which was part of the security company where he now worked, but Tara hadn't really given much thought to what that training entailed. After all, Owen was a computer geek. Computer geeks didn't have much need for ninja skills, did they?

He'd been teased as a child because his skills and tal-

ents lent themselves to academic pursuits instead of sports.
Even his own father had undermined Owen, calling him
weak and inept because he wouldn't try out for the football team in high school.

Tara wished some of those people could see Owen right
now, ready to take on two possibly armed men in order
to protect her.

The door to the van opened, and light invaded the back
of the van, blinding Tara for a long panicky moment, until
a rush of movement from Owen's side of the door spurred
her into motion. Her vision adjusted in time for her to see
Owen jamming the pillowcase over a man's head and giving him a push backward. The man fell over like a bowling
pin, toppling the other man who stood right behind him.

Owen grabbed Tara's hand. "Jump!" he yelled as he
jerked her with him out the back door of the van.

She saw the two men on the ground struggling to right
themselves. It wouldn't be long before they did, she realized. The thought spurred her to run faster. Thank God
she'd opted for low-heeled pumps for her wedding, she
thought as she ran across the blacktop road and into the
woods on the other side, her hand still firmly clasped in
Owen's.

The pumps proved themselves more problematic once
they hit the softer ground of the woods. Behind her, the
men they'd just escaped started shouting for them to stop,
punctuating their calls with a couple of gunshots that made
Tara's blood turn to ice. But, as far as she could tell, none
of the shots got anywhere near them.

"Come on," Owen urged, pulling her with him as he
zigzagged though the woods. It took a couple of minutes
to realize there was a method to his seemingly mad dash
through the trees. They were moving from tree to tree,
finding cover from their pursuers.

What was left of her wedding dress was a liability, she realized with dismay. The white fabric stood out in the dark woods like a beacon. At least Owen's tux was black. He blended into the trees much better than she could hope to do.

"You go without me," she said as they took temporary cover behind the wide trunk of an oak tree. "I'm the one they're after. I stick out like a hooker in a church in this dress. You could find help and send the police after the van. You could tell Robert what happened."

Owen looked at her as if she'd lost her mind. "I am not leaving you," he growled.

The sudden urge to wrap her arms around his neck and kiss him caught her off guard. She'd set aside those nascent feelings of attraction to Owen a long time ago, valuing his loyal friendship far more than she valued any sort of sexual attraction she might feel toward him. To have it come back now, in this awful situation, was confounding.

"Now!" Owen growled, and he tugged her with him through the underbrush to their next bit of cover.

Behind them, the sound of their pursuers was close enough to spur their forward movement. But the men following them weren't any closer, Tara realized. So far, she and Owen seemed to be staying ahead of the danger pursuing them.

But what would happen if they ran out of woods?

A brisk breeze had picked up as they ran, rustling the leaves overhead. Thank heaven for spring growth; two months ago, these woods would have been winter bare and couldn't have provided them with nearly enough cover. But even here in the Kentucky mountains, the woods couldn't go on forever, which could be a good thing or a bad thing. If they managed to find a well-populated town around the next copse, they'd be safe.

But if they ran into a clearing with neither cover nor the safety of numbers to protect them…

"How long do you think they'll keep chasing us?" she asked breathlessly as they crouched behind another tree.

"I don't know," Owen admitted. "I don't suppose you know why they grabbed you. Did they give you any indication?"

"No, it's like I told you—one of the men came to get me and the other put the pillowcase over my head before I could even get a good look at his face. Although he definitely asked for me by name. Ms. Bentley." She risked a peek around the side of the tree providing them with cover. "I don't see them anymore."

"I don't think we should move anytime soon. They may be hunkered down, waiting to flush us out."

Tara frowned. "How long are we talking?"

"I don't know. A couple of hours?"

She grimaced. "I suppose it's a bad time to mention that I desperately need to pee."

Owen gave a soft huff of laughter. "Can you hold it awhile?"

"Do I have any choice?"

"No."

"Well, there you go."

Owen gave her a look that made her insides melt a little. She might have decided years ago that she'd rather be his friend forever than risk losing him by taking their relationship to a more sexual place, but that didn't mean she wasn't aware that he found her just as attractive as she found him.

And right now he was looking at her as if he wanted to strip her naked and slake his thirst for her up against the rough trunk of this big oak tree.

Oh, God, Tara, you're hiding from crazy kidnappers and you choose now to conjure up that visual?

"I think I know where we are," Owen murmured a few minutes later.

Moving only her eyes, Tara scanned the woods around them, seeing only trees, trees and more trees. "How on earth is that possible?" she whispered.

"Because while you went to cheerleading camp, I went to Boy Scout camp."

"And what, got a badge in telling one gol dang leafy tree from another?" Staying still was starting to get to her already. She wasn't the kind of woman who stayed still. Ever. And the urge to look behind them to see if their captors were sneaking up on them was almost more than she could bear.

"No," Owen said with more patience than she deserved. "It's because I stayed in a rickety little cabin with five other boys about two hundred yards to our east."

She slanted a look at him. "How can you possibly know that?"

"See that big tree right ahead? The one with the large moon-shaped scar on the trunk about five feet up?"

She peered through the trees. "No."

"Well, trust me, it's there. And that moon shape is there because Billy Turley and I carved it in the trunk on a dare. Our camp counselor didn't buy that we were trying out our trailblazing skills like Daniel Boone before us."

There had never been a time in her life when she'd felt less like smiling, but the image conjured up by Owen's words made her lips curve despite herself. She and Owen had met around the time they were both in sixth grade. In fact, she could remember Owen taking that trip to the woods because she'd been over-the-moon excited about being invited to cheerleading camp, since only girls who went to the camp in middle school ever made the varsity squad in high school.

Oh, for the days when life was so simple that her biggest worry was crash-landing a herkie jump in front of twenty other judgmental preteen girls.

"I know you're about ready to squirm out of your skin," Owen said quietly, slipping his hand into hers, "but I have a plan."

She curled her fingers around his. "Okay. What is it?"

"As soon as I'm pretty sure our kidnappers have retreated, we'll head for the cabin."

She looked up at him, narrowing her eyes. "The one you stayed in twenty years ago when you were eleven?"

"I think it's still there."

"Maybe, but in what kind of condition?"

His lips flattened with exasperation. She felt his grip on her hand loosen. "Must you always be so negative?"

She tightened her fingers around his again. "Yes. But sorry."

He gave her fingers a light squeeze. "I suppose it's part of your charm."

"Sweet talker," she muttered.

"So we're agreed? We head for the cabin?"

"If it's still there." She looked up. "Sorry. Negativity."

"If it's still there," he agreed. "And we'd better hope it is."

The dark tone of his growly voice made her stomach turn a flip. "Why's that?"

"You know how the wind has picked up?"

"Yeah?"

"I think the rain may be getting here a little earlier than expected tonight."

Owen was right. Within a few minutes, the brisk wind began to carry needles of rain from which the spring growth overhead provided only partial shelter. Owen tried to tuck Tara under his coat, but the rain became relentless as daylight waned, darkness falling prematurely because of the lowering sky.

Tara wiped the beading water from her watch face. Nearly six. The wedding would have long been over by now, if she'd gone through with it. Robert must be going crazy, wondering what happened to her. Her car would still be in the parking lot, her purse in the bride's room. The only thing missing was the bride and her puffy white dress.

Would everyone realize something had gone very wrong? Or would they assume that Tara had succumbed to cold feet and bolted without letting anyone know?

Was Robert thinking he'd just made a narrow escape from a lifetime with a lunatic?

Stop it, Tara. This is not your fault.

Owen was right. She was way too negative. She added it to her mental list of things she needed to work on, right behind cellulite on her thighs and—oh, yeah—running away from dangerous, crazy kidnappers.

"You're thinking, aren't you?" Owen asked. "I always worry when you're thinking."

"I'm thinking I haven't heard anything from the kidnappers back there recently. I'm also thinking that there may be ants crawling up my legs. And I'm thinking if I have to hide behind this tree for a minute longer, getting soaked to the skin, I'm going to run crazy through the trees, screaming *I give up! Come get me!* at the top of my lungs."

Owen turned toward her, cupping her face between his hands. His fingers were cool, but the look in his eyes was scalding hot. "I know you're scared. I know wisecracking and complaining is how you show it. And you're right. We haven't heard those guys recently. I don't think they were eager to spend the rest of their day hunting you down in the woods when they know who you are and can take a chance on grabbing you another time."

She stared up at him. "You really think they'll try this again?"

"You said they asked for you by name."

"But why? I'm not rich. Robert's not even rich, not really. Not enough to warrant a risky daylight abduction."

"I know. But even if you can't think of a reason, they clearly had one." He dropped his hands to his sides. "It's time to make a run for it. You ready?"

"Born ready." She flashed him a cheeky grin, even if she felt like crying. It earned her one of Owen's deliciously sexy smiles in return, and he touched her face again. His fingers were cold, but heat seemed to radiate through her from his touch.

He grabbed her hand and started running, pulling her behind him.

Even though she'd convinced herself that their captors had given up and made their escape, every muscle in Tara's body tensed as she zigzagged behind Owen, her heart in her throat. Every twig that snapped beneath her feet sounded as thunderous as a gunshot, even through the masking hiss of the falling rain.

Two hundred yards to the cabin, Owen had said. Surely they'd run two hundred yards by now. That was two football fields, wasn't it?

Owen jerked sideways suddenly, nearly flinging her off her feet. He grabbed her around the waist as she started to slide across the muddy ground and kept her upright. "There," he said, satisfaction coloring his voice.

Tara followed his gaze and saw what looked to be a ramshackle wooden porch peeking out from the overgrowth about twenty yards away.

"You have got to be kidding me," she muttered.

His lips pressed to a thin line. "Shelter is shelter, Tara."

He let go of her hand and started toward the wooden structure with a brisk, determined stride.

She stood watching him for a moment, feeling terrible. The man had saved her life, and she'd been nothing but a whining ingrate.

Lighting flashed overhead, followed quickly by a bone-rattling boom of thunder that shook her out of her misery and sent her dashing through the muddy undergrowth as fast as her ruined pumps would carry her. She skidded to a stop at the edge of the porch and stared at what Owen had called a cabin.

It was tiny. She didn't have any idea how Owen and his fellow Boy Scouts had managed to squeeze themselves inside the place. The three shallow steps leading up to the porch looked rickety and dangerous, though apparently they'd managed to hold Owen's weight, for he was already on the porch, peering inside the darkened doorway of the small structure.

"I remember it as being bigger," he said quietly.

"You were eleven." She made herself risk the steps. They were sturdier than they looked, though the rain had left them slick. At least the stair railing didn't wiggle too much as she climbed to the porch and joined Owen in the doorway.

Years had clearly passed since any Boy Scouts had darkened the door of this cabin. What she could see in the gloom looked damp and dilapidated. The musty smell of age and disuse filled Tara's lungs as she took a shaky breath. "The roof leaks, doesn't it?"

Owen took a step inside. Almost immediately, he jerked back, bumping into Tara. She had to grab him around the waist to keep from falling.

Something small and gray scuttled out the door past

them, scampered off the porch and disappeared into the undergrowth.

"Possum," Owen said.

Tara grimaced. "So that's what I'm smelling."

He whipped around to look at her. "I'm sorry I've disappointed you. Again."

She grabbed his hand. "You saved me. I wouldn't have gotten out of there without you."

He gave her hand a little squeeze before letting go. "If it weren't for you, I'd have never gotten loose from that duct tape."

And he'd never have been in trouble if she hadn't called him to share her doubts about the wedding. Which maybe she wouldn't be having if she didn't still find Owen so darn attractive.

They could play this game forever, going all the way back to sixth grade when she saved Owen from a bully and he'd helped her pass math.

They were darn near symbiotic at this point.

"You're thinking again," Owen murmured.

"I am," she said. "I'm thinking if we're planning on hunkering down here until the rain passes, I'd like to make sure there's no possum surprises waiting for me in there. Any chance we could find a candle or two in this godforsaken place?"

"Maybe." Owen entered the dark cabin. A moment later, she heard more than saw him scrabbling around in a drawer. "Ha." He reached into the pocket of his tuxedo pants and pulled out something. A second later, a small light flickered in the darkness.

"You had a lighter in your pants pocket?"

"I wanted to be sure your candle lighting at the wedding went off without a hitch." He shot her a sheepish grin. "I take my man-of-honor duties seriously."

Her insides melted, and she crossed to where he stood, wrapping her arms around his waist and pressing her face to his chest. "You're the best man of honor ever."

He rubbed his free hand down her arm. "Oh, Tara, you're freezing. You really need to get out of those wet clothes."

"And into what?" she asked, her voice coming out softer and sultrier than she'd intended.

He stared back at her, wordless, his eyes smoldering as strongly as the flickering candle in his hand. The moment stretched between them, electric and fraught with danger.

And forbidden desires...

A loud thud sounded outside the door, and in a flash, Owen extinguished the candle and pulled Tara behind him.

There was another thud. Slow. Deliberate.

Someone was outside the cabin.

Chapter Three

Owen tucked Tara more fully behind him, squaring his shoulders in an attempt to look larger than he was. What he wouldn't give to have the pecs and deltoids of Mike Strong, who'd instructed him in hand-to-hand combat during his first grueling weeks of probationary training at Campbell Cove Security Services. Strong had insisted that Owen's lean, wiry build didn't mean he couldn't hold his own in a fight, but until today, he'd never had a reason to test that theory.

And given how badly his attempt to save Tara outside the church had gone, he wasn't confident that Strong would be proven right this time, either.

He could hear his father's voice, a mean whisper in his ear. "You're weak, Owen. Life ain't kind to the weak."

Grimly shutting out that voice, he searched the shadowy interior of the cabin for something he could use as a weapon, but the place had been stripped mostly bare a long time ago, from the looks of it. There was a rickety camp bed left in one corner, and the mattress of another lying on the floor nearby, but that was all. What he wouldn't give for one of those cheap little bow and arrow sets he and the other Scouts had learned to use that summer twenty years ago.

Not that he'd remember how to use it.

The footsteps on the porch moved closer, the steps careful. Deliberate. There was an oddly light touch to the sounds that didn't remind him much of the hulking men who'd shoved him into the side of the van earlier that day. These footfalls sounded almost—

A face peered around the edge of the door. Small, pale, freckled and terrified.

A kid, no more than ten or eleven. He froze there, his face framed by the bright red hood of his rain slicker. A second later, a second face appeared next to the boy's, smaller. More feminine. She had big, dark eyes and frizzy curls framing her face beneath her pink rain hood.

Owen took a step toward them. "Hello—"

The boy opened his mouth and screamed, triggering an answering shriek in the girl. They sped off into the rainy woods, their terrified wails turning to hysterical giggles of pure adrenaline rush before they faded from earshot.

Owen felt Tara's forehead press hard against his back. "Kids?"

"That could have been us twenty years ago." Owen turned to look at her. "Sneaking around Old Man Ridley's cabin, trying to catch him red-handed at murder."

Tension seeped slowly out of her expression, a faint smile taking its place. "Remember that summer he almost caught us?"

"One of the top ten most terrifying moments of my life." He laughed softly.

"Do you think those kids will come back with grown-ups next time?"

He shook his head. "Are you kidding? They'd probably be grounded for life just for sneaking around this old cabin." He pulled out the lighter and relit the candle he'd extinguished. "Come on, let's see what kind of shelter we can make of this place."

The place was grimy and drafty, but the tin roof seemed to have weathered the years without springing leaks, which had kept the interior dry and mostly free of mildew. The cot mattresses were a disaster, but Owen uncovered an old military footlocker half hidden by the remains of one of the cots. Inside, he found a couple of camp blankets kept well preserved within the airtight trunk. They smelled of the cedar blocks someone had placed inside the trunk to ward off moths.

"Here, wrap up in this." He unfolded the top blanket and wrapped it around Tara's shoulders, not missing the shivers rattling through her. "I wish we could risk starting a fire in that fireplace," he said with a nod toward the river stone fireplace against the near wall. "But the chimney's probably blocked by now, and besides, we don't want to risk smoke alerting anyone to where we are. Not yet."

She stepped closer to him, curling into him like a kitten seeking heat. "Just hold me for a minute, okay? They say body heat is the best heat."

Owen quelled the instant reaction of his body to hers, a talent he'd honed since their early teens, when Tara's femininity blossomed in time for his hormones to rev up to high gear. She'd put deliberate boundaries between them, first unspoken ones and then, later, when he'd wanted to push those barriers out of the way, spoken ones.

"I've never had a friend like you, Owen," she'd told him that night after the high school football game when he tried to kiss her in the car after he'd driven her home. "I need you to be Owen. My best friend. We can't risk changing that. Do you understand? Boyfriends are complicated. Relationships are volatile. I have enough of that in my life."

He couldn't argue with that. Motherless since just before they'd met, Tara had struggled to connect with her rough-edged, emotionally conservative father, who'd had to give up the military life he'd loved to take care of his daughter. Tara had felt as if he resented her for the end of his Marine Corps career, which had added to the existing friction between them right up until his death.

Owen had swallowed his desire and given Tara what she needed, as much as it had cost him to do so. But the desire had never gone away, married as it was to his enduring love for his best friend.

And at times like these, with her slender body pressed so intimately to his, what was left of her clothing clinging to her body and leaving little to his imagination, tamping down that desire was a Herculean task.

"Maybe the rain will stop soon," she mumbled against his collarbone, her breath hot against his neck.

"Maybe," he agreed. "Those children must live nearby, which is promising, because when this was a Boy Scout camp years ago, there were no houses in easy walking distance at all."

She burrowed deeper in his embrace. "I wonder how I'm going to explain walking around in the woods wearing a slip, half a wedding dress and my ruined silk pumps."

"Very carefully," he answered, making her chuckle. The sound rippled through him, sparking a shudder of pure male need.

"I don't think the rain is supposed to end before morning," she said with a soft sigh that heated his throat again. "We're going to need to find somewhere to sleep tonight. And I have to say, I'm not thrilled about sharing a cot where a possum was probably nesting."

"The blankets from that chest are pretty clean. We could cover the mattresses with those."

"Mattress," she corrected.

"Mattress?"

She looked up at him, her expression serious. "It's too cold in here for us to sleep apart. Right?"

He stared at her, his heart rattling in his chest like a snare drum. He swallowed hard and forced the words from his lips. "Right. Body heat is the best heat."

He was in so much trouble.

BAGLEY COUNTY SHERIFF'S DEPARTMENT investigator Archer Trask walked slowly around the small groom's room, taking in all the details of the crime scene. There was less blood than one might expect, to begin with. The victim had taken two bullets to the base of his skull—double tap, the big-city cops would call it. A sign of a professional hit.

But who the hell would target a groom on his wedding day?

"Vic's name is Robert Mallory. The third." The responding deputy flipped a page in his notepad. "Mallory Senior works in the Lexington DA's office, and he's already screaming for us to turn this over to the Kentucky State Police."

"Any witnesses?"

"No, but the bride is missing. So's her man of honor."

Trask slanted a look at the deputy. "You're kidding."

"Nobody's seen either of them since about an hour before the wedding."

"Bride's name?"

"Tara Bentley."

Didn't sound familiar. Neither did the groom's name. "Have you talked to the bride's parents?"

"She's an orphan, it seems." The deputy grimaced. "Her side of the aisle is a little sparse."

Trask rubbed his forehead, where a headache was starting to form. Why didn't he ever get a cut-and-dried case these days? "I want the groom's parents kept apart so I can question them separately. And any of the wedding party who might have seen anything. Do we have an estimated time of death yet?"

"Last time anyone saw him was around three, about an hour before the ceremony was supposed to start. Last time anyone saw the bride was round the same time."

Trask frowned. Missing bride, dead groom, professional-looking hit—nothing seemed to fit. "You said man of honor."

The deputy flipped back a page or two in his notepad. "Owen Stiles. Apparently the bride's best friend from childhood."

Stiles. The name sounded familiar. "What do we know about Stiles?"

"Not much. His mother is here for the wedding. She's the one who told us she couldn't find him. By the way, according to the man of honor's mother, their cars are still in the church parking lot."

Trask looked up at the deputy's words. "You're telling me the bride and her best friend took a flyer and left their cars behind?"

"Looks like. We've already checked the tags and they're registered to our missing persons."

Well, now, Archer thought. That was a surprising twist. "Let's get an APB out on both of them. Persons of interest in a murder for now. We need to check if either of them have another vehicle, too."

"I'll call it in." The deputy finished jotting notes and headed out of the room.

Trask looked down at the dead man lying facedown on the floor. Poor bastard, he thought. All dressed up and nowhere to go.

"Do you, Tara, take Robert as your lawfully wedded husband? To have and to hold from this day forward. For better or worse, in sickness and in health, forsaking all others…" The pastor's intonation rang in Tara's head, making it throb. She wanted to run, but her feet were stuck to the floor as if her shoes were nailed to it. She tried to tug her feet from the shoes, but they wouldn't budge.

Breathing became difficult behind the veil that had seemed to mold itself around her head and neck, tightening at her throat. She attempted to claw it away, but the more she pulled at the veil, the more it constricted her.

"Owen!" she cried, the sound muffled and puny. She knew he was here somewhere. Owen would never let anything bad happen to her.

"I'm here." His voice was a warm rumble in her ear, but she couldn't see him.

"Owen, please."

Arms wrapped around her from behind. Owen's arms, strong and bracing. The veil fell away and she could breathe again. Her feet pulled loose from the floor and she turned to face her rescuer.

Owen gazed at her, his face so familiar, so right, even in the shadows.

"You awake now?"

The shadows cleared, and she realized where she was. It was the old Boy Scouts camp cabin in the woods. Night had passed, and with it the rain. Misty sunlight was peeking through the trees outside and slanting into the cabin through the dusty windows.

And she was wrapped up tightly in Owen's arms on the mattress they shared.

"Yes," she answered.

"You were dreaming. Must have been a bad one."

She forced a smile, the frightening remnants of her nightmare lingering. "Just a stress dream. You know, late for class."

"You called out to me."

She eased away from his embrace and sat up. "Probably wanted you to do my algebra homework for me."

He sat up, too. The blanket spilled down to his waist, revealing his lean torso. She rarely saw him shirtless, and it came as a revelation. Owen might not be bulked up like a bodybuilder, but his shoulders were broad, his stomach flat and his chest well-toned. He'd talked often about Campbell Cove Security's training facilities, which were apparently part of the company's connected training academy, but she'd been so wrapped up in her wedding plans she hadn't listened as closely as she should have.

"Did you hear it, too?" he asked in a half whisper, and she realized he'd been talking to her while she was ogling his body.

She lowered her voice to match his. "Hear what?"

"Voices. I think I'm hearing voices outside. Listen."

Tara listened. He was right. The voices were faint, but they were there. "A woman and a man," she whispered. "Can't make out what they're saying."

"Maybe one of those kids did tell their parents about seeing us last night." Owen rose, grabbing his shirt from where it lay on the floor nearby and slipping it on as he crossed to the cabin's front window. Tara noticed that grime had smudged the snowy-white fabric.

"Can you see anyone?" she whispered.

He nodded. "They look normal."

"By normal, I assume you mean nonhomicidal."

He turned to flash her a quick grin. "Exactly."

"Maybe we should go out and meet them. It'll look less suspicious."

"Good idea." He glanced her way. "Wrap the blanket around your bottom half. It'll be hard to explain half a wedding dress."

Smart, she thought, and grabbed the blanket that had been covering them to wrap around her. She joined him at the door. "Ready?"

He took her hand. "Let's not tell them what really happened. Too hard to explain. I'm just going to say we're newlyweds whose car broke down in the storm."

"Okay." She twined her fingers with him and followed him onto the porch, surprising the couple approaching the cabin through the underbrush.

"Oh!" the woman exclaimed as they came to a quick halt. "I reckon y'all are real after all."

"You must be the parents of one of the kids we scared last night," Owen said with an engaging smile. "Sorry about that."

The woman, a plump brunette with a friendly smile, waved off his apology. "Don't you worry about that. Those young 'uns had no business bein' out here in the middle of a rainstorm. But we figured we should at least come out here and make sure you weren't in some kind of trouble."

The man grimaced at the cabin. "Y'all had to sleep here last night?"

"Sadly, yes," Owen said. "Our car broke down late yesterday afternoon, and then the rain hit, so we had to settle for what shelter we could find. And then, to our complete horror, we discovered we'd both left our cell phones at the church. So we couldn't even call for a tow."

The woman took in their appearances—the beaded bodice of Tara's torn dress, Owen's grimy white tuxedo shirt and black pants—and jumped to the obvious conclusion. "You're newlyweds, aren't you? Bless your hearts—this is where you spent your wedding night?"

Owen laughed, pulling Tara closer. "It'll be quite the story to tell on our golden anniversary, won't it? I don't suppose we could borrow a phone to call for help?"

"Of course you could." The woman dug in the pocket of her jeans and provided a cell phone. "Here you go."

"Thank you so much." Owen took the phone and went back inside the cabin to make the call, leaving Tara to talk to the friendly couple.

"Do you live close?" Tara asked.

"Half a mile. Kind of hard to see the place through all the trees. If it was winter, you'd probably have seen us and not had to spend the night here," the husband said. "I'm Frank Tyler, by the way. This is my wife, Elaine."

"Tara B—Stiles. Tara Stiles, and my husband's name is Owen." Tara smiled, even though her stomach was starting to ache from the tension of lying to this nice couple. But Owen was right. As crazy as the "newlyweds with car trouble" story was, the truth was so much more problematic.

Owen came back out to the porch, a smile pasted on his face. But Tara knew him well enough to know that his smile was covering deep anxiety. It glittered in his eyes, tense and jittery. He handed the phone back to Elaine Tyler. "Thank you so much. I've called someone for a tow, so we're set."

"Glad we could help. You know, we could drive you to where your car is parked."

"Not necessary. I've arranged for someone to meet us on Old Camp Road. Easy walk from here to there. You should get back to your family." Owen shook Frank Tyler's hand, then Elaine's. "Thank you again."

"Yes, thank you so much," Tara added, smiling brightly to hide her growing worry. Who had Owen called and what had he heard?

When the Tylers were out of earshot, Tara moved closer to Owen. "What's wrong?"

He caught her hand, his expression pained. "Tara, I don't know how to break this to you. Robert's dead."

She stared at Owen, not comprehending. "What?"

"He's dead. Shot, from what my boss told me."

She covered her mouth with one shaky hand, not certain what she was feeling. Her fiancé was dead. The man she'd been close to marrying. Even if she had become convinced he wasn't the man for her, it didn't mean she hadn't cared deeply for him.

And now he was gone? Just like that?

It was crazy. It had to be wrong.

"This has to be a mistake," she said, her legs suddenly feeling like jelly.

Owen led her to the steps and eased her into a sitting position on the top step. Ignoring the uncomfortable dampness of the wood, she turned to look at Owen as he settled down beside her and wrapped one strong arm around her shoulder. "I'm so sorry, sweetheart."

She leaned her head against his shoulder. "There's more, isn't there?"

He leaned his head against hers. "Yes."

She sighed. "Just get it over with."

"Robert was murdered at the church around the time you and I were taken by the kidnappers. Nobody knew where we went, so—"

"So now we're the prime suspects," she finished for him.

Chapter Four

"How long do you think it'll take your boss to get here?"

Owen looked away from the empty road, taking in the lines of tension in Tara's weary face. "He should be here soon. It's not that far from the office to here."

He didn't know how to comfort her when his own nerves were stretched to the breaking point. How had they gone from kidnap victims to murder suspects in the span of a few hours? And how could they ever prove their story? The only evidence left was a wad of duct tape still hidden in his tux pants, which was hardly dispositive. Any ether left in Tara's system would be long gone by now, and any ether that might have been deposited on her hair and clothing would have been washed away by the rain.

"What are we going to do, Owen?" Tara looked tiny, wrapped up as she was in the drab camp blanket. "What did your boss say we should do? Turn ourselves in?"

"He just told me to sit tight and let him figure it out." Owen didn't like admitting that he didn't have a clue what they should do, either, but he'd never been a suspect in a murder before.

"Do you trust him?"

How to answer that question? Owen technically had three bosses—Alexander Quinn, Rebecca Cameron and Maddox Heller, the three former government employees who now ran Campbell Cove Security Services. Cameron, a former diplomat, and Heller, a former marine, seemed nice enough, but Owen's department, Cybersecurity, was mainly under the hawkeyed control of Quinn, a former spy with an epic reputation for getting things done no matter the cost.

Owen didn't know if it was ever wise to trust someone like Quinn, who saw even his employees as expendable if it meant securing the safety of the country he'd spent decades serving. But Owen had no doubt that Quinn was dedicated to the cause of justice. And if he and Tara ended up in jail for something they didn't do, how would justice be served?

"I think he'll want the right person to go to jail for what happened to Robert," he said finally.

Tara's narrow-eyed gaze told him she hadn't been mollified by his answer. "Well, he'd better get here soon, because it won't take long for those nice people we met this morning to find out about Robert's murder on the morning news and start to wonder about that half-dressed bride and groom they saw hiding in the woods."

She was right. Owen checked his watch. Where the hell was Quinn? "I wish I had my phone."

"Is that him?" Tara nodded toward a small, dark dot at the far end of the narrow two-lane road. It grew bigger as it came near, resolving into a dark blue SUV. It stopped about forty yards down the road, and a sandy-haired man got out.

Not Quinn but Maddox Heller. Owen didn't know whether to be worried or relieved.

Heller motioned for them to come to him. Grimacing, Owen started walking. The rain had tightened the leather of his dress shoes, which were pinching his feet. Tara didn't look any happier about the walk, wobbling a little in her grimy pumps and taking care not to step on the hem of her blanket wrap.

"Sorry," Maddox said when they reached the SUV. "I wanted to be sure you weren't being used as bait for an ambush."

Tara pulled herself into the front seat and sighed deeply. "Twenty-four hours ago, my life was so simple."

Heller gave her a sympathetic look. "I'm sorry about your fiancé. Are you warm enough? Let me turn up the heater."

Owen sat on the bench seat behind them, closing his hand over Tara's shoulder. He felt her skin ripple beneath his touch, but when he started to pull his hand away, she caught it and held it in place.

"For now, I'm taking you to a safe house. We'll get you some clothes and something to eat, and you can try to get some sleep. I can't imagine you slept well in a cold cabin."

"What about the police?" Tara asked.

"Quinn wants to look into that issue before we decide what to do. For now, he wants you to just stay put."

Easy enough, Owen thought. He wanted nothing more than a hot meal, some warm, dry clothes and to sleep for a week.

"Do you know how Robert was killed?" Tara asked as Maddox reversed the SUV and headed back the way he'd come. "Owen said he was shot, but when? How?"

"The details are sketchy. We have some friends in the local sheriff's department, but they're hunkered down at the moment, as you can imagine, just dealing with the press and with your fiancé's family."

Tara rubbed her forehead. "I didn't even think about his poor parents. Who would do something like that? And why?"

Owen squeezed her shoulder. "We're going to find out. I promise."

She looked at him over her shoulder. "You can't promise that."

"I promise to do everything I can to figure this out and keep you safe."

She smiled wanly. "I know you'll try."

The drive to the safe house took about twenty minutes, taking them out of the woods and down a long country road dotted here and there with farms and pastureland where horses grazed placidly in the morning sun. Halfway there, Maddox Heller turned on the radio and tuned in to a local news station, which was covering Robert's murder with almost salacious excitement.

They learned nothing new, however, and Tara bluntly asked Heller to turn it off.

The safe house was a small, neat farmhouse nestled near the end of a two-lane road sheltered on either side by apple trees. There were no other houses on the road, no doubt by design. Even the house itself was sheltered on three sides by sprawling oak trees that hid most of the property from view unless someone was driving by on purpose.

"It's fairly rustic," Heller warned as he led them up the flagstone walkway to the river stone porch. "But you'll have what you need, and the property is protected by a state-of-the-art security system."

"Will there be anyone protecting us?" Tara asked. "I mean, if those guys who grabbed us try to find us again."

Heller glanced at Owen. "Owen's trained for the basics. The security system should do the rest, and we'll have an agent check on you regularly until Quinn decides how to proceed. You shouldn't be here long."

Tara glanced Owen's way. He wasn't sure if she was looking for reassurance or expressing skepticism. He smiled back at her, hoping it would suffice as a response either way.

Heller showed them how to set and disarm the security system. "You can set your own codes if that makes you feel more secure, or you can leave the code as is. We have an override code in case there's trouble, but only Cameron, Quinn and I know that code, so you should be very safe."

He led them deeper into the house. It was rustic, as Heller had warned, but everything looked to be in good working shape. There was wood in the bin next to the fireplace, and the kitchen appliances proved to be up-to-date. "We stocked the fridge and freezer, so you'd have enough to eat for a few days if things don't resolve sooner," Heller told them as they left the kitchen and entered the hallway that led to a couple of large bedrooms near the back of the house. He guided Tara to the room on the right. "There are several sizes of clothing you can choose from in there. We took up a collection from all the women we could reach on quick notice. Hopefully, you'll find a few things that work. Let me know if you don't." He nodded toward the other room. "I grabbed some of the stuff you had stashed at work, and got a few of the taller guys to lend you some clothes," he told Owen.

Heller followed Owen into the room and closed the door behind them. "You okay? Quinn said you had a knock on the head. Did you lose consciousness?"

"Briefly," Owen answered. "I'm fine."

"I could have Eric come take a look at you, although Quinn wants to keep as few people as possible in the loop on this, at least until he can get a better idea what's going on."

"I haven't had any symptoms. My head doesn't even hurt where I hit it, except a little tenderness in the skin."

Heller took a look at the lump on the side of Owen's head, frowning. "Don't take chances. Head injuries aren't anything to mess around with."

"I'm fine."

"What about Tara? Any lingering effects from the ether exposure?"

"Not that I can tell. I'll keep an eye on her."

Heller opened the top drawer of the tall chest next to the bedroom door and withdrew a lockbox. He set it on the bed and opened it with a key he pulled from his jeans pocket. Inside, nestled in foam padding fitted snugly to it, lay a Smith & Wesson M&P .380. "There's ammo in the drawer. Quinn said you'd been trained to use one of these."

Owen stared at the pistol, trying not to feel queasy. "I have, but—"

"No buts. You're trained to use it. Which means you also know when not to use it. Trust your training. And your own good sense." Heller handed Owen the key. "Quinn sent over a team from your department to set up a computer. You should be able to access the office server through an untraceable remote access program. I'm told you're the one who created the system, so I'm sure you know how to make it work."

Owen managed a weak smile, his gaze wandering back to the open pistol case. "Computers I can do."

Heller clapped his hand over Owen's shoulder. "You can handle all of it. Remember your training. Let it do the work for you."

Owen walked Heller to the front door. "Any idea when we can expect to hear something from you or Quinn or whoever?"

"Soon. I can't be more specific until Quinn's finished his investigation." Heller's smile carved dimples in his tanned cheeks, making him look a decade younger. "We're on your side, Stiles. Try to relax. We'll be in touch."

Owen blew out a long breath after he closed the door behind Heller, his heart pounding in his chest. What the hell had he and Tara stumbled into? And how was he supposed to protect her when he was shaking in his boots?

"There's a gun on your bed."

Tara's voice made him jump. He turned to look at her. "Heller left it for me, in case we need it."

Her eyes narrowed. "Do you know how to use it?"

"Yes."

She looked tired and scared, her arms wrapped protectively around herself. Still in the tattered remains of her wedding dress, she looked small and vulnerable, two words he'd never before associated with Tara. The Tara he knew was fierce and invincible. Seeing her so uncertain, so fragile, made his stomach ache.

"You need a shower and some sleep." He crossed to where she stood, rubbing his hands lightly up and down her arms. "Come on, let's see if we can find the bathroom."

She flung her arms around him suddenly, pressing her face to his chest. Her arms tightened around his waist, her grip fierce. "Thank you."

He wrapped his arms around her, wishing he could ease the tremble he felt in her limbs. "For what?"

"You came to find me, even when I told you not to worry." She looked up at him. "You always do."

"Always will," he promised.

Her gaze seemed to be searching his face for something. He wasn't sure what. Reassurance? Reliability?

Tell me what you want, Tara, and I'll give it to you.

"You're right about one thing. I need a shower and about a week of sleep," Tara said, pulling away from his embrace.

He needed a shower, too, but he felt suddenly wide awake, as if the reality of their dilemma had flooded his veins with adrenaline. He needed to figure out why Robert had been murdered and how it related to Tara's kidnapping.

Tara had disappeared into her room, and the sound of

running water coming from behind the closed door meant there must be a bathroom connected to her room. His bedroom didn't have an en suite bathroom, but the large bathroom just down the hall was more than convenient.

He took a quick shower, changed into a pair of jeans and a thick sweatshirt, and settled down at the desk nestled in the corner of his bedroom, where one of his colleagues in the computer security section had provided a high-tech setup.

Everything was up and running, so he connected to the Campbell Cove Security system and quickly found the files on Robert Mallory's murder. The details were sketchy, but the agent Quinn had assigned to compile information, Steve Bartlett, had pulled together a timeline of the murder, including the details Owen had provided to Quinn over the phone.

The coroner would narrow down the time of death, but witness testimony suggested that he'd been killed between two thirty, when his father had talked to him briefly as the groom was dressing, and around three thirty, when the best man had stopped in the groom's dressing room for a last minute pep talk and found his body.

Tara had been abducted about ten minutes after three, which gave her only a partial alibi for the murder, unless the coroner could nail down a more precise time of death for Robert. Had her abduction been part of the murder plot? But why grab her? Why not just shoot her the way Robert had been shot?

Owen rubbed his gritty eyes. Adrenaline might be keeping his brain awake, but his body was aching with exhaustion. He needed rest. To give his brain a break so he'd be focused and clearheaded enough to make sense of the tangled threads that might—or might not—connect the abduction and the murder.

The only thing Owen was sure about was his own involvement. He wouldn't have been anywhere near Tara and her kidnappers if she hadn't made that phone call to him. He had been in the church vestibule with the bridesmaids and would have remained there until Tara arrived for the start of the ceremony.

He had been collateral damage. Tara had been the target.

But why?

"I couldn't sleep."

His keyed-up nerves jumped at the sound of Tara's voice behind him. He swiveled his chair to look at her and felt an immediate jolt to his libido.

Her dark hair, still damp from the shower, fell in tousled waves over her shoulders. She'd found a long-sleeved T-shirt that fit snugly over her curves. It was thin enough for him to see that she wasn't wearing a bra.

He forced his gaze down to the slim fit of the gray yoga pants that revealed the rest of her curves, the well-toned thighs and shapely calves. She was always worrying that she was a little too curvy, but he thought she was perfect. Soft and sleek in all the right places.

"I couldn't sleep, either." He had a lot of practice suppressing his desire for her. He put it to use now, ignoring the stirring sensation in his jeans and concentrating on the fleeting expressions crossing Tara's face.

She had never been one to wear her feelings on her sleeve, and over the years she'd gotten pretty good at hiding her thoughts, even from him. He wasn't sure now if he could read her emotions, but she couldn't hide the sadness shadowing her green eyes.

He crossed to where she stood and waited. If she wanted his comfort, she'd take it.

She caught one of his hands in hers, a fleeting brush of

her fingers across his. Then she dropped her hand back to her side. "I wonder if the story has made the local news," she murmured, wandering toward the hallway.

He followed her into the front room, where she sat on the sofa, picked up the remote on the coffee table and turned on the TV. He settled beside her as she started flipping channels, looking for a local news station.

He hated to tell her the story might already have made the national cable news channels by now. It was sensational enough to draw the attention of news directors looking for stories to fill their twenty-four-hour formats.

He was right. She settled on one of the cable news stations, her attention arrested by a photograph of her own face filling the screen. "Fugitive Bride" was the graphic that filled the bottom of the screen in big, blocky letters.

"Oh, lovely," she muttered.

Unfortunately, the cable station didn't have any extra information about Robert Mallory's murder, though there was plenty of innuendo about the bride's untimely disappearance. The newsreader skirted the edge of libel. Barely.

As the news host moved on to a different story, Tara turned off the TV and lowered her head to her hands. "Robert's parents must be distraught."

"I'm sure they are."

"They must believe I killed him. It's what everyone believes, right?"

"No, of course not. No one who knows you believes that."

"Not that many people know me. Do they?"

He wanted to contradict her, but what she said was true. Tara had never made it easy for people to get to know her. Even Owen, who'd been her closest friend since childhood, knew there were pieces of herself she didn't share with him and probably never would.

She was good at her job as an analyst for a global security think tank based in Brody, Virginia, just across the state line. But how many of her colleagues there really knew her? They knew her qualifications, her educational background, her experience in security analysis gained working for a defense contractor for several years right out of college.

But did they know what she liked to do when she was home alone? Did they know she was a sucker for kittens, dark chocolate and flannel pajamas? Did they know that she made lists she wouldn't throw away until she'd marked off everything written there?

Did they know there was no way in hell she'd ever have killed Robert Mallory?

"Why would someone kill Robert and kidnap you?" he asked aloud.

"I don't know."

"It seems weird, doesn't it? Kidnapping you might have made sense if they were looking for ransom. I know you said Robert wasn't rich enough for kidnapping for ransom to make sense, but his parents are. So I could see the kidnappers pressuring Robert to pay up for your release, if they knew he could ask his parents for money."

"But instead, Robert was murdered. By the same people?"

"Obviously not the same people as our kidnappers, but maybe someone they were working with?"

"But why?" Tara asked. "If kidnapping me was to collect a ransom, why on earth did they kill Robert?"

"I don't know," Owen admitted, turning to face her. He took her hands in his, squeezing them firmly. "But I promise you this—we're going to figure this out. And we're going to make sure nothing like this happens to you again."

She gave him a look somewhere between love and pity before she released his hands and rose from the sofa. She crossed to the window and gazed out at the sun-bleached lawn that stretched from the side of the house to the sheltering oaks encroaching on the farm yard.

She looked terribly, tragically alone. And not for the first time in his life, Owen wondered if she'd ever really let anyone inside her circle of one.

THE WARRANT IN HAND gave Archer Trask and his team the right to search Tara Jane Bentley's small bungalow for any firearm she might own. As she was already a person of interest in a murder, he did not have to announce his presence before forcing entry, since doing so might give her time to flee if she was inside the home. But when he opened the front door, all optimistic notions of finding Tara Bentley hiding out at home went out the window.

The place had been trashed, top to bottom, and from the faintly sour smell in the kitchen, where the refrigerator contents lay in a spilled or broken mess across the tile floor, it hadn't happened in the past few hours.

Next to him, one of the deputies uttered a succinct profanity.

Trask got on his radio and ordered a crime scene unit to meet him at Tara Bentley's house. He didn't know if this destruction had anything to do with what had happened to Robert Mallory, but someone had tossed this place, clearly looking for something.

But what? What secrets was Ms. Bentley keeping? And did those secrets have anything to do with Mallory's death?

He stepped gingerly back through the living room at the front of the house, pausing as a framed photograph lying on the floor caught his eye. The glass was cracked, but the photo remained intact. Dark-haired Tara Bentley, grinning at the camera, leaning head-to-head with a dark-haired man with sharp blue eyes. His smile was a little less exuberant than hers, but he was clearly happy to be with her.

"Owen Stiles," Trask murmured.

"Sir?" a passing deputy asked.

"Stiles," he repeated, showing the man the photograph. "Bentley's partner in crime."

"You think the bride killed the groom and ran off with the best man?"

"Not the best man. The man of honor. He was standing up for the bride, not the groom." Trask put the photograph back on the floor where he'd found it and walked out the front door, motioning for the other deputies to follow him. They crossed back to their vehicles to wait for the crime scene unit to arrive.

Leaning against the front panel of his unmarked sedan, Trask pulled out his phone and dialed a number. A deep voiced man with a distinctive drawl answered on the second ring. "Heller."

"Mr. Heller, it's Archer Trask. We met back in December when I was looking into the threats against Charlie Winters."

Heller's voice was wary. "I remember."

"I need to talk to you about one of your employees, Owen Stiles. I can be there later today, if you can see me?"

There was a brief pause. "Of course. Three o'clock?"

"I'll be there." He pocketed his phone and looked around the neat property, trying to picture Tara Bentley there. The place was small but well maintained. He suspected the house would have been the same if someone hadn't trashed it.

"What were they looking for, Tara?" he murmured aloud. *And where are you now?*

Chapter Five

The blank notepad on the desk in front of her seemed to be taunting her. With a grimace, Tara picked up her pen and wrote a single word across the top of the pad: *Why?*

Why had those two men kidnapped her? Why had someone killed Robert? Were the two events connected?

Surely they had to be. It would be too much of a coincidence if they weren't.

She wrote those two questions beneath the header. Below that, she wrote another word: *What?*

What had the kidnappers wanted from her? What had they been planning to do with her? Ask for a ransom? Trade her for someone else, like a hostage exchange? If so, for whom?

A quiet knock on the bedroom door set her nerves rattling. "Come in," she called, turning to watch Owen enter her bedroom.

"I thought you were going to take a nap," he said.

"I tried," she lied. She hadn't tried, because the questions swirling through her head wouldn't let her rest.

The look Owen sent her way suggested he knew she was lying, but he didn't call her on it. Instead, he sat on the edge of the bed and leaned toward the desk beside it. "Making lists?"

"It's what I do."

His lips curved in a half smile, carving distinguished lines in his handsome face. He really had no idea how beautiful a man he was, but she knew. He'd been something of a late bloomer, growing into his lanky frame and thin, serious face. By the time adulthood had fulfilled the nascent promise of good looks that had only occasionally flashed into view during his awkward adolescence, his quiet nature and tendency toward shyness had already left an indelible mark on his personality.

He was brilliant at his work as a computer wizard, possibly because of his tendency to hide behind the computer screen, where he was the king of his own little world. His circle of close friends was even smaller than Tara's, and hers wasn't exactly expansive. In fact, Robert Mallory had been the first person she'd let get close to her in years. And now that he was gone, she was feeling a crushing amount of guilt at having led him on when she was beginning to admit to herself that she'd never really loved him the way she'd claimed to.

Owen picked up the notepad. "You think your kidnapping and Robert's murder are connected?"

"Do you think it's likely they're not?"

He thought for a moment before replying. "No. But damned if I can figure out what the connection might be."

Tara rubbed her gritty eyes. "That's where I am. I have no idea why anyone would have abducted me. Ransom is the usual reason, but if that was the motive, why on earth would someone kill the only person with the potential to supply the money?"

Owen's gaze narrowed. "These are the thoughts keeping you from sleep?"

She frowned. "You think that's strange?"

"I think you're avoiding what's really driving your unease."

Here we go, she thought. Owen was going to psycho-analyze her again. As usual. She leaned back in her chair and folded her arms across her chest. "I suppose you're going to tell me what I'm avoiding?"

His lips pressed into a thin line of annoyance, as she'd known they would. But his irritation didn't deter him. "Your fiancé was murdered today. You were kidnapped, rather roughly, if those bruises on your arms are any in-dication. But rather than deal with the fear and grief you must be feeling, you're making lists." He picked up the notepad and flipped it onto the bed beside him. "This is what you always do."

"And this is what you always do," she snapped, snatch-ing the notepad from the bed and putting it back on the desk in front of her. "You think you know what I'm feel-ing and when I tell you you're wrong, you tell me I'm sub-limating my emotions or something."

"Because you are."

"Says you."

"Yes," he said.

Infuriating man! She turned back to the desk and picked up her pen, determined to shut out him and his unsolic-ited opinions.

"I'm sorry," he said a moment later, after she'd struggled without any luck to come up with another entry for her list. "I've known you so long, I tend to think I know ev-erything you're thinking or feeling, but obviously, I don't. So why don't you tell me about your list?"

Even though she suspected his apology was just a back-door attempt to get back to his psychoanalysis of her emo-tional state, she hated when she and Owen were at odds, so she handed him the list she'd made. "Like I said, I think my kidnapping and Robert's murder have to be connected. But I don't know how."

He read over her jotted notes. "Good questions," he noted with a faint quirk of his lips. "I'll tell you what sticks out to me, if you like."

She waved her hand at him. "Please."

"What *did* they want from you? If you're right, and Robert's murder was connected to your kidnapping, then I don't think ransom could be the motive for your kidnapping."

"Agreed."

"So what would they have accomplished by kidnapping you?"

"I don't know."

"You don't have money. You're not a romantic rival someone needs to get out of the way—if Robert had some obsessive stalker, she'd have kidnapped you by herself, not hired two thugs to take you, and she probably wouldn't have killed Robert, at least not this early in the game."

"Your mind works in some really scary ways," Tara muttered.

His smile was a little wider that time. "It's part of my charm."

"Okay, so no ransom, no crazy jealous chick."

"You do have one thing that someone might want," Owen said after a brief pause. "Your work."

She frowned. "But how many people really know what I do? Most of my friends think I'm a systems analyst, and frankly, they don't know or care what that is anyway."

"But you're a systems analyst for one of the top security and intelligence think tanks in the country—the world, in fact. And more to the point, you have a pretty astounding security clearance level for a civilian contractor. I'm your best friend in the world, and even I don't know exactly what it is you and your company are planning these days, except that it must be pretty damn big if you couldn't take a couple of weeks off for a honeymoon."

Owen was right. The project she was working on these days was huge and considered top secret in her company. Only a few people she worked with knew what her part of the job entailed, and that was on purpose, since she had been tasked with planning a supersecret security symposium that would be drawing some of the highest-ranking security and intelligence officers from friendly—and even a few not-so-friendly—nations across the globe. Not even her fiancé, Robert, knew the full scope of what she was doing these days, though he'd been insatiably curious.

She frowned, a terrible thought occurring to her. "What if Robert was killed in an attempt to find out what I was doing for my company?"

"You mean they tried to get information from him and something went wrong?"

She swallowed with difficulty. "Or they realized he didn't know anything and wasn't any use to them, so..."

"They killed him," Owen finished for her. "I suppose it's possible, if your job is really what's behind what happened today."

She rubbed her neck, where tension was building into coiling snakes of pain. "I'm so tired I can't think, but I can't seem to turn my brain off."

Owen reached out and caught her hand. "I'll give you a neck rub. That'll help, won't it?"

She met his gaze, seeing no guile there. Owen wasn't like most other men. His offers of kindness had no ulterior motives. That was one of the reasons she trusted him in a way she'd never trusted anyone else in her life, not even Robert. To Owen, a neck rub was just a neck rub.

She turned her chair until her back was in front of him. The elastic band holding her ponytail had slipped a little, so she reached up and tightened it, giving him a clear view of her neck.

A moment passed before his hands touched her neck. They were neither hot nor cold, just pleasantly warm against her flesh. He eased his way into the massage, first with light strokes that sent minute shivers rippling down her spine. But soon, his fingers pressed deeper into her muscles, eliciting a flood of pleasure-pain that sent tremors rumbling low in her belly.

A neck rub might just be a neck rub for Owen, she realized, but it had never been, and never would be, just a neck rub for her.

He wasn't anywhere near the perfect man of her wish list. He was too much the introvert, too prone to shutting out the world and burrowing into his own head when he got interested in a project. He lacked the driving ambition that might have made him the next Steve Jobs or Elon Musk. His occasional social awkwardness, which seemed to hit him at the worst possible moments, was such a contrast to the sort of social charm and ease that Robert Mallory had checked off her must-have list.

And yet he was deliciously sexy in the way that a really smart, really decent man could be. He had a wicked sense of humor and a delight in all things absurd that always seemed to be able to bring her out of even the worst mood, on those days when the weight of her world seemed insupportable. His intensely blue eyes could mesmerize her when he was talking about something he was passionate about, whether it was some intricacy of computer science she couldn't understand or his love of baseball, an obsession they shared.

And his hands. He had the best hands, long-fingered and strong, with a deft dexterity that could turn a simple neck rub into pure seduction.

"Are you being nice to me now to make up for pissing me off earlier?" She kept her tone intentionally light, struggling against his spell.

His low voice hummed against her skin. "Is it working?"

Spectacularly, she thought. "If I say yes, you might not try as hard."

"Nonsense. I always strive to do my best."

If he were anyone but Owen, she'd be seriously contemplating sex right about now, she realized. But he was Owen, and Owen was off-limits, so she eased away from his touch. "That was just what I needed. I think maybe I can get a little sleep now."

As she'd known he would, Owen stepped away from the bed. "You do that. I'll try to get some sleep myself and then if you're awake in a few hours, we'll see about something for supper."

Impulsively, she caught his hand as he turned to go and pulled him into a tight hug. His arms enfolded her, strong to her unexpectedly weak.

"It's going to be all right," he murmured against her temple. "We'll figure all this out, I promise."

She let go and covered her emotion with a soft laugh. "We've had our share of figuring our way out of trouble, haven't we?"

He gave her ponytail a light tug. "Tara and Owen, the terrors of Mercerville."

"That was mostly me," she said wryly.

He smiled. "True."

She watched him leave the room and close the door behind him, feeling suddenly, terribly alone.

MADDOX HELLER was not alone in his office when Archer Trask arrived for their meeting. He took in the three people sitting in the small office space with unexpected trepidation, for he wasn't a man easily intimidated. But Heller had called in the other two chief officers of Campbell Cove Security, the enigmatic Alexander Quinn, a former CIA agent and a man who seemed to grow inexplicably more mysterious with each revelation about his past; and the elegant and beautiful Rebecca Cameron, a woman who Archer Trask knew primarily by her reputation as an accomplished diplomat and a brilliant historian. It was she who rose to greet him, extending her graceful, long-fingered hand for a shake.

"I hope you don't mind if Alexander and I join the meeting," she said with a friendly smile that brought sparkles to her dark eyes and carved handsome curves in her otherwise ageless face. She smelled good, Trask thought, her scent delicate but intoxicating. She was probably his elder by at least five or six years, but she had a youthful grace that made him feel ancient next to her.

"Saves you the trouble of questioning us separately," Maddox drawled, flashing a quicksilver smile that Trask didn't quite buy.

More like prevents me from separating you in the effort to catch you in a discrepancy, he thought. He took the seat Maddox offered, situated in front of their chairs, subtly surrounded by them.

As if he were the one being questioned.

"How long has Owen Stiles worked for your company?" he asked before someone could interrupt to offer him coffee or some other distraction.

"Almost a year now," Quinn answered. "He was one of our earliest hires and has worked out very well."

"He's in your IT department?" Trask asked, knowing it was a leading question. He already knew Stiles worked in Cybersecurity, although even his best intel hadn't managed to uncover exactly what cybersecurity meant to a company like Campbell Cove Security. Was he an analyst? Or was he a white hat hacker of some sort?

Or perhaps both?

"He's in Cybersecurity," Quinn answered blandly. "He analyzes security threats in both government and civilian networks and comes up with solutions to close the gaps that terrorists try to exploit."

Quinn came across as open and honest on the surface, but Trask didn't buy it. The only problem was, he wasn't sure Quinn was actually lying. He might be telling the truth, or he might be leaving out something important. Trask honestly couldn't tell.

"Do you have any idea where he is now?"

"No," Quinn answered. "We've been trying to find him, as you can imagine. He's vital to our work here, and his disappearance is troubling."

Trask narrowed his eyes, looking past Quinn to Rebecca Cameron. Her expression was as placid as the surface of a lake on a still day, reflecting her surroundings more than revealing anything beneath the surface. As for Maddox Heller, he simply shot Trask a look that was somewhere between a smile and a smirk, as if he knew exactly how frustrating this interview was turning out to be.

Clearly, they had circled the wagons around their employee, and nothing Trask asked in this particular interview would cause them to break ranks. So he changed direction.

"Do you know Tara Bentley?"

He spotted a slight flicker in Heller's expression before he pasted on that smirky smile again. "She asked Owen to be her man of honor in her wedding, so I know they're good friends."

"I believe they grew up together," Quinn offered blandly.

"Since middle school, didn't Owen say?" Cameron offered. "Sweet, to have stayed friends so many years, don't you think?"

"Have any of you met her?"

"Briefly, I think. She's come by to take him to lunch a couple of times, hasn't she?" Cameron smiled at her co-workers.

"But other than that, you know nothing about her?"

There wasn't even the briefest of pauses before Alexander Quinn answered, "No. Nothing at all."

OWEN HAD GONE to his bedroom with good intentions, but moments after he'd stretched out on the bed, the call of his computer overcame his weariness. Planting himself in front of the computer array, he considered his options.

Something had been bothering him since Maddox Heller rescued him and Tara from the road near the old Boy Scout camp. At the time, he'd been too wet, tired and hungry to ask any questions, but now that he was dry and warm, with a light lunch still filling his belly, he'd had time to realize something wasn't quite right about the situation.

For one thing, Maddox Heller had asked almost nothing about what had happened to them. He'd taken Owen's terse explanation over the phone at face value, asking no questions of any import. He'd simply accepted that Tara and Owen must be telling the truth, no matter how strange the circumstances of their abduction and despite the utter dearth of proof of their story.

Yes, he'd been their employee for a year now, but he knew that if one of the people working under him in the Cybersecurity section at Campbell Cove Security had come to him with such a strange story, he'd have asked a few more questions himself.

So why hadn't Heller?

He bypassed the normal remote desktop access to his work computer and instead decided to exploit a back door he'd created to anonymously monitor any computer activity company-wide. But to his astonishment, he found that his back door was blocked.

What the hell? Had Quinn ordered his full network access to be revoked? Why? Did he suspect Owen of something nefarious after all?

Maybe that was why Heller hadn't asked any extra questions. Maybe they were trying to contain Owen and Tara, keeping them under control in the secluded little safe house until they could finish an investigation.

He kept digging, trying other potential network access points until he managed to get back into the system through another narrow gap in security. It wouldn't take long for someone to notice the network intrusion, so he had to work fast before he was detected.

He went right to the most likely source of information— Alexander Quinn. If anything worth knowing about was going on at Campbell Cove Security, Alexander Quinn would know about it.

He was running out of time, fast, when he stumbled across a file about five levels deep in his user directory. It was hidden among Quinn's download files, though the file itself seemed to have been created in the directory rather than downloaded.

What caught Owen's eye was the file name: Jane0216.

Jane was Tara's middle name. And February 16 was her birthday.

Acutely aware of the ticking clock, Owen quickly copied the file to his personal cloud server account and backed out of the network. He was pretty sure his intrusion hadn't been detected; he'd seen no signs of anyone trying to block him out. He made a mental note to shore up the security for the network entry point as soon as he could. And he was going to do a little digging around when he got a chance to see how the cybersecurity team at Campbell Cove Security had blocked him out of his usual entry point.

But first he wanted a look at that mysterious file.

It was password protected, of course. But one of the courses Owen taught at Campbell Cove Academy was on password cracking for law enforcement. In fact, Owen had written a program for password cracking, using a set of queries that helped create a list of likely passwords based on an individual's unique set of personal connections and statistics. Of course, Quinn posed a particular problem, since both his past and present were shrouded in mystery. Owen was too smart to use the usual password prompts, but with a little creative thinking, combined with his knowledge of Quinn's past exploits, he managed to sniff out the password in a couple of hours.

"'DaresSalaamNairobi_080798,'" he read aloud with a satisfied smile. The boss had made a mistake after all, using a seminal moment in his history as a CIA agent to create his password. Quinn had once told Owen that it was August 7, 1998, not September 11, 2001, that had been the real start of Osama bin Laden's war against the United States. "He and Zawahiri killed over two hundred people in those attacks on our embassies in Tanzania and Kenya, including friends of mine. But it happened halfway around the world, so people just didn't pay attention, even though the intelligence community was practically screaming for them to wake up."

Holding his breath, Owen opened the file.

It was a background check on Tara Bentley, he saw. Detailed and intrusive, chronicling her life back to childhood. It appeared to cover all the details Owen knew about Tara and a few he didn't.

"What on earth is that?"

Tara's voice, shockingly close behind him, made him jump. He whirled around in his desk chair to look at her and found her staring at the computer screen, her eyes wide with horror.

"You have a file on me?" she asked, her pained gaze meeting his.

"Not me," he said, reaching out to take her hand, overwhelmed by the need to connect with her before she withdrew from him completely. "This isn't my file. I found it on the Campbell Cove Security network. Specifically, on my boss's computer."

"Maddox Heller?" she asked, her expression still a vivid picture of dismay. She felt violated, Owen knew, and he didn't blame her.

"No. Alexander Quinn."

"The CIA guy?" She looked confused. "Why would he be keeping a dossier on me?"

"That," Owen said, "is what we're going to find out."

Chapter Six

Weekends weren't technically days off at Campbell Cove Security. Most of the security experts who worked for the company had signed on knowing they were on call 24/7. But Alexander Quinn wasn't a heartless beast, despite his reputation. He knew several of his agents were married and many had children, and he had already seen the murky world he and his fellow agents navigated rip apart too many marriages and families. After the meeting with Archer Trask, he'd sent Heller home to his pretty wife and adorable children, and even Becky Cameron had wandered off to do whatever it was she did on her time off.

His part of the building was very quiet, though he knew there were a few classes going on in the academy section and some of the unmarried employees actually preferred to work weekends and take their days off during the week. Now and then he heard the faint tap of footsteps down a distant hall or the muffled shout coming from the academy wing, but he seemed to have the executive office area to himself.

Which was why the sound of a ding on the computer behind him sent a frisson of alarm racing through his nervous system.

He turned to look at the computer and found a query box blinking back at him.

"Why do you have a file on Tara Bentley?"

His eyes narrowing, he tapped an answer on his keyboard. "Because she's important to you."

There was a long pause before another message popped onto the screen.

"Do you know why she was kidnapped?"

How to answer that question? In truth, while Quinn had some ideas what might be behind the woman's abduction, he didn't know anything for sure. Her work at the Security Strategies Foundation was, in part, classified, requiring a certain level of security clearance.

Technically, based on his own company's contract with the US government, Quinn's clearance was sufficient to access that level of information, but there were protocols of information sharing that would take time to work through. And unless the government deemed the situation to be a national security risk, Security Solutions could always refuse to share the information.

"I have ideas," he finally typed.

After another significant pause, another message appeared on screen. "You didn't supply us with phones. Why?"

Quinn didn't suppose Owen would buy the idea that he'd just forgotten about phones. So he told the truth. "I didn't want the two of you to try to contact anyone on the outside."

Owen's next message was blunt. "Because you haven't decided what to do with us?"

Exactly. But Owen had a point. Talking to him on the computer, without the benefit of hearing the tone of his voice, was less than informative.

"I'm coming to see you in person," he typed. "I will explain everything and we can talk strategies. I'll be there in an hour. Now get off my computer."

He waited for a reply, but no more dialogue boxes appeared on his computer screen. He finally turned back to his desk and picked up his cell phone.

Becky Cameron answered on the second ring. "Not a good time."

"I'm going to go see our guests. Don't suppose you'd like to join us?"

There was a protracted pause, then a sigh. "Actually, I'd love to. But I can't. I'm in the middle of something and can't get away. But I'm very curious to hear your thoughts about the situation. Maybe we could meet tomorrow evening? I was thinking about driving into Whitesburg to try that new Greek restaurant that just opened."

Quinn raised an eyebrow. Becky was an old friend, one of his closest, in fact, but she was almost militantly protective of her private life. He supposed she might see the dinner invitation as just a way to combine work with her need for food, but driving all the way to Whitesburg seemed a little more personal than that.

"I can meet you there," he said, more curious than he liked to admit. "Seven?"

"Perfect. I'll see you there and you can catch me up."

She had to know they couldn't talk about Owen Stiles and Tara Bentley in public that way. So what was she up to?

Despite his reputation for embracing all things enigmatic, Quinn really didn't like a mystery, especially when it involved one of his closest colleagues.

"DO YOU TRUST HIM?" Tara managed not to nibble her thumbnail as she waited for Owen's reply. She'd spent most of her teen years trying to break her nail-biting habit and she'd be danged if she started doing it again now. She might be hiding from both kidnappers and the law, but that was no excuse for bad grooming.

"I don't know."

Owen was cleaning the kitchen counters, even though they were virtually spotless. It was his version of nail biting, she supposed, though he generally fine-tuned his computer rather than cleaned the house when he was puzzling over a troubling problem. She supposed the new computer system was too state-of-the-art to provide him quite enough distraction for their current dilemma.

"That's not reassuring," she said.

He stopped wiping the counter long enough to offer her a halfhearted grin. "I know."

"He used to be with the CIA. Which could be a good thing or a very bad thing."

"The problem with Quinn, in my admittedly limited experience, is that he's a big-picture guy. He's going to look out for the country first, his company next and then individuals fall in line behind those two things. Which is why I began to suspect Quinn may think what happened to us is connected to something bigger."

Such as the symposium she was supposed to be planning. The event so important that she and Robert had planned to postpone their honeymoon until late summer so she could get things done.

Tara perched on the bar stool in front of the counter Owen had resumed cleaning, taking care not to leave fingerprints on the nice, shiny surface. "There's something I've been doing at work that has been my entire focus for months now. Nobody else knows all the details except for me and the company's operating officers. Now I'm no longer there to do the job. What does that do to the equation?"

"You tell me." Owen stopped wiping and draped the towel over the edge of the sink. "If something happens to you, who takes over your job?"

"It would have to be one of the three partners. They were very careful to keep all the information about my project secret, with good reason."

Curiosity gleamed in his bright blue eyes, but he didn't ask her anything about her project. "So that's why you postponed the honeymoon."

"Yes."

"Could someone outside the company know what you were planning?" he asked.

"Yes, of course. It involves other people outside the company, and any of them could have experienced an intelligence leak. But that's one reason why the details of the project were so closely guarded. Even if someone found out what was going on, they wouldn't have the vital details to work with because those details won't be settled until about a week before it comes together."

"So it's an event."

"Owen, I can't tell you anything else. I'm sorry."

He smiled. "Understood. But if it's an event, then perhaps someone wants to sabotage it in some way. Would that be a possibility?"

She didn't reply, but Owen's expression suggested he'd read the answer in her face.

"Maybe that was the point of the abduction," he suggested. "To get the information out of you under duress. Or am I being too dramatic here?"

"It's possible," she admitted. "Without going into details, it's very possible that someone would like to get his hands on the information I have. I'm a more vulnerable target than any of the directors of the company would be, and nobody else has the information."

At the time the directors had approached her to run the project, she was over-the-moon delighted about the responsibility, knowing it meant the company valued her organizational and analytical skills as well as her reliability and discretion. While she'd consulted with the directors regularly, they'd allowed her to take the reins as far as planning the logistics of the symposium was concerned. She'd been the point person with all the countries and dignitaries invited, the face of their very prestigious think tank.

But now she was beginning to realize the steep price that such a high-profile position of authority could exact. The job had quite possibly made her a target.

She might still be a target, she realized. Her disappearance and the mystery surrounding Robert's murder would likely cause her bosses to shore up their already tight security. The kidnappers would have a difficult time getting through their defenses.

But she was still largely defenseless. If Owen hadn't come to her aid, she probably wouldn't have been able to escape the kidnappers. But even that situation had been nothing more than pure luck. The kidnappers had underestimated their resourcefulness, and they hadn't prepared for Owen's surprise arrival. They'd also been sloppy, binding her hands in front of her instead of behind her. She doubted they'd be that careless a second time.

While she'd been pondering her vulnerability, Owen had put up the cleaning supplies and washed his hands in the sink. He turned to her now, drying his hands on a paper towel, his eyes narrowed. It was his "I wonder what you're thinking" expression, and she realized that she was far more tempted right now to tell him everything about her secret project than she'd ever been with Robert.

She supposed that was the difference between a whirlwind romance and twenty years of enduring and unbreakable friendship. That fact only made her more certain than ever that she'd made the right choice when she began feeling attracted to Owen. Boyfriends were unpredictable and, in her experience, undependable.

Owen was her rock. It was a mistake to sleep with your rock.

Wasn't it?

A sharp rap on the door rattled her nerves. Owen tossed the paper towel in the waste bin and headed for the front door. Tara trailed behind him, her heart pounding with anxiety.

Owen checked the security lens. "It's Quinn. You ready?"

Tara took a couple of deep, bracing breaths and nodded. "Ready."

Owen opened the door to a broad-shouldered man with sandy hair and intelligent eyes the color of dried moss. He wore a neatly groomed beard a couple of shades darker than his hair and liberally sprinkled with silver. He looked to be in his midforties, but in his eyes Tara saw an old soul, a man whose life had been one struggle after another. The weight of the world was reflected not in lines on his face but in the shadowy depths of those hazel-green eyes.

He was dangerous, Tara realized with a flutter of alarm. But he also seemed like someone who'd be invaluable in a fight, as long as you were on the same side.

He was not an enemy she wanted to make.

"You must be Tara Bentley." Quinn shook hands with a firm, brisk grip. "I've heard a good deal about you."

"You've mean you've snooped around my life and uncovered a great deal about me," Tara corrected, her voice edged with tart disapproval.

"Fair enough." Quinn nodded toward the sofa. "Shall we sit and talk?"

TARA SAT IN the armchair, leaving Quinn and Owen to share the sofa. It put her at a slightly elevated angle, which made her feel more in control of the situation. "Do you know why we were kidnapped?"

Quinn's lips quirked slightly. It wasn't quite a smile, but there was a hint of humor in his eyes. "I believe it might have something to do with your work at Security Solutions."

"And why was Robert killed?"

"I don't know." His voice softened. "My condolences on your loss."

"Thank you."

"What do you know about my job?" Tara asked.

"I contacted your company directors and explained my concerns about my cybersecurity director disappearing along with their top analyst. We had an illuminating discussion about the work you've been doing."

"Why would they tell you anything illuminating?" Tara asked, wary of being tricked into revealing more than she should.

"Because I have a security clearance as high as theirs. I'm a security contractor for the government. I know things that few federal employees know about the government's security apparatus."

"Do I need to go take a walk so you can speak freely?" Owen asked, starting to rise.

"No," Quinn said. "Your own security clearance is high enough for you to hear what Ms. Bentley and I have to say."

"You first," Tara said as Owen sat again.

The quirk returned to Quinn's lips, a little broader this time. Definitely his version of a smile, Tara thought. He inclined his head slightly toward Tara before he spoke. "Your bosses didn't give me the details of the project, of course, for the sake of situational security. But I know that you're planning a global symposium on new terror tactics and strategies for preventing them from succeeding.

You've invited over seventy nations to participate. I don't know where or even when the meeting will take place, but I know it's going to happen on US soil, and someone very much wants to know the details."

"Which is why they kidnapped Tara," Owen murmured.

"Yes." Quinn looked at Tara, his expression hard to read. "You are the most wanted woman in a lot of terror-sponsoring countries. Any number of groups, foreign and domestic, would love to get their hands on the information you know. Your bosses at Security Solutions don't know why or how you disappeared, so obviously they're deeply worried. It's not just the local authorities who are looking for you."

"I have to turn myself in, then," Tara said.

Quinn cleared his throat before he spoke. "That does seem to be the best course of action."

"I didn't kill Robert."

"I know that. And there's no evidence to connect you to his murder. I think at this point, you're primarily wanted for questioning, just to clear up why you disappeared and where you've been."

"We can't provide any evidence of what happened to us," Owen warned. "All we have is our word."

"And you're not a disinterested witness," Quinn agreed. "But neither of you has any reason to kill Robert. Since no marriage had taken place, there's no profit motive for Ms. Bentley. There's not a whiff of conflict between the two of you, according to interviews with Robert's family and your friends. It's not like you and Owen are secret lovers who killed your fiancé so you could run away together."

Tara glanced at Owen. "No."

There was a flicker of something in Quinn's eyes as he looked from her to Owen. "Is there anything I need to know about the events of yesterday that either of you haven't already told me?"

"There is one thing," Tara said, "although nobody knows about it but Owen and me. I was planning to call off the wedding right before I was abducted."

"I see."

"Owen didn't know beforehand," she added. "I didn't tell him until after we escaped."

"I suspected," Owen said. "She called me and—"

"The less I know about that, the better," Quinn interrupted. "If you don't have a lawyer, Campbell Cove Security can provide one."

"Thank you. That would be helpful," Tara said. "How will this work?"

"I think, because of the threats against your life, we shouldn't schedule the time to turn yourself in. You, Owen and the lawyer will show up unannounced at the Bagley County Sheriff's Department and ask for Deputy Archer Trask, the investigator in charge of the Robert Mallory homicide investigation. The element of surprise will be your best safeguard against a repeat of yesterday's abduction attempt."

Tara glanced at Owen. He met her gaze with an almost imperceptible nod. She looked at Quinn again. "Okay. That sounds good."

"Tomorrow morning would be best. Get a good night's sleep, take time to shower, shave and dress in your Sunday best. You're the victims, not the perpetrators. You need to be confident and at ease. I'll return in the morning with your lawyer, we'll go over the case and then we'll drive you to town."

"Sounds like a plan," Owen said with a faint smile.

Quinn flashed that half quirk of a smile toward Owen. "You did well, under difficult circumstances. We will get you both through the rest of this."

"Thank you."

She and Owen walked with Quinn to the door. He turned in the open doorway, his features dark and indistinct against the bright afternoon sun. "We'll do everything in our power to protect you, Ms. Bentley. Know that."

"Thank you. I appreciate it." She watched, her heart thudding heavily in her chest, as if his words had been a warning instead of a promise.

She was a target. She'd known the possibility existed, but until Quinn had said the words aloud, the notion had been just that. A notion, something possible but not certain.

Now the cloud of threat hanging over her head felt heavy with foreboding, as if she were trapped without any hope of escape.

The touch of Owen's hands on her shoulders made her jump. She turned to look at him and felt the full intensity of his blue-eyed gaze.

"We will get through this. Tomorrow, we'll turn ourselves in and the police will protect you."

"What if they can't? It's a small county in a small state. They're not prepared or trained to provide protection from determined terrorists."

"Then Quinn will put agents in place to watch your back." The visit from his boss had apparently shored up Owen's defenses. He sounded strong and confident, and the firmness of his grip on her shoulders seemed to transfer that sense of strength into her, so that by the time he let her go and nodded for her to precede him into the hallway, she felt steadier herself.

Maybe everything really would be okay.

OWEN STOOD OUTSIDE the groom's room, trying to gather his courage to go inside. On the other side of the door stood the man who was about to take Tara away from him, and he was supposed to be wishing him good luck.

How could he do it? How could he shake Robert's hand and tell him to take care of the woman Owen loved more than anyone else in the world? How was he supposed to be okay with any of this?

Do it because Tara needs you to. Do it because it's the only way you'll be able to stay in her life.

His heart pounded wildly. His palms were damp with sweat. Though he'd met Robert dozens of times since he first started dating Tara, the man had remained little more than an acquaintance. There had always been a wary distance between them, as if Robert understood that Owen would never really be all right with his presence in Tara's life. And Robert would never truly be comfortable with how important Owen was to Tara, either.

But if they both wanted to stay in her life, they were going to have to create some sort of truce, however wary and fragile it might be.

He took a deep breath and reached for the door.

But a scraping noise from within the room stopped him midstep. The world around him seemed to disintegrate, and he was suddenly lying on his back, darkness pressing in one him, heavy and cold. It took a moment to realize he was in an unfamiliar bed in an unfamiliar place.

The safe house. He'd been dreaming. Groping for the small digital clock on the bedside table, he squinted to see the time. Only a little after eight, he saw with surprise.

As he rubbed his eyes, he heard another faint scrape of metal on metal. It seemed to be coming from the front of the house.

Tara? Maybe she hadn't been able to sleep.

But when he rose from the bed, he grabbed the unloaded Smith & Wesson .380 from the locked box he'd stashed in the bedside table drawer. He'd put the ammo in the dresser across the room, the way he'd been trained—don't keep the ammo with the gun. The rule had always seemed reasonable to him, as it would make it hard for an intruder to load the gun and use it against him. But now that he was trying to go out and face a potential threat, the extra step seemed to slow him down.

He had to protect Tara, even if it meant carrying a gun and facing the unknown.

Heart pounding wildly, he opened the bedroom door.

Chapter Seven

A furtive sound roused Tara from slumber. She sat upright in bed, her pulse roaring in her ears. Straining to hear past the whoosh of blood through her veins, she tried to remember what, exactly, she'd heard. Was it a scrape? A tap? It hadn't been as loud as a knock.

It's an old house, she told herself. Old houses made noise. A lot.

Then she heard the noise again. It was a scrape, like metal against metal. It came not from her room but from somewhere down the hall.

Someone trying to enter the front door?

Suddenly, Owen seemed an impossible distance away, even though his bedroom was just across the hall. She didn't think the sound was coming from there, but with her door closed, it was impossible to know for certain.

Owen had the gun. She hoped to goodness he really did know how to use it.

She eased her bedroom door open, holding her breath at the soft creak of the hinges. In the distance, thunder rumbled, and for a moment Tara wondered if it had been the gathering storm that had wakened her so suddenly. But it had barely been audible at all, certainly not loud enough to stir her from a dead sleep. And the noise she'd heard earlier definitely hadn't been thunder.

She slipped out into the hallway, the wood floors smooth and cool beneath her feet. The temperature had fallen along with the night, and she shivered as she crept across to Owen's room.

As she reached for the door handle, it twisted in her hand, startling her. She jerked back, stumbling over her own feet.

In the murky gloom, she felt as if she were tumbling backward into an abyss, the world turned upside down.

Then arms wrapped around her, stilling her fall. Owen's arms, his familiar scent unmistakable. He pulled her tightly to his bare chest, his own heart galloping beneath her ear as he held her close.

The moment seemed to stretch into infinity, as all her senses converged into an exquisite flood of desire. His skin was hot silk beneath her hands as she clutched his arms. He smelled like soap and Owen, a clean, masculine essence that had always made her feel safe and happy, even when the world around her was going crazy. The bristle of his crisp chest hair rasped against her breasts beneath the thin fabric of her tank top, bringing her nipples to hard, sensitive peaks.

She forced herself to shut down all those sensations, the way she'd been doing since she turned fifteen and began to realize that the gangly boy next door was becoming an attractive young man.

"Did you hear the noise?" Owen whispered, his voice barely breath against her hair.

She nodded.

He eased her away from him, and in the flash of lightning that strobed through the window at the end of the hall, she saw the gleam of gunmetal in his hand as he slipped down the hall toward the front of the house.

She stayed close behind him, unwilling to allow him to

confront whatever danger lurked ahead alone. She might not have been trained for danger the way he had been, but she was fit, she was resourceful and if she'd let herself admit it, she was also angry as all get-out.

She might not have loved Robert the way a wife should, but he was a good man. A sweet man. He hadn't deserved to die, and the thought that he'd taken a bullet because someone was after her made her want to break things. Starting with the killer's head.

Owen paused in the doorway to the living room, and Tara had to stumble to a sharp halt to keep from barreling into him. Reaching behind him, he caught her hand briefly, gave it a squeeze, then entered the larger room.

The scraping noise came again, louder this time. It was coming from outside the house.

"Stay here," Owen whispered urgently. "I need to know you're not in the line of fire."

Her instincts told her to ignore his command, but she made herself stay still, pressing her back against the living room wall as he edged closer to the front door and took a quick look through the peephole in the door.

He backed away, glancing back at her. He shook his head.

Outside, the wind had picked up again, moaning in the eaves. The first patter of rain on the metal roof overhead was loud enough to set Tara's nerves jangling. Owen crossed quietly to where she stood, rubbing her upper arms gently. "I'm pretty sure it's the wind rattling something outside. Maybe a loose gutter or a window screen. I don't see anyone lurking around."

"They wouldn't be out in the open, would they?"

"Probably not." He glanced back toward the door.

She followed his gaze. It was an ordinary wooden door, but somehow, in the dark, with her heart racing and her skin tingling, it seemed more like an ominous portal to a dangerous realm. "Someone could be trying to lure us outside."

"Or we could be letting our imaginations run away with us, the same way we used to do sneaking around Old Man Ridley's cabin twenty years ago," he countered. "I really do think it's just the wind."

She let out a huff of nervous laughter. "You're probably right."

"The only way to figure that out is to go outside and try to find the source of the sound. Do you want me to do that?"

Part of her wanted to say yes, just so she'd know one way or the other. But it was cold and rainy, and even if there were a threat outside, which she was starting to doubt, they were safer inside than outside.

"No," she said. "I think you're right. It's just the wind rattling something outside. I'm sorry for being such a scaredy-cat."

"You want to try going back to bed and ignoring all the creaks and scrapes outside?"

"Could we maybe light a fire here in the living room and camp out on the sofa instead?"

His lips curved. "We could do that. Let me grab a shirt and a blanket."

"I'll pop some popcorn," she said, starting to finally feel a little more relaxed.

Owen had a way of making everything a little easier to bear.

OWEN WOKE IN STAGES, first vaguely aware of light on the other side of his closed eyelids, then of a warm body tucked firmly against his side. Tara, he thought, his eyes still closed. He could smell the scent of shampoo in her hair and the elusive essence of the woman herself. The soft warmth of her body against his felt perfect and necessary, as if it were an extension of himself he couldn't bear to live without.

He opened his eyes to morning sunlight angling through the east-facing front windows of the farmhouse. He'd left his watch in the bedroom, but that much light had to mean the day was well under way.

Giving Tara a gentle nudge, he said, "Wake up, sleepyhead."

She grumbled and burrowed deeper into the cocoon formed by his side and the sofa.

"It's probably after eight. Quinn and the lawyer will be here soon."

She gave a muffled groan against his side and added a soft curse for emphasis. "I was having the best dream," she complained, lifting her head and looking at him through strands of her hair.

Even makeup-free, with her normally tidy brown hair mussed and tangled, and her morning breath not quite as sweet as the rest of her, she was still the most desirable woman he'd ever known. His morning erection became almost painfully hard.

She shook her hair away from her face and stared at him, too closely curled against his body to have missed his physical response to her nearness. He waited for her to make a joke and roll off the sofa to make her escape to the bedroom, but she didn't move, her eyes darkening as exquisite tension lengthened between them.

"I don't know what I'd do if I didn't have you," she whispered.

This was the point where he would crack a joke and make his escape, but he was pinned between her and the sofa. And even if he weren't, he didn't think he'd have been capable of moving away from her luscious heat, especially when she reached out with one slim hand and touched his jaw.

He couldn't find his voice. Didn't want to risk saying anything that would ruin this moment. It felt as if he were standing on the edge of a cliff, ready to jump into a beautiful void. What lay below might be a crystalline sea, cool and cleansing, with a whole universe of wonders and pleasures lying just beneath the surface. Or he might find himself dashed on sharp rocks to lie bleeding and dying for his gamble.

What was it going to be?

From somewhere in the back of the house, two alarm clocks went off with a loud, discordant blare.

Tara and Owen both laughed, snapping the tension of the moment. "We'd better get moving," she suggested, rolling off the sofa and straightening her tank top and shorts.

He pushed to his feet, shifting his own shorts to hide the worst of his erection. "How about scrambled eggs for breakfast?"

"We need something a little more decadent," she said, pausing in the doorway of her bedroom. "I'll make French toast."

Not exactly the sort of decadence he'd been thinking about when he woke up in her arms, but he could make do.

By the time he got out of the shower, he could smell eggs cooking from down the hallway. He laid out one of the suits he'd found in the closet, hoping it would fit, but went to the kitchen in fresh boxer shorts under a shin-length black silk robe.

"Are you worried about today?" she asked as she flipped a couple of the egg-crusted pieces of bread onto a plate and handed it to him.

"A little." He set the plate on the small breakfast nook

table and retrieved the bottle of syrup from the refrigerator. "I know we didn't do anything wrong, but we don't have any real proof of our story."

She brought her own plate of French toast to the table and sat across from him. "I have half a wedding dress."

"Which could have been torn in any number of ways." He handed her the syrup bottle. "But you really didn't have any motive to kill Robert."

"What if they think you did?"

He paused with his fork halfway to his mouth. Syrup dribbled on the table and he put down the fork and grabbed a napkin. "Because you and I are so close?"

"Best friends forever." She managed a weak smile. "You know people have always mistaken us as a couple. Ever since high school."

Their closeness had broken up more than one of his romantic relationships over the years. Not without reason. "But we've only ever been friends."

"Because we choose to be only friends. But we both know there's an attraction between us that we could build on if we ever chose it. Robert knew it. He just realized that I wasn't ever going to risk my friendship with you that way, so he didn't feel threatened." A cloud drifted over her expression. "He was remarkably understanding."

Owen wasn't sure that understanding would have lasted. Or that he could have allowed the status quo between him and Tara to continue once she was married.

Which, he supposed, *makes me a viable suspect in Robert's murder.*

THE LAWYER ALEXANDER QUINN provided was younger than Tara had expected. Anthony Giattina was tall, broad shouldered and sandy haired. He spoke with a mild southern accent and there was a sparkle in his brown eyes as he shook hands with her and Owen after Alexander Quinn's introduction.

"Call me Tony," he said. "I think we can get this handled with a minimum of fuss."

"Has Mr. Quinn told you what happened?"

"I told him I wanted to talk to each of you first. So I know the basics from news reports—your fiancé was murdered and you disappeared." His eyes softened. "My condolences."

"Thank you."

"We need to get on the road," Quinn interrupted. "You'll ride with Tony so you can talk in private. I'll follow." He nodded toward the two vehicles in the driveway and started walking toward them. He got behind the wheel of a large black SUV while Tony Giattina led them to a sleek silver Mercedes sedan parked behind Quinn's vehicle.

Owen waved Tara to the front seat and settled in the back behind her.

"So, from the beginning," Tony said after they were on the road. "Did either of you witness anything connected to Robert Mallory's murder?"

"No," Tara answered. "I didn't."

"I didn't, either," Owen said.

Tony's gaze flicked toward the backseat. "You sound uncertain."

"I saw him briefly when I arrived at the church," Owen said in a careful tone that made Tara turn to look at him, as well. "I was planning to talk to him before the wedding. Wish him well, that sort of thing. But I got the call from Tara before I could enter the groom's room."

"The call from Tara?" Tony asked.

"I was having cold feet," Tara confessed. "I called Owen because I wasn't sure I was doing the right thing, and he's always been my best sounding board."

"And what did the two of you decide?"

"I had no part in it," Owen said. "She told me nothing was wrong and hung up before I could ask her more questions. That's why I was on the way to the bride's room when I spotted what I now know was Tara going out to the parking lot."

"Runaway bride?" Tony arched one sandy eyebrow in Tara's direction.

"No. A man knocked on the bride's room door, and when I answered he told me there was a delivery outside for me."

"And you went with him?"

"I thought it might be a misdirected wedding gift."

"And was there a delivery?"

"No. As soon as I got outside, someone put an ether-soaked pillowcase over my head and threw me into a panel van."

There was a long moment of silence as Tony digested what she'd told him. He finally cleared his throat and spoke. "Go on."

She was beginning to lose him, she realized. Of course she was. She and Owen had both realized early on that their story sounded like pure fantasy.

"I think it was at that point that I happened upon the scene," Owen said before she could speak. "I saw two men pushing Tara into the van. I ran to try to stop them, but one of them punched me and I slammed headfirst into the van. I lost consciousness at that point and didn't come to until sometime later, inside the van. My hands were bound behind my back with duct tape."

"I see," Tony said in a tone that suggested he didn't see at all. "For how long were you in the van?"

"I'm not sure. It might have been an hour or more. We ended up about twenty minutes away from the church, though, so I think maybe the men driving the van took a twisty route, maybe to be sure nobody had seen them and taken chase."

"You think."

"I can't be sure. We weren't able to hear them plotting their next move or anything like that." Owen's voice took on a sharp edge. "Look, I can tell you're skeptical of what we're saying. Maybe you're not the lawyer we need."

"You're going to have to sell your story to people a lot more skeptical than I. And I never said I don't believe you."

Tara glanced at Owen. He met her gaze with a furrowed brow.

"How did you manage to get free?"

"I got the pillowcase off Tara's head. They'd left it on when they threw her in the van, so I guess they were hoping it would keep her sedated for the trip." Owen's voice darkened. "The idiots could have killed her."

"When I woke, I was a little disoriented from the ether. My hands were tied in front of me," she said.

"Their mistake," Owen murmured, his voice warm. "They didn't anticipate both of us waking up and working together, I think."

"Do you have any idea who took you or why?"

"We're not sure," Tara said quickly. "We're both wondering if it was connected to Robert's murder."

Tony slanted a look toward her. "You're taking his death well."

She looked down at her hands, which were twisting around each other in her lap. She stilled their movement. "I don't think it's real to me yet. I didn't see his body. Maybe if I did…"

"The police will be wondering why you're so composed."

She looked up sharply at the lawyer. "Do you want me to pretend to be hysterical?"

"No, of course not."

"I cared about Robert. I loved him. I can't even wrap my brain around the idea that he's gone."

"You said you were having cold feet."

She glanced at Owen. He was looking down at his own hands, his expression pensive.

"I was going to call off the wedding."

"Why?"

"Because I realized that I wasn't in love with him. Not the way I should have been if I were going to marry him."

"Did he know that?"

"No. The kidnapper grabbed me first."

"I see." Tony tapped his thumbs on the steering wheel. "Why do you suppose the kidnappers took Owen into the van rather than killing him and leaving him in the parking lot?"

"I have no idea," she answered.

"I suppose a body in the parking lot would have raised an alert sooner than the kidnappers planned," Owen added.

"A body in the groom's room raised the alert quickly enough."

"Hidden behind a door, not out in the open in a church parking lot," Owen pointed out.

"I wonder if they were planning to use you as leverage against me," Tara murmured.

Owen looked at her, his gaze intense.

"Leverage to do what?" Tony asked, sounding curious.

"Whatever they kidnapped me for. Anyone who knows anything about me knows about my friendship with Owen. We've been nearly inseparable since sixth grade. We went to the same schools, including college. On purpose. Maybe they realized they could use him against me, to force me to do whatever it was they wanted from me."

"And you really have no idea what that could be?" Tony sounded unconvinced.

"It's all a mystery to me," Tara answered.

Tony fell silent after that, though Tara suspected the mind behind those brown eyes was hard at work, figuring out all the legal angles of their dilemma.

She hoped it would be enough.

Within a couple of minutes, they were entering Mercerville, the Bagley County seat. The sheriff's department was located in the east wing of the city hall building, with its own entrance and parking area. Tony pulled the Mercedes into an empty visitor parking spot and cut the engine.

"I'm going to call the lead investigator on the case now. I want him to meet us at the door. I don't want to just walk in unannounced."

"Quinn said we shouldn't give them any notice we were coming."

"You want to be sure you meet with the lead investigator. That requires a courtesy call ahead of time to be sure he's here. We don't want to be handed off to someone down the food chain." He made the call. From what Tara could glean from his end of the call, the lead investigator was in and would meet them at the door.

Tony ended the call and turned to face them both. "Don't offer any information they haven't asked for. Nothing. Understood? If a question confuses you, let me know and we'll stop the interviews to confer. If I think the questioning is treading on dangerous territory for you, I'll step in. Agreed?"

"Yes," Owen said.

"Agreed." Tara looked at Owen. He met her gaze with a half smile that didn't erase the anxious expression in his eyes. She felt a flutter of guilt for her part in putting Owen in this position. If she hadn't been so stupid as to leave the safety of the church with a stranger—

Movement outside the car caught her eye. Turning her head, she spotted a man in the tan uniform of a Bagley County sheriff's deputy. He was tall and broad shouldered, with a slight paunch and a slightly hitching gait that seemed familiar. As he reached the sheriff's department entrance, he turned his head toward the parking lot.

She sucked in a sharp breath.

Owen put his hand on her shoulder. "What is it?"

"That deputy." She nodded toward the front of the building, where the deputy had just pulled open the door.

"What about him?" Tony asked.

"That's the man who lured me out to the van."

Chapter Eight

Owen had seen only a flash of square jaw and a long, straight nose as the deputy disappeared through the glass door of the sheriff's department, but it was enough to send adrenaline racing through his system. The skin at the back of his neck prickled and his muscles bunched in preparation. Fight or flight, he thought, remembering the lessons of his threat response classes at Campbell Cove Academy.

Flight, his instinct commanded. He was outgunned and on the defensive here.

"Let's get out of here," he growled to Tony.

"What? Are you insane?" Tony turned to stare at him. "You came here to turn yourself in to the authorities. If you leave now, you're just going to make things worse."

"Owen's right." Tara's voice was deep and intense. "If that man is a cop, they will never believe us over him. You know how it works."

"You can't know that—"

Owen snapped open his seat belt and tried to unlock the back door of the car, but the child-safety locks were engaged. "Unlock the door," he demanded.

Tony shook his head. "I'm telling you as your lawyer, this is insane."

"You're fired." Tara reached across the console and grabbed the key fob dangling from the ignition. Before

Tony Giattina could stop her, she pressed one of the buttons and the lock beside Owen made an audible click. He opened the door and exited the car.

Cool spring air filled his lungs, dispelling the faint feeling of claustrophobia he'd experienced while trapped inside the backseat. Tara was already out the passenger door, turning to him with wide eyes.

"What now?"

Owen looked back at the black SUV that had followed them to the sheriff's department. Quinn was already stepping out of the vehicle, his gaze sharp, as if he could sense the rise in tension. If anyone knew the danger they were in, it was Quinn, Owen realized. His wily boss understood that, sometimes, playing by the rules could get you killed.

Grabbing Tara's hand, he started resolutely toward the SUV.

Quinn's eyes narrowed at their approach. When Owen was close enough, Quinn muttered, "Hit me."

Owen's steps faltered. "What?"

"Hit me," Quinn said, taking a step forward. "I can't help you openly, but you can't go in there."

"How do you know…"

Quinn tapped the earpiece barely visible in his ear. "Hit me, damn it."

Without another second's hesitation, Owen let go of Tara's hand and punched Quinn as hard as he dared. His boss sprawled backward into the front panel of the SUV, his keys falling to the ground beside him.

As Owen bent to pick them up, Quinn murmured, "Not the safe house. It's compromised now. There's a stash of cash in the glove box. Use it and try to get in touch when you can." Shaking his head in a show of grogginess, he dragged himself clear of the SUV's wheels.

Tony Giattina was out of the Mercedes, his phone to

his ear. Probably calling in the escape attempt, Owen realized, which meant they had only seconds before half the sheriff's department would be pouring through the doors into the parking lot.

"Let's go," he growled as he opened the front door of the SUV. Tara climbed into the passenger seat and turned to look at him, her expression terrified.

"Maybe I was wrong," she said, sounding far less confident than she had seemed a few moments earlier.

"You weren't," he assured her, putting the SUV in Reverse. He cut off a car approaching from the left, earning an angry horn blow, and headed east on Old Cumberland Road. He could take a few twisty back roads over Murlow Mountain and reach the Virginia border in less than an hour.

But what then?

"They'll have an APB out on this car in no time," Tara muttered, fastening her seat belt. "They'll scan our license plate and we'll be done for."

She was right. He had to switch the plates with another vehicle. Preferably another black SUV, but any vehicle would do, at least for a while.

Meanwhile, he stuck to the twisty mountain roads that wound their way slowly but steadily eastward toward the state line. He'd traveled with his brother in Virginia a couple of years earlier and had learned, to his surprise, that travelers could overnight in their vehicles at rest stops. That would give them accommodations for tonight, at least, until they could figure out what to do next.

But first, he needed to find a big shopping center where they could pick up supplies.

"Is anyone following us?" Tara twisted around in her seat, nibbling her thumbnail as she peered at the road behind them.

"I don't see anyone, but I'm not exactly an expert at tailing. Or being tailed."

Tara looked at him. "Do you have a plan?"

"Yes, but I'm not sure you're going to be thrilled about it."

"Better spill, then."

"Did you know that it's legal to overnight at public rest areas in Virginia?"

"Please tell me that's a non sequitur."

"I'm going to stick to back roads for another hour or so. Then I'm going to drive down to Abingdon. I think there's probably some sort of shopping center there where we can pick up some supplies—food, blankets, water."

"Those had better be thick blankets," Tara muttered.

"I'm not sure what to do about the license plates, though."

"You'd think, with your boss being a former super-spy, he'd have extra license plates stashed in the trunk or something."

Owen slanted a quick look at her. "Do you think?"

"I don't know. He's your boss."

Even after a year, Owen knew very little about two of his three bosses. Maddox Heller was an open book, garrulous and friendly. His pretty wife and his two cute kids visited often, and the previous summer, Heller had invited everyone in the company out to their house on Mercer Lake for a Labor Day cookout.

But Rebecca Cameron was a very private person, despite her friendly, good-natured disposition. And Alexander Quinn was a positive enigma.

However, if there was one thing Owen knew about his inscrutable boss, it was that the man always seemed prepared for any eventuality. Including the possibility of having to go on the run at a moment's notice.

There were very few turnoffs on the curvy mountain

road they were traveling, but within a few minutes, Owen spotted a dirt road on the right and slowed to turn, hoping he wasn't driving them into a dead-end trap.

"What are you doing?" Tara asked.

"I'm going to find out if Alexander Quinn is as wily as he seems."

Almost as soon as they took the turn, the dirt road hooked sharply to the right. Owen eased into the turn and the SUV was immediately swallowed by the woods, which hid not only the road from their view but, more important, hid them from the view of the road.

He pulled to a stop and cut the engine. "If you wanted to stash something secret in this SUV, where would you start?"

"The glove compartment is too obvious," Tara said.

"Quinn did tell me there was stash of cash in there."

Tara opened the glove box. Inside was a wallet, weather-beaten and fat. She pulled it out and opened the wallet. "Lots of receipts," she said as she riffled through the papers inside. "And a ten-dollar bill. I don't know your boss well, but if this is what he thinks qualifies as a stash of cash..."

Owen unbuckled his seat belt and leaned over to look. The distracting scent of Tara's skin almost made him forget what he was looking for, but he managed to gather his wits enough to search the glove compartment. Besides the wallet, there was only the car registration, a card providing proof of insurance, and a thick vehicle manual.

But Quinn had clearly told him there was a stash of cash in the glove compartment. Was this some sort of trap? A test?

He sat back a moment, thinking hard. Assuming Quinn had been playing things straight, why would he have said there was cash in the glove box if there wasn't?

Narrowing his eyes, he leaned over and looked into the

glove compartment again. There could be no cash hiding in the registration paper or the insurance card. But what about the manual?

"What are you doing?" Tara asked, leaning forward until her head was right next to Owen's in front of the open compartment.

Owen turned to look at her, his breath catching at her closeness. Her green eyes seemed large and luminous as her eyebrows rose in two delicate arches.

He forced his gaze back to the glove compartment and pulled out the manual. Easing back to his own side of the SUV, he opened the manual.

There was a fifty-dollar bill slipped between the first two pages.

He flipped through the book, a smile curving his mouth. Nearly every page sandwiched money. Dozens of tens, about that many twenties, several fifties and even a handful of hundreds. Nearly five thousand dollars in cash, Owen realized after adding up the sums in his head.

"Does he usually carry that much money in his vehicle?" Tara asked when Owen told her the sum.

"I have no idea." He handed her the manual full of money. "Leave it in there for now. I'm going to see what else I can find in this SUV."

"I'll check up here in the cab," Tara said as he opened the driver's door. "You see if there are any underfloor compartments."

Fifteen minutes later, they had uncovered a set of Tennessee license plates, another fifty dollars in change hidden in various places around the SUV, a Louisville Slugger baseball bat, a small smartphone with a prepaid phone card taped to its back, a duffel bag full of clothing and survival supplies and a dozen MREs—military-issued meals that could be prepared without cooking utensils or even a fire.

"He likes to cover all his bases," Tara said, looking at their bounty.

"I'll switch out the license plate and put the Kentucky one in the compartment where I found the Tennessee plates," Owen said. "Then I'm going to see if there are any minutes left on that phone."

"Do you think that's a good idea?"

"It's a burner phone. Quinn said to get in touch when we could. I think this is how we're supposed to do it."

Tara shook her head. "Not this soon. The police might be keeping an eye on him. Let's wait a day or two before we call him."

Owen gave her a considering look. "Okay. You're right."

"Don't sound so shocked." She shot him a quick grin. "Go change the tags and I'll see if I can find any more treasures."

Owen took a screwdriver from the small toolbox inside Quinn's survival kit and switched out the Kentucky plates for the Tennessee ones.

"What now?" Tara asked.

"I'm a little tempted to see where this road leads," Owen admitted, peering through the trees to the twisting dirt road ahead.

"You've got to be kidding me."

"I doubt anyone would think to look for us here."

"Where exactly is here?" She leaned forward, as if doing so might somehow reveal more of the road than was currently visible.

"I have no idea."

She shook her head. "I liked your idea of sleeping in the car at a rest area better. At least rest areas have bathrooms and vending machines."

"We have MREs, plus some protein bars and several bottles of water in the survival kit."

"Unless there's a relatively clean bathroom stashed in that kit, my opinion stands."

He sighed. "You used to be more adventurous."

"And you used to be less reckless. When did you change?"

When I realized playing things carefully was getting me nowhere, he thought. *When you met Robert and threw yourself headfirst into a romance with him because he ticked off all the items on your wish list.*

"If you want to go to Virginia and find a rest stop, that's what we'll do. But let's wait here until dark. It'll be easier to escape attention in the dark."

She sighed. "You have a point."

"Don't sound so shocked," he said with a grin.

His echo of her earlier words was enough to earn him a small laugh. "I know I shouldn't be happy you got sucked into my mess, but I'm really glad you're with me. I'm not sure what I would have done if you hadn't been there in that van when I regained consciousness."

He reached across the space between them and brushed a stray twig of hair away from her cheek. "You'd have done what you always do. You'd have come out on top."

Her smile faltered. "I don't feel as if I've come out on top."

"We're not through fighting yet, are we?" He should drop his hand away from her face instead of letting his fingertips linger against her cheek. But with Tara showing no signs of unease, he couldn't bring himself to pull away. He liked the way her skin felt, soft and warm, almost humming with vibrant life.

"I suppose this is a bad time to mention I could use a bathroom break." Tara gave him an apologetic look.

He checked his watch. "Don't suppose you could wait another four hours or so?"

She shook her head.

So much for waiting until after dark to hit the road. "Well, can you wait another hour? I was planning to drive to Abingdon anyway so we could pick up some supplies. We should be there in an hour or so."

"Yeah, I can wait that long."

"If we can find a thrift store, we could stock up on some clothing without making a big dent in our resources," he suggested.

"Good idea. It would be nice to have something that actually fits again." She tugged uncomfortably at her too-tight T-shirt.

He forced his gaze away from her breasts. "I might be able to pick up a laptop computer at a reasonable price, too."

She glanced at him. "Is that a necessity? Five thousand dollars isn't going to last long if we make big purchases."

"I need to be able to stay up on what's happening in the outside world while we're hunkered down."

"Won't you need an internet connection to do that?"

"Yes, but there are ways to do that without being entirely on the grid." He got the SUV turned around on the narrow road and headed for the main road again, hoping the stop hadn't allowed their pursuers to catch up with them. At least they were no longer wearing the Kentucky tags the police would be looking for.

"Do you think we should come up with disguises?" he asked aloud.

"Such as?"

"You could cut your hair. Dye it another color. I could keep growing this beard and buy some gamer glasses—"

"Gamer glasses?"

"Tinted-lens glasses gamers wear to cut down on screen glare. Good for computer users, too. I can probably find some if I can track down a computer store or gamer's store in Abingdon."

"You should buy the hair dye. I'll buy the glasses. In case anyone's paying attention."

"Good thinking." He had reached the main road and he pulled over to a stop, sparing her a quick look before he got back on the blacktop. "So, we find a shopping center. I'll go with you to the computer store to pick out what I need, but you can pay for it. Then we do the opposite when we pick up your hair dye. You pick, I pay."

She flashed a wry grin. "As long as the first place we stop has a bathroom."

"YOU'RE TELLING ME you don't have any sort of security system in your vehicle?" Archer Trask gave Quinn a look of disbelief. "In your line of work?"

"Rather like the doctor who ignores his yearly checkup." Quinn shrugged. "I'm afraid it's a failing many of us have—focusing more on our clients' security needs rather than our own."

Trask didn't appear to believe him, but Quinn didn't care. Trask could prove nothing, and Quinn had access to enough legal help to keep the Bagley County Sheriff's Department from doing any harm.

Meanwhile, he needed to get back to his office and convene a task force to dig deeper into the Tara Bentley case. First line of attack—find out the name of the deputy who'd helped kidnap her and Owen. If he'd been able to get a decent look at the guy himself, he knew Giattina, who'd been parked closer, must have, also. As soon as Quinn finished this pointless interview with Trask, he planned to find Giattina and compare notes. He'd already warned Tony against sharing information with the police that Owen and Tara had revealed while he was acting as their lawyer. Attorney-client privilege was something Tony took seriously, so Quinn doubted he'd have revealed anything about the suspicious deputy to the investigators interrogating him.

Trask gave Quinn a copy of his statement to sign. "We have your license plate number and the description of your vehicle. We'll find Owen Stiles and Tara Bentley sooner or later." Trask frowned. "If you should hear from them, I'm sure you'll warn them that their decision to flee hardly makes them look innocent."

Quinn signed the statement. "Of course. Am I free to go?"

"You'll let us know if you hear anything from the fugitives?"

"Of course," Quinn lied.

He caught up with Tony Giattina outside, where the lawyer waited by his Mercedes, talking on the phone. His dark eyes met Quinn's, and he said something into the phone, then put it in his pocket. "Would you like to tell me why you're aiding and abetting fugitives?"

Quinn nodded toward the Mercedes. With a sigh, Tony unlocked the car and joined Quinn inside.

"You knew what was going on," Tony said with a grimace. "Is my car bugged?"

Quinn reached under the dashboard and pulled out a small listening device. "I'm sorry. I needed to hear what they had to say to you."

"You breached attorney-client privilege."

"I'm not an attorney."

"No," Tony said with a grimace. "You're a damned spy."

"Former."

"Former, my shiny red—"

"They're in trouble. And I believed them when they told you they recognized one of the Bagley County Sheriff's Department deputies as one of the men who kidnapped them."

"You think the cops were in on what happened to them?"

"Not the whole bunch of them, no. But at least one. And possibly more."

"So why didn't they stick around and identify the guy instead of punching your lights out and running for the hills?"

"Because who would believe them?" Quinn waved at the listening device sitting on the console between them. "You didn't believe them, and you're their lawyer."

Tony fell silent a moment. "What do you expect from me?"

"Your silence. They told you about the kidnapper as part of your attorney-client relationship. It remains privileged until such time as they give you permission to reveal it."

"You don't want me to tell what I know? If you and my clients are right, there's a kidnapper working as a Bagley County deputy, and you want that information kept silent?"

"I do."

Tony shook his head. "That makes no damn sense."

Quinn reached for the listening device and slipped it into his pocket. "What do you think would happen if we told what we know? Let's say Trask believes us. He'd track down the deputy you saw, get your identification of the man and start questioning him. Which would be a disaster."

"Why would it be a disaster?"

"Because I've come to believe the people behind Tara Bentley's kidnapping are up to something far more dangerous than a simple abduction. And if we tip our hand, we may not find out what their plan is until it's much too late."

Chapter Nine

"Wow. Is that you?"

Tara looked up at the sound of Owen's voice, but it took a moment to realize that the gangly hipster in the saggy gray beanie shuffling toward her was her best friend. The cap looked ancient and well used, and it went well with the rest of his slouchy attire, from the baggy faded jeans to the oversize navy hoodie with the name of an obscure eighties' metal band on the front. The sleek design of his amber-lensed glasses should have looked out of sync with the rest of his slacker aesthetic, but somehow the glasses seemed perfectly at home perched on his long, thin nose.

"I almost didn't recognize you," she said as he set a large shopping bag from an electronics store on the hood of the SUV.

"Likewise." He waved his hand toward her hair. "I like the purple."

She patted her now-short hair self-consciously. The budget hair salon in the Abingdon shopping center had done a decent job giving her a spiky gamine cut, but the spray-on color she'd added was way outside her normal comfort zone.

"We need to hit the road, but I had an idea for the SUV." Owen pulled a small bag from inside his jacket and reached inside, withdrawing a small stack of bumper stickers. "Start sticking them on the back of the SUV."

The stickers, she saw, embraced every social justice issue known to man, including some that contradicted each other.

"It would be better if this were a Volkswagen Beetle," she muttered when he rejoined her at the back of the SUV after he'd stashed his new computer inside.

"You make do with what you have," Owen said with a shrug. "The main thing is, it doesn't look like the SUV that left Kentucky this morning."

She tugged at the ends of her hair. "And we don't look like the people who left Kentucky this morning."

"Exactly." He cocked his head. "Don't suppose you could get your nose pierced?"

She gave his arm a light slap. "No."

"Maybe your belly button?"

"Get in the car."

From Abingdon, they took I-81 north, heading for the next rest stop. Spotting a sign for a sub shop at one of the interstate exits just south of the rest area, Owen pulled off the highway to grab a couple of sandwiches for their dinner.

By the time they finally reached the rest stop, the afternoon had started fading into twilight. Owen found a parking place a few spaces away from the nearest car and parked.

"Home, sweet home," he murmured.

"Let's take a restroom break," Tara suggested. "Give me a couple of dollars and I'll buy some drinks to go with our dinner."

The bathrooms were blessedly clean and human traffic at the rest stop was just busy enough for Owen and Tara to be able to blend in without any trouble. She bought the drinks and, while she was there, picked up a few of the brochures for south Virginia campgrounds and attractions.

She showed Owen one of the brochures over dinner. "It's a campground about two hours east of here. We pay a small fee for a campsite. There's a communal restroom within walking distance, and a charging station for electronics. They even advertise free Wi-Fi."

Owen looked at the brochure, his brow furrowed. "There is a tent stashed in the back of the SUV..."

"We stay here tonight, and then tomorrow we can settle in there. Maybe you can put that computer you bought to use."

"How's the salmon?" Becky Cameron asked.

"Delicious." Quinn tried to remain expressionless, not sure he was ready to let his colleague know that her sudden desire to socialize was beginning to make him uneasy. He turned keeping people at arm's length into an art form. Becky knew that better than most, having worked with him off and on for more than fifteen years.

"Are you ever going to tell me about your adventure this morning?" she asked, delicately picking at her own pan-seared trout.

"Not much to tell."

She gestured with one long-fingered, graceful hand toward the bruise shadowing his jawline. "Owen Stiles packs a nice punch."

"We taught him well."

"You don't seem particularly incensed at the idea of having your vehicle stolen by a trusted employee."

"Life is full of surprises."

Becky smiled, showing a flash of straight white teeth. "Subject dropped."

"That's for the best," he agreed, glancing around the crowded restaurant. "For the here and now, at least."

She nodded, taking a dainty bite of the trout. "We can catch up at work in the morning."

A few minutes of thick silence stretched between them before Becky spoke again. "You're wondering why I invited you here when I know as well as you do that there are certain topics we can't discuss in public."

"The question did cross my mind."

Becky's smile was full of sympathy. "I don't mean to be so enigmatic. That's your bailiwick."

He managed a smile. "But you clearly brought me here for a reason."

"Socializing isn't reason enough?"

He quirked one eyebrow, making her smile.

"Right," she said, the smile fading. "I wanted to talk to you about something not connected to work. And I was afraid if I tried to approach you at the office, I would lose my nerve."

Now he was intrigued. "I can't imagine you ever losing your nerve, Becky. About anything."

"It's about Mitch."

Suddenly, the half filet of salmon he'd eaten felt like a lump of lead in his stomach. He laid down his fork and took a drink of water to cover his sudden discomfort. "Has something changed?"

"Maybe." A furrow creased her brow. "There's some indication that he might not have died in the helicopter crash in Tablis."

Quinn froze in the act of straightening his napkin across his lap. "I saw the crash myself. We searched the area thoroughly for over a week. Men under my watch died trying to recover all the bodies. But it was the rainy season, and the current in the river where they crashed was brutally swift. Several bodies washed downriver and were never recovered."

"I saw film of the crash. I know how unlikely it is that he survived."

Quinn reached across the table and covered her hand with his. "I know you want to believe there's a chance he survived."

"I don't know what I want to believe, Quinn. It's been nearly ten years. If he survived, why didn't he try to reach someone? I know it's grasping at straws. It's just—what if he's out there? Maybe he doesn't remember what happened or who he is. Maybe he just needs to see a familiar face to trigger the rest of his memories."

He gave her hand another squeeze before letting go. "I don't think it works that way. But if you want me to put out some feelers with some of my old contacts in Kaziristan—"

"I'd appreciate it," she said with a grateful smile. She looked down at her plate. "I don't know about you, but I think my appetite is gone."

"You want to get out of here? Maybe we could head back to the office and talk about the subject we were supposed to talk about?"

She nodded. "You go ahead. I'll get the check and meet you there."

"I can wait," he said, feeling an unexpected protectiveness of her. He'd never thought of Becky as someone who needed anyone or anything. Even her relationship with Mitch Talbot, a marine colonel she'd met when she was stationed at the US embassy in Tablis, Kaziristan, had seemed lopsided. She was the diplomat, a woman of culture, education and power, while he was a gruff leatherneck more at home in fatigues leading his men into combat.

But clearly, she'd loved him deeply if she was willing to

put her reputation and her connections on the line to find him ten years after his presumed death. Was she setting herself up for a fresh new heartbreak?

She was obviously going to look for the man, whether Quinn helped her or not. And even though the thought of trying to dig up those old bones made him positively queasy, it was the least he owed her.

After all, he was the man who'd sent Mitch Talbot to his death.

MORNING WAS JUST a hint of pink promise in the eastern sky when Owen woke from a restless sleep. At bedtime the night before, he and Tara had tried to sleep on the narrow bench seats, but after the second time Tara tumbled off the seat into the floorboard, they decided it made more sense to fold down the seats and use the now-flat cargo area to deploy the sleeping bags stashed among other survival gear in the underfloor storage area of the SUV. Given the dropping temperature outside, they decided to zip the two bags into one spacious double bag. Curling up back to back, they'd fallen asleep in relative warmth, if not comfort.

At some point during the night, however, they'd ended up face-to-face, their limbs entangled beneath the down-filled cover of the sleeping bags.

For a heady moment, Owen wanted nothing more than to stay right where he was for the rest of his life, his skin against hers, her warmth enfolding him with a sense of sublime rightness he had never felt with anyone but her.

It would be so much easier if he could have found that feeling of completion with another woman. He'd tried more than once over the years to move on, to seek a relationship, a life, where Tara Bentley wasn't the most important part of it. It had taken a long time for him to come to terms with the fact that as long as Tara was in his life, she would always be the most important part of it.

Which meant the only way to move on with his life would be to let her go completely.

He gently extricated himself from her sleeping embrace. She made a soft groaning noise that echoed inside his own chest, but he forced himself to keep moving rather than return to the warmth of her body. Trying not to wake her, he unzipped his side of the sleeping back, wincing at the rush of cold outside its down-filled insulation. He grabbed his jacket from the front seat and added it to the sweatshirt and jeans he'd worn last night for warmth before he opened the door and stepped out into the chilly morning air.

Across the rest area parking lot, a handful of other travelers were up and moving, taking advantage of the bathrooms and vending machines. One machine seemed to dispense hot coffee, he noticed, swirls of steam rising from cups held by weary travelers exiting the building.

He pulled up the collar of his jacket and tugged the ratty beanie over his head, grimacing at the need for disguise. It was too dark for the glasses, so he left them in his jacket pocket as he slouched his way across to the rest area center.

After a quick bathroom break, the siren song of coffee drew him to the vending machine. He bought a couple of cups and tucked them to his chest under one arm while he studied the vending machine selections. Sweet or salty? Tara wasn't much of a breakfast person, but they couldn't be sure when they'd be able to eat again, so she needed something with some protein. A bag of peanuts and a pack of cheese crackers would have to do.

He didn't immediately notice a new arrival at the rest area center, so it was with a flutter of shock that he turned away from the vending machine to find a Virginia State Police officer standing only a couple of yards away.

He froze at first, his heart beating a tattoo against his ribs. Coffee sloshed in the cups pressed against his chest, almost spilling down his shirt.

Turning as slowly as he dared, he settled the cups and edged toward the side of the room, where a few travelers were looking through the brochure racks advertising local tourist stops.

He glanced back toward the policeman. He seemed to be looking for something.

Or someone?

Owen edged toward the door with his purchases, hoping he wouldn't do something stupid like trip over his own feet and draw attention toward himself. Tara was asleep in the SUV, with no idea how close they were to being discovered.

One foot in front of the other...

"Excuse me, sir? Have you seen this woman?" The voice, so close, made him jerk with surprise. Some of the coffee spilled onto the pavement in front of the rest-area door.

Slowly, he turned to face the policeman. The man was holding a printed flyer with a woman's photograph on it. Owen nearly melted with relief when he realized the woman on the flyer wasn't Tara.

"I'm sorry, no," he said, faking a midwestern accent. "Just driving through."

"If you see anything, give us a call." The policeman started to hand Owen a card, then belatedly realized his hands were full. He slipped the card into the pocket of Owen's jacket. "Have a safe trip."

"Thanks." Owen gave a nod and headed quickly across the parking lot to the SUV.

Tara was awake when he opened the door. He set the coffee and snacks on the floorboard and glanced over his shoulder. The policeman had remained outside the rest area center, talking to travelers as they entered and exited the place.

Following his gaze, Tara asked with alarm, "Is that a cop?"

"He seems to be looking for a missing woman. I nearly had a heart attack when he stopped me to ask if I'd seen her."

"Do you think he recognized you?"

"He didn't seem to." He looked at Tara. "Stop staring at him. He'll think we're up to something."

"We *are* up to something. Sort of." Tara forced her gaze away from the policeman, letting it settle on Owen's vending-machine bounty. "Coffee. Thank goodness."

"You need to eat something, too. I bought you some peanuts for protein."

"Yes, Mom." She tore open the packet of peanuts. "Want some?"

Owen's appetite was gone. Even the coffee, which he'd been craving just a little while ago, seemed entirely unappetizing. "Go ahead. I'll worry about getting us ready to get back on the road."

They'd filled the gas tank back in Abingdon, so they were good for several more miles before they'd have to worry about stopping for fuel. The tires looked fine, and all of the SUV's gauges were reading in the normal range. He settled in the driver's seat, his nerves finally steady enough for him to sit still without fidgeting.

"I think enough time has passed now that we can leave without looking as if we're running away," he said, glancing over his shoulder at Tara.

She licked salt off her fingertips and looked back at him. "Even though that's what we're doing."

"You have a better idea?"

She shook her head. "Let's get out of here."

"You can stay in the back and get a little more sleep if you want."

"No, I'm wide awake. Hold on and I'll come up front." She exited the back door and climbed into the front, first putting Owen's cooling cup of coffee in the console's cup holder. "You should drink that before it gets cold."

He looked at it and shook his head. "You can have it if you want."

She climbed into the passenger seat and buckled in, then picked up the cup. "If you insist."

They fell silent until they were well clear of the rest area and moving east on I-81. As they passed through the scenic town of Rural Retreat, Tara set down her empty coffee cup and turned in her seat to look at him.

"Maybe we should call your boss," she suggested.

"I'm not sure it's safe."

"Is it that? Or is it that you don't want to ask for help."

He angled a quick look at her. She gazed back at him, a knowing look in her eyes that made him feel completely exposed.

"I know you don't like asking for help," she added, her tone gentler. "I know why."

"I'm not afraid to call Quinn if we need him."

"But you're afraid if you call him now, he'll see you as weak. Just like your father used to accuse you of being."

He pressed his lips to a thin line, annoyed. "Not every decision I make in my life is influenced by what my father said to me when I was fifteen."

"Then call Quinn. He told you to get in touch, right?"

"Yes, but—"

"No buts." She pulled the cell phone from the caddy at the front of the console, where it had been charging all night. "Call him."

"I'm driving."

"I'll dial. Just tell me the number."

With a sigh, he gave her the number of Quinn's business cell phone. "It's still awfully early," he warned.

"Didn't you once tell me you think Quinn never sleeps?" She put the phone on speaker and dialed the number.

Quinn answered on the first ring, "Don't tell me anything about where you are. Just tell me if you're all right."

"We're fine," Owen answered, surprised at the relief that flooded him at the sound of his boss's voice. He wasn't close to Quinn at all, having barely spoken to the man more than a dozen times since he took the job at Campbell Cove Security. But just knowing he had someone besides Tara out there, trying to watch his back, was enough to bolster his sagging spirits. "We've disguised ourselves and the vehicle, so we're trying to find somewhere to hunker down until we can formulate a plan for our next steps."

"I think your next steps should include trying to figure out who wants the information Tara has in her head that they can't find anywhere else."

"That's where you could give us some help," Tara interjected. "I know what information they're looking for, but I'm not in the know about which groups might be looking for that information. Do you have a dossier on the groups most likely to be trying to make a big show of force at the symposium?"

"That's going to be a lot of dossiers," he warned.

"What about the deputy we saw? Maybe if we could get an ID on him, we could dig deeper and figure out who he associates with," Owen suggested.

"On it. The Bagley County Sheriff's Department inconveniently doesn't have a website, but Archer Trask has cooperated with us on a previous case he was investigating, so I'm going to see if I can exploit that relationship to get information without raising his suspicions."

"You're going to try to outcop a cop?" Tara asked skeptically.

"We have our ways." There was a hint of amusement in Quinn's voice. "I'll handle that end of things. Meanwhile, you need to stay off the grid as much as you can. You found the cash and all the supplies?"

"We did," Owen answered.

"You're a scary man, Alexander Quinn," Tara added.

"I like to be prepared," he said. "Call again in four hours. If everything is good, tell me that it's not. If you're in trouble, say everything is okay. Understood?"

Owen exchanged glances with Tara. Both her eyebrows were near her hairline, but she said, "Understood."

Quinn ended the call without another word, and she put the phone back in the console holder.

"So," she said, "where exactly do we plan to hunker down?"

"I think we need to find that campsite I was telling you about. And fast."

The sooner they were off the road, the less likely it was that someone would spot their SUV and start wondering if it might be the missing vehicle from Kentucky with the two fugitives inside.

Chapter Ten

"I can't believe you bought marshmallows."

Tara looked up from the shopping bag she was unpacking to find Owen holding a bag of the puffy white sweets. "I don't go camping without marshmallows. Or hot dogs," she added, pulling a pack of wieners from the shopping bag.

Owen sighed, but she saw the hint of a smile cross his face. "I hope you got mustard, too."

She waggled the mustard bottle at him. "And ketchup for me."

He made a face. "I appreciate the fact that you're trying to make this a fun experience—"

"I'm trying to get through this without losing my sanity," she corrected, her voice rising with a rush of emotion. "If I treat this like one of our nights out camping at Kingdom Come State Park, maybe I can get through this thing without being institutionalized."

Silence fell between them for a long, tense moment before Owen finally spoke. "I'm sorry."

She shook her head. "You have nothing to be sorry for. You're in this mess, too, and it's all because of me."

"No, I meant I'm sorry about Robert. I haven't really said that to you. I know you loved him, even if you didn't love him enough to go through with the wedding. And you haven't really had a moment to yourself to just grieve."

"I don't have time to grieve. I have to figure out this whole mess. It's about me and what I know. It's my responsibility."

He stood up from where he crouched by the fire pit he was building and crossed to where she stood by the SUV. He cupped her face between his hands, and emotion surged in her chest, making her feel as if she were about to explode. She tamped down the feelings roiling through her and forced herself to meet his soft-eyed gaze.

"You don't have to do this alone. Any of it."

Blinking back tears she didn't want to spill, she managed a smile. "I know you're on my side. You always are."

Something flickered in his gaze, an emotion she couldn't quite read, and he dropped his hands from her face and stepped a couple of feet away. "I'll put the hot dogs in the cooler." He picked up the pack of wieners and walked back to the campsite.

Even though he was only a few feet away from her, she suddenly felt as if she were alone, cut off from anything and anyone important to her. It was a hollow, terrible feeling.

She shook off the sensation. She wasn't alone. She hadn't been alone since the sixth grade, when Owen Stiles had literally stumbled into her life, dropping his lunch tray at her feet and soiling her favorite pair of Chuck Taylors. Once she got past the desire to strangle him, she'd found a friend who'd never, ever failed her.

He wouldn't fail her now. If there was anything in her life that was constant and permanent, it was Owen Stiles. His friendship was everything to her, which was why she'd fight anyone and anything, including her own libido, to keep him in her life.

While she was picking up camping supplies at a store in the nearby town of Weatherly, Owen had been busy setting up camp. The tent he'd found stored in the SUV now stood next to the campfire. It was larger than she'd expected, but still cozy enough that they should be able to stay warm in the night.

"Did you find any nightcrawlers?" he asked as she crossed with the rest of the supplies to where he crouched by the fire pit.

"Of course. No grocery store this close to a campground would be caught dead without a bait shop section." She sat cross-legged on the ground next to him and dug in her grocery bag until she retrieved two small plastic bowls full of dirt. There were little pinprick holes in the plastic lid of the containers. "Here. Have some worms."

"There's a curve of the river that runs near here, according to the online map." He pulled the cell phone from his pocket and waggled it at her, a smile flirting with his lips. "I don't know how Daniel Boone made it across the wilderness without Google."

A gust of wind lifted Tara's short locks and rustled the grocery bag. She looked up through the trees to discover that the sunny sky that had greeted them earlier that morning was gone, swallowed by slate-colored clouds scudding along with the wind.

"I don't think we're going to get to have marshmallows or hot dogs tonight," she said with a heavy sigh. "I bought a few cans of soup, though. I think we could probably heat one up using the camp stove before the rain hits."

"You're being a good sport about this," Owen commented as he gathered up the supplies he'd laid out on the ground by their would-be campfire. "I know how you like your creature comforts."

"It's not like this is your mess, Owen. You didn't drag me into this. It's the other way around."

"I dragged myself into it."

"Trying to help me."

"You'd have done the same." He finished stowing away the equipment in the waterproof duffel and stuffed it into the tent, leaving out only the portable camp stove and a small saucepan. He looked up at the sky. "We probably have another fifteen minutes before the bottom falls out of the sky, so what kind of soup do we have there?"

She pulled out three cans. "Chicken noodle, vegetable and beef, and chicken-corn chowder."

"The chowder sounds good. Filling."

She put the other two cans back in the shopping bag and pulled the tab ring on the can of chowder. It opened with a quiet snick. "Hope there aren't any bears nearby."

"Me, too." Owen added the butane canister to the camp stove and turned the knob until it clicked and a flame appeared at the center of the burner. "Oh, look, it works."

"You weren't sure it would?" Tara asked.

"I hoped it would." He set the saucepan on the burner and reached out for the can of soup.

Tara handed it to him and crouched beside him. "I didn't think to buy any paper bowls."

"There are plastic bowls and eating utensils in the duffel bag."

She retrieved them and sat down beside Owen in front of the stove. "I still think your boss is some sort of madman, but at least he's a madman who knows how to prepare for any eventuality."

"I imagine he learned about being prepared the hard way. I've heard some stories—all told in hushed tones, of course—about some of his adventures during his time in the CIA."

"Do you believe them?"

"Most of them, yeah. You don't get the kind of reputation Quinn has if you spent your years in the CIA behind some cushy desk in an embassy."

The advent of the clouds overhead had driven out most of the warmth of the day, and there was a definite damp chill in the increasing wind. Tara edged closer to Owen, glad for his body heat and the warmth drifting toward her from the camp stove. The soup was already starting to burble in the pan.

"Maybe we should eat inside the tent," she suggested. "I think it's going to rain any minute."

He looked up at the sky. "Good idea. Here, hand me the bowls and I'll spoon this up. Then you can take the food inside and I'll clean up out here."

Tara took the bowls of soup Owen handed to her and ducked inside the tent. Their sleeping bags covered most of the tent floor; as they had the night before, they'd zipped the bags together in order to take advantage of each other's body heat. With the sudden dip in the temperature, Tara had a feeling it was going to be a damp, chilly night.

Owen appeared through the flap of the tent, carrying the extinguished stove and the cleaned-up cooking pot. He left the stove just inside the tent to cool but stowed away the cooking pot, then took his food from Tara. He nodded at her untouched bowl. "Eat up before it gets cold."

She took a bite of the hearty chowder. It was pretty good for canned soup. "I don't suppose Quinn has sent you the dossiers we asked for."

Owen pulled the burner phone from his pocket. "To be honest, I haven't checked. I was keeping the phone off to conserve the battery, since I don't want to risk putting any sort of drain on the SUV's engine until we're on the road again."

They had agreed not to camp too close to the campground amenities, wanting to avoid interaction with other campers. The restrooms were only a hundred yards away, hidden by the woods, but the office was another hundred yards away, which meant the charging stations available to campers were also that far away.

"I'm getting a Wi-Fi signal from the campground. It's not the strongest, but it's better than nothing."

"Think it'll be strong enough for a file to download?"

"There's an email trying to download. It's slow going, but I'll bet it's from Quinn. Nobody else would have the email for this phone." He stuck the phone back in his pocket. "Let's finish eating. I'll check again when we're finished. Maybe it'll have downloaded by then."

Tara suddenly felt anything but hungry, but she forced herself to eat. If they were going to be running for their lives over the next few days, she needed her strength. Food wasn't a luxury. It was a necessity.

She managed to remain patient until her bowl was empty. She set it aside and looked up at Owen. "Can you check the email again?"

He gave her a sympathetic look and pulled out his phone. "Looks as if it's finished. Let's see what we've got."

She scooted closer so she could see the phone screen. The file attached to the email appeared to be a portable document file. Owen clicked the pdf file and a summary page appeared. Tara scanned the words, which informed them that the following files contained background details on the employees of Security Solutions. According to Quinn's notes, he was also trying to come up with potential connections between the sheriff's department and Security Solutions along with trying to connect members of the sheriff's department to any of the known terror groups who had both the motive and the means to stage a significant terror event on American soil.

"What do you expect to find in these dossiers?" Owen asked.

"Connections," she answered. "I'm thinking it would have to be someone who's in a position to take any of the information I might have supplied to the kidnappers and do something with it."

"Who might that be?"

"Well, obviously, my bosses, but since they already have the information I have, they wouldn't need to bother with a kidnapping."

"Do you have an assistant?"

"Yes, but Karen wouldn't be next in line for the job if I suddenly disappear."

"But could she use the information you have if she could get her hands on it?"

Tara thought about it. "Theoretically, anyone could. But it's likely that by now, my bosses have already changed all the details of the event. Either postponed it or moved venues."

"So maybe you're not in danger anymore."

The same thought had just occurred to her. "Maybe. But why do I still feel as if I'm in danger?"

"I think maybe because Alexander Quinn thinks you still are, and if he does, he must have a reason." Owen set aside his empty soup bowl and pulled the burner phone out of his pocket. "Let's find out why."

"Will he answer?" she asked as he dialed the number.

"He'd better."

Tara scooted closer so she could hear the other end of the call. The phone rang twice before a drawling voice answered, "Roy's Auto Repair."

"I'm calling about my green Cutlass GT," Owen said, arching his eyebrows at Tara.

"I'll check, sir." After a brief pause, the voice on the

other line continued. "Still checking, but Roy told me to ask how you're doing today."

"Just lousy," Owen answered.

"Sorry to hear that." The voice on the other end of the line suddenly sounded like Quinn. "Thought I said I'd call you."

"You did. But we have a question."

"Shoot."

"Why exactly do you think Tara is still in danger, when you have to know her bosses have already changed the details of the project?"

SHEFFIELD TAVERN WAS less a bar and more a restaurant that happened to serve liquor at a bar in the back. On this Monday afternoon, the bar crowd was laid-back and sparse, though it would probably pick up later in the evening.

Archer Trask had agreed to meet Maddox Heller for an early dinner at the tavern more out of curiosity than any real desire to deal with the Campbell Cove Security agent, given the way his previous day had gone. But the chance that Heller might provide some needed information about what, exactly, had sent Tara Bentley and Owen Stiles on the run again was worth putting up with bar food and average beer.

To his surprise, Heller brought his wife, Iris, a tall, slim woman with wavy black hair and coffee-brown eyes. She smiled at Trask, extending her hand as Heller introduced them.

As Trask shook Iris's hand, he felt an odd tingle in his hand, almost as if static electricity had sparked between them. But if Iris noticed, she didn't show it.

Trask took a seat across the table from Heller and his pretty wife, looking curiously from one to the other. "I'm wondering why you asked me to meet you here."

"Alexander Quinn requested that I contact you about something that's arisen in the Robert Mallory murder case," Heller said. "He's on other business, or he'd have asked to speak with you himself."

Something about this meeting didn't quite feel right, but Trask decided to play along as if he weren't suspicious. "Not sure there's much point talking to y'all, considering you weren't there."

"Actually, there is." Heller bent down and picked up the worn leather satchel he'd brought with him to the tavern. He unbuckled the latch and flipped the satchel cover open. "You see, my wife, among her many other talents, is an artist. And we've begun to use her talent in some of our cases where we work with witnesses—"

"She's a sketch artist, you mean," Trask interrupted, beginning to lose his patience. His day had been long already, and the rest of the week stretched out in front of him like a series of endless frustrations and dead ends. "But unless she saw who shot Robert Mallory, I don't see how she can help us."

"Has anyone told you what Tara Bentley says happened to her the day of her wedding?"

Trask tried not to show his sudden spark of interest, but he couldn't help sitting up a little straighter. "No. I assume she and her partner in crime told their lawyer something about their disappearance, but he invoked the lawyer-client privilege thing, so we're still in the dark. Damn inconvenient, that. Kind of makes it hard to do my job, you know?"

"She was kidnapped," Heller said bluntly. "Two men in a white cargo van. Owen Stiles happened upon them in the middle of it and was knocked out and thrown into the van, as well."

Trask stared at him in disbelief. "You've got to be kidding me."

"Yeah, that was about the reaction Owen and Tara were expecting," Heller drawled, looking so disappointed that Trask started feeling a little guilty for his instant reaction.

Then he got angry about feeling guilty. "It's a ridiculous story. Did they happen to tell you why someone would kidnap a bride on her wedding day when, oh, by the way, the groom ended up facedown in his own blood in the groom's room?"

"They don't know why. That's part of the problem."

"How did they get away?"

"Their captors miscalculated when they bound Tara's hands. They bound them in front of her with duct tape rather than behind her, and she was able to undo the tape around Owen's hands. He freed her, and that gave them time to prepare for a blitz attack on their captors when they stopped and opened the doors to transfer them wherever they were planning to take them."

"What then?" Trask asked, glancing at Heller's wife to see how she was reacting to the story Heller was telling. She had a placid look in her eyes, tinged by a hint of jaded knowing that suggested she'd seen and heard far stranger things in her life.

"They were able to get away, although the kidnappers pursued them in the woods for a while. Finally, the kidnappers retreated, and Tara and Owen found an old abandoned cabin for shelter from the rain that night."

"What then?"

"They got in touch with us, and we got them a lawyer. You know the rest." Heller's expression was completely neutral, which in his case was a tell. There was a little more to the story about how Bentley and Stiles got from point A to point B, but Heller wasn't going to share. Trask supposed in the long run, it wasn't that big a deal. What he really wanted to know was why they changed their minds about turning themselves in.

"They decided against turning themselves in while they were right outside the police department," Trask said. "Why?"

"Because yesterday morning, when they showed up to turn themselves in, they spotted one of the men who kidnapped them entering the sheriff's department, dressed in a deputy's uniform. Alexander Quinn saw the man, too, and he described him in detail to Iris. She made this sketch." Heller pulled a sheet of paper out of his satchel and laid it on the table in front of Trask.

Trask looked at the sketch. It was extremely well drawn, full of details and nuance. He recognized the face immediately.

"You know him, don't you?" Heller asked, his tone urgent.

Trask looked up at Heller, too stunned to hide his reaction. "Yes, I do."

"Who is he?"

Trask shoved the sketch back across the table, his stomach roiling. "This is bull. Just like the story Bentley and Stiles shoveled your way."

"Who is the man in the sketch?" Heller persisted.

"Maddox," Iris said in a warning tone, clutching his arm.

Something passed between Heller and his wife, and the man's bulldog demeanor softened. When he spoke again, his voice was gentle with a hint of sympathetic understanding. "You obviously recognize the man. Even if the story Tara and Owen told is bull, like you think, there must be a reason they chose this man as the scapegoat. Who is he?"

"He's my brother," Trask growled, his stomach starting to ache. "All right? He's my brother."

Chapter Eleven

The long pause on the other end of the line only convinced Owen that he and Tara were right. Quinn had his own agenda, as always. He and Tara might be valuable pawns in this particular chess game, but pawns they were, nevertheless.

"It doesn't matter whether or not her bosses have changed the details of the project," Quinn said finally. "What matters is letting your opponent continue to believe you're better armed than he is."

"What does that even mean?" Owen asked, trying not to lose his temper. Getting angry wouldn't get him any closer to uncovering Quinn's motives.

Tara put her hand on Owen's arm. "It means Mr. Quinn wants the people who kidnapped me to think there's a reason I'm not rushing back to civilization with my story."

"There is a reason. One of the guys who kidnapped us is working for the cops."

"They'll be wondering what information we're trying to protect by keeping you hidden," Quinn explained. "They'll want to know what that information might be, and they'll take risks to find out."

"But how does that help us if we don't know who they are?" Tara asked.

"We know who one of them is," Quinn corrected after

a brief pause. "I just got a message from Maddox Heller. I don't believe you know this, but his wife is working for us as a freelance sketch artist. I gave her the description of the deputy you say kidnapped the two of you."

"You saw him?" Tara asked.

"Yes."

"Unbelievable," Owen muttered. "I barely got a glimpse of him myself. How did you get a good enough look to give anyone a description?"

"Close observation is what I do. It's what I've done for decades now." Quinn's tone was abrupt. "The point is, Heller showed Archer Trask the sketch Iris made, and now we have an ID on the man who kidnapped you."

"Who is he?" Owen asked.

"He's Virgil Trask. Archer Trask's older brother."

"Trask identified him?" Tara looked at Owen, her eyes wide.

"Reluctantly, according to Heller. I haven't briefed him yet. He left a text for me on my other phone."

"Unbelievable," Tara muttered. "The kidnapper is the brother of the cop trying to bring us in."

"This could end up working in our favor," Quinn said. "Their relationship is going to force Trask to either play this investigation strictly by the book or risk being accused of a cover-up. He knows it, and he knows we know it, too."

"But is he going to take seriously the possibility that his brother is involved with a terrorist plot?" Owen asked.

"It doesn't matter. He knows *we're* taking it seriously, and we have the clout to make waves if he doesn't at least explore the possibility."

Tara shook her head. "What if he takes himself off the case? Won't that be the protocol if his brother is now a suspect?"

"If it were a large department, yes. But the Bagley

County Sheriff's Department has only three investigators, and one of those is on maternity leave. The other one is Virgil Trask."

"Great. He's an investigator, too?"

"We're on top of this." Quinn's tone was firm and, if Owen was reading him correctly, impatient. "I'll call back before ten. You continue lying low." He ended the call abruptly.

"Your boss is a sweetheart, isn't he?" Tara's tone was bone dry.

Owen looked at the phone display. The battery was getting low. He dug in Quinn's duffel for one of the portable chargers Quinn had packed. As he plugged in the phone to charge, he looked up at Tara, waving the portable charger in front of him. "This is why we need to trust him. He's always prepared. He's always a step ahead of whatever problem he faces."

"You make him sound like a superhero."

"No, just a man who's seen the worst the world has to offer and knows what it takes to face it." Owen pushed the phone aside and shifted position until he was face-to-face with Tara, their knees touching. The sense of déjà vu made him smile. "Remember the last time we shared a tent like this?"

The tension lines in Tara's face relaxed. A smile played on her lips. "The summer before we started high school. We sat just like this in the tent and swore we'd be friends forever."

He smiled back at her. "High school should have posed a problem for us. You, the cute little cheerleader with all the popular boys in love with you, and me, the socially awkward computer geek…"

She reached across the space between them and took his hand. "You, the brilliant, funny, kindhearted friend who never, ever let me down."

He twined his fingers through hers, his pulse picking up speed until he could hear it thundering in his ears, nearly eclipsing the steady syncopation of rain on top of the tent. "Then why do you think I'll let you down if things change between us?"

She stared at him in shock, as if he'd just reached across the space between them and slapped her. She pulled her hand back from his. "You know how I feel about this."

"I know you're afraid of things changing between us."

"You should be, too." She had turned away from him and now sat with her shoulders hunched. "I don't know what I'd do without you."

"You wouldn't be without me. Don't you see that? You'd just be with me in a different way. A deeper way."

She shot a glare at him over her shoulder. "You don't know that's how it would go. What if we discovered we weren't good together that way?" She shook her head fiercely. "I can't risk that."

Owen didn't push her. It would be useless when she had so clearly closed her mind to the idea that they could have something more than just friendship.

He pulled his jacket on like armor, protecting himself against both the dropping temperature outside and the distinct chill that had grown inside the tent with his tentative attempt to address the ongoing sexual tension between them.

But he didn't know how much longer he could keep denying what he felt for her. Maybe she was happy living this half life, but he was all too quickly reaching the point where something had to give.

ARCHER TRASK POURED himself two fingers of Maker's Mark bourbon and stared at the amber liquor with an ache in his soul. It would be one thing if he could just laugh off the allegation against Virgil with full assurance, but he couldn't really do that, could he? Virgil might be wearing a badge now, but he'd spent most of his youth caught up in one mess or another.

Their father's money had spared him the worst consequences of his reckless spirit, but even after Virgil left behind his teenage years, there had been whispers of questionable behavior, hadn't there? Complaints from prisoners of rough treatment. A tendency to rub some of his fellow deputies the wrong way.

But getting involved in a kidnapping?

Archer swirled the bourbon around in the tumbler, his mouth feeling suddenly parched. Just a sip wouldn't hurt. A sip and the burn of the whiskey to drive away the chill that seemed to seep right through to his bones.

But as one of the sheriff's department's three investigators, he was always on call, especially with Tammy Sloan out on maternity leave. He couldn't afford to show up on a call with liquor on his breath.

He pushed the glass away and picked up his cell phone. Virgil's number wasn't exactly first on his speed dial. In fact, as brothers, they weren't much alike at all. Trask had always chalked that fact up to having different mothers— his father's first wife had died suddenly of an aneurysm when Virgil was a small boy. Maybe that loss so early in his life had led to his wild ways when he reached adolescence. Or maybe Virgil had just been one of those people who could only learn by making his own mistakes.

Trask pushed the number for his brother and waited for Virgil to answer. Three rings later, Virgil's gravelly voice rumbled across the line. "What's up, Archie?"

Trask gritted his teeth at the nickname. "Just haven't talked to you in a while. We always seem to miss each other at work."

"You can thank Tammy Sloan for that. Squeezing out another kid and leaving us to pick up her slack."

"What are you working on these days?"

"Car theft ring over in Campbell Cove, mostly. You've got that rich kid's murder, don't you?"

"Yeah. Wonder why you didn't catch that call? You're senior in rank."

"I was off that weekend. Out of town."

"Yeah? Where'd you go?"

"Camping up near Kingdom Come. Me and Ty Miller. Thought we'd see if we could pull a few rainbow trout out of Looney Creek, but we got skunked."

"Rainbows won't be stocked in Looney Creek for another month."

"Reckon that's why we got skunked." Virgil laughed. "Why the sudden interest in my itinerary?"

"Just wondering why you weren't the one called to the church. It's turning out to be a real puzzle."

"So I hear. Grapevine says the girl and her boy on the side nearly turned themselves in to you yesterday morning but something spooked them away. Any idea what?"

"No," Trask lied, his stomach aching. "Not a clue."

"If you need a little help, let me know. This car theft ring ain't going anywhere anytime soon, and I could spare some time for my little brother."

"I'll keep that in mind." Trask realized he was gripping his phone so hard his fingers were starting to hurt. He loosened his grip and added, "We should meet up for lunch soon. Catch up with each other."

"Sounds like a real good idea. I'll call you tomorrow and we'll set up a time. Listen, I hate to rush you off the phone, but I've got some catch-up paperwork to do—"

"Understood. Talk to you tomorrow." Trask hung up

the phone and stared at the glimmering amber liquid in the tumbler still sitting in front of him.

Just one sip wouldn't hurt, would it?

He shoved himself up from the table and grabbed the tumbler. At the sink, he poured the glass of whiskey down the drain. The fumes rising from the drain smelled vaguely of charred oak and caramel.

He wasn't sure what his brother had been doing the day of Robert Mallory's murder, but he was pretty sure Virgil was lying about going camping with Ty Miller up near Kingdom Come State Park.

The question was, why was he lying? To give himself an alibi for something? Or to give an alibi to Ty Miller, his longtime best friend and former partner in crime?

One way or another, Trask had to find out where Virgil had really been the day of the Mallory murder.

No matter where the investigation took him.

IT WAS CHILDISH to blame her mother for dying. Only a foolish little girl would sit at the end of her mother's bed and curse under her breath at a woman who hadn't planned to drive in front of a truck with brake trouble. And Tara couldn't afford to be a foolish little girl anymore. She was the woman of the house now, or at least as much a woman as a girl of nearly eleven could be.

She was starting a new school this year, and Mama was supposed to go with her to sixth grade orientation. Daddy would be useless, grumbling his way through whatever presentation the teachers had planned, muttering things like "shouldn't be coddling young'uns this way" and "when I was this age, I was working in the fields all day, school or no school."

Now orientation was going to be horrible. And it was all Mama's fault for going away.

She pushed off her mama's bed and crossed to the window, looking out across their lawn at the house across the street. A new family was moving in, her father had told her. The Stiles family. Daddy had been in the Marine Corps with Captain Stiles, and he said the man was a good enough sort *for a gol dang officer.*

He hadn't actually said gol dang, but Mama had taught her she shouldn't cuss or use the Lord's name in vain, and even though she was really, really mad at Mama right now for going away just before sixth grade started, she still lived by Mama's rules.

A boy came out of the house across the road. A tall, skinny boy with dark hair that flopped across his forehead and braces on his teeth that glittered in the sunlight as he said something to his father as he passed.

The old man answered in a voice loud enough for Tara to hear it all the way across the road, though she couldn't make out the words. Whatever the man had said, it made the boy look down at his feet until the man had entered the front door with the boy he was carrying and closed the door behind him.

Then the boy's head came up and for a moment, Tara was certain he was looking straight at her.

She felt an odd twist in the center of her chest and stepped back from the window, not sure what she had just felt.

TARA WOKE SUDDENLY to darkness and a bone-biting cold that made her huddle closer to the warm body pressed close to her own. Owen, she thought, because of course it would be Owen. It had always been Owen, ever since she'd first laid eyes on him the day of her mother's funeral.

The unchanging constant in her life.

He made a grumbling noise in his sleep, and his arm

snaked around her body, spooning her closer. A humming sensation vibrated through her to her core, spreading heat and longing in equal measures. Oh, she thought, how easy it would be to let go and just allow this tension between them to build and swell to fruition.

She had a feeling it would be amazing, because Owen himself was amazing, a man of both strength and gentleness. She'd seen his passion—in his work, in his hobbies, and yes, even his passion for her, which flickered now and then like blue fire behind his eyes when he couldn't control it.

Keeping things platonic between them was difficult but necessary. Because Tara had lost enough in her life. She wasn't a coward, and she knew how to take calculated risks in order to achieve rewards.

But she could not lose Owen. She couldn't. Things between them had to remain constant or she didn't know what she would do.

Even when her body yearned for him, the way it was doing now. When it softened helplessly in response to the hardness of his erection pressing against the small of her back.

His hand moved slowly up her body, tracing the contours of her rib cage before settling against the swell of her breast. One fingertip found the tightening peak of her nipple through her T-shirt and flicked it lightly, making her moan in response.

Was he awake? His breathing sounded even, if quickened. Maybe he was seducing her in his sleep, giving sway to the urges they both kept so tightly reined in during their waking hours.

If he was asleep, it didn't really count, did it?

His fingers curled over the top of her breast, cupping her with gentle firmness. He caressed her slowly, robbing her of breath, before he slid his hand down her stomach. His fingers dipped beneath the waistband of her jeans and played across the point of her hip bones before moving farther down.

Closer. Closer.

He jerked his hand away suddenly, a gasp of air escaping his lips and stirring her hair. He rolled away from her, robbing her of his heat.

His breath was ragged now, ragged and uneven, a sure sign that he was no longer asleep.

"Tara?" he whispered.

She stayed still, her body still thrumming with hot need that would never be satisfied. That, she understood with aching sadness, was the cost of keeping her relationship with Owen the same as it had ever been.

But she could spare him the embarrassment of knowing she'd been awake for his dream seduction. Spare him knowing how very much she'd wanted him to keep touching her, to keep driving her closer and closer to the brink of ecstasy.

Behind her, Owen blew out a soft breath and sat up, being careful not to jostle her as he rose to his feet and headed outside the tent.

As soon as she was certain he was out of earshot, she rolled onto her back and stared up at the top of the tent, her heart still pounding wildly in her ears. She felt flushed and unsatisfied, and the urge to finish what Owen had started burned through her.

But she'd earned this frustration. She was the one who'd decided that it was too risky to test the sexual waters between them.

She would just have to live with the consequences.

Chapter Twelve

That had been close. Too close.

Owen let the water in the sink grow icy cold and splashed it on his face and neck, despite the chill bumps already scattered across his flesh from the walk through the woods this cold March morning. Another early riser, an older man brushing his teeth at the next sink over in the camp's communal men's room, glanced at Owen with curiosity but kept his comments to himself.

Owen could remember only a few tantalizing fragments from his dream, but the very real memory of Tara's hot flesh beneath his exploring fingers remained vibrant in his mind.

Thank God she'd still been asleep. Thank God he'd awakened before he'd allowed himself any further liberties with her.

He soaped up his hands and rinsed them, as if he could somehow wash away the sensation of her skin on his fingertips, but the feeling remained, on his skin and in his head.

He should feel ashamed. Dirty, even. But all he felt was a ravenous need to finish what he'd started in his dream.

He tried to gather his wits, get himself under control before he returned to the tent. But the man staring back at him in the mirror looked fevered and hungry, his blue eyes dark with the memory of touching Tara the way he'd longed to touch her forever.

He closed his eyes and bent his head, feeling tired. Tired of pretending he didn't feel what he most certainly did. Weary of denying himself the very natural desire he felt for Tara.

If he were going to be around her, he'd have to find a way to rein in that desire for good. He just didn't know if that was possible, which left one other option.

He could leave her life for good. Put her behind him, cut himself off from the constant temptation she posed and try to live without her.

As terrible as the idea of excising Tara from his life seemed to him right now, the thought of a lifetime of pretending he didn't want her as much as he loved her was even worse. It was a lie to behave as if he was okay with being nothing more than her friend.

He wasn't okay with it. He couldn't keep doing it.

The bearded man at the next sink had apparently watched the spectacle long enough. "Are you okay?" he asked.

Owen lifted his chin with determination. "I will be," he said.

He felt the other man's gaze follow him out of the bathroom. Outside, frigid air blasted him, reigniting a flood of goose bumps down his arms and back. Only belatedly did he realize that he shouldn't have drawn attention to himself the way he had. Even now his face might be plastered across TV screens throughout Kentucky and nearby states. How long before someone realized the scruffy-faced, bleary-eyed man in the hipster beanie they'd seen in the campground bathroom was the fugitive from Bagley County?

He didn't know whether to hope Tara was still asleep or

awake when he got back to the tent, but when he ducked back into the tent to find her up and snugly dressed in a down jacket she'd bought back in Abingdon, he found he was relieved. The extra clothing she wore seemed like armor donned specifically to cool his ardor, which made him wonder if she'd been awake for at least part of his unconscious seduction.

But the smile she flashed his way was pleasant and unclouded by any sort of doubt, so he decided she couldn't know what he'd almost done.

"I'm starving," she announced. "I was thinking, we should probably use up the eggs and bacon in the cooler, don't you think? Before the ice melts and they start to spoil? And I bought a little bottle of syrup back in Abingdon in case I got the chance to make my famous French toast. What do you think? French toast and fried bacon?"

He forced a smile. "Who could say no to French toast and bacon?"

"I'll go get the stuff from the cooler. Can you get the camp stove started?" She passed him in the opening of the tent, her arm brushing his. Even with the added layers of clothing they both wore, Owen could swear he felt the same tingle in the skin on his arm he'd felt in his fingertips when he woke that morning with his hand under her shirt.

He lowered his head until his chin hit his chest. How was he going to keep up appearances with her? Already, he was one raw nerve, acutely aware of her constant nearness.

It had to be because they were forced together by these circumstances, stuck in a situation where neither of them could go far from the other for any length of time. Back home, he could escape to his own apartment, indulge his fantasies about her and, on occasion, indulge his body's demands as well, without Tara having to know about any of those feelings or urges.

But there was nowhere to escape to now, no way to channel his desires without Tara knowing what was going on. He was stuck between the blissful heaven of being close to her and the burning hell of not being able to do a damn thing about it.

He forced himself out of the tent and went about the business of firing up the camp stove, glad for the distraction. But it lasted only as long as it took Tara to return from where they'd parked the SUV with the styrene cooler they'd picked up during their shopping trip. He felt her before he heard her footsteps crunching through the undergrowth. Her presence skittered up his spine like the phantom touch of fingers.

"I thought I'd bring the cooler to us so we didn't have to keep going back and forth to the SUV," she said as she set it beside him. "The ice has barely melted at all. I guess the cold snap helped slow the melting. I think we're good with the perishables for another day or so."

"Good," he said, mostly because he could think of no more cogent response. He backed away and let her take over at the camp stove, turning his back to the sight of her while pretending to take in the rain-washed beauty of the sunrise just visible through the trees to the east of them.

"I wish we'd thought to buy a radio," Tara said over the thumping of her spoon whipping the eggs into a batter. "I'd like to know what the news folks are saying about us after this weekend."

"Probably better not to know," Owen murmured. "I'm sure Quinn will keep us up with the latest news."

"I don't know," Tara muttered. "He's not exactly been a font of information to this point."

"He called when he said he would last night."

"And told us blasting nada."

He couldn't stop a smile. Tara had a thing about making

up her own versions of profanities in order to avoid cursing. She'd told him once that her mother loathed swearing, even though she indulged her leatherneck husband's proclivity toward salty language. Tara didn't talk much about her mother at all, but he'd gotten the feeling that her attempts to temper her own language were a result of her mother's influence.

"Maybe there's nothing to tell yet," he said.

"It has to have hit the news by now, at least in Kentucky. Robert's family is very influential in Lexington."

"I'm sure it's been on the news."

"Which means whatever photos of us they could find are being plastered all over local Kentucky news stations. And maybe Virginia ones as well, if they've figured out we were headed for here."

She was right. But what else could they do at this point? They'd already changed their appearances. His beard was growing in thick enough to change the way he looked, and the beanie and glasses made him even harder to recognize. Tara was almost unrecognizable with her new spiky haircut and ever-changing streaks of spray-on color in her hair.

He knew a few ways to go completely off the grid. Change their names, assume new identities with documents that would pass all but the most in-depth scrutiny. But that would be the act of someone who'd lost all hope of justice prevailing.

Had they really reached that point?

"Maybe we should have turned ourselves in to that Virginia state policeman I almost ran into back at the rest area," he said.

"They'd just send us back to the Bagley County Sheriff's Department and we'd be right back where we started." Tara rubbed her eyes, smearing the remains of her heavy mascara and eyeliner.

Without thought, he reached across the narrow space between them and ran his thumb under her right eye to wipe away the worst of the smears.

Instantly, heat flared between them, searing in its intensity.

She trembled beneath his touch, her eyes darkening with unmistakable signs of desire. He'd seen such a reaction in her before but never this strong, this undeniable.

And in that instant, he knew. "You were awake."

She licked her lips. "Yes."

"Why didn't you stop me? Why didn't you wake me up?"

She looked away, closing her eyes. "Because I didn't want you to stop."

He touched her again, tipping her chin up to make her look at him. Her eyes fluttered open and again he was struck by the potency of desire he read in her gaze. "Tara…"

She drew away from him, shaking her head. "We can't, Owen. You know why we can't."

"Because you're afraid that it'll all go wrong and you'll lose me."

"I can't deal with losing you, Owen."

"Do you know what I was thinking about this morning? When I went to the restroom?"

She stared back at him mutely, the desire in her eyes replaced by apprehension.

"I was thinking that if things between us didn't change, I was going to leave Kentucky. Go to Texas or California or, hell, I don't know, maybe Idaho. Anywhere you weren't, so I could get you out of my system once and for all. Because I don't think I can live in this endless limbo, Tara. Maybe you're okay with our relationship staying as innocent and platonic as it was when we met in sixth grade. But I'm not."

She stared at him in horror. "You don't mean that."

"I do, Tara. I'm sorry. I know you want to keep things the way they are, but people change. Circumstances change. I love you. Desperately. In every way a person can love another person."

"I love you, too."

"Then you have to let me go."

She shook her head violently. "No." She rose to her knees, reaching across the space between them to cup his face between her palms. "I don't want to let you go. I can't. You're all I have anymore."

He saw her expression shift, as if she finally realized what she was asking of him and why. Her eyes narrowed with dismay, and she looked so stricken that he wanted nothing more than to put his arms around her and promise her everything would be okay.

But he couldn't do that anymore. He'd finally reached his breaking point.

He put his hands on hers, gently removing them from his face. "I can't be your safety net, Tara. I don't want to do it anymore. If you can't take a chance on us, then that's fine. I'll accept it and go so we can both finally move on."

Tears welled in her eyes, but she blinked them away, anger beginning to drive away the hurt he'd seen in her expression before. "You promised you'd never let me down."

"I know." He hadn't let go of her hands, he realized, as if holding them was as natural as breathing. He gave them a light squeeze before letting go. "I just don't believe the status quo is good for either of us anymore."

Anger blazed in her eyes now, giving off green sparks. "Is this an ultimatum? Sleep with me or I won't be your friend anymore?"

"That is totally unfair, Tara! You know that's not what I'm talking about here." He turned away from her, anger beginning to overtake his own pain.

"That's the only thing we don't have between us, don't you see?" She caught his arm, tugging him back around to look at her. "We have everything else. Friendship. Understanding. Loyalty."

"We don't have marriage together. Children together. We won't make a family together or grow old together. If you think you can find a man or I can find a woman who'll put up with what we do have together, you're wrong."

"Robert was going to."

"Tara, Robert was already trying to push me out of your lives."

She stared at him, shocked. "No, he wasn't."

"Not where you could see it, no."

She sat back on her heels. "Why didn't you tell me?"

"I didn't want to come between you that way."

"If I'd known what he was doing, there wouldn't have been an us to come between," she said fervently. "Robert knew what you are to me. I made it clear from the beginning. One of the reasons I thought we could work together was that he took your presence in my life so well."

"Please, don't do this." Owen sighed, hating himself for even bringing up Robert's issues with him. "I don't want you to remember him badly."

"My life is so upended right now and I honestly can't understand why." She raked her fingers through her spiky hair, looking faintly surprised to find it so short. "I mean, intellectually, I can understand that someone wants to get his hands on something I know, and I also get that it's information that's dangerous for someone with bad intentions to know. But like I said earlier, I'm sure what I know has already been changed by my company. I'm as out of the loop now as anyone else."

"Is there anything you knew that could still be dangerous if someone else knew it?" he asked, glad for the change of subject. Despite his declaration to Tara about cutting the cord between them, he wasn't any more eager to do so than she was.

"I honestly don't think so. Whoever's taking over my job now that I'm gone is probably far more in danger for what he or she knows than I am now."

Owen frowned. "You think your bosses would already have put someone in your position?"

"I'm sure they have. It's not a job that can go unfilled for long, especially with the upcoming symposium details having to be changed so close to the planned time of the event."

So there was now someone else who knew the details of the symposium, Owen thought. Who was in the job only because Tara was now unavailable.

"What would happen if you went back to Mercerville and managed to get yourself cleared of Robert's murder?" he asked. "Would you get your job back?"

"If my bosses were satisfied that all the charges against me were bogus, I'd say yes. We had a good relationship and I was good at the job."

"Even if they'd already replaced you?"

"I think so. It would be hard for someone to come in and learn my job in a few weeks, much less a few days. What I did, nobody else in the company duplicated."

"So how did they find someone to replace you?"

She seemed to give it some thought. "I guess they would have promoted my main assistant, although he wouldn't be able to pick up everything I was doing very quickly. It was a pretty complex system, with lots of security protocols in place. Plus, I had a more personal relationship with the people we were inviting to the symposium than anyone else in my section would have. That kind of interpersonal connection can be hard to maintain. Lots of personalities and egos involved."

Owen nodded. "Who is your primary assistant?"

"Chris Miller."

Owen pulled out his phone and typed in a text to Quinn.

"What are you doing?" Tara asked.

"Telling Quinn to do a deep background check on Chris Miller."

"You think Chris is involved in this mess?"

"I don't know," Owen admitted. "But we have to look at all the angles. Maybe the real reason Robert was killed was to make sure you couldn't go back to your job before the symposium began."

"Because I would be a suspect."

"We couldn't figure out why they kidnapped you. Maybe that's why."

"I thought they wanted to get the information out of me."

"Which would have been far messier than just making sure you were a suspect in a murder and unsuitable for classified work."

Tara cocked her head. "So by staying out here on the run, we're actually playing into the hands of the people who kidnapped me and maybe even killed Robert?"

"Maybe we are."

"So why is your boss making sure we stay where we are?"

That, Owen thought, was a good question. Alexander Quinn had a way of positioning his own allies as pawns in a bigger game. He would do everything possible to protect them, but sometimes collateral damage happened. An unfortunate but inescapable result of the high-stakes game Quinn and the people at Campbell Cove Security played.

"I guess maybe he's already figured out what's going on," Tara murmured, her eyes narrowed with thought. "Maybe Chris Miller is already on Quinn's radar."

Owen wouldn't be surprised if that were true. "But if he is, can he move fast enough to stop whatever plot is underfoot?"

"I don't know. It all depends on whether they moved the symposium back or up."

"What do you think they did?" Owen asked. "If you could read the minds of your company officers?"

"Up," she said after a moment more of thought. "If they moved the symposium up rather than back, it wouldn't leave bad actors much time to put their plot together."

"All the more reason to keep you on the run. Even if you went back now, you'd have to work through all the red tape and the explanations of why you fled in the first place. You wouldn't have time to get back to your job before the symposium took place."

Tara's lips twisted with irritation. "Damn."

Owen lifted his eyebrows at her curse.

One side of her mouth curled up in amusement at his reaction. "Sorry, but sometimes a profanity is the only word that'll do."

"So, what do you think we should do next?" he asked.

Her green-eyed gaze lifted to meet his, full of determination. "I think it's time to go home."

Chapter Thirteen

"So Ty Miller works evenings?" Archer Trask peered through his windshield, sunlight glaring off the back windshield of the vehicle in front of him. The rain that had soaked the area the previous night was long gone, replaced by blinding sunlight and rising temperatures.

"That's right," the receptionist on the other end of the line replied.

Ahead of him, the light turned green and traffic started to move. Trask put his phone in the hands-free holder. "What about Friday evening? Was he working Friday?"

"Let me check the schedule." There was a brief pause, and then she answered, "No, he was off Friday and Saturday."

"Is he working tonight?"

"Yes. He's scheduled to work every night through Friday of this week."

Trask grimaced. "Okay, thank you." He ended the call and stared at the road ahead, frustrated. So far, his brother's alibi seemed to be holding, although Trask hadn't gotten ten far. For one thing, he didn't want Virgil to know what he was doing, because his brother would certainly want to know why he was trying to establish his alibi.

And for another, he wasn't sure he should be giving any credence to the story Heller had told him in the first place.

It was a secondhand, maybe even thirdhand story from a pair of people who were currently on the run from the law. Some people, including his boss the sheriff, might not appreciate him spending time trying to prove his brother's innocence when there was an actual murder case on his plate.

The problem was, Trask was pretty sure Robert Mallory's murder was connected to whatever had happened to Tara Bentley the day of her wedding. He no longer thought she'd willingly left the church. But that left a lot of possibilities open, possibilities that didn't necessarily involve kidnapping.

Maybe Owen Stiles had spirited her away, not willing to watch her marry another man. Everyone seemed certain they were just friends, but Archer knew it was hard to keep sex out of the equation, friends or not. Tara Bentley was a healthy, attractive woman, and Owen Stiles was a healthy, reasonably good-looking man. The situation was ripe for sexual tension.

Had Stiles killed Mallory? Of the two fugitives, he seemed the more likely suspect. Jealousy, possessiveness, lust, obsession—all potential motives for murder.

But if he'd murdered Tara's fiancé, why was she still with Stiles? Was her friendship stronger than her love for and loyalty to the man she planned to marry? Or had she been the one whose feelings transcended friendship?

He rubbed his head as he reached the intersection with Old Cumberland Highway. If he turned left, he'd be heading back toward Mercerville and the sheriff's department, where three days' worth of paperwork awaited him. If he turned right, he'd end up in Cumberland, not far from Kingdom Come State Park.

He wondered if anyone in the area remembered seeing his brother and Ty Miller at the camping area outside the park the previous Friday.

When the light turned green and traffic started to move again, Trask signaled a right-hand turn.

"ARE YOU GOING TO tell Quinn what we're doing?" Tara looked up from stashing the last of the supplies in the duffel and stretched her back. "Because I don't think he's going to be happy that we're changing the plan he's working, whatever it is."

"Too bad. It's not his life. It's ours." With his usual precision, Owen folded the tent into a tidy square. He crossed to where she stood and slipped it inside the duffel before zipping it shut.

He stood close enough that she caught a whiff of the soap he'd used earlier when they risked heading into the more crowded camping area to use the campground's shower facilities. Not for the first time, she'd spent her shower time trying not to think of Owen naked under the spray of his own shower, water sluicing down his chest to catch briefly in the narrow line of hair that bisected his abdomen before dipping farther south.

But her imagination had seemed so much more potent, so much harder to deny, now that she'd actually felt his fingers against her flesh, moving with sexy determination, making her shiver with need.

Was this how it was for him, too? This trembling ache in her core when she looked at him, the way even his voice could send little flutters of awareness up and down her spine?

She was beginning to understand why he'd snapped earlier this morning. Wanting something you knew you could never have was painful. The pain didn't go away just because you were the one putting up all the obstacles, as she was coming to understand. Was it even worse when you were the person who wanted all the obstacles to disappear?

She had to clear her throat before she spoke. "It's probably better if we don't give him any forewarning."

"You do realize he knows exactly where we are, don't you?" Owen met her troubled gaze. "All of the Campbell Cove Security vehicles have GPS trackers on them."

"Even his personal vehicle?"

"Even his personal vehicle. While we were in the general camping area, I logged on to my computer and went through one of my back doors at the company to check the GPS monitoring. There we were, one stationary red dot on the map."

"So when we start heading back to Kentucky—"

"Quinn will know," Owen finished for her. He picked up the duffel and took a quick look around the campsite area to make sure they hadn't forgotten anything. They'd already packed all the other supplies, including the camp stove, into the back of the SUV. "But we should have a few hours of travel before he starts getting suspicious. Should we be planning our next moves during that time?"

"Probably should be," Tara agreed as she followed him through the undergrowth to the rocky path where the SUV was parked. "Except I'm not sure I know what those next moves should be."

"You don't think the first thing we should do is turn ourselves in?" He put the duffel in the back of the SUV and turned to look at Tara. "Isn't that the best way to get you reinstated at Security Solutions?"

"Theoretically, yes. But what if it doesn't work? What if we're locked away and nobody believes us? We need proof of our theory, and the only way to get that is to—"

"Don't say it."

"We have to break in to my office."

Owen shook his head. "Your office, which has probably had security doubled or tripled over the past few days? That office?"

"Yes. You're right, they've almost certainly hardened the security, but they're trying to keep terrorists out, not me."

"I'm not so sure about that."

"Okay, I guess it's possible they're trying to keep me out, as well. But either way, they're not trying to keep *you* out."

"Tara, I don't know anything about your company's security measures."

"You don't know yet. But you've spent the past few years as a white hat hacker, haven't you?"

"That's not what I call it."

"But it's what you are, right?" He gave a slight nod, and she pushed ahead, the idea making more sense the longer it percolated in her head. "With my knowledge of the company and its general protocols, and your knowledge of computer systems, I'm betting we can get inside the office building without being detected. Even at code red security, only certain areas of the building will be under twenty-four-hour surveillance."

"It seems to me that any part of the company where we might be able to discover anything helpful would be one of those areas of the building." Owen nodded toward the driver's door. "You want to drive or do you want me to?"

"You drove all the way here. I'll drive back. Maybe you could catch up on some sleep."

He looked skeptical as he climbed into the passenger seat.

While he buckled in, she addressed his previous protest. "You're right that the parts of the building where the most top secret material is kept will be under constant surveillance. But my office isn't one of those spaces. I went to the classified material when I needed it. I didn't take it out of its place of safekeeping."

"So your office won't be considered a high security risk area."

"Exactly."

"If that's so, how does getting into that area help us?"

"Because Chris Miller and I shared office space. Not right on top of each other, but in the same section. If I'm able to successfully get into my office undetected, I may be able to get into his office and see if there's anything incriminating to find."

"Do you expect there to be?" Owen asked curiously.

She considered the question carefully. "Honestly, I don't know. The only thing about Chris Miller that's ever given me pause is that he's a little too friendly."

Owen frowned at her. "Friendly how?"

She glanced at Owen. "Not that kind of friendly. I just mean, he doesn't have a suspicious bone in his body, which is weird for a guy who works in security. I've had to warn him about phishing emails, that kind of thing. He opened an email not too long ago and nearly let loose a virus in our system. I figured out what he'd done just in time to warn our IT guys and they stopped the program before it could open up any holes in our cybersecurity."

"How does he even keep his job? For that matter, why on earth would he be next in line for your job?"

She made a face. "Nepotism. Chris's uncle is the founder of our firm."

"Maybe he's the weak spot in your company's security without even knowing it," Owen suggested. "Someone could be using him. Manipulating him to get the information they want."

"More likely than not," she agreed. "Which is why I need to get into the office and see what he's been up to. It might help me find out if anyone has been trying to exploit his position to get secure information."

Owen remained silent for a long time while they headed southwest on I-81 to Abingdon. Only as they exited the interstate and began heading due west toward Kentucky did he speak again. "You realize if we get caught, it will make it nearly impossible to prove our innocence."

"I know. But it may be our only chance to find out what's really going on and who's behind it in time to stop whatever they're planning. That's reason enough to take the risk, don't you think?"

As Tara braked at a traffic light, Owen reached across the space between them and touched her face with the back of his hand. "Has anyone ever told you what a brave person you are?"

She stared back at him, a shiver running through her at his touch. For a moment, as their gazes locked and the air in the SUV's cab grew warm and thick, she found herself wondering if she'd made the wrong choice all those years ago when she felt the tug of attraction to Owen and ruthlessly subdued it. What if he was right? What if they could have everything? Their deep and enduring friendship and the heady promise of intense passion?

Wasn't that what everyone really wanted? To have it all?

The traffic light changed to green. Owen dropped his hand away from her cheek and nodded for her to drive on.

She headed west on Porterfield Highway, feeling chilled and unsettled.

WORKING FOR A small law enforcement agency had its benefits and its drawbacks. For the most part, Archer Trask liked the slower pace of his job at the Bagley County Sheriff's Department. There was enough petty crime to keep him busy most of the time, and in such a small place, he generally got to know the citizens he helped as people rather than impersonal names and case file numbers, the way he had done when he worked a couple of years in the Louisville Police Department before returning home to Bagley County.

But one of the drawbacks of working for a small agency was the glacial pace at which the wheels of information gathering turned. Which was why it had taken almost a day for a simple background information request about the security company where Ty Miller worked to make its way to his email inbox.

He had just spent a frustrating hour trying to track down anyone in the Cumberland area who might have seen his brother and Ty Miller up near Looney Creek on Friday, but the problem was, Kingdom Come State Park wouldn't open until the first of April, and most of the people who weren't park visitors had been too busy at their own places of work on Friday to notice if a couple of middle-aged men had wandered by with fly rods and tackle boxes that day.

In fact, he had begun to think he'd wasted a whole day chasing a false lead when his phone pinged with the email notification. He pulled over onto the shoulder and checked the message. It was from Don Robbins, the deputy he'd assigned to dig up background information on Cumberland Security Staffing.

He read through the list of companies that hired the staffing company to provide security personnel for their firms. There were a couple of shopping strip centers, a movie theater, a couple of mining companies and even a church or two that had showed up on the list of clients.

It was only on his second read through that Trask came across a familiar but unexpected name.

He stared at the email for a moment, then dialed a phone

number, unease wriggling in his stomach as he waited for an answer.

"Security Solutions," answered the female receptionist.

"This is Deputy Archer Trask. Is this Diane?"

"Yes, Deputy," she said, her tone warming as if she were pleased that he'd remembered her name. "How can I help you?"

"Diane, does your company still use Cumberland Security Staffing?"

There was a brief pause before she replied, "I'm not really supposed to answer that question."

"Could you put me through to someone who can?"

There was another pause. "I've been asked not to disturb any of the officers this afternoon." She lowered her voice. "Is it urgent for you to know this information right now?"

"Yes," he answered. It was urgent to him, at least.

"We do employ them. They provide our four night guards."

"Can you tell me the names of the guards?"

"I don't know if I can do that—"

"Okay, maybe you can tell me this. Is one of them named Ty Miller?"

After a long pause, Diane whispered, "Yes."

"Thank you, Diane. You've been very helpful."

He hung up the phone and stared at the narrow road stretching into the mountains ahead of him. So Ty Miller was a security guard at Security Solutions, the company where Tara Bentley worked. And according to Maddox Heller, Tara Bentley was kidnapped by two men outside the church where she was supposed to marry Robert Mallory, who had mysteriously turned up murdered in the groom's room.

Tara Bentley, who had told her lawyer that his brother Virgil was one of the men who'd kidnapped her.

His brother, Virgil, whose alibi for the day of Robert Mallory's murder and Tara Bentley's alleged kidnapping was Ty Miller. Who worked for the same company as Tara Bentley, albeit indirectly.

Trask rubbed his temples, his head aching with the sudden twists and turns his murder case had started to take. Worse than the complications was the fact that he didn't know what he was supposed to do next. Bring his brother, the deputy investigator, in for questioning? Interrogate Ty Miller about his whereabouts on Friday, even though he had less probable cause to question him than he had where Virgil was concerned?

He needed to find Tara Bentley and Owen Stiles. They were the only people who really knew, firsthand, what had happened to them the day of Robert Mallory's murder.

"WHY ARE YOU back in Kentucky?" Quinn's voice was tight with annoyance over the cell phone speaker.

Owen glanced toward Tara. She gave a nod. "Tell him."

"How secure is this line?" Owen asked Quinn.

"About as secure as any cell phone can get. Someone would have to be listening for your transmissions specifically to find you. Or get very lucky."

"I'm not sure that's secure enough."

"Then perhaps we should meet," Quinn said.

"Where?"

"Where Maddox picked you up Saturday," Quinn answered. It was oblique enough a response that only Owen, Tara, Maddox Heller and Quinn would know where he meant.

"I can do that," Owen said. "In about an hour?"

"I'll see you there." Quinn hung up.

Tara glanced at Owen. "Do you think he'll try to talk us out of it?"

Owen thought about the question for a moment, then shook his head. "No. I think he'll devise some ingenious way for us to get away with it."

For the first time in many miles, Tara shook off her troubled expression and managed a smile. "I think maybe I'm starting to like Alexander Quinn."

"Don't go crazy, now," Owen joked, to cover his own anxieties starting to rise to the surface the closer they got to Bagley County. He wasn't as sure as Tara that breaking into her company office was a smart thing to do. The risks were high and the possibility of rewards was scanty in comparison.

Maybe he'd been right that Quinn would support their crazy scheme, but he wasn't sure he'd consider that good news.

Chapter Fourteen

So far, Ty Miller hadn't answered any of Trask's calls,
and attempts to catch him at home had so far proved futile. However, a check with the receptionist at Cumberland Security Staffing had revealed that Miller would be
working the night shift at Security Solutions tonight, starting at eleven.

In the meantime, Trask had been studying his file on
Robert Mallory, trying to examine the case from a different angle. Mallory's death had seemed to be the main
event, with Tara Bentley's disappearance a side story. But
what if that assumption was wrong? What if Tara's disappearance were the focus of the crime, with Mallory's
murder a peripheral event?

Had Mallory stumbled onto something that had led to
his murder? Could he even have been complicit in whatever had led to his fiancée's kidnapping?

"Assuming she was kidnapped," he muttered as he
checked the clock on his office wall. Only a little after
five. Almost five more hours to go before he could head
to the Security Solutions compound and wait to catch Ty
Miller before he started work.

With a sigh, he returned his attention to the files. He
preferred legwork to paperwork, but at least this particu-

lar bit of paperwork involved trying to pull together the scattered threads of a mystery.

Starting with Tara Bentley.

Who was Tara Jane Bentley? He knew the basics—the only daughter of former Gunnery Sergeant Dale Bentley and Susan Bentley, both now deceased. She was born in Campbell Cove, grew up there and only left town to attend the University of Virginia.

Trask paused, reaching for a second stack of papers. Hmm. Owen Stiles had also attended the University of Virginia. Coincidence? Unlikely.

He set aside questions of their unusually close friendship, since it would only lead him back to mundane motives for Robert Mallory's murder, and that road hadn't been leading him anywhere definitive.

For the past five years, Tara had worked at Security Solutions, a nonprofit think tank dedicated entirely to analyzing security threats both global and domestic and searching out strategies for prevention and even prediction of future events, helping security experts to stay ahead of the terrorist threat rather than reacting after an event took place.

Since joining as an analyst, she'd moved quickly up the company ladder to director of global relations, whatever that meant. Because the company was a nonprofit entity, she wasn't exactly rolling in dough, though his tiptoe through the company's public profile suggested she made a decent salary.

But he'd already examined the idea of a profit motive in Robert Mallory's murder, at least where Tara Bentley was concerned. Mallory's income had been generous, and would've grown considerably as he took over more and more of his father's law practice. He'd recently become a partner, and if Tara Bentley had gone through with marrying Mallory, she could have led a financially comfortable life indeed. But she wasn't going to see a penny of his money now, since he'd died before the wedding.

So what had really happened the day of the wedding that had left Mallory dead and Tara Bentley running for her life?

Could it have anything to do with his brother Virgil and his elusive alibi for the day in question?

Trask leaned back in his chair and rubbed his burning eyes, feeling further from the truth than ever.

"WE ALMOST WENT to this school," Tara commented as Alexander Quinn walked with her and Owen down the long corridors of Campbell Cove Security. "It closed about two years before our freshman year. Do you remember?"

"Vaguely," Owen said, looking around. "I guess I never really gave any thought to what this place was before it became Campbell Cove Security."

"It was scheduled to be demolished before I came in and bought up the property and the building." Quinn's tone was brisk, as if he was annoyed by the trip down memory lane.

Tara kept her mouth shut for the rest of the walk. When they reached the end of the corridor, instead of turning right or left, Quinn led them forward through a dark red door marked Exit.

Outside, twilight had fallen while they were in Quinn's office, updating him on everything they'd done since their last contact. Tara had been expecting a little more push-back from Quinn about their breaking-and-entering plan, but he'd been remarkably positive about the idea, with a couple of caveats.

"First, if something goes wrong, there can be no direct links back to my company," he said firmly. "So that means I can't send you any of my agents to help you out with your plan. Just Owen, and he's not going to be there in any company-related capacity."

"Understood," Tara said quickly.

"And second, if you do end up in trouble because of this, I'm not going to be able to help you the way I have so far. You'll be on your own completely. Can you deal with that?"

Despite the tightening sensation in the pit of her gut, Tara had nodded.

"We have to figure out what's really going on before we risk going to the police again," Owen added with more resolve than Tara felt. "There could be a terror plot already in motion, and this could be our chance to stop it cold."

"Which is exactly why I'm going along with this crazy plan," Quinn said with a smile. "And why I'm going to help you figure out all the angles so we can avoid any of the obvious pitfalls."

Among the obvious pitfalls, Tara had learned, were the exact security protocols followed by Security Solutions' night security team. Quinn refused to reveal just how he'd come by the information, but he was able to tell them when the security patrols would be in what part of the building. "It's not smart to stick to a set plan," he'd commented with disapproval, "but I guess that's the price of outsourcing your site security instead of building your own in-house staff."

Tara's guess about the company's security focus had been correct. Except for a single walk-through of the company's nonsecure office wing early in the shift, just after eleven o'clock, the security patrols would spend the rest of their eight-hour shift patrolling the secure areas. None of the guards had keys to the securest rooms, where the classified material was, Quinn told them. "You won't be able to get in there, either," he warned.

"We don't think we'll need to," Tara assured him.

Over the next couple of hours, they'd worked out a plan that even Quinn agreed might get them in and out of the building without detection. He admitted he'd already checked with Tara's bosses to see if they'd done anything about revoking her credentials. They hadn't, they'd admitted. They weren't ready to give up on her innocence, and blocking her credentials seemed too much like admitting she could have done something wrong.

"Foolish sentimentality" had been Quinn's succinct assessment, but at last it made it more likely she could get through inside her office building without triggering any alarms.

"They'll have evidence of an ingress," Quinn warned, "and they'll have the code number used to enter, if they decided to check the security system logs."

"If I don't trigger an alarm, they won't have any reason to check," Tara told him. "And even if they do, all they'll see is that someone entered the office building using the security code for my department. But everyone in the department uses the same code number to disarm the alarm."

Quinn's stony expression was as good as an eye roll. "Our nation's security is in good hands."

"Well, it'll work in our favor this time," Owen murmured.

They'd shared a pizza with Quinn while going over a quick checklist of things they wanted to accomplish and how they planned to go about it. There was a brief discussion about using night vision equipment to aid in their getting safely inside the security perimeter, but they all agreed that since both Tara and Owen lacked experience with night vision equipment, the goggles would be more of a detriment than an asset.

Finally, Quinn had handed over a couple of heavy backpacks and led them down the corridor to this exit into the encroaching woods behind Campbell Cove Security.

"We're being banished to the woods?" Tara murmured as she struggled to keep up with Owen's long strides behind Quinn.

"I have no idea," Owen admitted.

Ahead of them, Quinn strode confidently through the dark woods, avoiding obstacles in the underbrush as if he knew exactly where they were, even though the path beneath their feet was little more than a tangle of weeds and vines, anything but well traveled.

About a hundred yards into the thickening woods, they reached a small clearing of sorts. There were no trees in the small area, but kudzu vines took up the slack, nearly covering what looked like a small shack in the middle of the woods.

"It used to be one of the school's outbuildings," Quinn told them as they approached the kudzu-swallowed building. Only the door remained vine free, and even it would have been difficult to pick out at a cursory glance, painted with a mottled green camouflage pattern that nearly perfectly matched the surrounding kudzu. "We left the kudzu when we cleaned it up and put it to use. Cheaper than camo netting."

Inside, the place was remarkably clean. It was little more than a room with a couple of camp beds, a tiny kitchen area with a sink, a one-burner electric cooktop and a mini refrigerator. The door in the back of the building led to a small but usable half bath with a tiny shower and an even tinier sink.

"Please tell me this works," Tara said as she eyed the shower with near desperation.

"It all works. Electricity and plumbing should get you by until you have to leave for your rendezvous with Security Solutions," Quinn said. "I had someone park the SUV in the woods due north of here, just off the road into Mercerville. They've topped off your fuel tank and changed out the license plates again, just in case." He slanted them a wry look. "Got rid of the bumper stickers, too."

"Thought of everything," Tara murmured.

"You'll stay here until then. I thought you might both enjoy a hot shower and a hot meal. From this point forward, I expect no contact from either of you unless you achieve your ends. Agreed?"

Tara glanced at Owen. He gave a brief nod.

"Agreed," Tara said. Owen echoed her response.

"Clean up after yourselves and try not to knock off any of the kudzu." Quinn opened the door, quickly slipped out and closed it behind him.

The silence that fell afterward made Tara feel as if she were about to smother. The small outbuilding itself wasn't cold, nor was it overly warm, but it felt closed in, suddenly, after days of living outside or in an SUV.

"I'll be magnanimous and give you first dibs on the shower," Owen said. He had taken a seat on one of the camp beds and was digging through the backpack Quinn had supplied. He pulled out each piece and laid it on the bed, revealing a couple of changes of clothes, a pair of hiking boots and a handful of protein bars. Owen waved one of the protein bars at Tara as she sat on the bed opposite. "He meant what he said about cutting us loose, but at least he gave us a change of clothes and a couple of meals to get us through to the next hidey-hole."

"Yay?" Tara pulled out the clothes Quinn had provided for her. They looked as if they'd fit well enough, though she longed for her own closet and her own wardrobe.

What she wouldn't give to be in her cute little house in Mercerville, cuddled up in front of the fireplace.

With Owen, an unrepentant little voice whispered in her ear.

She grabbed the change of clothes and headed for the small bathroom. "I'll try not to use up all the hot water."

Easy enough, she thought as she turned the cold tap all the way on.

ARCHER TRASK EYED the clock as he closed up the file folders. Three hours to go, and he wasn't any closer to a theory about Robert Mallory's murder than he'd been when he started.

Unless he wanted to believe his brother and Ty Miller really had kidnapped Tara Bentley and killed her fiancé.

But what was the motive? Trask's brother was a pretty ordinary guy. Divorced, no kids, worked a tough job and spent his off time hunting, fishing and four-wheeling. About the average for a guy from Bagley County, Kentucky. He wasn't particularly religious or political, as far as Trask knew, which would seem to rule out those particular motives.

As far as Trask knew. Which was the problem, wasn't it? Even when they were younger, he and Virgil had never been close. Virgil was a decade older than Trask, and he'd never had much time for his younger half brother, too busy raising hell with his friends to do any brotherly things with his tagalong sibling.

After a while, Trask had stopped trying to be close to Virgil, which had seemed to be fine with him.

There was quite a lot about Virgil that he didn't know, wasn't there?

Really, if anyone knew Virgil at all, it was their father, Asa. He had always had a soft spot for Virgil, even during the worst of his delinquency. *We used to call it sowin' wild oats*, Asa would say when Trask's mother complained about Virgil's latest misdemeanor.

Trask had long suspected that Asa had never really gotten over his first wife. Marrying Trask's mother, Lena, had been a matter of expediency—he had a young boy who needed a mama, and he was a man who needed a warm body in his bed. Lena Lawrence had been a beauty in her youth, and she'd fallen hard for the older widower with a child.

Trask suspected she'd long ago given up on true love and was still married to the old man much for the same reason he'd married her in the first place—neither of them wanted to go through life alone.

He picked up his phone and dialed his parents' number. His mother answered, her voice warm, "Archer, how are you?"

With some embarrassment, he realized it had been at least two weeks since he talked to his mother. "I'm good," he said quickly, realizing she might be wondering if he was calling with bad news.

Of course, in a way he might be.

"I heard you're workin' that murder case at the church."

"Yeah. I can't really talk about it."

"Oh, I know. Your daddy's always tryin' to get Virgil to spill the beans about his cases, too, but Virgil tells him just enough to make him want to know more, then laughs and says it's police business and he can't spill the beans." Even though there was laughter in his mother's voice, Trask could tell she didn't like Virgil's form of teasing. "Makes your daddy crazy."

"Speaking of Virgil, have you seen much of him lately?"

"Some, here and there. He's been spendin' a lot of time with Ty Miller. You remember Ty, don't you?"

"Yeah, I remember Ty. What are they doing, hunting and fishing?"

"No, they just seem to hang out in Ty's garage with some of their friends, smokin' and talkin' if he's not on duty."

"Really?" That didn't sound much like Virgil, who'd never been much of a joiner. "Who's he hanging out with besides Ty?"

"Oh, I don't know. I think I saw one of the Hanks boys there a couple of weeks ago, and Chad Gordon. Jenny Pruitt mentioned to me at church Sunday that her boy, Dawson, was hanging out with Ty, too." His mother's voice darkened. "She sounded a little worried about it, to tell the truth."

"Why's that?"

"I don't rightly know. I told your daddy about it, but he said not to worry, Virgil's a deputy now and we don't have to mind his business anymore." Lena laughed. "Thank goodness for that. He was a handful."

"I suppose we both were."

"Oh, you had your moments," Lena said, "but I never had to worry about bailing you out of jail in the middle of the night. Listen, I know it's a little late, but I'm betting you're calling from work, aren't you? I have some leftover supper—we had fried chicken, green beans and mashed potatoes. Your favorite. You want to drop by on your way home?"

"That's real tempting," Trask said, meaning it. "But I've got to work for a few hours longer tonight. But I'll definitely take you up on the offer the next time you cook my favorites."

"Oh, okay, then."

The disappointment in her voice almost made him give up on his idea of confronting Ty Miller at work tonight.

What would it really accomplish? So far, even the accusation against Virgil was third hand. He had yet to speak to Tara or Owen Stiles, face-to-face or otherwise. Hell, the only reason Ty Miller was on his radar at all was that Virgil had unwittingly named him as his alibi.

But Archer needed to hear that alibi himself, read Ty Miller's face and decide whether or not he was lying for Virgil.

"I'm really sorry," he told his mother. "I'll drop by and see you just as soon as I get a minute of free time."

"I'll look forward to it," she said, her tone loving. He felt an ache of love for his mother throbbing deep in his chest. He didn't know if she was living the life she wanted, but she was the sort of person who made do with what she had and looked for the bright side of every situation.

She deserved a more thoughtful son than he had been lately.

"Love you, Mama. I'll talk to you soon."

"I love you, too, sweet boy. You be careful, all right?"

"Will do." He hung up the phone, his eyes going toward the clock.

A little after nine. Almost showtime.

THE COLD SHOWER had done nothing to calm the urgent throb of heat at her core or the itchy, unsettled feeling that she was walking into the heart of danger with so many important things left unspoken.

If they were right that Robert's murder was about keeping Tara on the run, then they might encounter someone armed and very dangerous at her office tonight. She, Owen and Quinn had gone to great lengths to tie up all the loose ends and make tonight's break-in go as smoothly and safely as possible, but even Quinn had acknowledged the risk.

She had no family to say goodbye to. Her friends were

mostly people Robert had known or a handful of women she'd gone to high school or college with and rarely talked to anymore now that their lives had gone in different directions.

Owen was her family, her circle of friends, her rock. And she had denied him the only thing he'd asked of her in all the years of their friendship.

He was a man. They were attracted to each other. She was asking a lot of him to deny those feelings while continuing to be her friend.

But she couldn't bear life without him. He was her true north.

The heat in her core spread up into her belly and breasts, sending a quiver down her spine as the door to the small bathroom opened and Owen stepped out, wearing only a pair of jeans and a towel around his neck. His hair was still damp from the shower, a trickle of water sliding down his chest to follow the dark line of hair that dipped beneath the waistband of his jeans.

Friends with benefits. Wasn't that what people called it these days? She knew there were other terms for it, vulgar terms, but what she felt with Owen wasn't vulgar or base. She loved him. She just wasn't ever going to risk being *in* love with him. That complicated everything beyond hope.

But being his best friend, who he happened to sleep with now and then—that was something she could handle, wasn't it?

Owen gave her an odd look as he swiped the towel down his chest a couple of times before he tossed it aside and met her in the middle of the small room. "Is something wrong?"

She nodded, trying to find her voice. But her mouth was dry and her heart was pounding, drowning out all her thoughts.

"What is it?" Owen asked, his voice dropping to a gravelly half whisper.

"I was wrong," she said, her own voice coming out raspy. "I was wrong about us."

His brow furrowed, but he waited for her to speak.

Instead of words, she chose action, rising to her tiptoes and curling her fingers through his damp hair. She moved closer, sliding her other hand up his chest, reveling in the crisp sensation of his chest hair beneath her palm.

Owen opened his mouth as if to speak, but she didn't let him get that far. With a sharp tug of her hand, she pulled his head down and covered his mouth with hers.

Chapter Fifteen

She tasted like honey and heat, her lips soft and her tongue insistent, parting Owen's lips and demanding entry. He was powerless against her, just as he'd always known he would be. Tara was his soft spot, his Achilles' heel. In the end, he could never deny her anything, and that was why he was still by her side, long after a sane man would have walked away to find greener pastures. Tara was his one and only, and for all his talk of walking away, he now understood he never would do so.

Her hands seemed to be everywhere—on his shoulders, his sides, the tips of his fingers and the skin just above his hip bones. He was on fire, an unquenchable heat that seemed to grow and spread wherever she touched him.

Finally, her fingers dipped to the zipper of his jeans, and while every inch of his flesh seemed to sing with joy, a mean little voice in the back of his head asked a question.

What is she really offering you?

As if she'd heard the sudden note of discord, Tara stilled her hand and pulled back to look at him, her eyes dark with desire. "What's the matter?"

He wanted to tell her nothing was wrong, to proceed with what she'd been doing. Everything would work out the way it was supposed to.

But he'd never been a guy who worried about the future

when the future came. He was the guy who had his week planned on a spreadsheet. He was that much like Tara, he supposed, or maybe all these years of friendship had made her control freak side rub off on him.

He had to know what she was really offering before he agreed to take it. For better or for worse.

"What are we doing here?" he asked softly.

She gave him a quirky half grin. "Been that long?"

"Been forever, but that doesn't really answer my question."

Her fingers fluttered lightly against his rib cage, sending shivers down his spine. "I'm seducing you."

"I thought you were against our pursuing a romantic relationship."

A small frown creased her forehead. "I'm not against a sexual relationship. I think we could handle that, don't you? Solves the sexual tension problem, but we don't muck up our friendship with other kinds of expectations."

His heart sinking, he pulled her hands away from his body. "Sweetheart, that won't solve anything."

"Why not? People do this all the time. Friends with benefits."

"That never ends well."

"We could make it end well." She rose to her tiptoes to kiss him again.

And he let her. Drank in the sweetness he found there, the passion and the promise of pleasure. Drank and drank, losing his will to resist. Maybe this could work, he told himself as he wrapped his arms around her waist and dragged her closer, flattening himself against her so he could feel all the soft curves and strong edges of her body. He had known her intimately for years, except for this part of her, the seductress with a wicked imagination and an unimaginably sweet touch.

But what happens when she's ready to start a relation-ship with someone else again? the mean little voice asked.

With a low growl of frustration and regret, he pushed her away.

"No, Owen, don't do this..."

"I have to," he said, sinking onto the edge of the nearest bed. "Someone has to be sensible about this."

"No, don't you see? We've been too sensible about this for too long. We should have known we could figure out a way to have what we both want. We always have." She sat beside him on the bed, too close. The scent of bath gel on her heated skin was intoxicating.

He caught her hands before she touched him again. "I don't want sex from you, Tara."

She looked confused. "But isn't that the problem?"

"No, sweetheart, it's not. Sex is just a part of what I really want."

Her eyes flickered with annoyance, so very Tara-like. She hated when someone contradicted one of her plans. And nine times out of ten, if he was the one thwarting her will, he'd have gone along with her just to see her beautiful smile when she got her way.

But this was too important a decision to give in to Tara just to see her smile. Their friendship was on the line. One way or another, something had to give, because he couldn't bear to be just her bed buddy and her best friend.

He wanted what she'd been so ready to offer Robert Mallory, even though Owen had known all along she'd never loved Robert enough to spend forever with him. He knew it because he knew, deep down, that he and Tara were supposed to be together.

But what he knew, or thought he knew, didn't matter at all if Tara didn't see it, too.

"I don't want to be your best friend forever or your

friend with benefits, because that will never be what you are to me." She started to speak, but he touched her lips with his fingertip, stilling them. "Tara, I love you. I have loved you since the time you pantsed Jason Stillwell for stealing my lunch money. That love has never faltered, even through your snotty cheerleader years and the time you decided that dating only frat boys at Virginia was the best way to reach your life goals."

She grimaced. "Don't remind me," she said against his fingertip. He dropped his hand and she flashed another quirky half smile at him. "I love you, too, Owen. You know that."

"I do. But do you love me enough to marry me?"

Her expression froze, and for a moment, she turned so pale that he thought she was going to pass out. But then her color came back, rising to fill her cheeks as if she'd pinched them.

"Marry you?"

"Yes. Rings, cake, children, forever and ever and ever."

"No. I can't marry you." She pulled away from him, pacing across the floor to stand near the kudzu-draped front window. She stared into the greenery, clearly seeing something else. "You know why I can't."

"Just because your parents' marriage was a mess doesn't mean yours will be. You were willing to marry Robert."

"Because he ticked off everything on my list," she said, her voice rising with distress. "It felt like a sign. This is the one."

"But he wasn't."

Her face fell. "No, he wasn't."

"Because I am."

She didn't look at him. Didn't speak.

With a sigh, Owen retrieved his watch from the small bench beside the table and checked the time. Getting close to eleven. In an hour, they should be just outside the Security Solutions compound, sneaking in through a small back gate that most employees knew nothing about. Even Tara hadn't realized the gate existed until Quinn showed her where to look on the property.

"We'll have to table this for now," he said. "Let's get dressed and packed up. We have a long walk to the SUV. If we wait too long after the guards do their check on the office buildings, we won't have as much time to look for evidence before we have to leave."

She turned away from the window, her expression composed. She walked past him to the other bed and sat on the edge to pull on a pair of thick socks. "Dress warmly," she said. "Judging by the air I felt coming through that window sash, it's getting really cold out."

He pulled on a long-sleeved black T-shirt and shrugged a thick black sweater over it. The jacket Quinn had supplied was also black, a medium-weight Windbreaker that should keep him warm enough as long as the clouds scudding overhead didn't start spitting out snow rather than rain.

The hike to the SUV was painstakingly slow in the dark, and the heavy silence that had fallen between him and Tara didn't help to make the forward slog any more enjoyable. He finally spotted the SUV's gleam through the trees about a hundred yards ahead and breathed a sigh of relief.

He handed over the SUV keys to Tara. "Your company. You drive."

She took them without a word or even a smile and climbed behind the steering wheel. He rounded the vehicle and got in the passenger seat, looking at Tara's grim profile as he buckled up. "I don't think we can accomplish this mission without talking to each other."

"I'm sorry. I just don't know what to say."

He shook his head. "There's nothing else to say about us, is there? You're not willing to risk our friendship for something more, and I've come to the conclusion tonight that I can't walk away from you, even if I know deep down it's what I should do. So we go on the way we always have."

She looked at him. "Can we?"

"I don't know what else we can do. Do you?"

She shook her head and faced front again. For a moment she didn't move at all, just sat still and silent, her gaze fixed on something outside the SUV. Then she released a soft breath and put the key in the ignition. The SUV's engine roared to life.

Moving forward in the deepening night, they fell back into silence again.

THERE. JUST WHEN Archer Trask was beginning to think the receptionist from the security staffing company was wrong, Ty Miller's black pickup truck turned into the driveway of the Security Solutions compound and parked near the gate.

Trask was reaching for his door handle when he realized that Miller wasn't alone.

Easing his hand away from the latch, Trask leaned over to open his glove compartment and retrieve the small set of binoculars he kept there. He lifted the lenses to his eyes and took a closer look at the passenger seat of Miller's truck.

His stomach twisted as he recognized his brother's craggy face.

Damn it, Virgil.

THERE WAS NO good place to park the SUV, but Tara pulled the vehicle as far off the road as she could, hoping the darkness and the trees that lined the access road would be enough to hide the vehicle from any curious eyes that might pass by at this late hour.

The only real perimeter to the Security Solutions compound was an aging chain-link fence about eight feet high. Razor wire twists had been added at some point in the recent past, but there wasn't any real security outside of the kiosk just inside the front gate, and even it wasn't manned after hours. Employees had a key card that would allow them to enter through the automated gate, and anyone else would have to wait until morning for the daytime crew to arrive.

Getting in without going through the front gate, however, would seem to require a climb over the tall fence and braving the vicious edges of the razor wire. But somehow Alexander Quinn had uncovered a utility gate near the back of the property that made it possible for public utility repairmen and also law enforcement to enter the property after hours if necessary. It was a convenience not known to many in the company, Tara was certain, because she'd never heard a thing about it, and she was placed fairly high in the company's hierarchy.

"I'd guess he learned of it from your bosses themselves," Owen opined when she remarked on Quinn's knowledge of the back gate. "Or maybe from some of his law enforcement contacts. Quinn always seems to know where to find information he needs and how to exploit it."

"You make him sound scary."

"Most of the time he is."

They located the gate after a frustrating search through overgrown weeds and grass outside the company grounds. A heavy chain had been looped through the gate latch, giving the outward look of a locked gate, but closer examination revealed there was no lock at the end of the chain.

All they had to do was unwind the chain to open the gate and enter.

"Now what?" Owen asked.

"We're about three hundred yards from the building, I'd estimate." Tara peered through the gloom, trying to get a sense of perspective. "There's a side entrance on the east wing of the building, where my office is located. It opens with a key card, but if for some reason you can't put your hands on a key card, it'll also open with a numerical code."

"Not very secure."

"Well, after the third time Clayton Garvey left his key card at home and had to go through the humiliation of fetching a guard to let him in, they changed the system."

"You'd think people who deal in security threats would be able to identify the ones in their own systems."

"Human nature." They were close enough now to see the building looming in the darkness like a sleeping steel-and-glass behemoth. "That's the door we're heading for."

They slowed down as they neared the entrance, taking care not to draw attention to themselves. Just because the security guards would now be focusing attention on the more secure parts of the building didn't mean she and Owen didn't have to take precautions as they entered and started moving around. There were cameras at the end of each corridor, and while these weren't controlled by motion sensors, she and Owen would still need to be quick in hopes of avoiding immediate detection.

The cameras record everything, which is why you need to wear the masks I've provided until you're out of range of the corridor cameras, Quinn had warned them. They stopped now, while still clear of the building's external security cameras, to slip on the knit masks Quinn had put in their backpacks.

"Ready?" Owen asked, making last-minute adjustments to his mask.

"Yes."

He motioned for her to lead the way.

UNTIL THE VERY last moment, Trask had planned to confront his brother before Virgil and Ty Miller ever set foot into the building. But then Virgil had stepped out of the truck wearing the same security company uniform that Ty wore, and Trask was suddenly uncertain about everything he'd believed he knew.

As he froze in place, his mind racing through all the possible implications, Ty and Virgil walked across the narrow space between the parking lot and the front entrance, disappearing inside the building.

The automatic gate was still slowly closing. Spurred into action, Trask jumped from his truck and raced through the gate with inches to spare. But when he tried the front door, he found it locked.

He hadn't noticed Virgil or Ty stop to punch in an alarm code after entering, so he might be able to pick the lock without setting off any sort of alarm.

Within a few moments, he felt the last of the pins in the lock open and he gave the door a tug. It swung silently outward and he slipped into the building.

Stopping to listen, he didn't immediately hear any other noises. Wherever Ty and Virgil had gone, they'd gone quickly. There was an elevator bank a few feet inside the foyer. Maybe they'd taken the elevator to another level?

He moved toward the bank of elevators, glad he'd worn soft-soled shoes. They made a tiny, almost imperceptible squeak on the polished floors, but at least he wasn't leaving echoing footsteps ringing behind him as he walked

He looked at the elevator indicator lights. Hmm. All

of them seemed to read Ground Floor. Wherever Ty and Virgil had gone, it appeared they hadn't gone by elevator.

Wandering a little deeper into the building, he spotted his first security camera. It stood still, which might mean it was showing a static image on a security monitor somewhere. If so, his presence here would need some explaining. Somehow he didn't think his bosses at the sheriff's department would be satisfied with whatever he managed to come up with.

Too late to worry about that now. He backtracked until he found an office directory sign. There were two wings, it appeared. The one he was in was called Administrative Services and included a long list of offices and names. Tara Bentley's office was on this floor, he saw, in an area marked Analytical Security Services Unit.

He had no idea what that meant, he realized. Or what, really, Tara did for Security Solutions. It was all very vague in general, the way a lot of job descriptions at security companies could be.

Owen Stiles's position at Campbell Cove Security was only slightly less mysterious, and that was only because Trask had a better grip on what "cybersecurity" meant than "analytical security services."

Maybe this was his chance to find out a little more about who his mysterious fugitive bride really was.

He turned right and headed for Tara Bentley's office.

Chapter Sixteen

The corridors were mostly dark, except for a few lights near the tops of the walls that shone at half strength every ten yards or so. Tara kept an eye on the security cameras as she walked quickly up the hall. She and a couple of her coworkers had noticed that just before each camera made a sweep of the service area, it twitched twice in the opposite direction of its eventual sweep. Then it would move in a slow arc before going stationary again until its next sweep.

The one down the hall started to twitch twice to the left. Tara grabbed Owen's arm and pulled him through the nearest door.

"Is this it?" Owen whispered.

"No, it's a conference room."

"Then why did we come in here?"

She told him about the camera sweep observation.

"How long will the sweep last?" Owen asked.

"Should be over now." She risked a quick peek into the hall and saw the camera sitting still again. She grabbed Owen's hand and they hurried up the hall, pausing as they reached a corner.

She took a quick look around the corner. It was empty, and the camera at the end of the hall was still. "Let's go."

Owen followed her forward as she led him swiftly down the corridor and around another corner. They managed to reach the door to her office without the cameras moving again.

But to her surprise, the door to her office was locked.

"These doors aren't usually locked," she whispered, giving the knob a second, futile twist.

"Let me take a look. You keep an eye on the cameras."

"Move in as close to the door as you can. I don't think the camera's view reaches into this alcove." Tara flattened her back against the door and watched with curiosity as Owen pulled a small leather wallet from his pocket. He unfolded the flaps to reveal a series of narrow metal rods of various sizes, all small. It was a lock-picking kit, she realized with surprise as Owen selected two of the metal pieces from the wallet and tucked the rest of them back in his pocket.

He inserted both pieces into the lock, wiggled them around in ways that made no sense to her whatsoever. But within a couple of minutes, the door lock gave a slight click and Owen twisted the knob open.

He entered first, with caution. Tara followed closely behind him, her hand flattened against his spine. "My desk is over here on the right. Chris Miller's desk is here to the left."

Suddenly, the light came on in the room, almost blinding her with its unexpected intensity. She squinted, wondering if Owen had flicked on the light. She was about to tell him to turn the lights off again when he stopped dead still in front of her, his back rigidly straight.

She realized with a sinking heart that he hadn't been the one who'd turned on the lights.

A drawling voice greeted them, a twist of humor tinting his words. "Well. This is an unexpected turn of events."

She turned around to see the man who'd lured her out to the church parking lot standing in front of them, holding a big black pistol.

"HEY!"

The voice that rang through the corridor behind him stopped Trask short. He turned slowly to find himself looking at Ty Miller, no longer dressed in his drab olive security uniform but a pair of khaki pants and a dark blue blazer over a white golf shirt.

No, that wasn't right. This man was younger, though his hair color, his features, even his general build were the same as Ty Miller's. In the low lighting of the nighttime building, it had been easy to see what Trask was expecting to see.

He hadn't been expecting to see Ty's brother Chris, even though he was also an employee of Security Solutions. It was after midnight now. What the hell was he doing here at this hour?

"Archer," Chris said as he stepped closer. "What are you doing here?"

"Looking for your brother, actually."

Chris looked puzzled. "Is he working tonight? He told me he was off this week. Guess he must be covering someone else's shift."

"What are you doing here this late?"

"I have an analytical paper to present tomorrow to the officers about the sym—" Chris bit off the last word. "For something we're planning. Anyway, I realized I left some files here in my office that I need to return to the secure section before morning, so I came here to get it."

"Do you mind if I come with you? This place is a little creepy at night. Don't tell my boss I said that."

Chris grinned. "It's our secret. And you're right. It's creepy as hell."

They headed down a long corridor side by side. The oppressive silence continued to make Trask's skin crawl. Then, suddenly, he heard the quiet murmur of voices com-

ing from somewhere down the hallway and faltered to a
halt. Chris Miller stopped short, too, an odd expression
on his face.

When Chris spoke, it was in a whisper. "Nobody's supposed to be in this wing at this hour. Security should already be on the other side of the complex."

Trask eased his hand beneath his jacket and closed his
fingers over the butt of his service pistol. He kept his voice
as low as Chris's. "One quick question. Did you know my
brother was working security here these days?"

Chris gave Trask an odd look. "No, he's not."

"Maybe he just started."

"No." Chris's voice rose a notch. He tamped it back
down to a hiss of breath. "If we'd hired new security people, I'd know. One of my jobs is to screen the personnel
Security Staffing sends our way. I'd know."

Damn it. Trask swallowed the bile rising in his throat
and nodded toward the continuing murmur of voices drifting up the hallway. "Let's go find out who's here."

"TY, GET OUT HERE." The man in the drab olive uniform
kept the muzzle of his pistol pointed directly at Owen's
heart. Owen forced his gaze away from the muzzle and
concentrated on taking in every detail of their captor's
appearance.

Definitely the same man he'd seen trying to shove Tara
into the panel van outside the church. Also definitely the
same man who'd been entering the Bagley County Sheriff's Department in a deputy's uniform the morning they
tried to turn themselves in.

"You're Virgil Trask," Tara said, her voice strong,
though Owen heard the slightest tremble on the last word.

"And you're a real pain in the ass, lady. Not real good
at stayin' put."

"What were you planning to do with me? What was the point of drugging me and dragging me away from the church?"

Virgil looked at her as if she'd lost her mind. "Do you think this is some sort of *Scooby Doo* episode? You think I'm going to stand here and waste time telling you all the details of my nefarious plot?"

"You can't just shove us out of here at gunpoint," Owen said. "Security cameras will catch it all."

Virgil shot him a withering look. "Who the hell do you think runs the security cameras around here?" He turned his head toward a door in the back of the room. "Ty, you comin' out here or not?"

A big broad-shouldered man emerged from the door, his arms full of files. "He left them here, just like he said, Virgil." The man Virgil Trask called Ty stumbled to a stop, dropping a couple of the file folders stacked in his arms as he spotted Owen and Tara. He muttered a soft profanity.

"Yeah," Virgil said with a grimace. "I was really hoping I wouldn't have to kill anyone just yet."

"Do it now, do it later," Owen said with a studied shrug. "It's what you have planned, isn't it? Killing a whole lot of people from a whole lot of countries who are wanting to clamp down on terror attacks across the globe? What I don't understand is why."

Virgil said nothing, but Ty Miller dropped the rest of the folders he held onto a desk nearby and took a belligerent step toward Owen. "You think those people are coming here to make us all safer? They're just looking at more ways to tie our hands behind our backs."

Virgil shot Ty a look of disgust. "Would you shut up, Ty? Let's just figure out a clean way to get rid of them and get back to what we're here for."

"Those files are from the classified section," Tara said,

taking a few steps toward the files Ty had just deposited. "Chris had them in his office?"

"Uncle Stephen let him take them out for some paper he's preparing to present to the directors. You know Chris, he doesn't get everything on the first read through."

Tara glanced at Owen, looking faintly horrified. "And he left them in his office?"

"Stop talking, Ty. I mean it." For a moment, Virgil's pistol swung toward his partner in crime. It was a tiny opening at best, but Owen had a feeling there wouldn't be another.

He launched himself toward Virgil, knocking him hard into the nearest desk. Virgil hit it with a loud grunt of pain, already swinging his pistol back around toward Owen.

But Owen had already jerked the backpack from his shoulders and held it in front of him, using it to shove the pistol wide as Virgil pulled the trigger. Big puffs of fabric and insulation flew from the backpack as both Owen and Virgil fell to the floor.

"Owen!" Tara screamed.

All the breath seemed to rush from Owen's lungs, and the world around him started to go black.

THE SOUND OF a gunshot was easy to mistake for other things. A vehicle backfiring, or even the crack of a baseball bat hitting a pitched ball.

But neither of those things could be found inside this building at nearly half past midnight. While Chris Miller froze in place, Trask's cop instincts sent him running toward the sound.

A woman's voice rose in a wail. "Owen!"

The sounds seemed to be coming from the office just down the hallway, the one marked Analytical Security Services Unit. Trask would bet what little money remained in his savings account that the woman's voice he just heard belonged to Tara Bentley.

He'd found his fugitives. He just hoped it wasn't too late.

As TARA STARTED across the room to where Owen had fallen, Ty Miller grabbed her arms and held her in place. She struggled against his hold, but he was as strong as a bull and his grip was already digging deep bruises in her flesh.

Still, she kept fighting, her heart racing with terror as she watched Owen go dreadfully still.

"Let me go!" She kicked back against Miller's legs, her boot apparently connecting with one of his kneecaps, for he let out a howl of pain and his grip on her arms loosened.

She tore out of his grasp and ran to Owen's side.

"Get back!" Virgil trained his pistol on her from his position on the floor, desperation tinting his deep voice. "Get back, or I'll shoot you, too."

She lifted her hands toward him. "Please, let me go to him."

Virgil shook his head. "Stay where you are."

"He's hurt!" She could see a dark, wet patch spreading on the side of Owen's jacket. "I have to stop the bleeding or he could die."

"He's going to die one way or another." Virgil nodded toward Ty, who grabbed Tara's arms and pulled her backward again.

"We need those files, Virgil," Ty said.

"I'll get them. You take the girl."

"What about him?" Ty asked.

Virgil looked down at Owen. "He'll bleed out sooner or later. Then we'll come back here to clean up."

Tara thought for a moment she saw Owen's hand twitch,

but after that he was completely still, and she guessed with despair that she'd seen only what she wanted to see.

He might already be dead, his heart stopped by Virgil Trask's bullet. He could be gone and there were so many things she still hadn't told him.

Like how much she loved him. How much the image of that forever love he'd talked about had burrowed its way into her soul that she understood now how impossible it would ever be to walk away from what he was offering.

Now, when it was too late, she finally got it.

Don't die on me, Stiles. Don't die on me before we have our shot at forever.

CHRIS MILLER HAD remained where he stood down the hall while Trask made his way to the closed door. Just as well, he'd probably be more of an obstacle than an aid.

Trask waited against the wall, trying to hear what was being said inside the room. He heard the low rumble of his brother's voice, and the broader country drawl of Ty Miller answering. They were talking about cleaning up after themselves. Something about files. The woman was begging them to let her go to someone. She'd cried out Owen's name, so maybe Stiles had taken that bullet he'd heard fired down the hall?

"Let me go!" Tara's voice rose again to a shriek.

"Get her out of here!" Virgil bellowed.

Trask flattened himself against the wall, waving down the hall for Chris Miller to get out of the way.

Chris scurried down the hall and rounded the corner, out of sight. Trask saw him reaching for his phone as he ran. Calling 9-1-1? Trask hoped so.

There was a hard thud against the door, followed by several more thumps.

Then splinters of wood flew from the door beside

his head in concert with another blast of gunfire. Trask ducked, his heart galloping in his chest.

"WHAT THE HELL, VIRGIL! You nearly hit me." Ty Miller released one of Tara's arms, giving her the chance to pull away. Her cheek stung where a splinter of wood from the gunshot had sliced through the skin, but she didn't think she'd been hit anywhere else.

She jerked free of Ty's grasp and turned to look at Virgil. But he wasn't standing there holding a gun as she expected. Instead, he was grappling on the floor with Owen, whose eyes were open and locked with Virgil's. His hand covered Virgil's on the pistol, and he shouted, "Get out of here, Tara!" without ever looking in her direction.

He was alive. The words sang through her whole body, sending a flood of sheer relief pouring through her like fizzy champagne bubbles. But reality crashed through the brief moment of jubilation. He was still wrapped in a death grip with a man who'd already shot him once. And another man was already moving toward them, ready to help his buddy overpower Owen.

She grabbed the chair that sat near the door and swung it at Ty Miller, catching the big man right in the small of his back. Something made a loud cracking noise, and it wasn't the solid steel chair she'd somehow managed to wield like a club. Ty howled with pain as he crashed to the floor, writhing in agony.

"Go, Tara! Go!" Owen shouted as he started to lose his grip on Virgil's arm.

"No!" she cried, picking up the chair again and heading to his rescue.

Ty Miller's hand clamped around her ankle, stopping her short. Losing her balance, she fell hard to the floor, the impact sending stars sparking through her brain for a moment. She pushed through the disorientation and kicked with her free leg, hitting Ty in the chin. He yelled out a stream of profanities but let go of her leg.

She scrambled up again and grabbed the chair, grunting as the full weight of the steel behemoth made itself known. Earlier, with adrenaline spiking her strength, it had felt almost featherlight, but the adrenaline was starting to drain away.

She gazed desperately at Owen, who had managed to grapple Virgil Trask toward the window.

Suddenly, the door behind her slammed open, and both Virgil and Owen froze to look at the newcomer. Tara turned as well and found herself looking at a dark-haired man holding a big gunmetal-gray pistol. He aimed the pistol's muzzle across the room at Virgil Trask.

"Put the gun down, Virgil. It's over."

Owen let go of Virgil and stumbled back, falling into a chair a few feet away. Tara ran to him, her heart in her throat.

"What are you doin' here, Archie?" The tone of Virgil's plaintive query was somewhere between anger and dismay.

"I'm here to put an end to all of this, Virgil. Put down the gun."

Virgil shook his head. "You don't know what this is, Archie. I caught your fugitives. He tried to kill me."

"That's a lie!" Tara shouted as she paused in the act of trying to find the source of the blood dripping on the floor beneath Owen. "These two men tried to kidnap me the day of my wedding. I think one of them killed my fiancé. They're after some secret information."

"I know," the man in the doorway said. "I'm Archer Trask. I'm the lead investigator on your fiancé's murder case."

"Come on, Archie! She's your top suspect, and I found her. I was going to bring her in."

"It's over. Just put down the gun."

"Archie, it's me."

Archer Trask stared at his brother sadly. "I know, Virgil."

Suddenly, Virgil's gun hand whipped up a couple of inches, and Tara shouted a warning.

It wasn't necessary. Gunfire blazed from Archer Trask's pistol at the same time Virgil pulled the trigger of his own weapon. The bullet Virgil fired went wide, hitting the doorframe behind his brother's head. His brother's bullet, however, hit Virgil in the chest.

For a minute, Virgil stared in disbelief at the bloom of red spreading across his shirt. Then he looked back at his brother, the stunned expression frozen on his face as he slid to the floor. His chin fell to his chest, and only the desk beside him and the wall behind him, now streaked with his blood, kept him from falling over.

Archer Trask walked slowly to his brother's side, gazing down at him with a look of pure grief. He nudged the pistol away from his brother's slack fingers with his toe, moving it out of reach. Then he crouched in front of Virgil and touched his fingertips to his brother's throat.

The look of sheer agony on his face told Tara what that trembling touch had revealed.

Archer sat back on his heels, tears leaking from his eyes. "Damn it, Virgil," he said.

Chapter Seventeen

"Do we have to do this now?" Tara looked at the grim face of Bagley County Sheriff Roy Atkins as he loomed over where she sat in one of the small interrogation rooms at the county hall complex. "I know Deputy Trask must have already told you everything that happened tonight. I just want to make sure Owen is okay."

"He's still in surgery."

Shock hit her like a fist blow. "Surgery? He's in surgery? Why is he in surgery? He was awake and talking, and the paramedics seemed to think he was okay—"

"He was shot in the side. They want to be sure he didn't sustain any life-threatening internal injuries, so they need to get the bullet out of him before it causes any worse problems."

"Surgery?" She pressed her hand to her mouth, terror twisting her insides. She had thought it was over. She just had to get through all the debriefings, convince the authorities that she had been running for her life, and then she and Owen could move forward with the life they should already have been living together.

This couldn't be happening. Not now.

Owen deserved the forever he wanted so desperately, and somehow she had to find a way to give it to him.

But she couldn't do it from here, halfway across the

county from where he lay on an operating table, fighting for his life.

A brisk duo of knocks on the door drew Sheriff Atkins's gaze in that direction. His look of mild irritation deepened when Tony Giattina walked confidently through the door and set his gleaming leather briefcase on the table between the sheriff and Tara.

"Don't say anything else, Tara," he said, looking at her with far more sympathy in his expression than had been there the last time she saw him. He was dressed in an expensive-looking suit and a crisp linen shirt that would have been more at home at a morning court appearance than a two in the morning visit to the county jail. "Sheriff, are you planning on holding my client overnight?"

For a moment, the sheriff looked as if he wanted to say yes. But finally, he shook his head. "Just don't leave our jurisdiction this time, Ms. Bentley."

"She wouldn't dream of it," Tony said blithely, offering Tara his hand. She took it and rose, following him out of the interrogation room.

Outside, the corridor was buzzing with more movement than she'd noticed when she was first brought in. A lot had happened, including the death of one of their own deputies. That he'd been the cause of his own death hadn't really sunk in at this point, and some of the deputies sent furious glares her way as she walked out of the building with her lawyer.

To no one's surprise, Alexander Quinn was waiting outside the sheriff's department. He nodded toward Tony before turning his attention to Tara. "Are you all right?"

"I need to see Owen. The sheriff said he's in surgery."

"He is. One of my colleagues is there with him, waiting for word. I'm here to take you to the hospital." He opened the passenger door of a dark blue SUV and helped her inside. As she buckled in, he climbed behind the wheel and reached for his own belt. "On the way, why don't you tell me everything that happened tonight?"

One way or another, she thought with resignation, she was going to have to undergo an interrogation after all.

THE LAST PEOPLE Archer Trask had expected to see sitting at the bar of the Sheffield Tavern were Maddox Heller and his pretty wife. He almost turned around and walked out when he saw the expressions of sympathy in their faces, but he braced himself against the unwanted kindness and walked over to where they sat.

The bar was nearly empty at this time of the morning. It would close in another hour, which would at least give him a polite reason to escape, he thought with bleak humor.

"We heard what happened," Heller said as Trask settled on the bar stool next to him. "I'm sorry."

"So am I," Trask said. He waved at the bartender. "Bourbon and branch. Light on the branch."

"We think we've finally figured out what your brother and Ty Miller were involved in," Heller said. He had a glass of what looked like water with a twist of lime and had drunk a little of it. Even the wife was nursing her glass of white wine, barely taking a sip at all as she looked from her husband's face to Trask's.

"I can guess at some of it," Trask said. "My mother told me Virgil had been spending a lot of time with Ty Miller and some of his friends. I had a chance to talk to Ty's brother, Chris, for a few minutes before the police and emergency services arrived. He said Ty had gotten involved with some group of preppers."

"They weren't just preppers. Preppers mostly just want to be left alone to prepare for whatever might come," Heller said. "Your brother and his friends were determined to make sure our country cut its ties with the rest of the world. Extreme isolationism, I guess you could call it."

Trask remembered a few of the more objectionable things he'd heard his brother say over the years. He could definitely see him falling on the side of "kick the foreign bastards out and don't let them back in."

"Quinn and his previous security company back in the mountains of Tennessee came across a very similar group of nihilists—the Blue Ridge Infantry. We think one of the men in this group of people had familial ties to some of the former members of the Blue Ridge Infantry."

"I've heard of them. They were in Virginia, too, and there were less organized groups here in Kentucky with sympathetic leanings."

"I think maybe Ty and your brother were in the process of trying to organize this Kentucky group into something more cohesive. Through Chris, they found out Security Solutions was planning a security event that involves several other countries. I think your brother and Ty must have realized that if they could create a big, deadly disruption of that event, their success would be a spectacular recruiting tool to pull off bigger and more influential attacks against the government they think has betrayed them. But they needed more information about the event to be successful."

"So they kidnapped Tara Bentley? Why? To get her to tell them what she knew?" Trask asked with a frown. "You think they were going to try to torture it out of her?"

"We thought that might be the case at first," Heller admitted. "But we couldn't quite make Robert Mallory's murder fit our theory."

The bartender arrived with the bourbon and water. Trask took a sip and grimaced. "Neither could I. It seemed to be completely out of the blue. No motive seemed to fit."

"They wanted Tara Bentley out of the way, and they

wanted the cops looking in a completely different direction," Heller said. "If they'd killed her, where would your
investigation have taken you?"

"To her. Her connections. Her job," Trask answered.
"But instead, it was her fiancé who died. And she was
my prime person of interest instead of the victim. I didn't
even look at her work as a possible reason for what happened until recently."

Heller nodded. "Your brother was a cop. He would have
known the direction you'd look in."

"Leaving him and Ty free to look for the information
they would never have gotten from Tara."

"They planned to stash her somewhere until they got
what they wanted from her second-in-command."

"Ty's brother, Chris." Trask took another sip of the
bourbon. It burned all the way down, leaving him feeling
queasy and unsettled. He pushed the drink away. "They
found some files tonight."

"We heard. Security Solutions has already sent people
from their secure documents division to return them to a
place of safekeeping."

"I don't think Chris was intentionally involved."

"We don't think so, either," Heller agreed. "He was just
too careless for the job he was tasked to do."

Trask stood up, feeling stifled and claustrophobic in this
place. He pulled a couple of bills from his wallet and put
them on the bar next to his drink. "I gotta get out of here."

Heller and his wife followed him outside. "Trask,"
Heller said, stopping him in his tracks.

He turned to look at them. "I really need to be left
alone."

It was the wife, Iris, who reached out and took his hand.
As had happened the last time they met, he felt a strange
zip of energy flow through him where her fingers touched

his flesh. "I'm so sorry about your brother. If you need anything, you give us a call, okay?"

She flashed him a faint smile, removed her hand and walked away with her husband.

Trask turned to watch her go, rubbing his hand where she'd touched him. Just a moment ago, he'd felt as if he'd never feel normal again. But now...

Now he felt as if there just might be a sliver of hope out there after all.

"HE'S OUT OF SURGERY. He did just fine." A tall, beautiful African American woman rose as Quinn and Tara entered the surgical waiting room. "I tried to reach his parents, but I got no answer."

"I think they're in Branson, Missouri," Tara said. "They go there every spring, before the summer tourist rush kicks in." She rubbed her gritty eyes, surprised to find tears trembling on her eyelashes. "I want to see him."

"I know. They'll take him up to his room as soon as he's out of recovery." The woman offered Tara a gentle smile. "I'm Rebecca Cameron. I work with Quinn at Campbell Cove Security."

"Right. Owen's mentioned you."

Rebecca put her arm around Tara's shoulders. "Come on. I'll take you to his room."

The empty room looked so sterile. Tara found herself futilely wishing the hospital gift shop downstairs was open so she could at least buy a nice vase of spring flowers to make the place look more homey and welcoming.

As if she had read Tara's thoughts on her face, Rebecca patted Tara's back. "I suspect all he really needs right now is you." With an encouraging smile, Rebecca left her alone in the room.

It seemed to be forever later when a nurse and an attendant wheeled Owen into the hospital room on a gurney. He wasn't exactly awake, but his eyes were fluttering open and closed and his arms flailed weakly as he tried to help the attendant move him from the gurney to the bed.

The nurse finished settling Owen and put his IV bag on the pole beside him. She turned to smile at Tara. "Are you Tara?"

Tara nodded.

"He asked if you were here when he first started coming out of the anesthesia."

Tara crossed to Owen's bedside. His eyes were closed again, but when she took the hand without the IV, he squeezed weakly.

"Tara?" he mumbled.

"Right here, Owen. Where else would I be?"

The nurse smiled at her again. "I'll be back in a bit to check his vitals. You can stay in here with him if you want. I could get you a reclining chair if you like. To make it more comfortable."

"That's fine. Thanks. No hurry. Just when you can get to it." She waited until the nurse walked out the door, and then she bent closer to Owen. "You gave me a scare, you big, brave idiot. Don't ever do that again."

His eyes fluttered halfway open, though his pupils seemed incapable of focusing. "Admit it. You were impressed by my show of manly courage."

"Terrified is more like it," she confessed, her heart surging with relief to hear him making jokes. "I didn't need proof of your strength, you know. I've always thought you were the strongest man I know."

"No matter what my father thought?"

"By now, we both know he's a fool. So stop trying so hard to prove it, okay?" She touched his cheek. "For the dozen years you scared off my life span, you owe me big, mister."

His dry lips cracked into a lopsided, painful-looking smile. "Yeah? You got a payment in mind?"

She leaned even closer, lowering her voice to a whisper. "How about you marry me?"

His eyes struggled to focus. "Was that a proposition?"

"It was a proposal." She picked up the roll of tape the nurse had left on the bedside table after she taped down his IV cannula. Stripping off a piece, she wrapped it around his left ring finger. "See? I got a ring and everything."

A raspy laugh escaped his throat. He winced, and when he spoke again, his voice was hoarse but full of humor. "Why, Miss Tara, this is so sudden."

"Say yes, Owen."

"Yes, Owen." His eyes fluttered shut.

She drew up the chair beside his bed and sat there with a goofy smile on her face, her fingers twined with his.

OWEN WOKE TO sunlight angling through a window, falling across his eyes and making his head hurt. He turned his head with a grumble and found himself face-to-face with Tara.

She was just starting to wake, her eyes fluttering open. She gave a slight start when she saw him watching her. Pulling back from the bed, she laughed sheepishly. "Good morning."

He winced in pain as he shifted position in the bed. "That's a matter of opinion."

"Are you in a lot of pain? Do you want me to call the nurse?"

"No, please don't. She kept waking me up all night."

Tara brushed his hair away from his face. "Oh, come on, you slacker. You slept through the last couple of vitals checks. I was awake for all of them." She rubbed her red eyes. "God, I need about a week of sleep."

"How did you get the police to let you come here?" His throat felt as if he'd swallowed glass. Probably the breathing tube they'd have administered before surgery.

"Quinn sicced Tony Giattina on them. They didn't know what hit them."

"Tony's speaking to us after what we did to him?" He was surprised.

"Well, that's still up in the air." Tara touched his face, her expression gentle. "You look terrible."

"Thank you. You don't know how much better that makes me feel."

"I thought I'd lost you." Her fingers moved lightly over his forehead, her touch strangely tentative, as if she weren't sure whether she had a right to offer him comfort. "When I realized you'd been shot, I was so scared."

"I'm okay. Everything's okay." He put his hand over hers. As he did, he noticed a piece of tape wrapped around his left ring finger. A vague memory drifted through his brain. Tara holding his hand, talking about debts. But the rest of the memory eluded him, somehow distant and unreachable.

"I love you," she murmured, pressing her lips against his palm. "I was so afraid I'd never get to tell you that again."

"Oh, I already knew that." He gave a weak wave of his other hand, wincing a little as the IV cannula shifted in his vein. He was aching all over and felt as if he'd gone about ten rounds with a freight train, but a sense of peace began to settle over him. Everything was going to be okay now. His wound would heal and he and Tara would get their lives back.

"What are you smiling about?" Tara asked, rubbing her cheek against the back of his hand. He liked the feeling, liked the way it sent little flutters of life through his otherwise lifeless body.

"Just thinking that it's finally over. The truth will come out, one way or another, and we'll get to go back to our lives again."

"Do you remember anything about last night?"

"I remember running into Virgil and Ty. I remember getting shot. Then someone shot Virgil."

"Deputy Trask," she said, her voice darkening. "Virgil's younger brother."

Owen grimaced. "Poor bastard."

"What do you remember after that?"

"You holding my hand. Paramedics. Lots and lots of lights, and then it's a blank." He narrowed his eyes at her. "Did I miss something?"

"Quite a bit," she said with a wry half smile.

"I remember seeing you after surgery," he added. "If that's what you're getting at."

"Yes, I was waiting for you when you came up after recovery."

"You told me I owed you big."

"That's right." Smiling, she ran her finger lightly over the edge of the tape on his finger. "I also told you the payment I wanted."

He looked at the tape on his finger, then back at her face. What he saw in her eyes made his heart turn a little flip in his chest. "Did I agree to your terms?" he asked, emotion swelling through him to settle like a lump in his throat.

Tears glittered in her eyes. "Yes, but you were a little loopy at the time."

"So maybe you should tell me again. What do I have to do to even up things between us?"

A smile crept over her lips. "Marry me, Owen Stiles. Make me your wife."

He caught her hand in his, pressing it against his chest. "Why, Tara?"

She frowned, as if she hadn't expected the question. "Because I love you."

"You loved me yesterday and the day before that. But you weren't anywhere near thinking about marrying me. Don't make a big decision just because we've gone through a crisis."

"I'm not. I was already thinking about it before you were shot. It's just, staring down the barrel of a gun really clarifies things for you, you know? I realized that I might not get the chance to tell you that the one thing I wanted more than anything in this world was to live the rest of my life with you. To be with you in every way. It suddenly seemed so stupid to be afraid of having everything with you. I trust you completely. With my life. And with my heart." She stroked his cheek, the tears spilling down her cheeks. "I know now that we belong together in every way. I believe that with all my heart."

He had trouble pushing words past the lump in his throat. "So ask me again."

Her eyes met his, deadly serious. "Will you marry me, Owen Stiles?"

"I do believe I will," he answered, pulling her down for a kiss.

* * * * *

Look for the continuation of Paula Graves's
CAMPBELL COVE ACADEMY *series when*
OPERATION NANNY *goes on sale next month.*

You'll find it wherever
Mills & Boon Intrigue books are sold!

"Bex," a harsh whisper sounded. "Move. Now."

Bex's eyes flew open. Impossibly, Max stood towering over her, ski-mask guy limply hanging over his shoulder, his arms dangling toward the ground. Max jerked his head, motioning for her to run straight ahead to the aisle directly in front of them.

Stunned that she was alive and could run, she ducked and darted from the alcove, then stopped just past the endcap and looked behind her.

He yanked out his pistol and shoved it toward her. "Remember how to use one of these?" he whispered.

She swallowed, then nodded. "I haven't fired one in years."

Something dark passed in his eyes, and she knew he was remembering one of the many times he'd taken her to target practice so long ago.

And seeing him now, so calm and focused, she knew that if anyone could save her, it was Max.

But who would save her from him?

SECRET STALKER

BY
LENA DIAZ

MILLS &
BOON®

First Published in Great Britain 2017
By Mills & Boon, an imprint of HarperCollins*Publishers*
1 London Bridge Street, London, SE1 9GF

© 2017 Lena Diaz

ISBN: 978-0-263-92867-9

46-0317

Our policy is to use papers that are natural, renewable and recyclable products and made from wood grown in sustainable forests. The logging and manufacturing processes conform to the legal environmental regulations of the country of origin.

Printed and bound in Spain
by CPI, Barcelona

Lena Diaz was born in Kentucky and has also lived in California, Louisiana and Florida, where she now resides with her husband and two children. Before becoming a romantic suspense author, she was a computer programmer. A former Romance Writers of America Golden Heart® Award finalist, she has also won the prestigious Daphne du Maurier Award for Excellence in mystery and suspense. To get the latest news about Lena, please visit her website, www.lenadiaz.com.

Thank you to my editor, Allison Lyons,
and my agent, Nalini Akolekar.

This one's for George. Because he reads every book I
write, and pretends to love romance novels, all to make
me happy. Best. Husband. Ever. I love you, babe.

Chapter One

The whispers started thirty seconds after Bexley Kane walked down aisle three in the Piggly Wiggly on Magnolia Street. Not that there was a Piggly Wiggly on any other street in the tiny town of Destiny, Tennessee. With a population the size of a large high school in other parts of the state, this town could only support one grocery store. And one movie theater. And one Waffle House. But, oddly enough, there were four Starbucks. Too bad not one of them was anywhere close to Magnolia Street. Bex sure could use a venti caramel macchiato right now.

Head high, shoulders back, she began filling her cart as quickly as possible while pretending not to notice the other shoppers talking behind their hands as she passed. But, come on, did they really believe that she didn't know they were gossiping about her? She could well imagine what they were saying.

Is that who I think it is? What's it been, ten years? Why is she back in town?

You didn't hear? Her mama done passed away. I heard she died of a broken heart, on account of her daughter didn't visit even once after she got run out of town.

You think Chief Thornton will arrest her this time?

Is there a statute of limitations on murder?

"Miss Kane, nice to see you today," Mr. Dawson gave Bex a genuine, welcoming smile from behind the deli counter. "I was hoping I'd see your lovely face at least one more time before you left Destiny. You here for lunch? We've got a brand-new batch of pickled pigs' feet." He proudly thumped a large jar on top of the display case that looked like a science experiment gone horribly wrong.

Bex very nearly lost her breakfast. She averted her gaze from the nauseating sight and smiled at one of the few people in Destiny who hadn't treated her like a pariah in the week that she'd been back.

"Hello, Mr. Dawson. I called in an order for some lunch meats and grilled chicken. Could you see whether it's ready, please?"

"Gladys must have taken that order. I'll check the cooler. Won't take but a minute." He opened the massive walk-in refrigerator behind him and headed inside.

Bex checked her grocery list. The only thing left to get was mustard, one of several things she'd forgotten the first time she'd been in the store. After today's shopping trip, she should have enough to tide her over for several more days, until she finished taking care of all of the details of her mother's estate. Then she could hop into her car and leave Destiny in the dust. Again. And this time, she'd never come back.

If she remembered correctly, Mr. Dawson kept the condiments across the aisle from the meat case. Since little else had changed in this town, she doubted that had, either. She turned around—and locked gazes with the one person she'd hoped to avoid.

Max Remington.

His golden-brown eyes stared at her in shock for all of three seconds. Then they filled with anger. His jaw clamped tight and, without a word, he circled around her and headed to the sandwich counter at the other end of the deli.

Gladys miraculously appeared as if from thin air, eager

to take Max's order. Bex couldn't help noticing that he was all smiles and *yes, ma'am*s, *no, ma'am*s when speaking to the older woman. But he couldn't even spare a hello for his former lover.

His curt dismissal shouldn't hurt. After all, she was the one who'd left him. But he'd been her first love. And she'd built him up in her mind over the years as her handsome hero, dreaming of what life could have been, should have been, if she'd said yes that night.

And if Bobby Caldwell hadn't died.

She grabbed a jar of mustard and allowed herself the guilty pleasure of admiring Max from beneath her lashes—all six feet two of him. At eighteen, he'd been the cutest, sweetest, most popular boy at Destiny High. At twenty-eight, he was a devastatingly handsome man with bulging biceps and muscular thighs filling out the gangly frame of his youth. His dark hair was short on the sides, thick and wavy on top. He'd been clean shaven when she'd been with him. Now his angular face was framed by neatly trimmed stubble, as if he was considering growing a beard but hadn't yet committed.

He dressed pretty much the same as he had back then: nothing fancy, just a no-nonsense button-up blue linen shirt neatly tucked into a pair of crisp jeans. In deference to the chilly autumn air outside, he wore a lightweight navy blue jacket. And as he turned to point to something in the display case for Gladys, the white lettering on his back reassured Bex that she'd made the right decision all those years ago—the letters spelled Destiny Police Department.

Good for you, Max. You chased your dream after all.

"Will you be needing anything else, Miss Kane?"

She forced her gaze away from Max, her face flushing with heat when Mr. Dawson glanced down the counter, then back at her, obviously noting her interest in her former high school sweetheart.

He handed her a brown paper sack that was stapled closed. "Your order's inside. Just show the cashier that code on the bag at checkout and she'll ring up the manager's special. That'll save you a couple of dollars."

"Thank you." She lowered her voice. "I really appreciate how nice you've been to me. You're one of the few people who's made this trip bearable."

"You don't need to thank me for doing what's right. It's a downright shame how nasty folks can be. They ought not to be throwing stones without taking a long, hard look at themselves first."

She smiled again, painfully aware that Max and Gladys had stopped talking the moment she'd thanked Mr. Dawson. Was Max looking at her? Had he decided to acknowledge her existence after all?

The sound of his boots echoed on the tile floor as he strode toward her. She clutched the bag and jar of mustard against her chest, frozen in place while she desperately tried to think of something, anything, to say.

He stalked past without even looking at her.

Bex's breath rushed out of her, deflating her like a popped balloon.

Someone cleared their throat. Mr. Dawson. He was watching her with a sympathetic expression on his face. Beside him, Gladys looked decidedly less friendly, a frown wrinkling her brow, her hands on her generous hips. There was no doubt about whose side she was on. Not that there were any sides to take. A fight required two people, and Max hadn't cared enough about the outcome to even stick around for the first volley.

Bex nodded her thanks to Mr. Dawson before putting her items in the cart and heading toward the back of the store, as if there was something else she needed. What she *really* needed was a moment to compose herself.

Not wanting to risk another encounter with Max, she

strolled along the rear aisle toward the other side of the store, putting off checking out until she was certain he'd be gone.

Maybe she should just get in her RAV4 and hit the road right now. She could hire someone else to pack up her mom's house. Settling the last legal details of the estate through the mail instead of working with her lawyer in person would delay things. But at least she wouldn't have to endure one more person's disapproving stare. And her heart wouldn't have to face Max again.

She tried to convince herself that it wasn't cowardice that had her wanting to run— it was self-preservation. Because it had taken years to tape and glue the pieces of her broken heart back together. But shattering it again had only taken one angry look from Max Remington.

MAX SHUFFLED IMPATIENTLY in line behind Mable Humphries. It was the express lane, ten items or less. But she had thirty items. And the only other register that was open had three customers waiting with overflowing carts.

He blew out a frustrated breath, then forced a smile when the elderly woman looked at him.

"How are you today, Mrs. Humphries?" he asked.

"You sure are sweet to ask, Detective Remington. My joints have been aching something fierce today, and not just from the chill outside. I think we're in for a storm soon. Don't you?"

He gave her a noncommittal answer and she prattled on about her aches and pains. He wished he could just ignore her outright or tell her to hurry up. But the manners his mother and father had drilled into him couldn't be ignored.

Except, apparently, where Bexley Kane was concerned.

A twinge of guilt shot through him over the way he'd treated her. Or, rather, *ignored* her.

Destiny was too small for him not to have heard the

rumors. He knew she was back in town because of her mother's recent passing. But he hadn't been prepared for actually coming face-to-face with her after all these years. He'd just…reacted. All the lines he'd rehearsed in case he ever saw her again had disappeared in a fog of rage and hurt. So he'd done the only thing he could safely do. He'd kept his mouth shut.

As Mrs. Humphries droned on, Max nodded in the appropriate places but otherwise tuned her out.

Bex. It was hard to believe that she was really here. Was she staying? Permanently? Based on her comments to Mr. Dawson about him making her "trip" bearable, Max didn't think so. Maybe he should have paid more attention to the gossip swirling around town about her instead of taking pains to avoid it every time her name came up. Then maybe he'd know what Bex's plans were so he could take the necessary precautions to ensure that he didn't run into her again.

He'd already done his duty by Bex's mom, the sweet woman whom he and half the town had expected would become his mother-in-law one day. He'd gone to the memorial service her church had put together, a service without a casket or even an urn since her body had been shipped out of town to be interred somewhere else. As far as he knew, Bex hadn't bothered to go to the church. For his part, he'd arrived early and left fast, just in case she did show.

His mourning was done in private, when he'd planted some white lilies in Mrs. Kane's garden as a tribute to her. They'd always been her favorite, and he'd planted a new lily in her yard every Mother's Day for the past ten years.

"It sure was nice running into you, Detective." Mable's gnarled hand gripped his with surprising strength. "Hope to see you at the town picnic next weekend. I'm making some of my famous sweet potato pie."

"I wouldn't miss it, ma'am." He gently extricated his hand and returned her wave as she pushed her cart to the exit.

The young brunette at the cash register scanned Max's sandwich and handed it back to him.

"You want to make that a meal deal with chips and a drink? I can have someone run to the deli and—"

"Just the sandwich, thanks." He quickly paid and let out a breath of relief that he was finally about to get out of purgatory. He wasn't even hungry anymore. All he wanted to do was return to the police station, immerse himself in work and try to forget all about Bexley Kane.

"Everybody do what we say and no one gets hurt!"

Max jerked his head toward the entrance. Five masked gunmen with assault rifles had just run in through the front door and were pointing their guns toward the handful of customers at the other register.

The cashier beside him started screaming. One of the gunmen swung his rifle her way. Max dived over the counter, pulling the girl to the floor seconds before the countertop above them exploded in a hail of gunfire.

Chapter Two

Bex flattened herself against a cereal box endcap, pressing both of her hands against her mouth to keep from crying out.

Rat-a-tat-tat-tat-tat-tat!

Bam! Bam!

She dropped to the floor, her breaths coming out in short pants. What in the world was happening? Who would fire guns inside a Piggly Wiggly? The answer, of course, was obvious. Someone was holding up the place. But she still couldn't believe it was happening. Not here. Not in the tiny town of Destiny.

Thank God Max had plenty of time to have left before the gunman or gunmen had shown up.

And wasn't that a crazy thought, being glad the police officer was out of harm's way when he was the one person who might have been able to help her and any others trapped inside?

A scream sounded from the front of the store. Someone else shouted. Footsteps pounded down an aisle not too far from where Bex lay on the floor. If someone was holding up the store, wouldn't they have forced the manager to open the safe in the front office? They wouldn't be running down aisles and still shooting minutes later, would they?

Bam! Bam!

That sounded like a pistol.

Rat-a-tat-tat-tat.

Automatic gunfire.

She pressed a hand to her throat. Was that a gunfight? Whoever had the pistol was at a serious disadvantage.

Another shout sounded. More footsteps.

Bam!

"Where is she?" a man yelled. "She wasn't with the ones who locked themselves in the cooler."

"How the hell should I know? Reggie said she was ready to check out. She should have been up front when we got here."

"Find her. And find that stupid cop. He's screwing everything up and I'm gonna blow his brains out."

Oh, no. Please, God, don't be talking about Max.

But in her gut, she knew they were. He was the only policeman she'd seen in the store just a few minutes before the gunmen came in. No one else could have gotten here this fast. He either hadn't left when she'd thought he had, or he'd run back into the store when he saw the gunmen go inside.

Footsteps sounded again, much closer this time. If they turned down the back aisle that ran the width of the store, they'd see her. She had to move, hide. Or better yet, find Max and get them both out of the store.

Right, like she was GI Jane or something. The only danger she faced on a typical day was whether she might get a splinter in her finger from one of the pieces of furniture that she sold at her antique store.

Move, Bex. Hurry!

She sent up a quick, silent prayer then pulled herself forward in an army crawl.

MAX CROUCHED DOWN, his pistol out in front of him while he whispered into his cell phone and made his way down aisle five toward the front of the store again.

"Searching for remaining three gunmen. What's your ETA?" he asked his SWAT team lead, Dillon Gray.

He reached the end of the aisle and looked left, then right, before crouching by the endcap. He paused, listening for sounds that might indicate where the gunmen were hiding.

"Roger that," he whispered in answer to the instructions over the phone. "I've got five customers and four employees locked in the cooler from the inside with good cover. There are coats in there, so they're okay for now. Searching for additional customers. You guys need to get in here ASAP, full SWAT gear. These yahoos may be stupid and disorganized. But that makes them unpredictable and dangerous."

A noise sounded from the east end of the store. He looked down the next aisle. Clear. He jogged to another endcap, heading east.

"Negative," he whispered in response to Dillon's next question. "No clue what they want. As soon as the cashier screamed, they started shooting. Erratic though, as if they don't know how to handle those M16s they're waving around. Thankfully no one's been hit yet except the one gunman I took out."

With his fellow SWAT team members apprised of the situation, he put his cell phone away so he could focus on finding the one customer he knew was unaccounted for.

Bex.

As PLANS WENT, hiding behind a waist-high clothing rack of "I Dig the Pig" Piggly Wiggly T-shirts probably wasn't the best one Bex could have made. But when she'd seen the end of a rifle emerging from one of the side aisles, she'd dived behind the closest cover she could find. Unfortunately, the T-shirts were apparently good sellers. There were barely enough left to conceal her.

She held her breath as the gunman crept past her hiding space. He was dressed in black jeans and a black T-shirt and was wearing sunglasses. She supposed that was his idea of a disguise, but he clearly was young—probably barely out of high school. The other gunman she'd seen a few minutes ago had a black ski mask over his face and the build of someone older, maybe late twenties. Both of them were carrying wicked-looking rifles.

The guy in sunglasses turned down the aisle she'd left just a minute earlier. She let out a shaky breath, then crept to the side of the display, ready to zip down another aisle to get to the front of the store. That's where she'd last heard the sound of a pistol. And she was betting that pistol belonged to Max.

She leaned forward, looked left, right, then—*oomph!* A hand clamped over her mouth and she was yanked backward behind the shirts.

Chapter Three

Bex struggled against her captor, twisting and writhing in his grasp.

He pressed his cheek against hers and held her so tight she could barely move.

"Be still, Bex. It's me, Max."

She froze, then went limp with relief.

He slowly lifted his hand from her mouth, as if he didn't quite trust her not to cry out. She half turned to look at him, nodding to let him know she wasn't going to sob hysterically and give away their position. Or at least she didn't think she was. Cowering from gunmen was an entirely new experience for her. She could very well start screaming like a madwoman any second.

Apparently Max had more faith in her than she did. He loosened his arm around her waist and let her go. She was about to ask him what she should do when he edged to the right of the display. His whole body was tense, alert, as he ducked lower and slid his pistol into the holster at his waist. What was he doing?

A gunman, the one in the ski mask, stepped out from behind a stack of bagels and English muffins, his gaze zeroing in on Bex through a gap in the clothing rack. She ducked behind another shirt, expecting to feel a bullet slam into her any second. The gunman rushed forward, his sneakers visible beneath the clothes.

Bex jerked her head toward Max. But he wasn't even looking at her. He was poised like a runner, one leg down, one up, balancing on his fingertips like he was about to take off in a sprint. Ski mask guy stopped directly in front of the rack, looking down at Bex. He started to raise his gun.

She squeezed her eyes shut. The air rushed beside her. The squeak of a shoe sounded on the floor. She heard a grunt, then…nothing. She was still alive. No bullets had ripped into her body and thrown her to the floor in a pool of her own blood.

"Bex," a harsh whisper sounded. "Move. Now."

Her eyes flew open. Impossibly, Max stood towering over her, ski mask guy hanging limply over his shoulder, his arms dangling toward the ground. Max jerked his head, motioning for her to run to the aisle directly across from them.

Stunned that she was still alive and *could* run, she darted forward, stopping a few feet down the aisle and looking back.

Max was lowering the unconscious—dead?—gunman to the floor under the rack. Bex swallowed, hard. Moments later, Max stopped beside her with a confiscated rifle in his hand.

He frowned. "Are you all right?"

She looked past him at the body visible beneath the obscenely cheery pink and green shirts. A shiver ran up her spine over their close call but she forced a nod.

After a quick look to the far end of their row, Max checked the rifle's loading, then yanked out his pistol and shoved it toward her.

"Remember how to use one of these?" he whispered.

She swallowed. "Sure. But I haven't fired one in years."

Something dark passed in his eyes, and she knew he was remembering one of the many times long ago when he'd taken her to target practice. When other boys waffled between wanting to be a pilot or a fireman or maybe a professional football player, Max had never wavered in his desire to be a detective and SWAT officer like cool Chief Thornton, who'd visited Destiny High every year on career day.

Max had loved the idea of piecing clues together and solving crimes as his main gig. And then, when the situation called for it, putting on full SWAT gear and storming some criminal's compound to rescue hostages. It had been his dream. And seeing him now, so calm and focused, she knew that if anyone could save her and the other customers, it was Max. But only if she followed his instructions and let him do his job.

She took the pistol, careful to point it away from him and keep her finger on the frame, not the trigger, as he'd drilled into her so many times.

He gave her a nod of approval and pivoted toward the back of the store again, then the front, as if scoping out their situation. Then he dropped to his knees and peered in between the bottom shelf and the one above it on both sides of the aisle they were on. He hesitated, as if thinking something through. Then he was pushing boxes of noodles and pasta behind the jars of spaghetti sauce. When he'd cleared a spot a couple of feet wide, he grabbed her arms and shoved her toward the opening.

She wanted to protest that she wasn't nearly as small as he apparently thought she was. But the sound of footsteps, and Max's head jerking toward the front of the store, had her squeezing into the impossibly small hole and pulling in her legs after her as tightly as she could. The sharp scrape of the metal shelf against her arm had her clenching her teeth. But she didn't make a sound.

He leaned down, held a finger to his lips motioning for her to be quiet, and then he was gone.

She clutched the pistol in both hands, her pulse pounding so hard she felt light-headed. A tiny tapping sound started above her head. She twisted to see what was causing it and realized she was shaking so hard her shoulders were making the shelving above her rattle against its brackets. She drew several deep, slow breaths and concentrated on trying to calm down. The tapping stopped. Then she heard it, another sound—footsteps.

Coming toward her.

Her finger shook as she moved it to the trigger. Wait. It could be Max. She moved her finger back to the gun's frame.

Oh, God. Please let it be Max coming back for her.

The tapping started again. She clamped her jaw and forced herself to hold still. The footsteps stopped. Was it one of the gunmen? Had he heard her?

Ever so carefully, she peeked through the gap above the boxes of pasta to her left but couldn't see more than a few feet. Looking the other way yielded more of the same— boxes and jars blocking her view.

A squeak. Someone's shoe against the floor?

Her hand started shaking violently, the pistol bobbing in her grip. A trickle of sweat rolled down the side of her face.

Another sound. *Oh, God.* Someone was behind her. She was surrounded. The person in her aisle shuffled forward, his shoes squeaking again.

Bam! Bam! Bam!

Gunfire sounded from the front of the store. She sucked in a breath.

Bang!

Another shot rang out.

A new sound—scuffling feet not far from her hiding place. A muffled curse. A dull crack. More footsteps, hurrying toward her now.

This was it. He was coming for her.

She steadied the pistol, blew her breath out, tried to re-member everything Max had taught her all those years ago. Exhale slowly, move your finger to the trigger, squeeze—

"Bex, it's me. Don't shoot."

She blinked. Max? Wait, he wasn't whispering.

She moved her finger away from the trigger just as he crouched down in front of her and peered into her hid-ing place.

"Max?" All of her questions and fears were in that one hoarsely uttered word.

"It's okay," he said. "It's over."

He gently took the pistol from her violently shaking hands, shoved it into his holster. And then he was scooping his arms beneath her, pulling her out of the maze of pasta and sauces and lifting her up against his chest.

The sight of a dark heap on the floor had her throw-ing her arms around Max's neck and squeezing her eyes tightly shut.

"Is he...is he—"

"He's alive. Don't worry about him. I've got you, Bex. Everything's going to be all right."

She should have told him to put her down, that she was perfectly capable of walking on her own. But she wasn't entirely sure that was true. Her whole body seemed to have turned into a mass of shaking nerves. She squeezed her eyes tightly shut and selfishly buried her face against Max's chest while he carried her to the front of the store.

She sensed others around them now, heard someone ask Max something but didn't catch his murmured reply. More sounds—voices, boots scuffling across the floor. Her traumatized mind grasped what was happening, that help had finally arrived, that the SWAT team must be clearing the store and securing the scene. But she couldn't seem to force her eyes open or loosen her grip around Max's neck as he carried her outside.

Chapter Four

Max leaned against a Destiny PD patrol car in the Piggly Wiggly parking lot, in a circle with the five other officers who made up the SWAT team, all in full tactical gear except him. Since the danger was over, they were talking in detective mode, trying to figure out what had just happened.

There'd been no fatalities. The only people to get shot were two of the gunmen, courtesy of Max, and they were on their way to the hospital. The three other bad guys were on their way to the county lockup. But the grocery store and surrounding area were still bustling with firefighters and police officers and would be for quite a while as they sorted through the mess.

Chief Thornton, who'd been talking to the fire chief, shoved his way between team lead Dillon Gray and his best friend, second in command Chris Downing. The others—Donna Waters, Colby Vale and Randy Carter—widened the circle to make room.

Thornton looked at each of them, a ferocious frown on his brow. "Where's the new guy?"

Max's lips twitched at the shrugs and carefully blank looks on Dillon's and Chris's faces. The chief was having a heck of a time trying to force everyone to accept a new member onto their SWAT team and detective squad.

Blake Sullivan was still learning the ropes of Destiny PD and no one was exactly rolling out a welcome mat for him.

The guy was former military and had been a detective in Knoxville before relocating here. He'd made it clear on his first day that he expected to step right into the action. It had been a bitter pill for him to realize he had to spend several months as a uniformed beat cop first—as they all had—to learn the station's routine and his way around the county before becoming an active member of the team.

Thornton turned around, looking for his beleaguered new hire, then put his hands on his hips. He'd obviously spotted Blake, fifty yards away, looking bored as he leaned against the ambulance where Bex was being examined by an EMT.

"Why isn't he wearing tactical gear like the rest of you?" Thornton demanded, directing his question at Dillon.

"When Max's call came in, we had to hustle," Dillon said. "Didn't have time to coddle a newbie and bring him in on the assault."

The chief narrowed his eyes. "This would have been a perfect opportunity to show him the ropes. Next time the team is activated, you had better include him. You hear me?"

"Yes, sir. I hear you."

Max grinned. He wouldn't bet a plug nickel that Blake would be included on their next callout. At this point, it was a matter of principle. Blake would have to show some humility before Dillon would back down. And judging by how distant and arrogant the new guy seemed most of the time, that moment of acceptance wasn't going to happen anytime soon.

"Colby, go get Blake." The chief jerked his head toward the ambulance.

Colby sighed and jogged across the parking lot.

"And you, Max, stop grinning like the village idiot

and tell me if you recognize any of the gunmen. Chris snapped their pictures as they were brought out, minus the ski masks and sunglasses some of them were wearing." The chief motioned for Chris to pass his phone to Max.

Max flipped through the images on the screen, then shook his head and returned the phone to Chris.

"None of them look familiar. I don't think they're local."

"He's right," Dillon said, not even glancing Blake's way as Colby ushered him into their circle. "We all grew up here. I may not know everyone in town by name, but I know most of them by sight. I've never seen any of those men before."

"Let me have a look." Blake held out his hand.

Chris arched a brow.

Max shoved him. "Give him a break. What could it hurt?"

Chris shoved him back but handed his phone over.

Blake's jaw tightened. One of these days the guy would probably explode like a spring that had been wound too tight. Max wasn't sure he wanted to be there when that happened.

"Well?" the chief asked, impatience heavy in his tone as Blake carefully examined each picture.

He handed the phone to Chris. "The second one and the last one are gangbangers from my hometown. I don't know their names. But they have the same tattoos on their forearms as other gangbangers I've arrested."

"They're gang members from Knoxville?" the chief asked.

Blake nodded. "Those two for sure. Can't speak for the other three. I can call my old squad, send them the photos to help us get IDs. Maybe the other ones just don't have their tats yet. They have to earn them. But we can assume they're all in the same gang."

"We don't assume anything around here," Dillon said. "We deal in facts."

Blake's shoulders stiffened, but he didn't rise to the bait.

Colby asked, "Why would street thugs drive forty-five minutes to storm a small, rural grocery store with assault rifles? They could have made a much bigger haul in Knoxville."

"They didn't get a haul at all. Didn't even try," Max said. "As soon as they came in, they started firing wildly into the air—except the one who shot at me. They split up as if looking for something, leaving only two guys to control the customers up front. But they didn't seem to have a clue what they were doing. I was able to signal the manager to hustle the employees and customers into the cooler while I drew the gunmen's fire. If they were there for money, they'd have all stayed up front and forced the manager to open the safe."

Dillon crossed his arms, looking thoughtful. "They came here looking for something."

"Maybe they were looking for some*one*." Max nodded toward the other end of the parking lot.

As one they all turned to see Bex, still sitting in the back of an ambulance.

The chief motioned to Chris. "Text those pictures to all of our phones. Max, show the pics to Miss Kane and ask her whether she recognizes any of them."

Max straightened away from the cruiser. "Dillon's the lead. He should question her."

A look of surprise flashed across Dillon's face, but he took a step toward Bex anyway.

The chief put his hand on Dillon's shoulder to stop him. "No. Max is going to interview her. The rest of you can change out of your gear and get initial statements from the other witnesses. The EMTs should be done checking them out soon. One of our officers is putting them in the break room as their medical reviews are done, unless any of them need to be hospitalized. You know the routine. Get those statements."

Colby clapped Max on the shoulder in a show of solidarity as he and the others headed to their vehicles to shed their gear. When only the chief remained, he faced Max with his hands on his hips.

"Go on, son. Spit it out. You look like you're chewing on nails."

"You, more than anyone, know my history. You hired me right out of high school, right after...everything. Dillon or one of the others should interview Miss Kane. Not me."

"That it? That's all you got to say?"

He wanted to say a whole lot more. But he respected his boss too much to let loose with a string of curses. "Yes, sir. That about sums it up."

"Good. Glad we got that settled. Because you're a professional and I've never had reason to say otherwise. Don't give me a reason today. Miss Kane was clinging to you like a lifeline when you carried her out of the store and it took ten minutes of your sweet-talking to get her to let you go. You may not be comfortable, given your past. And I understand that, I really do. But this isn't about you. This is about finding the truth, conducting an investigation. Right now, whether either of us likes it or not, you're our best option for getting her to answer our questions. Now, I ain't normally one to explain my decisions and don't plan on doing this again anytime soon. So I suggest you get over there and *do your job, Detective.*"

Heat flushed up his neck. His face was probably beet red. Feeling like a high school kid who'd just been scolded by the principal for skipping class, Max gave his boss a curt nod and strode across the parking lot.

Before Max was even halfway there, he noticed an older gentleman in a dark gray suit working his way between the cars and fire trucks toward Bex's ambulance. Max hesitated. The man was Augustus Leonard, one of only two lawyers in town. Why did a lawyer want to talk to Bex?

THE EMT, DON, steadied Bex's left forearm on a raised metal board that he'd slid out from the wall of the ambulance. From the amount of bandages, antibiotic sprays and other first aid equipment lying around, Bex would have thought her arm had been severed. She was embarrassed at all the fuss he was making over such a small cut.

Pausing with a needle poised between what looked like tweezers, he said, "Ma'am, are you sure you won't go to the hospital and have a doctor stitch you up? You may need X-rays. There might be other injuries you don't even know about yet."

She shook her head. "I don't have anything more serious than this."

"You're one lucky woman. It could've been a lot worse."

Bits of memories flashed through her mind—gunshots, crouching behind the T-shirt rack, her stomach clenching with dread as the gunman with the ski mask raised his arm, ready to shoot her. She shivered and considered the bandage on her arm. He was right. It could have been so much worse.

"You're right. And I assure you I'm very grateful that I'm only getting stitches."

"Stitches? What stitches?" a gravelly voice said from the open doors of the ambulance.

Bex looked over, smiling to see her lawyer looking all proper and perfect, his white hair neatly in place, his handlebar mustache sticking out on each side like skinny white toothpicks. She started to lean toward him to shake his hand, but Don frowned at her, holding her injured arm steady.

"Sorry, Don." She waved at her lawyer. "Mr. Leonard, nice to see you. What are you doing here?"

He arched a bushy brow. "I might ask you the same thing, Miss Kane. Imagine my concern when I look out my office window and see a SWAT team racing into the grocery store. Even worse, a few minutes later, you're carried out by Detective Remington and placed in this ambulance. And now I hear something about stitches. Do tell, please, what's going on? How badly are you hurt?"

She nodded toward her left arm. "Not bad at all. Just about to get a couple of stitches, that's all."

"More than a couple," the EMT murmured as he pricked her skin with the needle.

The shot he'd given her to numb her arm did its job, but she couldn't help wincing and looking away.

"How did you get cut?" her lawyer asked.

"It happened when I crawled in between some shelves. Some gunmen held up the store and I had to hide. I really am okay. Thanks to Max—ah, Detective Remington."

"Who else was hurt?" he asked. "I saw two men brought out on stretchers."

"I have no idea. I haven't heard about anyone else in the store, or the details about what happened. I hope those men will be okay."

"They were the bad guys," Don said without glancing up from his work. "Heard it over the radio. Two of the gunmen were shot and taken to Maryville. I don't think any of the shoppers were injured."

Bex turned her head again as he poked the needle into her skin.

"Hurts?" Augustus asked.

"No, I just…don't like needles."

"It's a shame your mother refused to let you come see her in Destiny all these years and then your first time back you end up in the middle of a robbery." He shook his head.

"Dorothy shouldn't have kept you from your own home all this time. It wasn't right. For what it's worth, I did try to talk some sense into her. But she was too worried about you, was determined to keep you away."

"I just wish she would have agreed to move in with me. But she insisted on staying here," Bex said.

"Destiny was her home. She had a lot of friends here, her volunteer work at the church. I doubt she'd have moved for anyone."

"Well, I guess it all worked out. Mama enjoyed the trips to see me. She got a little thrill every time I had a limo pick her up."

"You spoiled her."

"She deserved it. I only wish I could have done more for her while she was alive. No matter how well my business did, she refused to let me buy her anything expensive. Half the gifts I mailed her were returned. I sent her a houseful of furniture once and she wouldn't sign for it, wouldn't even let the guys unload anything from the truck."

He smiled. "That's Dorothy for you." He leaned forward and patted her good hand. "My condolences again. I know you loved her very much. Her heart attack was such a shock to us all."

She blinked against the burn of unshed tears. "Thank you. No sense in dwelling on the past anymore, though. I need to wrap things up here and get back to my own home as soon as I can, make sure Allison isn't ready to quit after being left in charge of the antique shop so long."

"Allison?"

"My assistant. And friend. Once I pack up everything, when do you think I'll be able to put the house up for sale?"

She risked a quick look at her injured arm. Four stitches in, probably a few more to go. She looked away before Don dipped the needle in again.

"Another few weeks at best, a month at the worst. Your

mother's will is fairly straightforward. But there are some tangles to unravel with the various properties she had around the county and ensuring there are no liens before I can get them transferred to you as the owner."

"You're referring to the farmland my daddy used to have? Aren't those plots leased out to local farmers? The same ones who've been on that land since Daddy died years ago?"

"Yes, but it won't take long to clear them out. Shouldn't be a problem. It's a standard eviction process."

"I don't want them cleared out. Just transfer the deeds to them."

He blinked like an owl. "Pardon?"

"I don't need the land, Mr. Leonard. And I'm doing well with my antique store. I'm not rich by any stretch. But I've got what I need. No reason to be greedy. Those men have worked that land for years. They've earned this. It's the right thing to do. Mom and Dad would approve, I'm sure."

He looked like he wanted to argue but he gave her a crisp nod. "Very well. It's your land, your money. I'll draw up some papers to make the transfer. It will take more time than originally planned, of course."

"Thank you. I understand."

Don jostled her arm as he leaned past her to put away the needle. But when she started to pull back, he stopped her.

"I need to bandage that before we're done," he said.

She sighed and relaxed her arm.

Don cleaned up the tabletop to prepare for bandaging her cut.

"If the paperwork takes much longer, can we plan on doing it through the mail? Including the sale of my mom's house?"

He frowned. "Why would you want to do that? You're

here now. If a few more weeks is too long, I can try to put a rush on things."

"I don't want you to have to hurry on my account. But after, well, after today, I'm more inclined to finish packing up the house and just go. Can't I sign some kind of power of attorney over to you?"

His brows raised again, making her think of snow-white caterpillars.

"You can, certainly. But most people prefer to give power of attorney to someone they know and trust rather than to their lawyer."

"My mama trusted you. That's good enough for me."

He puffed out his chest, his face turning a light shade of red. And suddenly Bex wondered whether he'd felt more toward her mother than simple friendship. And whether those feelings were returned. If so, her mother had never said anything. But then again, her mother might have worried that Bex would feel funny about her finally dating someone after all these years. And, truth be told, she would have felt...odd about it.

A car crash had taken Bex's father from them when Bex was in middle school. The loss had been devastating for her and her mother. Imagining her mom with anyone other than her daddy made her feel sad. But happy, too. Her mother deserved some male companionship in her life. And if she'd found it with the honorable Mr. Augustus Leonard, then that was a very good thing.

Mr. Leonard cleared his throat. "Thank you for your faith in me, Miss Kane. I have a form at the office you can fill out for the power of attorney. When you're finished here, I can walk you over. Martha's a notary. She can witness our signatures and notarize the document."

"Can you raise your arm a few inches?" Don asked.

Bex lifted her arm so he could wrap some gauze over the stitches.

"Sounds like a plan," she said to her lawyer. "The sooner I can get out of Destiny the better. There's nothing left for me here except bad memories."

Movement near the ambulance doors had her looking up, and right into Max's eyes. Again. And just like in the grocery store, his jaw tightened and his eyes darkened.

"Max. Um, hi. How long have you been standing there?" she asked.

"Long enough." The bitterness in his voice surprised her. Had he heard what she'd said to Mr. Leonard? Why would it matter? He certainly didn't have any feelings for her anymore, as evidenced by how he'd treated her at the deli.

Or did he?

He motioned toward the bandage. "What's wrong with your arm?"

She blinked and looked down, having forgotten all about her injured arm. "It's just a little cut."

"More like a gash," Don said. "Eight stitches."

"How did that happen?" Max elbowed his way past the lawyer and hopped into the ambulance. He grabbed Bex's left hand to inspect the EMT's work as if he would demand a redo if it didn't meet his standards.

Bex frowned and tugged her arm out of his grasp. "I assume it happened when you…when I hid between the shelves. It's not a big deal. I'm fine. Really."

He studied her a moment, then promptly ignored her, speaking instead to the EMT.

"Why didn't you take her to the hospital?"

"She said she didn't—"

"I refused to go to the hospital," she said.

"Well?" he asked the EMT, as if she hadn't spoken.

Don's brows rose to his hairline. "I, ah, Miss Kane didn't want to go to the hospital. She asked me if I could take care of her arm here."

"What about the risk of infection? Those grocery store shelves aren't exactly sterile."

The bewildered look on Don's face hardened. "I know how to clean a wound, sir. And I asked Miss Kane about getting a tetanus shot, but she insisted that she didn't need one."

Max turned to face her. "You either get the shot or you're going to the hospital."

Bex rolled her eyes and grabbed her purse from the bench beside her.

"I'm not an idiot, Max. I'm up-to-date on my shots. And I don't need you, or anyone else, bossing me around." She shook the EMT's hand. "Thank you, Don. I appreciate your help."

She went to hop down from the ambulance, but Max gently pushed her back and hopped down first. Then he lifted her out before she realized what he was about to do.

The feel of his warm hands around her sent a delightful shock of awareness up her spine, making her stiffen in surprise.

His jaw tightened and he dropped his hands, taking a quick step back. Before she could correct his obvious misinterpretation of her reaction, Mr. Leonard stepped forward.

"I'll escort you back to my office."

"She needs to answer some questions about the shooting," Max said, a thread of steel in his deep voice.

Eager to avoid any kind of confrontation, Bex stepped between the two men and shook Mr. Leonard's hand. "Thank you, for everything. If you don't mind, I'll go to your office some other time to sign that power of attorney."

"Very well. My door's always open for you, Miss Kane." He tipped his head politely. "Detective Remington." Then he headed across the parking lot toward his office, one of a handful of businesses and restaurants on Magnolia Street.

Max waved Bex back from the ambulance so Don could close the doors and prepare to return to the hospital.

Bex crossed her arms, not quite sure which Max Remington was standing before her now—the one full of anger at the deli, or the one who'd nearly broken her heart with kindness as he'd soothed her after carrying her out of the store.

"I never really thanked you before. You saved my life today."

"Just doing my job." His voice was curt, clipped.

She sighed. Deli Max was back.

"Chief Thornton wants me to show you some pictures of the gunmen to see whether you recognize them. And I'm sure he'll want me to interview you about what happened," he continued. "I figure it will be easier at the station. We can take my truck. I'll bring you back to your car when we're done."

He reached for her good arm, but she jerked back, her stomach churning with dread. At the mention of the police station, her body flushed with heat, in spite of the chill in the air. She shook her head and took a step away from him.

"I'm not going to the police station."

He frowned. "Why not?"

She glanced past him at Thornton, who was talking to a uniformed officer about thirty yards away. "I...don't have fond memories of that place, as you can imagine. And I never intend to go there again. So, unless you're arresting me, the answer is no."

She hurried toward her car, which, thankfully, was no longer blocked by a fire engine, as it had been earlier.

"Bex. Wait."

The irritation in his voice as he followed her had her practically running and pulling out her keys. She stopped beside a blue Honda and reached for the door handle just as Max caught up to her. He braced a hip against the door and crossed his arms as if daring her to try to open it.

Which was fine, since this wasn't her car.

She stepped back, her hands on her hips. Then she took another step, then whirled around and ran to her Toyota RAV4 SUV two spaces over. By the time Max realized she'd played a trick on him and started toward her, she was zipping out of the parking space.

He stood watching her in her rearview mirror, his hands fisted at his sides.

Running from him was childish. Especially since he was a police officer and she'd have to answer his questions eventually. But facing angry, cold Max was more than she could take right now after everything else that had happened. How could she stand there, talking to him as if he was a stranger, when even now her body yearned for his touch?

It might have been ten years since she'd last kissed him, a decade since she'd felt the comforting weight of his body pressing her down into the mattress. But from the moment she'd seen him at the deli, all those years had fallen away as if they'd never happened. And her emotions were just as raw now as the day she'd left.

She wanted, needed, some time to herself. To decompress, to reflect about what had happened today and get her emotions back under control. Trying to do that with a man she'd once loved looking at her like he despised her was more than she could bear, more than anyone should have to bear after the kind of crisis she'd just lived through. No, tomorrow would be soon enough. She'd face Max tomorrow.

The sound of a powerful engine had her looking in her rearview mirror again. A shiny black four-by-four pickup was coming up fast behind her. And sitting in the driver's seat was an achingly familiar silhouette.

Max Remington.

Chapter Five

Normally the ride from the grocery store to her mother's house would have taken Bex twenty-five minutes. Today, with Max riding her bumper, it took half that. She barreled into the driveway on the left side of the house and slammed her brakes. Max braked hard behind her, narrowly missing her car.

He hopped out of his pickup and stalked up to her window before she'd even cut her engine.

"Get out."

Even with the window rolled up, she could hear the anger vibrating in his deep voice.

"Go away."

He shook his head. "Open the door, Bex."

She gave him a very unladylike gesture and reached for the gearshift, fully intending to drive across the lawn back to the road.

"Gonna run again, Bex?" he taunted. "You're good at that."

She stiffened.

"You drove twenty miles over the speed limit. I can arrest you for that."

"There was a maniac following me. I was in fear for my life."

If his jaw tightened any more his teeth would probably break.

A long breath huffed out of her as her anger drained

away. This wasn't how she wanted things between the two of them. She'd blindsided him by coming back and deserved a little consideration. He'd also saved her life today. Repaying him by pushing his buttons and making his job difficult wasn't right. She cut the engine, grabbed her purse and waited.

Looking suspicious at her sudden change of heart, he seemed to almost reluctantly step back, just enough for her to open the door and get out of her car.

As she headed toward the wide, covered front porch than ran the width of the cottage, he was hot on her heels, so close she could feel his body heat against her back. And just like that, her skin prickled with awareness and her belly tightened, her body's natural response to Max being that close.

She couldn't believe he still had this kind of impact on her, after all these years and after everything that had happened. It was irritating, and made it really hard to keep her raw emotions at bay.

"You don't have to hang so close," she told him as she climbed the steps.

"Just making sure you don't run again," he taunted.

She stopped, then whirled around to face him. But he was too close. She had to climb two more steps to be able to meet his gaze without craning her head back.

"Was that supposed to be funny?" she demanded.

"Not even a little bit."

He arched a brow, daring her to bring up the past, to go down a road she had no intention of traveling. Down that road lay too much hurt. And danger. For both of them.

She let out a pent-up breath and turned around, climbing the rest of the steps and crossing the wide porch. After unlocking the front door, she turned the knob. And suddenly he was pushing past her into the living room.

"Please, won't you come in," she muttered behind him, closing the door and flipping the dead bolt.

He did a quick turn around the room, glancing through doorways into the kitchen, the hall, the bathroom, all while keeping his hand on his holster. She supposed it was second nature to do things like that, the instincts of a cop automatically checking the security when they went anywhere.

When he returned to the entry, he eyed the dead bolt but didn't say the obvious—that she'd never have locked a door when she was growing up here. Most people in Destiny didn't lock their doors. Bex's mother certainly hadn't. The dead bolt had been frozen when Bex had arrived and she'd had to spray it with oil to get it to work.

Feeling silly now for having locked it, she flipped the bolt again, leaving the door unsecured, even though her big city instincts had her fingers itching to flip the bolt.

For a man who'd been all bent out of shape about wanting to talk to her, Max didn't seem to be in any kind of hurry to talk now. Instead, he strolled around the room, examining the stacks of boxes containing her mother's things, reading the labels on each one. When he reached the fireplace, he stared in silence at the dark square above it where a picture of the two of them from their senior prom used to hang. She expected him to ask her what she'd done with it, perhaps in a sarcastic or accusing tone. She'd die before she told him that she'd carefully packed it away and put it in a box to go back home with her to Knoxville. But he didn't ask.

Instead, he turned around and headed toward the archway that led into the eat-in kitchen on the front left side of the house.

"Got any coffee? I sure could use some even though it's inching toward dinnertime now," he said.

She frowned and hurried after him. "I thought you

wanted to interview me about what happened at the store? Show me some pictures or something?"

He hesitated, then pulled his phone out. A moment later, he flipped through pictures of five men, holding each one up for her.

"Recognize any of them?"

"No. Are those the gunmen?"

He didn't answer, just put his phone back in his pocket. After opening the cabinet to the right of the sink, he took down two coffee cups, acting just as familiar and comfortable with the house as he'd been as a teenager. As if the years between had never happened.

A few minutes later he had the old-fashioned coffee-maker spitting and gurgling a thin stream of dark coffee into a carafe.

"Cream and sugar still?" He took the creamer out of the refrigerator, which Bex had topped off just this morning, and grabbed the sugar bowl from the kitchen table.

"Yes. Still." She pulled out one of the chairs and plopped down. "I'm surprised you remember where Mom kept everything."

His lips thinned. "I practically lived here in high school. Your mom was like a second mom to me. We kept in touch. I didn't write her out of my life just because you wrote me out of yours."

She sucked in a breath, old hurts washing over her. The last time she'd seen Max suddenly felt just as fresh and painful as it had the first time around—as if all the years in between had never happened. She should apologize, explain. He deserved that. But how could she?

Especially now that he was a cop.

He set the cup of creamy white coffee in front of her and a cup of strong, black coffee in front of himself before finally sitting across from her.

He rubbed his neck and let out a deep sigh, stretching

his long legs out in front of him. He looked so tired, as if the weight of everything that had happened today had drained the fight right out of him.

"Why did you come back, Bex? After all these years, why come back at all? It's not like you went to the memorial service."

She almost choked on the coffee she'd just sipped. She forced the now tasteless liquid down her throat and shoved the cup away. She rose from her chair, fully intending to order him to leave.

"Bex. Please. I'm not trying to fight. I really want to know." He watched her intently, waiting for her to make the decision.

She drew a deep breath then sat down again. "I had a private funeral for her in...outside Destiny."

He nodded. "I figured. Which is kind of my point. Why come back? You didn't have to. You could handle everything remotely. From wherever you live now."

Silence filled the room, his unasked questions hanging between them. Where did she live? Where had she gone? Where would she go once she left again?

She considered telling him. It wasn't exactly a big secret anymore, as it had been when she'd fled. Privacy was a fantasy these days. Finding someone was as easy as doing a search online, even if they'd changed their name—which she hadn't done.

If Max really wanted to find her, he could. Especially as a police officer. He'd be able to track her down. And yet, all these years, he'd never once tried to find her. Had never walked up to her condo or visited her little shop, asking for answers. So she wasn't going to give them now.

"I needed to settle her estate, go through her things, pack up the house."

He didn't say anything, just waited.

She glanced around the kitchen, at the fading yellow

drapes hanging above the sink. The horrible red-rooster wallpaper on the wall above the stove, wallpaper that she'd hated while growing up here but that somehow seemed perfect now.

She smoothed her fingers against the faded, chipped laminate-topped table. Her mother had refused to let Bex replace it with one of the gorgeous antiques from her store. Mom had insisted she loved the cheap, worn table. But Bex knew that what her mom really loved were the memories she'd shared with Bex's father at this worn-out table, before a tight curve on a dark road had taken him away from both of them.

"Bex?"

She forced her hands to stop rubbing circles on the fake wood. "I guess I just…needed to see…home, one last time. I wanted to go through her things, remember her, decide what to keep, what to give away."

"Was there any other reason that you came back?" he asked, his deep voice soft, barely above a whisper.

He was giving her an opening. It shocked her to realize that, to see the longing in his eyes, bared before her. And, God help her, she wanted so much to tell him that, yes, she came back to see him, too. But that wasn't true. No matter how much she wished it could be. Once she left this time, she knew she'd never see Max again.

She slowly shook her head. "No. No other reason."

He blinked, and like throwing a switch, his eyes shuttered, his expression went blank. "Well," he finally said. "Guess that answers that." He gave her a bitter smile. "I loved you, Bex. All those years ago, I loved you in every way a man can love a woman—with my mind, my body, my heart, my soul. And I thought you loved me, too. I would have done anything for you back then. Anything. Together we could have faced whatever really happened the night Bobby Caldwell died. We would have gotten married, raised a couple of kids by now." He shook his head, a muscle flexing in his cheek. "But all that's water under the bridge now, isn't it? You've sure as hell moved on. Guess it's high time I moved on, too." He pulled his phone out of his pocket. "If going to the station's too difficult, so be it. We'll do the interview here. You don't mind if I record it, do you?"

She sat as still as a statue, staring at him in shock, reeling from everything he'd just said. And one thing in particular—that it was time he moved on. What did that mean? That in all these years he'd never dated anyone? That he'd been, what, waiting for her?

She'd dated, a handful of times. But her first dates were always last dates. Because no one had ever measured up to Max. She'd never once considered that he might have been existing in that same limbo that she had all this time. And now she wished that she could tell him the truth.

That she hadn't moved on. And never would. That a day hadn't gone by that she didn't think of him.

He arched a brow. "Bex? I've turned on the recording app. Do you consent to having your statement recorded?"

She blinked, then nodded.

"You have to say it out loud."

"Oh, um." She cleared her throat. "Yes, I consent to having my statement recorded."

"Excellent." He shoved the phone to the middle of the table between them. "First we have to get the logistics out of the way. State and spell your first and last name for the recording. Then list your address and place of employment."

She frowned. "Is that really required?"

He nodded.

She sighed and told him what he'd asked, admitting that she lived in Knoxville, giving him the address of her condo. And she told him about her antique store. Then she went on to answer his questions about everything she'd done the day of the grocery store shooting.

The interview started out stilted, on her side at least. But answering his questions was almost a healing therapy for her emotional wounds. It helped her go numb, almost dead inside, and get through this.

Going over the same questions over and over was grueling, tiring and reminiscent of when the chief had grilled her years ago. Thornton had trained Max well. She felt just as guilty this time as she had ten years ago, even though this time she had nothing to feel guilty about.

He finally stopped the recording and put his phone away. "I guess that's it. For now."

Relieved, she grabbed both of their long-empty coffee cups and carried them to the sink. After rinsing them, she turned around. Max was still sitting at the table, studying her as if he had a million more questions and was looking to her for the answers. Afraid that he might start the interview all over again, she headed toward the archway into the family room.

"Thanks again for protecting me this morning." She waved toward the front door. "You can see yourself out. I've got packing to do."

She headed into her bedroom, the one she'd had her whole life until she'd left at eighteen. Taking the master bedroom hadn't even tempted her. It would have felt... weird, sleeping in the room her mother had slept in just a few short weeks ago.

Her suitcase was in the closet, so she grabbed it and dropped it on top of the bed, then flipped it open. She'd packed light, with just a week's worth of clothes, and had laundered everything yesterday. It wouldn't take long before she could head out. She opened the top dresser drawer and grabbed a stack of underwear and bras.

"You're not sticking around?"

Startled, she jumped, then pressed a hand against her chest. Max lounged in the doorway to her bedroom, looking impossibly appealing.

"Sorry," he said, even though he didn't look sorry. "Didn't mean to startle you."

She shoved her armload of underwear into the suitcase and headed to the dresser for more clothes. "I'm going home."

"When?"

An armload of shorts and T-shirts went into the suitcase. "Today. Now. Just as soon as I'm packed."

"Don't you want to stick around and find out why those gunmen went after you?"

She hesitated, her arms full of jeans. "What are you talking about? They robbed the store. You make it sound like it all had something to do with me."

"I'm thinking maybe it did. They didn't rob the store. They were searching up and down aisles looking for you. At least, that's what it seemed like to me."

She slowly lowered the jeans into the suitcase. "Why would they be looking for me?"

He shrugged, not offering anything else. Probably because it was part of his investigation.

"All the more reason to leave, then." She headed for the closet to get her shoes.

Max wandered around the room, picking up a few odds and ends from her childhood—little horse figurines on her dresser, a cross necklace her mom had given her on her sixteenth birthday. And then he looked up, at the wall over her dresser, and froze.

Bex could feel her face growing warm. "Mom left my room exactly the way it was the day I left."

He was in most of the pictures, with her, because they'd always been together, from middle school on. It seemed that every fun or cherished moment in her life had Max in it—her first dance, the field trip to Animal Kingdom at Disney, playing video games at the arcade in the mall one town over from Destiny. And there was their graduation photo, the last one taken of the two of them. They'd walked together, hand in hand in their black graduation robes, each of them boasting the gold stoles of the National Honor Society. Both of them smiling and happy.

"Figures I'd find you both here, in your bedroom. Just like old times, huh?"

Bex and Max both turned to see Bex's old high school nemesis, Marcia Knolls, standing in the doorway. Max's hand had automatically gone to the gun holstered at his hip, but he relaxed when he saw who was standing there.

"What are you doing in here?" he demanded. "You should have knocked."

"I did. You two were apparently too busy to hear me." She smirked at Max. "Does your girlfriend know about all those police interns you've been screwing?"

Bex blinked, then looked at Max.

His eyes narrowed, and he took a step toward Marcia.

Bex hurried to step between them.

"Marcia, hey. It's been a long time. Is there something I can help you with?"

Marcia glared at her, hands coiled into fists at her sides. Surprisingly, Bex wasn't even mad at her for her crude comment about her and Max. Instead, she felt sorry for her. Marcia was one of those people who'd been miserable the whole time Bex had known her and had blamed others for that misery. It was clear that she hadn't changed, that she was still just as miserable and lonely as she'd been back in high school.

"I heard about the shooting," Marcia said. "Figured I'd stop by and see if you were okay." She glanced at Max. "Looks like you're doing just fine, already slipping back into old habits."

Bex doubted Marcia had stopped by hoping she was okay. If anything, she was looking for some juicy gossip.

"There was a shooting at the Piggly Wiggly. But thanks to Max, everyone is fine. He saved my life, and the lives of everyone else in that store." She could feel the weight of his stare, as if he was surprised or wondering if she really felt that way.

"Yeah, well, too bad he couldn't save everyone years ago," Marcia taunted. "Then maybe Bobby would still be around."

"What do you really want, Marcia?" Max asked. "You can cut the crap about caring about Bex. No one in this room believes that."

She gave him a resentful look. "I was just wondering when Bex plans on leaving." She waved toward the suitcase. "I'm assuming soon?"

"And why do you want to know?" Max demanded.

Her face reddening slightly, Marcia said, "Mama sent me over with a casserole and her condolences on your mother's death, Bex." She cleared her throat. "Not that you really cared, did you? You never bothered to visit her."

Max stepped even closer. "Not that it's any of your business, but Bex saw her mother a lot, just not in Destiny. And they spoke on the phone every Sunday evening, without fail. Now, unless you have something nice to say to a woman who's grieving the loss of her mother, you need to leave."

Bex almost felt sorry for Marcia. Her face went pale and she seemed taken aback. "I wasn't trying to be mean." She aimed a pleading look at Bex. "I'm sorry about your mom. I really am. It's just that when I see you, it makes me think of Bobby. And I just—"

"Out. Now." Max used his much larger body to force her into the hallway.

Bex was about to tell him to go easy on Marcia when

the other woman turned and ran from the house. Max followed her, and soon the sound of the front door slamming echoed through the little house.

If she hadn't been anxious to leave before, Bex was anxious now. She'd meant it when she'd told her lawyer that there wasn't any reason left for her to stay. Marcia was only one of many who blamed Bex for Bobby's death. And Max wasn't exactly warming up to her. Not that she could blame him.

Bex stuffed a few more things into her suitcase and zipped it closed.

"She's gone," Max said from the doorway. "You're really leaving, right this minute?"

"I think it's for the best. I'll stop at my lawyer's office in town, then I'm off to Pigeon Forge for a couple of weeks to clear my head before going home."

He was reaching for her suitcase but stopped with his hand on the handle. "Pigeon Forge?"

It dawned on her what he was thinking about, and she belatedly wished she'd thought more carefully before answering him. She nodded and refolded an afghan at the foot of the bed that didn't need folding. Pigeon Forge, nestled in the foothills of the Smoky Mountains, had been their place, where she and Max had gone on many trips their junior and senior year. Always with friends, to satisfy her mom that they were well chaperoned. But she and Max had found plenty of time to sneak away to be together. It had been the happiest time of her life. And it had become her habit since leaving Destiny to go to Pigeon Forge every time her life seemed like it was falling apart. The moment she'd found out about her mother, she'd reserved her usual cabin in the Smokies for once she was finished with her duties in Destiny. Now she wasn't sure it was a good idea anymore. Rather than healing her soul, it just might crush her.

Without a word, Max picked up her suitcase and carried it out of the room.

Bex sighed and followed him, grabbing her purse and car keys along the way.

Once he'd placed the suitcase in her trunk, he straightened and leaned against her car. "I may need to contact you with more questions as the investigation goes on."

"Mr. Leonard has my contact information. He'll be able to get in touch with me."

"It's probably better that you're leaving. Bobby Caldwell's death is a fresh wound again now that you're back in town. A lot of people, like it or not, believe you got away with murder. Marcia's just one of them."

She paused beside the driver's door. "Just like you."

"No."

She looked up at him. "You don't think I killed Bobby?"

He swore and ran a hand through his hair. "Whatever… resentments I have toward you, I never once believed you had anything to do with Bobby's death."

She wasn't sure what to say to that. "You told Marcia I saw my mom, that I called her every week. How did you know that?"

He shrugged. "Small town. Word gets around."

"Only if my mom told someone about it. And she wasn't the type to gossip, not about me. And her close friends wouldn't share that type of information, not with you. The only way you could have known is if Mom told you."

He didn't say anything.

"You're the one who planted the lilies, aren't you?"

Again, he remained silent. But the truth was in his eyes.

"You really did visit my mom regularly, didn't you, Max? Why?"

He straightened away from her car. "Just because you pushed me out of your life didn't mean your mom did. I always planned on marrying you, Bex. From the moment we started hanging out in middle school. I thought of your mom as my future mother-in-law for so long I couldn't just turn that off when you threw my proposal in my face."

She sucked in a breath. "I didn't throw it in your face."

He waved his hand in the air. "Just go see your lawyer and run off to Pigeon Forge. You've probably got some guy waiting there for you. Don't let me keep you."

She glared up at him, her hands on her hips. "And don't let me keep you from those interns you're sleeping with, either."

His jaw tightened and he held the door open for her.

Her anger evaporated in a shaky sigh. Tears burned at the backs of her eyes. "Can't wait for me to leave, can you, Max?"

Something passed in his eyes—regret? His anger seemed to rush out of him, too, and he looked tired and resigned.

"This is never how I wanted things to be between us. But it's probably for the best, Bex."

She nodded. "I'm just glad you're okay. I was so scared when I heard that gunman saying the cop had interfered and they were going to kill him. I figured that was you. I was so scared. I was trying to find you to warn you when I got trapped behind that display of T-shirts."

"You were looking for me to warn me? Are you insane?"

She stiffened. "Apparently so. Take care, Max. I mean it. I want you to be happy and safe. No matter what you think of me, that has never changed. I've always wanted what was best for you. That was the driving concern in every decision that I made."

He frowned at her words. "Bex, what are you—"

She shook her head, realizing she'd said too much. She stepped into the opening to get in the car. A loud boom sounded and the windshield exploded.

Max grabbed her and shoved her to the ground.

Chapter Six

Max crouched down beside a thick oak tree to examine an impression in the dirt. A shoe print, narrow, small and recent—probably the shooter's. He glanced over his shoulder, just able to see Bex's house through the scrub brush. She was inside now, probably hunkered down in a back bedroom with one of Destiny's finest guarding her. But her car, with its shattered windshield, sat where they'd left it when he'd rushed her inside the house and called his SWAT team. The windshield was in a direct line from where he was, which pretty much confirmed that he'd found where the shooter had stood when he'd tried to kill Bex.

A static sound in his earpiece had him turning around. Twenty feet away, at his two o'clock, Colby crouched in full SWAT gear like Max was now wearing, and pointed toward Max's eleven o'clock. He held up one finger, then made a circular motion. The shooter was close. Colby had spotted him. Too close to risk speaking into their earpieces, thus the hand signals. Max nodded to let him know he understood, then he looked to his left and made the same motions to Chris, who was also a good twenty feet away.

The rest of the team was out here, too. When Max had called them from Bex's house, the strategy had been set— half the team would approach from the west, driving the shooter back toward the rest of the team. The plan had worked. And now the shooter was trapped between them.

Max waited, glancing from Colby to Chris, until they both signaled that the whole team was in sync. The static crackled in his ear again, and this time he heard Dillon's voice, so low he wouldn't have heard it if he wasn't listening for it.

"Three, two, one, go."

Max crept forward, as silently as possible, in perfect unison with his team. Sweeping his assault rifle out in front of him, he used the scope every few feet, hoping to see what Colby had seen. Five painfully slow minutes later, the shadowy figure of someone peering out from behind a tree, clutching a rifle, had Max freezing in place.

Ever so carefully, he signaled his teammates. Shooter spotted. He also signaled that this was his takedown. He was the closest. Hell, even if he wasn't, he'd have demanded the right to finish this. Bex might not be his anymore, but he still cared about her—a fact that had been ruthlessly revealed to him today. And he wasn't about to stand by while someone else took down whoever had tried to kill her. No, this shooter was his. And they were definitely going down.

Realizing the rifle was too bulky and cumbersome for such close quarters, he carefully set it against a tree. Then he pulled his pistol from his holster, motioned to his teammates and started forward.

The shooter ducked back behind the tree. Had Max been spotted? He stopped, listened, waited. When he didn't see or hear anything, he started forward again.

Fifteen feet.

Fourteen.

Thirteen.

Something snapped up ahead. He froze. Was that a twig? Or had someone just ratcheted a round into a chamber?

Sweeping his pistol in front of him, he scanned the trees

to his left, right. Chris and Colby were still within sight, just barely. They'd stopped, like him, and were waiting, listening.

Two minutes later, Max signaled his teammates and started forward again. His gaze was riveted on the tree where he'd last seen that shadow.

Steady and slow, inch by inch. He stopped a yard back from the thick tree. Breathing through his mouth, as quietly as possible. He played the waiting game once again. Then he heard it. Fast, shallow breaths. His prey was still exactly where he'd seen him, hiding behind the tree. And from the sound of it, he was practically hyperventilating—afraid.

Good. Max wanted him to experience fear, just like Bex had felt. He was about to spring around the tree when he spotted another shadow, a good thirty feet in front of him. The quick hand signal told him it was Dillon. And then the shadow disappeared behind cover. Dillon was letting Max know that he was close and in the line of fire. Time to switch strategies.

Max ever so carefully holstered his pistol. Then he slowly and quietly pulled the long serrated hunting knife from his boot. He listened to the shallow, rapid breathing. Crept a foot to his left, planning his approach. Without taking his gaze from the tree, he held a hand up in the air, letting his teammates know he was about to strike.

Three.

Two.

One.

He rushed forward, swinging around the tree. Wide, terrified eyes met his. He registered the identity of the shooter a millisecond before he struck, knocking the shooter's rifle skyward and dropping the unneeded knife to the ground as he tackled his prey.

The capture was far too easy for Max's liking. He'd

wanted, needed, that explosion of violence against the person who'd nearly killed Bex. But his thirst for vengeance had been discarded the instant he'd seen how scared and pale his opponent was and realized there would be no fighting back.

Underbrush crashed around him from all sides as the rest of the SWAT team swooped out of their hiding places and aimed their rifles toward Max's prisoner.

Marcia Knolls stared up at them, at the guns pointing at her head, then projectile vomited on Max's vest.

MAX STOOD NAKED from the waist up in front of Bex's guest bathroom sink, trying one last time to scrub the stained, reeking fabric of his bullet-resistant vest. Thanks to an always-packed go-bag in his truck, he had a fresh shirt hanging over one of the towel racks. But he didn't want to risk getting it soiled, so he hadn't put it on yet. He scrubbed at the cloth on the vest one more time, then, realizing it was pointless, he swore and tossed it to the floor.

"I could have told you it was a lost cause." Dillon stood in the bathroom doorway, a grin on his face. "Trade it with Blake. You two are about the same size."

"Yeah, I'm sure he wants a vest that smells like vomit."

Dillon shrugged. "As a newbie, you take what you can get."

"You don't really mean that."

Dillon shrugged again. But Max knew he was right, that their team leader wouldn't try to give Max's ruined vest to the rookie. Dillon might be playing hardball right now with Blake, but he didn't play dirty.

Max rested his hands on the countertop as he looked at Dillon in the mirror. "Speaking of Blake—"

"Yeah, yeah. I know. The chief is going to be ticked. But, honestly, this time I completely forgot about the guy. It didn't even occur to me to include him on the callout."

Max laughed.

Dillon frowned. "It's not funny. I'm going to get a thirty-minute lecture out of this. I probably won't hear right for a week after the chief yells at me."

Max grabbed a washcloth from the neat stack in the open shelving above the toilet. "Yeah, well. Maybe that will ensure that you remember next time." He wet and soaped up the cloth to scrub the sink.

"Oh, sorry," a feminine voice said. "I didn't know you were still changing."

Max turned around to see Bex backing up from the doorway, a handful of fresh washcloths and towels in her hands. Dillon melted back into the shadows of the hallway, leaving the two of them alone.

"Don't go," Max said. "You can put those up in here. Sorry about the mess I'm making." He plopped the wash-cloth into the sink and moved back so she could enter the small room.

She hesitated, her gaze falling to his chest, before she cleared her throat and looked away. "No problem. Are you kidding? You saved my life. Again. Make all the messes you want. I didn't remember whether I had enough towels still in here, with all the packing I did. Looks like there are plenty. I'll just put these back in the box—"

"Bex, wait." When she still turned to leave, he added, "Please."

She froze, then turned back toward him, a foot back from the doorway. "Was there something else you needed?"

He let out a deep sigh. "Are you okay?"

"Of course." She absently stroked her fingertips across the bandage on her left forearm. "Like I said, you saved my life. Thank you. That sounds so inadequate. But... thank you."

He braced his hands on the door frame on either side of her. "It can't be easy having someone try to kill you twice in one day. Especially with the two events appearing unrelated."

"Appearing? You think there's a chance that they are related?"

"I didn't say that. Just reserving judgment until we investigate."

"But the shooter, Marcia, she wasn't at the grocery store this morning."

"No. She wasn't."

"Did she say why she tried to shoot me?"

"She collapsed after I cuffed her. They took her to Blount Memorial in Maryville. Probably won't get to interview her until tomorrow. Assuming she doesn't lawyer up by then."

She seemed to ponder that for a moment, biting her lip as she considered all the possibilities.

"Don't think too hard on it," he said. "That's my job. I'll figure this out. Your job is to be careful, stay alert."

"Because someone else might try to kill me today?"

The bitterness and underlying fear in her voice had him automatically reaching for her, wanting to comfort her. But she hurriedly backed up before he could touch her.

He dropped his hand to his side and smiled as if it didn't matter. Because it shouldn't. What the hell had he been thinking to reach for her? Had he really expected that she'd want his touch? She was the one who'd left. She was the one who'd been gone for ten years. If she wanted anything to do with him, she knew where to find him. And she hadn't come back even once. She hadn't called, texted, sent a freaking email. Clearly, that horse had galloped away years ago, never to return. The sooner he got that through his thick skull, the better off he'd be.

"You can't drive home tonight with your windshield blown out. I'll ask the chief to assign someone to watch over you until your car is fixed. They can—"

"Follow me around? How long would it take your boss to tell them to haul me to the station like he's wanted all along? Thanks, but no thanks. I don't want police protection. I'll take my chances on my own."

"You're being stubborn. At least let me call a security company. They could assign bodyguards—"

"I'm fine, Max. Really. In spite of how things seem, I assure you I can and do usually take care of myself."

And then she was gone, taking her armload of towels with her.

Footsteps sounded in the hall and Dillon stuck his head in the door again. "Hey, man. One of the Piggly Wiggly suspects at Blount Memorial is already out of surgery. The chief wants me to head over there to question him the moment he wakes up, preferably before he asks for a lawyer. But Marcia Knolls is at the hospital being checked out, too, and already saying she wants to cut a deal, so I've got my hands full. Everyone else's plate is loaded already. Can you help me out?"

"You bet." Max grabbed his clean shirt and yanked it over his head.

Dillon hesitated. "Could be an all-nighter. You sure you don't want to hang here? With Bex?"

Max stared at him. "You sure you want to ask me that question?"

Dillon held up his hands in a placating gesture. "Hey, I had to ask."

Max glanced at his watch. Almost shift change for the uniformed officers. He grabbed his cell phone out of its holder. "Did I see Jake Cantor outside earlier with the other uniforms?"

"I think so, why?"

"Can you ask him to meet me in the living room on your way out? I need to ask him something."

Dillon gave him a long look, then sighed. "All right.

Keep your secrets. I'll send him in. Make it quick though. I'll meet you at my truck." He headed down the hallway.

Max did a quick internet search on his phone. When he found what he was looking for, he made a call, then went into the living room. When he spotted Officer Cantor standing by the fireplace looking impatient, he strode to him.

"Hey, Jake."

"Max. What's up? I was about to head back to the station to finish my reports for the shift change."

After a quick look around to make sure that Bex wasn't within earshot, Max said, "If you don't mind putting that off for a little while, I need your help. I've hired a bodyguard service to keep an eye on Miss Kane. But I need someone to watch over her until their guy gets here. I know you do security work on the side sometimes. I'll pay your fee—"

"No way, man. Keep your money. I can wait until your guy gets here. Not a problem. I take it Miss Kane doesn't know about this?"

"No. And I don't want her to. She sort of has a phobia about the police. Or at least, Destiny police. She refused our protection. So I can't ask the chief to assign anyone."

He looked confused over Bex's distrust of the local police, probably because he wasn't around back when Bobby Caldwell was killed—and the chief threw Bex in jail.

"Okay," Jake said. "This stays on the down-low. Like I said, not a problem. Give your bodyguard my cell number. I saw Miss Kane out on the lawn talking to one of the other detectives a few minutes ago. I'll keep an eye on her until he gets here."

Max shook his hand. "Thanks, Jake. I owe you one. When you talk to this guy, stress again for me that he and his team need to make sure Bex, Miss Kane, doesn't spot them. They need to be invisible."

"You got it."

Chapter Seven

Max shifted in the uncomfortable plastic hospital chair that he'd slept in most of last night. Beside him, lying in bed with one hand cuffed to the railing, was grocery store shooter Lenny Stinsky.

The all-nighter that Dillon had predicted had turned into all night and most of the next day. It was already nearing the dinner hour. But Max wasn't going anywhere, not when his long wait was finally about to pay off. According to Lenny's doctor, he was now healthy enough to talk and awake enough to understand his Miranda rights.

To be absolutely certain of that, to reduce the possibility of Lenny's statement being thrown out at trial, the chief had decided to be in on the interview. Which was why Max was sitting on one side of Lenny's bed while the chief was on the other. But since neither of them was proficient at playing good cop, this was going to be a tag team of bad cop, bad cop. Meaning they were going to lie through their teeth to try to get as much information as they could out of the little tattoo-covered delinquent.

As gangbangers went, Lenny Stinsky was the scrawniest, least tough-looking one that Max had ever seen. Not that he'd seen all that many in Destiny. Mostly he was going by what he'd seen on TV.

The kid was eighteen, just barely. But he looked so small and scared that he could have passed for fifteen.

Luck was definitely on Max and the chief's side today. Because the other guy Max had shot, a guy with a temper as hot as his hair was red, appeared to be the leader of the gunmen. He was far more jaded and too experienced to talk to the cops. He'd asked for a lawyer the second he woke up from the anesthesia. He'd also demanded to see Lenny. To keep him from talking, of course. But no way was Max going to let him get within a hundred feet of their little squealer.

Max scooted his chair closer to the bed and glanced at the chief sitting on the other side before asking his next question.

"So far you haven't told us much, Lenny. We need names. If you want a deal, you need to give us something worth dealing for. Now start over, and this time give us some details."

Lenny's eyes were wide and uncertain as he glanced from Max to the chief and back again. "What kind of deal do I get?"

"Nothing so far. You have to prove you've got something we want before we talk terms." Max glanced at his watch. "I really don't care which one of the five of you I deal with. The first guy to talk is the one we negotiate with. The rest of you can go to prison for the rest of your lives for all I care."

That wasn't true, of course. Three of the five had suffered only mild concussions from being knocked out and were in county lockup, refusing to talk, just like the other guy who'd been shot and was still in the hospital. Lenny was Max's only hope of getting any information anytime soon. But the little scumbag didn't need to know that.

Lenny's Adam's apple bobbed in this throat.

Max checked his watch again. "Time's up. I'm off to talk to one of the other guys."

"Wait." His hand shot up then jerked short, the handcuff rattling against the bed rail. He winced and lowered his arm. "Okay, okay. I'll start from the top. What do you want to know?"

"Who hired you, for starters? All you've told us is some guy approached you and your homies on a corner in Knoxville. What was his name?"

"I don't know."

Max started to stand again.

"Wait, wait. I'm not lying. I really don't know."

The desperation in the kid's voice told Max he was probably telling the truth. Which didn't bode well for their investigation.

He relaxed back in his chair again, settling in for a long interview. "He never gave you a name?"

Lenny shook his head. "No. I never really saw his face, either. It was at night. We were in an alley, goofing around, when he drives up and parks his car at the entrance, blocking us in. Chucky heads over to make him move, but the guy pulls a gun on him."

"Who's Chucky?" Max asked.

Lenny swallowed. "He...he's our leader. Red hair, about six feet tall, freckles."

The other guy Max had shot.

The chief tapped the bed railing to get the kid's attention. "You saw a guy pull a gun but you can't describe him?"

"Didn't say I couldn't describe him, just not his face. The car's headlights were shining toward us. All I could see was his outline, you know? And the gun. The guy was about six feet tall, average weight, not too skinny but not big, either."

Max rolled his eyes. "That describes half the guys I know. What about his hair color?"

"Didn't see it. Told you it was dark, and the headlights were on."

"What about the gun?"

"That's easy. It was just like the ones he gave us for holding up the grocery store."

"An M16?" Max asked.

Lenny shrugged. "Guess so. Never saw one before that night." He mouth curved. "Pretty badass gun."

A chill swept through Max at the delight on the kid's face. For the first time since the interview had begun, he believed he was seeing the real Lenny Stinsky, the gang-banger who had little to no respect for the lives of others.

"What about the car the guy drove?" Max asked. "What kind was it? Did it have a front license plate?"

The kid shrugged again. "It was one of those SUV things, dark color. Didn't see any plates. Like I said, the—"

"Headlights were too bright, yeah, yeah. Did he make the deal with Chucky or all of you?"

"All of us."

"How much?"

"Ten thousand."

Max scoffed. "You risked years of prison time for a split of two thousand dollars?"

Lenny shook his head. "Not a split. Each."

Max shot a look at the chief. "You're saying this guy came out of nowhere and hired the five of you for fifty thousand dollars?"

"Yep." A gloating look crossed Lenny's face, until he tried to cross his arms and couldn't because of the hand-cuffs. He yanked them against the rail and frowned.

"Did he pay up front?"

"I ain't sayin'."

Code words for he wasn't going to tell the cops where his money was. Max didn't bother going down that tan-gent. They'd follow the money trail later. What he needed right now was a name.

"What were the exact terms of the deal? Did you hear him? Or did Chucky relay the information?"

"You're kidding, right?" He shook his head like he thought Max was an idiot. "No way was any of us getting near him with that wicked-looking gun. We hung back and waited for Chucky to tell us what the guy said. The guy talked to Chucky, then tossed a duffel bag on the ground and drove off."

Max's stomach sank. The chief was already scrubbing his face and shaking his head. If everything Lenny had just told them was hearsay, they had the legal equivalent of zero in a court of law. And they couldn't base any potential search warrants off hearsay, either. Lenny was looking more and more like a dead end.

"Lenny, I'm going to ask you again. This is really important, so think hard before you answer. Did you personally hear anything the gunman said?"

"Oh, yeah. Of course."

Max gripped the arms of the chair. "Good, good. What exactly did you hear him say?"

"When Chucky headed toward the guy's car, the man said, 'Hold it right there. I want to make you a deal.' A couple of minutes later the guy was gone and we had the address to that store and a picture of the gal we were supposed to scare." He grinned. "And those sweet M16 rifles."

Max shook his head in disgust. He pushed his chair back and stood. The chief was slower, but he stood, too.

"I did good, right?" Lenny looked back and forth. "We got a deal? I don't do no time?"

Max wrapped his fingers around the foot rail and leaned toward him. "No, Lenny. We ain't got no deal. All you've told me is that you have no direct knowledge of who hired you to storm the Piggly Wiggly and that you can't even describe the guy or give us his name. In other words, you have nothing."

They headed toward the door.

The handcuffs rattled against the bedrail. "Wait, I told you what I know. Where are you going?"

Max let the door swing closed behind him and the chief.

The chief put his hand on his hips. "Which one is Chucky? One of the ones over at county lockup?"

"No. He's the other guy I shot, the one who asked for a lawyer."

"Figures." Thornton motioned with his thumb over his shoulder. "If this Lenny guy told us the truth, the other three gunmen won't be able to help us any more than he did, even if they weren't already asking for lawyers."

"That about sums it up," Max said.

The sound of footsteps coming down the polished tiled hallway had Max turning around, surprised to see Dillon striding toward them.

When Dillon reached them, Max asked, "What are you still doing here? Didn't you get Marcia's statement yesterday? Or did something else happen?"

"No, nothing else, thank goodness. But there was a delay with her statement. The doctors around here are a little too careful, if you ask me. They wouldn't let me talk to her yesterday at all, even though she called us. I had to wait for them to clear her."

"They're terrified of lawsuits these days," the chief grumbled. "Is she ready to talk now?"

"I just finished interviewing her. She answered every question I asked and then some. She's terrified of going to jail. But nothing she said ties into the grocery store holdup. Her going after Miss Kane with that rifle was apparently a spur-of-the-moment decision. Marcia fancies herself Bobby Caldwell's girlfriend and blames Miss Kane for his death. She said when she saw her with you, Max, that all those old feelings of anger came back. She was furious that Max and Bex were back together and she could never be with Bobby again."

"We're not back together," Max gritted out.

Dillon shrugged. "Just relaying what the witness—"

"You mean suspect."

"Fair enough. I'm just telling you what she said. She was jealous and angry and grabbed the rifle out of the trunk of her car. She claims she was only trying to scare Miss Kane."

"Right. And she just happened to have a loaded rifle in her car when she came over."

The chief cleared his throat, drawing their attention. "Not that I want to give Miss Knolls an alibi or reasonable doubt, but she has won the shooting challenges at the county fair three years running. The fair is coming up soon. It's likely she keeps her gun in the car to take back and forth to target practice these days."

Dillon grimaced. "You hit it on the head, Chief. That's exactly what she told me, that she was going to do some target practice after bringing over a casserole her mom made her deliver to Miss Kane. She also insisted that if she'd really wanted to shoot anyone, she wouldn't have missed."

The chief nodded.

"Please don't tell me you agree with that statement," Max said.

"Okay. I'll just keep quiet, then." The chief rolled his eyes.

Max swore. "So we have her on, what, a misdemeanor? Assuming we believe her story?"

"Well." The chief scrubbed the stubble on his chin. "We could charge her with attempted murder if we wanted to go that route. But a jury of her peers would set her free so fast your head would spin. Trying to pin the grocery store thing on her won't stick, either."

"Then you're just going to let her go? I don't care how proficient she is with a rifle. No one's perfect. She could have hurt or killed Bex when she pulled that trigger."

"I ain't gonna argue with you on that," the chief agreed. "We'll charge her with something, maybe reckless endangerment. Let her spend a few nights in jail to teach her a lesson. But unless Miss Kane wants to press more serious charges against her, she'll be out in a few days."

Max whirled around and headed down the hallway.

"Where are you going?" the chief called out.

"To get Bex to press charges against Marcia Knolls."

Chapter Eight

Bex parked her mom's ancient Ford Taurus in front of her lawyer's office and cut the engine. She would have much preferred to take her own, far newer SUV, but until she could get the windshield replaced, the Taurus would have to do. Hopefully she could get her car fixed soon and get out of town. It was as if the universe was against her, throwing obstacles in her path to keep her from leaving.

Just this morning, she'd come across more of her mom's things packed in the attic. And she'd spent most of the day sorting through them and figuring out where to take them. It wasn't like she could throw away homemade quilts and other keepsakes her mom had collected over the years. But Bex didn't have room in her condo to hoard everything, either. So she'd kept the more sentimental of the items and spent hours driving around Destiny delivering the rest of them to longtime friends of her mother.

That had taken even more time, of course, since she couldn't just walk up, leave her mom's things, and not stay and visit. That kind of rudeness would have made her mother ashamed to call her daughter. So she'd done her duty, answering her mom's friends' questions about what she'd been doing all these years. Telling them about the antique store she ran with her best friend in Knoxville, building a comfortable life for herself, if not an exciting one.

The close-knit group had known about her, of course.

They'd known that her mother visited Bex several times a year. They also knew that her mom had forbidden Bex to come to Destiny because she was so worried about the shadow of her past hanging over her head.

Her mom had been nothing if not protective. And her friends had served her well, keeping her secret until the very end. They were also steadfast in their support of Bex, flat out telling her they knew she was innocent, that she hadn't killed that stalker-boy. Their support had Bex so close to tears she'd almost broken down in front of them.

Now she was finally alone once again, back in town with another task to finish. But even though she was anxious to be done, she hesitated to get out of the car. Glancing in the rearview mirror at the grocery store across the street sent a chill of dread racing up her spine.

She'd been so lucky to have escaped not one but two shootings without serious injury. But she couldn't count on Max always being there to protect her. Bad things came in threes, didn't they? Her mom's death had been the first terrible blow. Hopefully the two shootings counted as the second and third bad things and nothing else would happen before she could escape this town again.

She shoved the door open and headed into the two-story office building. The exterior door opened onto a short hall with a bench and another door at the end that she knew from previous visits was the bathroom. She stepped past the bench and through the open doorway into the reception area.

Her attorney's assistant looked up from some papers on her desk and gave Bex a brilliant smile, as she did with everyone.

"Miss Kane, so nice to see you again. Are you here to make an appointment?"

Bex smiled at the elderly woman who was just as perfectly put together as her dapper employer. Martha couldn't be a day younger than seventy, but she got around just as well as women half her age and looked like she could have graced the pages of a fashion magazine. Bex had loved the kind woman the moment she'd met her and always felt lighter in spirit after talking to her.

"Hi, Martha. It's good to see you, too. I don't have an appointment, but Mr. Leonard said I could stop by anytime to sign a power of attorney."

"Oh, sure. Of course. I can take care of that for you. No appointment needed. Good thing, too. Because he's got someone in his office right now. I wouldn't want you to have to wait. Have a seat while I get the form." She waved toward the row of cushy leather chairs against the wall across from her desk.

Bex murmured her thanks and settled into one of the chairs as Martha headed down a hallway behind her desk to what Bex assumed was a storage room. The building was small, housing the one-lawyer office downstairs and living quarters for Mr. Leonard upstairs.

She glanced to her right at the closed door to her lawyer's office. She would have liked to tell him goodbye before leaving town. But even if she had to wait another day for her windshield to get repaired before she returned to Knoxville, she doubted she'd come back to her lawyer's office before then. In town, she felt too exposed, vulnerable.

Max's warnings, his encouragement for her to let the chief assign someone to protect her hadn't fallen on deaf ears. The only reason she'd refused the offer was because she didn't trust the chief, or any of the Destiny police, except Max. And he hadn't exactly jumped at the chance to be the one to protect her.

Max. Just thinking about him had her chest hurting again. Would he be happy once she was gone so he could get on with his life again, without her interference? Without her bringing up memories he'd much rather forget?

Leaving would make it more difficult for him to conduct his investigations into the shootings. But other than that, would he miss her? The idea seemed ludicrous given that every conversation they'd had was fraught with tension and anger. All she knew for sure was that she would miss him. Or maybe it was the idea of him—the way they'd been as a couple. Bex and Max, always together, so much so that friends had taken to calling them Mex—which she hated but that Max had thought was funny. So funny that he'd teased her that they should move to Texas someday and be Tex Mex.

It was amazing how quickly the years could melt away after seeing someone again. She wondered how long it would take before she could go a whole day without thinking about him. It had taken years to get to that point the last time. She didn't imagine it would be any easier this time. He wasn't the kind of man a woman could easily forget.

The click of sensible heels on hardwood floors heralded Martha's return. With clipboard in hand, she crossed the room before Bex could climb out of the chair she'd sunk into.

Martha waved her to stay seated. "No need to get up. I know how those chairs are. They grab you and hold on. Augustus needs to put something harder and less comfortable in here." She handed the clipboard and a pen to Bex. "You can read over this and fill it out right there. As soon as you're done, I'll make sure you signed everywhere you needed to sign and then I'll notarize it and give you a copy. Take your time."

Bex thanked her again and read through the form. Everything seemed straightforward. She initialed a couple of paragraphs where Martha had marked an X and then signed the bottom. Now to climb out of the person-eating chair. She set the clipboard on the little table beside her and grasped the arms of the chair.

Suddenly a large, familiar tanned hand appeared in front of her to help her up. She selfishly allowed her gaze to travel up him a bit more slowly than she should, enjoying every little piece of scenery the trip revealed—from his narrow jeans-clad hips with the oversize rodeo-style belt buckle to his flat waist, the soft-looking forest green shirt that revealed a small dark matting of hair at the V of his neck. But no matter how much she tried to prepare herself for the final destination, her breath still caught when she viewed his handsome, angular face and those amazing warm brown eyes that seemed to tug at her very soul whenever he looked at her.

One of his dark brows arched and a smile tugged at the corner of his mouth. "You okay, Bex? You seem a little preoccupied."

She put her hand in his, savoring the warm feel of his skin against hers as he effortlessly tugged her out of the chair. And loving that he seemed in a better mood today, gifting her with a smile.

"I was just thinking it was about time you showed up," she teased, feeling happier for some reason.

"You were expecting me?"

She reluctantly pulled her hand from his and smoothed her blouse over her khaki pants. "I'm getting used to you saving me. And I'm pretty sure my life was in danger in that chair."

His smile widened. "I've heard small children have disappeared in those monster chairs." He glanced around, nodded at Martha. "I thought I might find you here. When you're done, maybe I can take you to Eva-Marie's for dinner. I want to update you on a few developments. And maybe if I ply you with some of Eva's homemade pecan pie, I can convince you to work through your fear of the police station and come in to give a formal statement."

Her ridiculous happiness at seeing him faded and she shook her head. "I'm not ever going back there."

He cocked his head, as if he was sizing her up, planning strategies. "I want to make sure you're safe, Bex."

"I'm not taking any foolish chances. I'm going home as soon as feasible."

"Not to Pigeon Forge to relax a few weeks first?"

She shook her head. "No. I've…decided to go straight to Knoxville." Because now she realized that if she went to Pigeon Forge all she'd do was think of Max and the last time they'd been there. And that wasn't something she could handle right now.

"How about we have dinner and talk about your plans, and your safety? Plus, I need to talk to you about Marcia Knolls."

She shouldn't say yes. And she really didn't want to discuss anything to do with Marcia. But she heard herself saying, "You buying?"

"Of course."

"Okay. I'll join you, but only because I'm too financially savvy to pass up a free meal. And the bagel I had this morning has long since lost its ability to stave off the growling in my stomach. But don't expect any miracles. I'm telling you right now that nothing will make me agree to go downtown with you."

"Downtown? You make it sound like we're a big city. You've been gone way too long."

The reason for her being gone seemed to hang like a heavy cloud over both of them, making his smile fade and her body tense. The surprisingly easy camaraderie that had flowed between them a moment ago evaporated, leaving them both on edge and uncomfortable once again. She hated that this was how things were between them. But there wasn't anything that could be done about it.

Bex crossed to the desk and handed Martha the clipboard and pen. "You can mail me a copy later. No rush."

"Oh, nonsense. It'll only take a minute for me to notarize this and make you a copy. I'll be right back."

Bex was about to protest, but Martha was already heading down the hallway behind her desk again.

Max crossed his arms and rocked back on his boots. "I didn't see your RAV4 out front. Is it at Eddie's?"

Eddie's Auto Barn. Bex smiled ruefully. "That place is still around?"

"Yep. Ralph Putnam bought it from Eric Green last year."

"Has anyone ever figured out who the original Eddie was who started the garage?"

"Not as far as I know."

She smiled and felt a tug of nostalgia for the happy years she'd spent growing up here. "Maybe I'll ask Ralph to pick up my car and repair the windshield. I'm driving my mom's Taurus right now and haven't had a chance to put the RAV4 in anywhere to be fixed."

The phone in his pocket buzzed and he pulled it out. He tilted it to see the screen, then frowned. "I've got to take this. Be right back."

She nodded and he headed through the open doorway into the little hallway just outside. Feeling restless, Bex toured the reception area, walking the perimeter of the small room and studying the surprisingly nice artwork. She wondered whether a local painter had created it and leaned closer to look at the signature.

"No, she refused to come to the station. I don't think I can convince her, either."

She straightened, realizing she was unwittingly eavesdropping on Max's phone conversation out in the hall. She was about to move away when he said something else.

"You're changing your mind now? You're the one who

ordered me to talk to her in the first place. I'm telling you it's all ancient history with us. We were kids. It meant nothing. Our past isn't why she's refusing to go. It's her past, the Caldwell thing."

She sucked in a breath, his words cutting through her like knives.

Ancient history.

It meant nothing.

"You like that painting? My oldest granddaughter did that."

Bex turned around to see Martha standing behind her desk, papers in her hand, a proud smile on her face.

"Um, yes. It's quite lovely." She hurriedly moved away from the doorway toward the desk.

Footsteps sounded behind her, and she knew Max had entered the room again. She glanced at him and caught him frowning. He looked at the painting by the doorway, then her. Had he heard Martha talking to her? Did he suspect she'd overheard his call?

He looked like he was about to say something when the door to Mr. Leonard's office opened behind him, letting the sound of several male voices into the room. A wheelchair came into view first, and Bex frowned in surprise to see Robert Caldwell sitting there. The last time she'd seen him he'd been a strong bear of a man. Now he was pale, thin and sickly. Had losing his oldest son done that to him? She pressed a hand against her throat, feeling a stab of nausea at the thought. And then she looked up at the man pushing the wheelchair and took a quick step back.

"Bex?" Max whispered. "What's wrong?"

She blinked at the apparition in front of her. Bobby Caldwell. It couldn't be. How was this possible?

"Bex?" Max moved in front of her, bending down so their eyes met. "Pull yourself together," he whispered.

"But how can it be? Bobby is…" She worked her mouth

but couldn't seem to say it out loud, that Bobby was supposed to be dead.

His brows raised and a look of dawning came over his face. "That's Deacon, just back from a tour overseas, Iraq. He's Bobby's younger brother. Remember how much alike they always looked? I assure you that Bobby Caldwell hasn't come back from the grave."

She let out a shaky breath and nodded. "Yes, of course. It was just…a surprise. I'm fine." At his skeptical look, she straightened her shoulders. "I'm fine. Really."

He stepped back beside her. But she almost wished he hadn't. Because now the elder Caldwell had a clear view of her, and his eyes were filled with such hate that it had her stomach churning with nausea all over again. His face reddened and his eyes darkened almost to black.

Mr. Leonard, seemingly unaware of the tension in the room, stepped around the Caldwells to greet Bex. He took her hands in his. "Delighted to see you again, dear. Are you here to sign that form?"

"Um, yes. Martha already had me sign it. I was just about to leave. I didn't mean to intrude." She tugged her hands from his.

"Nonsense, nonsense," he said. "No need to rush." He nodded at Max. "Good to see you, Detective. I hope everything's okay? No other crises happening in our little town?"

Max shook his hand. "So far, so good." He stepped past the lawyer and shook Deacon's hand. "Deacon, good to see you. Thank you for your service. Glad to see you made it back in one piece."

"Thanks, Max. Good to be back." Deacon shook his hand.

Max nodded at the man in the wheelchair. "Mr. Caldwell."

"What's she doing here?" The older man's words dripped like venom from his mouth.

Bex curled her fingers into her palms.

Mr. Leonard turned around, his face mirroring surprise for a split second. Then a look of dawning came over him. He gave Bex an apologetic glance before facing his other clients.

"Robert, I'll have those papers drawn up in no time. Have Deacon bring you back in a week and we'll perform a final review."

Relief flashed in Deacon's eyes and he started forward, pushing his father's chair and looking eager to escape.

"Hold it," his father demanded, slamming one of the brakes on the wheelchair and almost overturning it in his zeal to stop. "I'm not going anywhere until I hear an explanation for why she's here. Augustus, if you're going to do business with this murdering piece of vermin, I'll take my business elsewhere."

Bex sucked in a breath, and Deacon's mouth fell open in astonishment.

Mr. Leonard sputtered and stammered, seemingly so shocked that he didn't know what to say.

Max had no such problem. He planted himself squarely in front of the elder Caldwell's chair and leaned down, both hands braced on the arms of the wheelchair.

"Calling Miss Kane a murderer is slander, Mr. Caldwell. And Destiny is just old-fashioned enough to still have laws on the books that give me the power to arrest you for that. I suggest you keep your insults to yourself unless you want to see the inside of a jail cell."

"Bah, Thornton would toss you out on your backside if you put one hand on me. And it's not slander if it's true. That, that—"

"Careful," Max warned, his eyes narrowed dangerously.

Caldwell glared at him before aiming his fury at Bex

again. "You killed my son. You shouldn't be free and walking around. You should be six feet under, just like him."

"Dad." Deacon sounded mortified. "Please, stop." He aimed a pleading look at Bex. "I'm so sorry, Bex. It's the cancer. He doesn't know what he's saying."

"The hell I don't. Stop making excuses for me, you dolt. You never did have the sense your brother had."

Deacon winced and shot Bex another pleading look, as if begging her to overlook his father's poor manners.

Bex was shaking too hard to say anything, so she simply tipped her head at Deacon, trying to let him know that she didn't hold his father's enmity against him.

Max leaned down and said something beneath his breath to the older man. Then he motioned to Deacon. "Get him out of here before I make good on my threat to arrest him."

Deacon flipped the brake and quickly wheeled his father out the door. The old man didn't say anything else to Bex, but his hatred and fury were clear as his glare followed her until the door closed behind the two of them.

Silence reigned inside the little office. Max looked like he wanted to shoot someone. Martha looked horrified, papers dangling from her fingertips. And Mr. Leonard appeared equally nonplussed, his mouth opening and closing as if he wasn't sure what to say.

Bex cleared her throat and ran a shaky hand through her hair, flipping the long strands back over her shoulder. "I'd better go. Thank you for your help this week, Mr. Leonard." She stepped toward Martha and held out her hand. "Is one of those for me?"

Martha blinked, then looked down at the papers. "Oh, yes, my apologies. Here you go." She held one of the papers out to Bex, her smile decidedly less bright this time.

"Thank you." Bex turned and hurried toward the door. It opened just as she reached it. Max was holding the door.

"Thanks," she whispered, barely able to force even one more word past her tight throat.

When they were outside, she hurried to the Taurus and opened the driver's door.

"Bex." Max's deep voice sounded behind her.

She cleared her throat but didn't turn to face him. She didn't want him to see how hard she was struggling not to cry. Because she wasn't this weak woman who cried every time something didn't go her way. Until she'd seen Max again after all these years.

"Sorry about dinner," she said. "I'm not hungry anymore."

"Bex, wait. Please. I need to explain—"

She slid into the driver's seat and shut the door to block whatever he was saying. The tears were flowing freely now. All she could hope was that the angle of the car and the tint on the windshield kept him from seeing that she was crying.

She dashed her tears away and a few moments later she was driving down the road, just like ten years ago, with Destiny, and Max, in her rearview mirror.

Chapter Nine

It was tempting to barrel down the highway to Knoxville
and pretend none of this had ever happened. But Bex rather
doubted her mother's old car would make it. And she was
too mentally exhausted right now to make that trip.

But she wasn't quite ready to return to her mother's
house, either. She was far too upset, and seeing the empty
house wasn't going to make her feel any better. So, instead, she wound aimlessly down the backroads until the
sun began to sink in the sky, going nowhere in particular,
trying to drive out her frustrations.

Driving on gravel roads was apparently a skill she'd
forgotten long ago. She was forced to slow down almost
to a crawl to keep her car from sliding on the loose rocks
and ending up in a ditch.

It suddenly dawned on her where she was, and what was
close by. She'd never intended to drive down this particular
road. But now that she was here, it seemed that fate had
raised its hand. And she started looking in earnest for the
turnoff she knew had to be close by.

It didn't help that the road was overgrown with weeds,
the edges hard to see, especially in the gloom from the oak
tree branches blocking out the fading sunlight overhead.
Maybe she should turn around and rent a four-wheel drive
before coming out here. Then again, if she didn't do this
now, she never would.

She wasn't sure why doing this was suddenly so important. After all, living in the past had never done anything for her before. But with the present so painful, maybe this was just the thing, to remember better times and pretend, if only for a moment, that all the bad had never happened.

"Where are you, where are you?" she muttered, peering through the trees on the right side of the road. Just when she thought she'd have to give up and turn around, she saw it—an old, weathered barn hundreds of yards away, perched upon a slight rise.

She slowed the Taurus, mildly surprised she was able to make the turnoff without wrecking the ancient car. The trees fell away as she accelerated across the fallow field, dried-up remnants of cornstalks, long since harvested, the only evidence of the last crop that had been planted here.

In her mind's eye, the barn was like a familiar Norman Rockwell painting, a beacon of happier times, welcoming her home. But she couldn't ignore reality for long. The barn was dilapidated, crouching like an evil gargoyle against the dead land surrounding it. Time had not been kind to the abandoned building. Holes had been punched in its rotten walls, probably by animals that had made their homes inside. She parked beside it, not too close, for fear a stiff breeze might blow the building over on top of her car.

Leaving her purse and keys in the Taurus, she made a slow circuit around to the front of the barn and stopped. Funny how so much had changed, and yet, everything was the same. The red paint that had once graced the structure was nearly gone. But the initials carved into one of the boards to the right of the door remained—MR + BK, with a Cupid's arrow running through the middle.

Max's words at the lawyer's office echoed in her mind. *Ancient history. It meant nothing.*

That last part was what hurt the most. *It meant nothing.* What had he meant by "it"? The seven years they'd been best friends? The three years they'd been serious boy-friend and girlfriend? That last year, when they'd finally gone all the way? They'd pledged their love to each other. Had it all been a lie on Max's part? Had everything he'd said in her mother's kitchen been a ploy to get her to talk?

It shouldn't matter. Good grief, she was approaching thirty now. A small-business owner with an established life in another town, with friends who didn't care about whatever past she'd left behind. This barn, those initials carved in the wood, they were the part of her life that re-ally *was* ancient history, just as Max had said.

But it was *her* history, a very important part that had made her the person she was today, for better or for worse. And she'd never realized until now just how stuck in the past she was, and that she'd never really cut the tether to Destiny. To Max. Part of her was still here. Part of her had never left.

Until now, she'd never wondered whether the love be-tween her and Max had been real or not. Just thinking that what she'd thought of as the very best part of her life, as a beautiful experience, might have meant nothing to him twisted a knife deeper into her heart.

Angrily brushing at the tears running down her cheeks again, she sent up a quick prayer that the building was sturdier than it looked and headed toward the enormous double doors built to accommodate a small tractor, or maybe a pair of draft horses in older times.

The rusty chain looped from one door handle to the other was more of a suggestion than an impediment to her getting inside. All she had to do was squeeze in the open-ing between the two doors after ducking beneath the chain. And suddenly it was ten years ago, as if she'd never left.

The missing and damaged boards allowed enough light to seep in for her to see that little had changed inside since she and Max had sneaked into this old barn that first night, and again several more times after that. He'd laid a blanket and pillow down onto a bed of fresh hay. They'd introduced each other to a world of passion that neither of them had ever experienced before. It was the most wonderful moment of her young life up to that point. She'd been so naive, believing that love would last forever. But nothing lasted forever, if indeed it had ever existed.

She wrapped her arms around her waist and stepped farther into the barn.

"What are you doing in here, Bex? It's dangerous. Didn't you see the No Trespassing signs out front?"

She whirled around, pressing a hand against her heart even as she recognized Max's voice.

His eyes narrowed as he stepped closer. "You've been crying."

"I'm fine. What are you doing here? This can't be a coincidence."

"I tailed you out of town." He held up his hands as if to stop any angry words. "I wasn't trying to be intrusive or nosy. But you seemed upset and I was worried about you driving while upset. I just wanted to make sure you got home okay." He looked around the barn. "Imagine my surprise when you turned in here."

She wasn't feeling charitable enough at the moment to believe that he'd followed her out of worry. In fact, she was more inclined to believe something else entirely.

"I didn't wreck. Yay me. But I'm thinking your true reason for following me is that your chief ordered you to. Well, you can turn around and go back to the station. Tell him you did your duty, tried once again to convince me to go to the station, and once again I refused. Go on. I don't need you here. And we both know you sure as hell don't want to be here. Not with me. If you ever did."

She turned her back on him and waited to hear his boots make a path to the doors. Instead, he moved closer. She could feel the heat of his body at her back even through her sweater. And she hated that what she wanted to do, what she really craved, was to take one step back and lean into him. She wanted to feel his arms come down around her, hold her and this time never let her go. And she hated herself for it.

"Bex, what's wrong?" His deep voice curled itself around her like an invitation.

It was insane that being this close to him could have such an impact on her. He was setting her on fire, making her body yearn for him, as if it remembered him and ached to be with him again. How could she want him when she hurt so much inside and her mind was screaming at her that she was a fool?

She didn't answer, couldn't answer, without revealing the war going on inside her.

His heavy sigh seemed loud in the quiet barn. "How long are you going to stand there? What did you plan on doing when you came in here?"

She shrugged. Let him think she was being difficult instead of that she was paralyzed by her own traitorous emotions. If he touched her right now, she knew she wouldn't be able to walk away. Perhaps it was the emotional roller coaster she'd been on since getting that shocking call that her mother had passed unexpectedly that made her so vulnerable. Maybe it was coming so close to death herself that had her yearning for what she'd once had but could never have again. A sob built in her throat. She ruthlessly held it back, clenching her hands into fists at her side.

Go away, Max. Can't you see you're killing me?

"At least let me escort you back to your mom's."

The confusion and irritation in his voice was exactly what she'd needed. It helped her snap out of her pity party and gave her enough of a flash of irritation at him to finally speak.

"No, thank you. I'm not ready to go back."

There. That had sounded strong, unaffected, confident. Hadn't it? Surely he hadn't heard the little wobble in her voice. It had only been a tiny little wobble.

"Bex?" His voice was softer this time. "Are you all right?"

She squeezed her eyes shut, drew two deep, bracing breaths. "Just go, okay? You don't owe me anything. It's not like we're in a relationship anymore."

Her voice was thick with tears, but there was nothing she could do about it. She just needed him to stop torturing her and leave before she melted into a puddle of misery. His hurtful words from back in town poured out of her in a sea of bitterness. "Whatever happened in the past was ancient history anyway. Didn't even matter."

"I knew it. I knew you heard that stupid phone call." He turned her around and put his hand beneath her chin, forcing her to look at him. "I'm sorry, Bex. I was a jerk back there, okay?"

"Back where? At the grocery store deli, when you ignored me? Or the lawyer's office, where you basically told your boss—or whoever was on the phone—that I wasn't even a blip on your life's radar? I'm guessing when we made love here that never mattered, either." Tears ran down her cheeks and she swiped them away. She swore. "I did *not* come here for this. I don't want to do this. Please, Max. Just go."

He grabbed her shoulders, his eyes dark with anger and frustration. "You're the one who turned down my proposal. You're the one who left. So why are you so angry at me?"

She shook her head, her throat tight.

He started to say something else, then stopped. Started again, then swore and yanked her against him. He wanted to kiss her. She could see it in the way his mouth tightened, the way his gaze dropped to her lips. And for one crazy minute, she wanted the same thing. She wanted his mouth swooping down on hers, consuming her in a wild, angry kiss that was nothing like the tender kisses they'd shared as teenagers. She wanted—needed—crazy right now. A kiss so unexpected and incredibly hot that they'd both be panting by the time they broke apart.

She blinked up at him, her shaking fingers pressing against her lips. Just the thought of him kissing her had her mouth tingling.

His nostrils flared as he watched her fingers. Then he shook his head, as if trying to clear his mind. And the moment, the spell, whatever it was, was gone. But the anger, the hurt, wasn't.

"Just because I don't want to share every intimate detail of my life with my boss doesn't mean our past was a lie. It meant something, Bex," he rasped, his voice ragged. "*We* meant something."

And then he was gone.

She didn't know how long she stood there, his words repeating themselves over and over in her mind, confusing her even more than she was before.

We meant something.

She stood there for a long time, until the shadows began to lengthen, until a noise in the loft spooked her and she berated herself for being silly. No telling what kinds of animals made their home here in this old, abandoned barn.

She slipped between the chains and headed to the Taurus. She'd just started to circle back toward the road when something in her rearview mirror had her slamming on the brakes. She stared long and hard at the mirror, which showed the front of the barn. But several minutes passed and she didn't see anything else.

Laughing nervously, she told herself her mind was playing tricks on her. The roof overhang must have cast a shadow across the doors to make it look like a man had slipped through the chains and run around the side of the building.

Chapter Ten

After wolfing down a hearty breakfast of bacon, eggs, biscuits and gravy at Eva-Marie's diner, Max leaned back against the corner booth. And settled in to wait.

He glanced at his watch, then at the door to the diner, dreading the upcoming conversation. He still wasn't sure why he was doing this. Then again, who was he kidding? He was doing this because of what had happened last night with Bex, or, what had *almost* happened. And how badly he'd wanted it to happen.

That alone, the fact that it had nearly killed him not to kiss her, told him that this meeting he'd set up this morning was the right thing to do. The honorable thing to do. Even though he had no intention of pursuing a relationship with Bex again. Thoughts of her were consuming his days, his nights, no matter how hard he tried to push them out of his head. And that made it impossible, and wrong, to remain in a relationship with someone else. It was time to end his three-week dating spree with police intern Monica Stevens.

Breaking up with someone in a diner made him cringe. He'd tried to schedule this discussion at her place, or his. But as soon as he'd called her this morning, saying they needed to talk, it was as if her sixth sense had kicked in. She'd become distant, defensive, and insisted that they meet here. In public. Why she wanted to do that, he had no idea.

Then again, as the door opened and she strutted inside, he realized exactly why she'd chosen this particular place. He'd wanted to spare her feelings and not make a scene. But she obviously had no such intentions toward him.

Monica strode down the center aisle, her heavily made-up eyes tracking him like a radar-guided missile. Her long, blond hair bounced around her shoulders. Impossibly tight jeans outlined her curvy figure, tapering down her long legs to a pair of bloodred stilettos that clicked across the black-and-white tiled floor. Every head turned her way, watching her deliberate progress until she stopped beside Max's booth.

He started to stand but she waved him back down.

"Don't bother acting the gentleman now." She put her hands on her hips. "You think I don't know what you're doing? This whole town is talking about your little girlfriend and how you carried her out of the grocery store all lovey-dovey." She rolled her eyes. "Now you're breaking up with me so you can go screw that boyfriend-stealer again. Admit it."

A gasp of outrage sounded behind her. Monica looked over her shoulder to see Sally, the waitress, holding a pot of coffee, her mouth hanging open.

"Go away." Monica made a shooing motion with her hand. "We're busy."

Max shot Sally an apologetic look before rising to his feet. "I'm sorry."

Monica rolled her eyes again. "It's a little late for that."

"I was talking to Sally."

Monica narrowed her eyes.

Sally glared at Monica's back and whirled around.

Max tossed some bills onto the table. "Let's go somewhere private."

Her hands went back to her hips. "Are you breaking up with me or not?"

He didn't have to look past her to know that everyone was listening for his response. She'd practically yelled her question. And the place had gone completely silent.

"Monica—"

"Answer me," she shouted.

He winced. "We've only been dating for a few weeks. I hardly think it qualifies as a breakup. But, yes, I've got a lot of things going on with the investigation and all. You deserve someone who can focus on you and right now that's not me. I think we should stop seeing each other—"

Whap!

Her hand slapped his cheek. The sting was nothing compared to the sting to his pride as she pivoted on her stilettos and marched out of the diner. He'd never made a woman angry enough to slap him before, and it bothered him that he'd done so now.

"Good riddance is all I can say." Sally stopped in front of him and refilled his coffee cup. "I could tell she was trouble from the minute the chief hired her. You never should've taken up with the likes of her."

Max sat back down, figuring another cup of coffee might do him some good. Since Sally was still standing there, expecting a reply, he shrugged.

"She's an intelligent, nice woman. I can't blame her for being upset. As soon as I knew that Bex was back in town I should have told Monica about our past. Obviously she heard the rumors from someone else. That had to embarrass her."

"Right. When would you have talked to her? After the first shooting or the second?" She shook her head in disgust. "The woman was a police intern, for goodness' sake. She had to know you were busy with the investigations and didn't have time to coddle her. Not that you should anyway." She looked past him, out the window, and her mouth quirked up in a smile. "You been wasting years on types like that Monica woman. When all along you should have been spending time with someone of quality, like her."

She waved toward the window, then took her coffeepot with her as she headed to the counter.

Max looked out at the parking lot, worried that Sally might be trying to fix him up with someone. Then he saw her. Bex. She'd just parked her mom's Taurus in the only space left at the end of the packed lot and was heading toward the diner.

A quick glance at the street confirmed that one of the bodyguards that he'd hired to keep an eye on her was sitting in his car at the curb. He must have seen Max's truck outside and figured she'd be safe inside.

About five inches shorter than Monica, without the stilettos, Bex had lush, dark-brown hair that fell just past her shoulders. And even though he couldn't see them this far away, he knew her eyes were an incredible sky blue that could darken like a storm whenever she was mad. Or when she was writhing beneath him in passion.

He frowned and shoved that dangerous memory far away. It wouldn't do to dwell on the past. He'd done enough of that yesterday. Seeing her go into that barn where they'd first made love had brought up all kinds of memories he didn't want to deal with again. He'd thought they'd been locked away somewhere tight all this time, or were gone altogether. And yet it had only taken one trip to a ramshackle barn to bring them all back again.

Who was he kidding?

Those feelings had been dredged up the moment he'd seen her standing at the deli counter at the Piggly Wiggly, her dark hair reaching past her shoulders. When he'd rounded the end of the aisle, the shock of seeing her had nearly driven him to his knees. But even though his mind

ordered him to stop, turn around, get out of the store before she saw him, his body had other ideas.

His legs had continued to carry him forward like a
starving man drawn to an incredible bounty that would
either save him or destroy him. He'd been fighting his insane attraction to her ever since. And when he'd followed
her into the barn, heard the tears in her voice, the hurt that
he'd caused, he'd been lost. He hadn't wanted to leave her
there. He hadn't been lying when he said he was worried
about her. But at the same time, he knew that if he'd stood
there even a second more, he'd have dragged her to the
ground and made love to her.

He scrubbed his jaw and shoved the coffee cup away
just as Bex walked inside. And just like when Monica had
come in earlier, everyone looked to the front. But unlike
earlier, Bex's entrance was met with greetings and smiles
and a few hugs. There might be a cloud over her in most
parts of town, but the old-timers in this diner seemed to
have no concerns about Bex's past and whether she was
guilty of murder. They were greeting her like old friends,
or at least, friends of her mother. It was mostly retired
folks in here this time of day. The younger crowd was
busy making a living.

When Bex reached his booth, he rose and tipped his
head.

"Morning, Bex. Everything okay?"

"Just peachy. Except that strange men I don't know
seem to be following me everywhere." Unlike her prede-
cessor, she kept her voice low so it didn't carry to the other
tables. And the rest of the patrons had turned around to
offer them privacy.

"Strange men?" he asked, glancing around.

She waved toward the car parked at the curb. "I assume
you hired him to keep an eye on me."

He let out a deep sigh. So much for the bodyguards

being invisible. "Guilty." He studied her a moment. "You don't seem angry." He waved her into the booth and sat across from her.

She shrugged. "Honestly, I was kind of surprised at how easily you backed down when I insisted that I didn't want anyone keeping an eye on me. I felt pretty silly later for not taking you up on your offer and was going to call someone myself when I spotted one of the men outside my house last night. From his mannerisms, I kind of figured he might be a security guy. But I called the police just to be sure."

Max waved Sally over, who came bearing a pot of coffee and an extra cup for Bex, along with a menu.

"Thanks, Sally." Bex smiled. "I appreciate the coffee but I'm really not hungry."

"Let me know if you change your mind." Sally hurried to another table to refill their cups.

"I'm surprised I didn't hear about the call," Max said. "What happened?"

She ruined her coffee with a liberal amount of cream and sugar. "A uniformed officer came over and checked the guy out, then told me he was a bodyguard of all things. But the guy wouldn't say who'd hired him. I let it drop, said not to worry about it, that I was pretty sure who was behind him being there. Thanks, Max. I do appreciate you making sure that I'm safe. Especially since my shadow isn't a cop."

"Ouch."

She winced. "Sorry. No offense. I don't hold it against you that you're a police officer."

He smiled. "Gee. Thanks. I feel so much better now."

She smiled back, then her smile faded. "I can reimburse you for whatever costs—"

"No."

She sighed. "I figured you'd say that. If you change your mind—"

"I won't."

"As stubborn as ever I see," she said.

"One of the many things we have in common."

Her bubble of laughter had several people looking at them, smiling as well, before returning to their meals. He couldn't help smiling, too. Seeing Bex looking happy was too contagious not to have him feeling lighter inside. Her eyes danced with merriment and it was as if all the years between them had never passed. This was the Bex he remembered, the Bex he'd loved.

"What are you thinking about?" he asked.

"You. And me. And Mr. Youngblood's orchard."

He grimaced. "Before or after I thought I could outrun that bull to get you some apples?"

"Oh, definitely after." She laughed. "I warned you not to try it. But you were too stubborn. Once you got an idea in your head you wouldn't let it go. Maybe you should have gone out for the track team. I swear I never saw a human being run that fast."

"Not fast enough."

"You were faster than the bull," she argued.

"But not faster than Mr. Youngblood's buckshot." He winced again, barely refraining from rubbing his posterior at the memory. "I couldn't sit up for a month."

"True." She rested her chin on her palm, a faraway look in her misty blue eyes. "But we had a lot of fun that month. I must have read you over twenty books while you were convalescing."

"You tortured me. At least three of them were romance novels. I've never lived that down with my brothers." He leaned toward her conspiratorially. "I still have to pay them hush money to this day."

"You wouldn't have to pay if you didn't actually like

them. Admit it. You've probably got a romance novel under your pillow right now and you read it every night."

He laughed. "I guess you'd have to come over to my place to find out."

Her smile faded, and the easy camaraderie that had sprung up between them evaporated. He wanted to kick himself for getting carried away and destroying the light atmosphere.

They both straightened, and she awkwardly cleared her throat.

"Where do you live anyway?" she asked, before taking a sip of coffee.

"I built a house on some land adjacent to my father's farm. Close enough to keep in touch but far enough away that I've got my privacy."

She nodded, then shoved her cup out of the way.

"I didn't mean to take up so much of your time. I know you're really busy with the investigation. Actually, that's the reason I'm here. I drove into town to take care of a few more errands and when I passed the grocery store I couldn't help thinking about what happened. That's when I remembered something that I didn't tell anyone before. I pulled over to call you when I saw your truck over here in the lot, so I decided to come tell you in person."

"Tell me what?"

"A name. When I was in the grocery store, hiding from the gunmen, I overheard one of them in the next aisle saying something about Reggie telling them that *she* was heading toward the front of the store. I'm not sure what they were talking about. But I figured this Reggie person might be someone who works at the store. And if that's the case—"

"Then there's an insider who might have helped the gunmen."

"Exactly. What do you think? Could that be helpful?"

"It's a lead to follow. Could very well be a great lead. Thanks, Bex."

"Of course. If I think of anything else, I'll let you know." She shoved out of the booth and stood.

Max stood, too. "You seem to be in a hurry."

She hesitated, her gaze dropping from his. Was she thinking about last night, about what had almost happened between them?

"Just…have a lot to do to wrap up loose ends. How much is the coffee? A couple of bucks?"

She reached into her purse but Max put his hand on hers.

"I'll take care of it."

She blinked, and looked like she wanted to say something. But then she cleared her throat as if changing her mind.

"Thanks, Max. Take care." And then she was rushing down the aisle and out of the diner.

Max watched her until she was driving down the street, her bodyguard following a few car lengths behind. Then he pitched some bills onto the table and headed out to his truck.

Once inside, he made a call to his boss and told him about the name that Bex had remembered.

"Where are you right now?" the chief asked.

"Eva-Marie's. Just had breakfast."

"Good. That's a hop-skip away from the Piggly Wiggly. This Reggie thing sounds like a great lead. And this is the perfect time to follow up on it. I sent Colby, Donna and Blake to the Pig to walk the witnesses through the shooting, step-by-step, to see if any of their initial statements change. Plus, we asked the manager to round everyone up who works there to come in, not just the ones on shift during the shooting. I wanted to see whether anyone saw anything suspicious in the days or weeks before, when maybe the shooters were casing the place to plan the assault. Everyone should be there right now. You can head on over and see if one of them is named Reggie."

"Will do. Wait, you said Blake is there?"

"You got a problem with that? The man isn't exactly a rookie at law enforcement. He's just new to us. He needs to be brought up to speed on how we do things."

Max grinned but was careful not to laugh. "You're the boss."

"Don't you forget that. Now get over there. And let me know once you find this Reggie guy."

WHEN MAX REACHED the doors to the grocery store, he flashed his badge to the deputy assigned to log everyone who went in or out. Then he was inside, taking quick stock of the situation.

A row of folding tables and chairs had been set up in the main aisle that ran the width of the store, just behind the checkout area. He counted fifteen civilians, mostly teenagers, sitting at the tables. They pretty much all had the same bored look that teenagers often sported these days as they apparently waited to be interviewed.

Many of them he recognized, by sight if not by name. In a town as small as Destiny, it was common to run into the same people at local stores and events, even if they never spoke. But there were still a few faces he didn't know, and some he couldn't see because they were blocked by others.

A short distance away were two more tables, each with only one civilian sitting behind it. Donna sat at one table, writing something down while her interviewee spoke animatedly with his hands to punctuate whatever he was saying. At the second table, Colby was the one asking questions, with Blake taking notes like a good apprentice should.

Colby spotted Max and waved him over. "Hey, if you're

here to help interview, we sure could use you. Drag one of those tables over here."

"Which one's Reggie?"

"Reggie?" Colby frowned and picked up a clipboard of names. "Reggie, Reggie, Reggie." He ran his finger down the line, then reversed direction. "Hmm, no Reggie here."

"You mean Gina," the man sitting across from him said. He pointed to one of the names on the sheet of paper. "Gina Oliver. We all call her Reggie."

"Why?" Colby asked.

He shrugged. "Her real name is Regina. To most people she's Gina. But to her friends, she's Reggie. Beats me why she uses that for a nickname. I like Regina a lot better."

"Which one is she?" Max asked.

The young man leaned back in his chair, scanning the faces of the other employees. "There she is, on the end."

"Red hair?" Max grabbed an extra clipboard and pen from the table.

"Nah, brown hair." He stood and pointed. "That's her, next to the redhead. The one in the green shirt."

The young woman he was pointing to looked at Max and her eyes widened—just like they had the morning of the shooting, when he'd pulled her to the floor, supposedly to protect her from the gunmen.

"Oh, she's definitely involved in this," he muttered. "She was the cashier in my line when the gunmen busted into the store."

He dropped the clipboard on the table and stalked toward her.

She jumped up from her chair and took off toward the entrance.

Max took off after her.

Some of the other workers whistled and made catcalls as Reggie shoved a display of potato chips over and raced past a cash register.

Max hurdled over the display, bags of chips crunching beneath his feet as he sprinted toward the door where she'd just disappeared. He ran through the opening and slid to a halt in front of the deputy stationed there.

"Which way?" Max demanded. "The girl who ran out of here. Which way did she go?"

He pointed to the right, and Max caught a glimpse of her brown hair before she disappeared around the corner of the building. Dang, she was fast. Remembering the layout of the store on the lot and what was behind it, he took a gamble and headed in the opposite direction.

"You're going the wrong way," the cop called behind him.

Max ignored him, pumping his arms and legs as he rounded the corner, then sprinted for the next corner. If he remembered right, the tall fence at the back of the property would force his prey back toward him. Sure enough, as soon as he reached the corner, Reggie ran out in front of him. He tackled her in midstride, turning with her in his arms to protect her as they both fell.

Her startled scream was abruptly cut off when they landed in a heap of arms and legs. Max cursed when his head slammed against the pavement, but he held on to the squirming girl.

"Stop fighting me," he ordered.

The fury in his voice must have shocked her into submission, because she immediately stilled.

The sound of running footsteps heralded the arrival of Colby, the stun gun in his hand his weapon of choice against the rowdy teenager in Max's arms. He stopped a few feet away and clipped the stun gun back on his belt.

"Looks like you got your man—or woman or child, as the case may be."

"Stop grinning and get her off me."

"Yes, sir," Colby teased. He yanked the girl up then put her on the ground again, facedown, while he cuffed her.

Max was slower to get up, brushing off his pants and then rubbing the back of his head. He winced when his fingers touched a particularly tender spot that was already becoming a knot.

"Hold still," Colby ordered as he patted down the now squirming girl, checking for weapons. He straightened, keeping one hand on Reggie's right arm. "You okay?"

"No," she whined. "He threw me down. I probably have bruises. I'm gonna sue both of you."

"I wasn't talking to you," Colby said. "I was talking to the police officer who had to chase your sorry butt."

She glared at him.

"I'm fine. Just a bump." Max lowered his hand. "Are you Gina Oliver? The one they call Reggie?"

"Depends on who's asking." If she'd been chewing gum she'd probably have spit it at him. "Why'd you chase me? I ain't done nothing."

"So it's just a coincidence that you were at the cash register when your friends came in firing automatic weapons, huh?"

She looked away. "Friends? Don't know what you're talking about. Like I said, I didn't do anything."

"Then why did you run?"

She shrugged. "You're a big guy. You scared me. I've seen TV. I know how you cops can be, beating people up for no reason."

Colby rolled his eyes. "I'll clear the break room. We can interview her in there."

Max grabbed her arm and led her around the side of the building, following Colby.

Reggie swore at him. "I'm just a minimum-wage cashier. I ain't broke any laws. I didn't do anything wrong."

"Then you've got nothing to worry about."

A few minutes later, Max had Reggie cooling her heels in the locked break room while he spoke to Colby and Donna in the hallway a few doors down, just outside the manager's office. Donna had run over to them when they brought Reggie back inside.

She was slightly out of breath from zipping across the width of the store to catch them. "Max, you'd better be careful, and fast with the questions. I just got the lowdown on Gina. She's Sam Oliver's daughter."

Max groaned. "The Olivers who live off Coonskin Hollow?"

"Yep."

Colby frowned. "I don't remember Sam Oliver. Should I?"

"He's caused some trouble here and there. Maybe you were on vacation and I was the lucky one those nights," Max said.

"It gets worse," Donna warned him. "Sam heard we brought Reggie in for another interview and is on his way over. Says to leave his girl alone and no one is to speak to her. Of course, legally, she's an adult."

"Which means I can ask her anything I want." Max checked his watch. "Lucky for me I took her phone when I patted her down again in there. And as long as no one else is allowed down this hallway, no one's going to tell her that Daddy dearest is on his way. When did he call?"

"Hasn't been that long," Donna said. "I figure if he drives the speed limit, you've got fifteen minutes."

"Meaning I probably have ten."

"That's my guess. Make it quick."

Chapter Eleven

As soon as Max stepped inside the break room, Reggie jumped out of her chair and rushed toward the door.

Max shut the door and stepped in front of her, blocking her way. "You try to leave without answering my questions and I'll slap you in jail."

"On what charges?" she demanded.

"Conspiracy to commit armed robbery, for one. I can think of at least half a dozen other charges. You don't believe me, try it."

She glared at him, then turned around in a huff and plopped down on the plastic chair.

He eyed one of the delicate-looking chairs, not confident at all that it would be able to hold him up. But he took his chances and carefully sat down. The chair squeaked in protest but seemed sturdier than it looked. He rested his forearms on the table.

"Which one of those five yokels the other day was your boyfriend?"

She shook her head. "None of them. I don't...I don't have a boyfriend."

"You're a pretty good actress. I bought your scared act and thought I was protecting you when the gunmen stormed the place. Let me guess. That whole screaming thing was to let your boyfriend know something had gone wrong with the plan. As soon as you saw me in line you were worried, because a cop being there didn't figure into the whole plan, did it?"

She wouldn't look him in the eye. "I don't know what you're talking about. Some guys with guns came in the store and one of them shot at me. If it weren't for you, I'd probably be dead. Not that I'm thanking you or anything."

"Yeah. I'm not holding my breath for a kumbaya moment with you, either."

"I don't even know what that means."

"That doesn't surprise me, either. Try going to church sometime. Learn a few hymns. Learn not to hang with gangbangers hell-bent on spending the rest of their lives in prison and dragging you with them."

She blinked, a shadow of fear flashing in her eyes before she looked away. Crossing her arms, she seemed to be trying for a jaded, world-weary look. If he hadn't seen her eyes, he'd probably have bought her routine. He wasn't kidding when he'd said she was a good actress. And he supposed there was a remote possibility that she really was telling the truth. But he wasn't counting on it. Not since Bex had told him one of the gunmen had mentioned a Reggie. He figured he'd lead with that and see where the conversation went from there.

"See, here's the thing, Reggie. I don't believe you. Wanna know why? Because one of the customers hiding in the store during the shooting overheard a couple of those gunmen talking about the whole thing. You know, the plan to go after Bex Kane? The plan where you called them when she came into the store. And later, you called them saying she was heading toward the front. I thought you looked familiar when I saw you at the register and now I know why. You walked past the deli when Bex was there. I'm guessing that was your reconnaissance so you could estimate how much longer it would be before Bex would check out. So your buddies could time it with their entrance. What did you do, fake a price check or tell the manager you needed a bathroom break when Bex walked into the store? So you could keep an eye on her and warn your buddies when it looked like she was about done shopping?"

Her eyes were like saucers now and looked like they were about to bug out of her head. He hadn't actually seen her near the deli. But based on what Bex had said, he figured she must have hidden close by, maybe one aisle over, peeking through the shelves to watch Bex. It only made sense. And from the borderline terrified expression on the girl's face now, he knew he'd guessed right.

He glanced at his watch. He didn't have much time before Reggie's father arrived. No question the man would put an end to the interview and insist on a lawyer if the cops wanted to talk to her again. Her dad was an ex-con and had no love for the police. He also knew the system, and his rights. And his daughter's.

He was lucky Reggie had even come back to the store with the other employees for an interview. The manager must have called her when her father wasn't home, or he'd never have let her come in. Max decided it was time to play hardball, to turn the screws and try to get as much info as possible before he lost his chance.

"The way I see it, Reggie, you have two options. One, I haul you off to jail and arrest you on attempted-murder charges."

"But I didn't do anything. I was with you. And then the manager put me in the cooler with the others. I had no part in this."

"I already told you I have a witness, so you can drop the act. There's no question that you knew about the assault ahead of time, helped plan it and now you're trying to cover it up. That's conspiracy to commit murder. Makes you just as guilty as if you'd worn one of those masks and pulled the trigger. You can forget college or whatever else you might have planned. You're going to spend your twenties inside a maximum-security prison."

She swallowed, hard. "What's the second option?"

He had her. If he could just get her to give him the info before Daddy dearest showed up.

"You give me their names, for starters. Oh, we know most of them. Some of them are turning deals in the hospital and lockup," he lied. He wasn't counting Lenny, since he didn't know enough to help with the case. "Then you have to tell me exactly why they were trying to kill Bex Kane."

"If…if I do that, do I still go to jail?"

"Prison, Reggie. Yeah, you're doing time no matter what. But I could put a good word in with the judge and try to get you in a minimum-security facility for a reduced sentence." He shrugged. "If you fully cooperate, who knows? Maybe you'll even get off with only probation."

He was lying through his teeth. But she didn't know that. A commotion sounded from out in the main part of the grocery store. It sounded like Colby arguing with someone—probably Reggie's father. Max was almost out of time.

"Tell me right now, Reggie. Names. Or I take you to jail."

She spewed the names out like a rapid spitting a kayak down a rain-swollen river.

He scribbled them down as the sound of yelling and shoes pounding on the floor outside got louder and louder.

"They weren't trying to kill her, either," she volunteered. "Did the ones turning deals tell you that already?"

She was so ready to sing, worried someone else would get a better deal than her. If he only had more time.

"Maybe, maybe not. Just hurry and tell me what you

know before I decide not to talk to the judge on your behalf."

"They were supposed to scare her, for one thing. And then they were gonna take her—"

More yelling sounded down the hallway, much closer now.

Reggie's eyes widened, and she looked toward the door.

Max slammed his hands down on the table, making her jump.

"Finish it, Reggie. They were going to kidnap Miss Kane? Is that what you're saying?"

"Yes. For a little while, at least. They definitely weren't wanting to kill anyone."

"You seriously expect me to believe that? They had assault rifles. They were searching for her. Of course they wanted to hurt her."

"They didn't. I swear. They were supposed to—"

"Reggie, shut your face!" A shout sounded from right outside the room. "Don't tell them cops nothing."

Her eyes widened again, and she chewed her bottom lip in indecision.

The sound of scuffles sounded from outside. Something heavy slammed against the wall. It sounded like half of the police force was trying to keep her father from coming into the room.

She obviously wasn't sure what to do. She kept glancing from the door to Max.

"Reggie, ask for a lawyer, you idiot!" her father raged outside.

She slid a look at Max, her earlier smug look returning.

"Think very carefully before you say anything else," Max warned her. "Remember, you need me to give a good word to the judge to help you get a reduced sentence. And I'll only do that if you tell me what those boys wanted when they broke into the store. What were they going to do? Why were they looking for Bex? Who hired them? Give me something, Reggie."

She looked toward the door again, where they could both hear her father yelling.

Max straightened. "Fine. You want to spend your twenties and thirties in prison, that's your choice." He turned around and strode toward the door.

"Wait!"

He turned around. "Yes?"

"They were supposed to take her someplace else. I don't know where, I swear. But they were supposed to make her talk, on camera."

"Talk about what?"

"They wanted her to confess to murdering some guy named Bobby something or other."

He grew very still. "Caldwell? Bobby Caldwell?"

"That's it. Yes. They were supposed to film her making a confession. And then they were supposed to give the film to—"

The door slammed open, the frame splintering in pieces where the locking mechanism used to be. Six-foot-six, three-hundred-pound Sam Oliver stood in the opening, looking like a bull ready to tear into a matador. He glared at Max then turned his glare on his daughter. He jabbed his finger in the air, pointing at her. "Don't tell him another damn thing."

She nodded, looking more terrified of her father than of Max, which, of course, meant his interview had just come to an end. If he'd had any doubts, they went away the second she finally found her voice again.

"I want a lawyer."

Chapter Twelve

She'd forgotten how bright and clear the night sky could be out in the country, the stars sparkling like little gems without the light pollution of a city to compete with them. Bex absently traced a finger on the arm of the white wicker couch in the little sunroom on the back of her mother's house. Only, it could be more aptly called a moon room right now, since it was past ten at night. She'd always loved this room, which her daddy had converted from a screened-in porch when she was in elementary school. He was handy like that, always doing projects around the house to make her mama happy.

"Are you okay, Bex?"

She let out a squeal of surprise and jerked around to see Max standing in the doorway between the kitchen and the sunroom. She pressed her hand to her chest, surprised her heart hadn't exploded from fright.

"Max? What on earth are you doing here? How did you even get in?"

"Sorry," he said. "Didn't mean to frighten you. I drove by, saw your lights on and decided to stop. I knocked, loudly, several times. But you must not have heard me all the way back here. When you didn't answer, I got worried so I used my key."

He held it up, then pitched it onto one of the little wicker tables scattered around the room.

"Your mom gave me that key years ago. I used to keep an eye on the place whenever she went on a trip out of town. She liked me to come inside, water her plants. But mainly she wanted me to make sure the pipes hadn't burst or anything else major happened." He cocked his head, studying Bex. "She never told me outright that she was visiting you in Knoxville. But it wasn't hard to figure out. Word gets around town when a limo shows up with out of town plates."

He stepped closer, rounding the couch. Then he stopped abruptly. Even with the room lit only by moonlight she could tell he was looking at her, his eyes glittering as they traveled down her barely clothed body.

Her face flamed hot and she grabbed an afghan off the back of the couch to cover herself. She was only wearing a nightshirt and panties. True, Max had seen her in far less. But that was a lifetime ago.

He sighed and pulled a folder out from under his arm and plopped it onto the narrow table in front of the couch. "We need to talk."

She waved toward the folder. "About whatever's in there?"

"That and more. I don't suppose I can tempt you into a late-night trip to the police station for an on-camera interview."

"Are you ever going to stop asking me that?"

"Not as long as my boss keeps bugging me to ask you."

She rolled her eyes again. "The only way I'll go there is if rocky road ice cream is involved. With fresh strawberries on top."

The corner of his mouth quirked up. "And chocolate syrup?"

"You remember."

"I remember a lot of things."

She tightened her grip on the afghan.

He gave her a sad smile this time. "This town still rolls up the streets at nine. The ice-cream parlor closed hours ago. Unless you want to grab something from Smiths? Not that a twenty-four-hour convenience store compares well to an ice-cream parlor."

If they kept skirting around memories of their shared past, she was doomed. She didn't respond to his ice-cream comments and tried to bring the conversation back to something less dangerous.

"You said you drove by and saw my lights on. I may not have been to your new house, but you said it's on land that borders your dad's property. My mom's house isn't anywhere near that."

"I didn't say I happened to be in the neighborhood. I was hoping you'd be up. Like I said, we need to talk."

"Okay, well, I guess I'll try to answer your questions. I just can't go back to the police station, okay? I'm serious. You have no idea how awful it was. Your boss locked me up in one of those cells for two days. I was eighteen and terrified. The only reason he let me out was because he didn't have enough evidence to charge me and the judge ordered me released."

"I know. I was there, remember?" His jaw worked. "Or I would have been, if you'd let me. I had to hear everything secondhand because you refused to let me visit you. The chief would have allowed that if you'd only told him to let me in."

"What did you expect me to do? You'd asked me to marry you and I turned you down. Then a few hours later I was in jail under suspicion of murder. I was confused, scared and angry. I couldn't deal with your hurt feelings on top of everything else."

His eyes flashed with anger. "My *hurt feelings*? You make it sound so trite. It was a hell of a lot more than hurt feelings. Why did you shut me out? Why didn't you..."

He closed his eyes, shaking his head. When he looked at her again, the anger seemed to have drained out of him. "This is a conversation we should have had a decade ago. It's too late to go over all that now." He flipped the folder open. "This is the reason I'm here." He spread out some pictures on the table, then frowned. "Mind if I turn on a light? The kitchen light isn't doing a lot of good out here."

She adjusted the afghan and cleared her throat. "Go ahead." She didn't bother to tell him where the switch was. He knew this house just as well as she did.

He crossed to the side wall, well away from any doorways, and leaned down by the baseboard to flip the switch. Light flooded the room from the ceiling fan overhead. He sat on the wicker chair across from her. "Your father had a thing for putting the switches in the craziest places, didn't he?"

"He called it his security system. Anyone breaking in wouldn't know how to turn on any lights."

"That's for sure. I bet it makes for some stubbed toes at night, though."

She shook her head. "I'm used to it. Except for all the boxes in the living room, of course. I'm still banging my shins against those, day or night."

His smile faded at the reminder that she was packing up the house to leave. He fanned the pictures out again.

She scooted forward, careful to keep the afghan tucked around her. "Those look like hospital photos. Five guys. The gunmen again?"

"Yeah. Better pics than the ones on my phone. Are you sure that you don't recognize any of them?"

"Do you know their names yet?" She picked up the first picture.

"We do now, yes. From a witness at the grocery store. Plus, Blake, one of the new detectives, worked with some of his contacts at his old job to corroborate the information. We'd have figured out their names anyway from their prints since they're all in the system. But that was taking a while. Regardless, I'm more interested right now in finding out whether you've seen them around, maybe watching you in the days leading up to the assault."

"Watching me? Like…stalking me?"

He nodded.

A shiver went down her spine and she set the first picture down, then carefully studied each of the remaining ones before shaking her head.

"Sorry, Max. I don't think I've seen any of these men before. Or, boys, really. How old are they?"

"They range in age from nineteen to twenty-two. But don't feel sorry for them. They're old enough to make better decisions. And this isn't their first brush with the law. They all belong to the same gang."

She gave him a sharp look. "We have gangs in Destiny now?"

He laughed without humor. "Even a town this small has its own version of gangs. But, no, they're not from here. That's why I want to make absolutely sure that you look carefully at their faces. Think back over the last few weeks, even."

After looking over the pictures again, she pitched them onto the table. "I haven't seen any of them before. They must be from Knoxville, since you're making such a big deal over whether I've seen them before."

He shuffled the pictures into the folder and leaned back against the chair. "Can't confirm or deny that."

"You don't have to. I can still read you, just like I always could." As soon as she said it, she wished she could take the words back. "I'm sorry. I'm not trying to rehash the past. Really, I'm not. It just seems like every conversation we have takes us there, sooner or later."

"Don't apologize. Sitting with you here is…weird,

strange. Not what I expected I'd be doing this week, that's for sure."

She smiled. "Me neither."

He checked his watch, then swore beneath his breath.

"My mama would have washed your mouth out with soap for that back in the day."

He grinned. "You're right. She would have. Guess I've picked up some bad habits I need to work on. I'll get to the point, since it's getting late. We've made a lot of progress on the investigation."

"Which one?"

He stilled. "Sorry, I forgot to tell you about Marcia with everything else that's been going on. She confessed to shooting the rifle but swears it was only to scare you. She said it wasn't planned, that she had her gun in her car and after seeing you here with me she got to thinking about Bobby—whom she fancied her boyfriend, even though from what I remember he was always telling her to get lost—and as she was driving away she pulled over and decided to try to scare you just to make herself feel better, I guess. She thinks you killed him."

She rubbed her hands up and down her arms. "Her and about half the town."

He didn't bother to deny the obvious. Half the town, or more, did think she'd killed Bobby Caldwell. She shivered again.

"Are you cold?" He started to shrug out of his jacket.

"No, no. I'm fine. Thanks. So you let Marcia go, right?"

"Hell, no. I want you to press charges against her for attempted murder."

"But she wasn't trying to kill me."

He gave her an incredulous look. "She shot a rifle at you."

She shook her head. "If she was trying to kill me, I'd be dead, wouldn't I? Marcia was an amazing shot even back

in high school. If she says she was just trying to scare me,
I believe her."

He shook his head. "You're saying you don't want to
press charges."

"That's what I'm saying."

He shook his head again. "Unbelievable. Fine, I'll tell
the chief. Back to the grocery store investigation. I've got
some questions for you. But first let me explain a few
things. I probably shouldn't be telling you any of this.
Well, no probably about it. The investigation is confiden-
tial, and I need your word that you won't share these details with anyone else."

"It's not like I'm receiving social invitations in this
town. Who would I tell?"

"I'm serious. Your lawyer, a clerk at the bank, anyone
at all. Not a word."

"Okay, okay. I won't tell anyone."

"When you and I talked at the diner, you told me that
one of the gunmen said Reggie told them a woman was
heading toward the checkout. That set off alarm bells for
me. It sounded like the gunmen had inside information,
someone inside the store, maybe an employee, letting them
know when it was the right time to come inside."

"The right time? Like when there weren't that many
customers?"

"More like when *you* were inside."

"Me? You really were serious earlier when you said I
might have been the target?"

He slowly nodded.

She listened in stunned disbelief as he told her about a
cashier named Reggie who'd partnered with the gunmen.
Her hand shook as she pulled the afghan closer. "You're
saying that someone is trying to…kidnap me? They want
to force me to…confess?"

"According to Reggie, yes."

"Well. I guess we know who's behind that. It's Mr. Caldwell, Bobby's father. Has to be."

He nodded. "Makes sense. That's the first person I thought of, too. He's got plenty of money, owns thousands of acres of farmland in this county, and his family comes from old money up in Chattanooga. Plus, he's made no secret over the years that he always thought you did it. After all, you and Bobbie had a…history."

She frowned and was about to dress him down when he held up a hand to stop her.

"I'm not blaming the victim here. I know he stalked you during your senior year. *History* was the wrong word."

"You think? Yet another reason I'm no fan of your boss, by the way. He didn't do anything to stop Bobby. No one did."

He winced.

She immediately regretted her outburst. "Except you. I know you tried to help me, got yourself in trouble more times than I can count by going after him."

"Fat lot of good it did. His father's security guys tossed me on my butt just about every time before I could get close to Bobby. I'm really sorry, Bex. I'm sorry I didn't do more. I know it was a really tough time for you."

"Tough?" She fisted her hands in the afghan. "No one could help me—not the school, not my mom, not you, not the police. I was miserable, Max. My life was a living hell that year." She sucked in a breath and looked at him, too late wishing she could recall her words. "I don't mean that you and I—I mean, it was also the best year."

"After Bobby was found," he continued, as if she'd never spoken, "his father kept lobbying Thornton to arrest you. But, like you said, there was never enough evidence. So after that initial forty-eight hours in the cell, he had to let you go."

"Yeah, nice guy. Holding a terrified teenager in jail after ignoring her calls for help for nearly a year."

"Bex, that was a long time ago. Looking back, can't you see there was more to it than that? He was also protecting you. From Bobby's father. Those two days were a cooling-off period for everyone. Thornton feels terrible about failing you, not being able to do anything about the stalking without proof. He was determined to protect you from the fallout."

"Let me guess," she said. "He told you that? Because he sure hasn't ever said anything like that to me."

"Not exactly. But I was there, too, spoke to him more than you in those early days, since you wouldn't let me visit you. I figured out what he was doing even if he was too gruff and stubborn to explain his actions." He shook his head. "He's never been one to explain himself. But I've worked with him since I graduated. Aside from odd jobs on farms and mowing yards, being a cop in Destiny is the only real job I've ever had. So I've had plenty of time to get to know him. He's a good man, Bex. Locking you up wasn't out of meanness or because he really thought you'd killed Bobby. Believe it or not, he cared what happened to you."

She stared past him, through the windows to the dark backyard, illuminated only by moonlight. Max might be able to see some good in Thornton. But she'd never experienced anything but the harsh reality of a policeman who did things by the book and wouldn't help her no matter how many times she pleaded for him to stop the stalking. And then the moment something happened to Bobby, he'd locked her up. She'd never forgive him for that.

"You think Robert Caldwell Senior hired those men to go after me?" she asked, refusing to discuss Thornton anymore.

He let out a deep sigh. "I think it's possible, highly likely. But while some of the other guys track down that lead and talk to Mr. Caldwell, I'm here to talk to you. Bex—"

"You want me to tell you about that night."

He nodded. "Your mother, God rest her soul, thought she was protecting you by not letting you talk to the police back then. But the problem is that it only makes you look guilty. Bobby's father has built this up in his mind for years, convinced that because you left town, you must have been guilty."

"I didn't leave until two weeks later. It's not like I just disappeared overnight."

"Doesn't make much difference. You never gave a statement. The investigation stagnated because of it. In Caldwell's eyes, you're guilty. Period. And he's gone ten years without someone paying for his son's death. You show up in town, he hears about it and bam, gunmen raid the store when you're there and go searching for you, paid by some anonymous guy."

"Anonymous?"

He nodded. "One of the gunmen in the hospital wanted to cut a deal. But the deal was to give us the identity of whoever hired him and the others to go after you. He couldn't give us his identity."

"How much money are we talking?"

"Ten thousand dollars. Each."

"Wow. Fifty thousand dollars is more than the average person could afford. But ten thousand apiece wasn't exactly making those guys rich. I wouldn't risk my freedom for a penny less than a million," she joked.

"I didn't say they were smart."

She smiled. "What exactly do you need from me? Do you want me to say I didn't do it? That I didn't kill Bobby?"

"That would be a good place to start."

The silence stretched out between them.

"Bex—"

"You need to leave."

His brows raised. "Back up. What just happened here?"

"Nothing happened. It's late and I'm exhausted. I need to get some sleep. So do you." Holding the afghan around her like a robe, she stood and headed into the kitchen.

Max followed her. She could hear him close and lock the door to the sunroom behind him. By the time he caught up to her, she had the front door standing wide-open.

His gaze flicked to the door, then to her. "What time do you get up in the morning? I'll bring breakfast and then we can continue with our conversation."

She shook her head. "I'm not answering any more questions. Don't bother stopping by."

His brows lowered in a deep slash. "I'm trying to help you, Bex."

"No. You're trying to solve a case and you think that by dredging up the past you'll find some clue. Well, you can do that all you want, but you'll have to do it without me."

He stepped closer, looking down at her with a deep frown wrinkling his brow. "I could arrest you for obstructing a police investigation."

"Go ahead. Then you and Thornton can share some stories over a couple of beers about how you both threw me in jail."

His eyes narrowed, but not before she saw the flash of hurt in them.

Her shoulders slumped. "I'm sorry, Max. I shouldn't have said—"

He stepped through the door without another word.

Chapter Thirteen

Bex towel-dried the breakfast dishes and packed them into a box. That was the last of them. From here on out, however many days she had left in Destiny, she'd use paper plates and disposable utensils. Tomorrow was trash day. She'd empty the refrigerator tonight and set the bags at the curb.

She'd already had her RAV4 taken to Eddie's to get the windshield fixed. Ralph, the owner, was going to sell her mom's Taurus for her. Movers were scheduled to arrive later in the week to take the boxes she'd designated to go to her condo in Knoxville. Then, as soon as her lawyer gave the okay, an auction company would hold an estate sale for everything else, including the house. In just a few short weeks, it would be as if her mother had never even existed.

A sob escaped before Bex even registered the tears flowing down her cheeks. Her knees buckled and she sagged to the floor.

"Oh, Mama. Mama, Mama, Mama. I miss you so much."

The grief hit her like a tidal wave, pushing her under, drowning her in darkness and sorrow. She'd cried when she'd first gotten the call from the hospital, of course. But that was nothing compared to the paralyzing pain that racked her now. She curled into a ball and cried until it seemed like there was no moisture left in her body to form any tears, until her throat ached from the strength of her sobs. And then she fell into an exhausted slumber right there on the kitchen floor.

When she woke up, only a short time had passed. But it felt like a lifetime. Her lifetime, her mother's, her family's. Nothing would ever be the same again. She'd never hear her mother's voice on the phone. Never see her smiling face when the limo pulled up to Bex's condo for one of her mom's trips to Knoxville. Never swap much-loved books in the mail with favorite passages highlighted in pink. Bex had thought she'd dealt with her grief before coming back to Destiny. But apparently she'd had to see the house all packed up to really push her over the edge and make her face her tremendous loss.

Feeling bruised from the emotional hit she'd just taken, she pushed herself up to sitting and rubbed her bleary eyes. This little house had been her home for eighteen years. She'd been happy here, the doted upon only child of two incredibly loving parents. Now both of them were gone. And Bex wasn't sure how she could go on without them.

She was tempted to curl back into a ball. But she could almost see her mother scowling at her and telling her to "suck it up, Buttercup." Her mom never suffered whining or pity parties. Bex wasn't going to insult her memory now by ignoring all the life lessons her mama had taught her.

After replenishing her parched body with a bottle of water, Bex went outside to check the mail that she'd forgotten to check yesterday. That was one more thing she needed to do, set up a forwarding address. She supposed she could do that online tonight.

The bodyguard assigned to watch her this morning sat in his SUV parked in the grass across the street, no longer bothering to pretend that she didn't know about them.

She waved and he waved back. Having him there made her feel safe. But she cringed at the thought of how much the twenty-four-hour security was costing Max. As soon as she sold her mom's house she'd pay him back. She'd caused enough problems for him. Having him lose his savings wasn't going to be added to that list.

She opened the mailbox and pulled out the short stack of envelopes—a final bill from the funeral home, the electric bill and a manila envelope with no return address or stamp. She hesitated, a cold prickle of unease flashing through her.

It wasn't uncommon for people this far from town to stick a note in each other's mailboxes. It was most likely a note from one of her mother's friends, wishing her condolences. But with everything that had happened since her fateful trip to the Piggly Wiggly, the envelope took on a more sinister appearance.

The sound of shoes crunching on dried leaves had her looking up to see the bodyguard crossing the road toward her. He stopped in front of her.

"Miss Kane, I'm Neil Granger. I couldn't help noticing the worry on your face. Something wrong?"

"Maybe. It seems silly, really, but this—"

"Didn't go through the post office." He frowned down at the envelope. "Mind if I open it?"

Since he was already pulling on a pair of latex gloves, she didn't bother answering. When he was ready, she handed it to him.

"Please step back," he said.

Her throat tightened at his request. Did he think someone had hidden something dangerous inside? It didn't seem possible, as thin as the envelope was. But she stepped back anyway, watching him carefully pat down the surface and examine the edges before pulling the flap open. He peeked inside, then his posture seemed to relax and he motioned her forward.

"It's some kind of picture." He reached in and pulled it

out. His gaze shot to hers, and he slowly turned the picture around.

Bex blinked in shock as the proof of her sins stared up at her from an eight-by-ten glossy photo. She couldn't fool herself any longer. This wasn't something she could run away from again. It was time to finally face her past.

MAX PROPPED HIS booted feet on top of his desk and leaned back in his chair, watching the sun burn away the last of the morning fog through the police station windows. Yet another chilly day had dawned with no viable leads about who had arranged for the gangbangers to go after Bex in the grocery store. To say that he was getting frustrated was an understatement.

One desk over from him in the expansive squad room, Colby was leaning back in his chair, too. Both of them had the case files up on their computer monitors and were tossing theories back and forth.

"The Marcia thing is still bothering me," Colby said.

"Tell me about it. I didn't expect her to be released so quickly. She should be toughing it out in a jail cell right now."

Colby jabbed a thumb over his shoulder at the chief, who was talking to Donna by the interrogation room. "His orders. When you didn't call back saying Miss Kane wanted to press charges, he wouldn't let us lock her up. Sorry, man."

"Nothing you could do. I'd just feel better if she wasn't on the loose with that rifle. If she told us the truth, then her emotions are running high and impairing her judgment. What's to stop her from deciding to go after Bex again?"

"And if she's lying?"

"Then maybe whoever hired the gang to hold up the grocery store hired her, too. What did we find on Caldwell senior? Do we have anything at all to link him to any of this? His belief that Bex killed his son is no secret. And he certainly has the funds to hire anyone he wants to do just about anything."

Colby dipped his head in acknowledgment. "Donna's been following that angle and so far she's got nothing. Obviously he's too sick right now to have gone to Knoxville. And we can't get a look at his finances to look for payments to any thugs without a warrant. Trust me. Donna tried. But the judge turned her down, said he needs something more than conjecture."

"Did she interview him?"

"Officially, no. He's refusing to talk to us. But she caught up to him outside the hospital before one of his chemo treatments. She barraged him with questions as his son, Deacon, pushed his father into the hospital. Didn't do any good and his lawyer called the chief later threatening a lawsuit for harassment if we pulled something like that again."

Max shook his head. "Other than what I got from Lenny Stinsky, we've got nothing from the shooters, either. None of them are talking. I'll give it to Caldwell senior, or whoever is behind this, they picked the right thugs to hire. Or maybe threatened them with some dire consequence if they talked."

He tapped his right hand on his thigh, thinking it through. "Lenny and the other one who was shot are still in the hospital. Maybe we can play them against each other, even with their lawyers present, and get one of them to take a deal."

"I thought Lenny Stinsky didn't know the name of the guy who hired them. That only leaves the Chucky guy. And he's a hard-core criminal. I don't see us getting him to go for a deal."

"He's facing hard time for the grocery store holdup."

Colby shrugged. "You can try to talk to him. I certainly didn't have any luck."

"Maybe I'll head over there in a little bit." Max tapped his thigh again. "Even if he doesn't have a name, he's got to have a better description, maybe even of the make and model of the car. If we can narrow it down, get the specific date when it happened, too, we might generate a viable lead on who was in that car that night."

"Like I said, I already tried. But hey, maybe after stewing in the hospital for a few days he's softened up. Or getting worried about heading to jail when he gets discharged. Caldwell seems like the logical money man. Maybe one of his security guys is the man who drove to Knoxville. I can work up a list of everyone who works for him and—"

"Already did."

They both turned to see Donna standing a few feet away. The chief was still on the far side of the room, talking to Blake this time.

"Did what?" Colby asked.

"Got a list of everyone working for Caldwell. I've even spoken to a few of them. But they all, of course, insist they haven't been to Knoxville. And ever since I tried to talk to their boss at the hospital, I'm persona non grata at the Caldwell estate. I haven't given up. But I'm spending most of my time on the computer looking into everyone instead of interviewing them. Slow going."

"Let's assume Caldwell is the money guy and one of his security guys hired the thugs," Colby said. "Why now? If his goal was to get Bex to confess to murdering his son, why wait ten years to go after her?"

"Cancer," Max answered. "He's going through chemo. And he sure didn't look well when I saw him at his lawyer's office. Maybe he decided he's got nothing to lose by breaking the law and going after Bex. Maybe getting her to confess to murdering his son and going to prison is his last dying wish. Who else has a motive to want her to confess?"

"Marcia Knolls," Donna and Colby both said at the same time.

Max slowly nodded. "She's got motive. She loved Bobby and has always blamed Bex for his death. But the same question goes for her. Why wait ten years?"

Donna frowned and looked deep in thought.

Colby shrugged. "Beats me. Unless seeing Bex in town was enough to make Marcia go ballistic, like she did when she shot that rifle. Her family has a big farm outside of town. They aren't exactly hurting financially. Maybe she's got a piece of that pie and decided to use it to hire those wackos to scare Bex into confessing."

"Okay," Max said. "Robert Caldwell Senior and Marcia Knolls are still suspects. And we still have nothing concrete to charge either one."

Colby and Donna exchanged a frustrated look.

"There's something else bothering me about this whole thing," Max continued. "If the goal is to get Bex to confess, why make such a public thing out of it? Those thugs could have kidnapped Bex at her mom's house at any time since she got here. She doesn't have any neighbors close by. It would have been easy. So why wait until she's in the grocery store to go after her? Either of you have a theory on that?"

"Not me," Donna said. "And the chief's waving me over again. Probably to fuss at me for pushing so hard on the Caldwells again." She rolled her eyes and headed toward the other side of the room.

"I don't have a theory either," Colby said.

"I might," Max said. "But it's a bit out there. I was hoping you had something better."

"Well, I don't so you might as well share. Who knows? Maybe you're onto something. Spill."

Blake, who'd just sat down at his desk two rows over, must have heard their conversation, because he suddenly rolled his chair over in front of Colby's desk and crossed his arms, daring either of them to tell him to go away.

Colby frowned, obviously unimpressed with Blake's challenging posture. "Don't you have something to do? Like issue parking tickets down Main Street?"

"Leave him alone," Max said.

Colby's mouth twitched, and Max knew he was trying to hold back a smile. Picking on the new guy was more of a habit than anything else at this point. But Blake was a serious kind of guy and was getting more and more wound up. For both Blake's and Colby's sakes, it was time to move on and let the new guy start contributing.

"What's your theory?" Colby asked.

The relief on Blake's face was palpable. He sat at attention in his chair, eagerly waiting to hear what Max had to say.

"Okay, the Pig isn't far from the station, so as soon as a nine-one-one call went out, it was only a matter of minutes before some uniformed cops would show up, a few minutes more for the SWAT team since they had to gear up. And it's right in the middle of the main business area where most of our restaurants and shops are."

"Right," Colby said. "Which doesn't make sense, as you already said."

"It doesn't make sense if your goal is to get Bex to confess. But what if that isn't the goal?"

Colby frowned. "We already know that was the goal. That's the only useful information Lenny gave us."

"No. Lenny said the goal was to scare Bex. Reggie's the one who said they were going to kidnap her to tape a confession. We don't have corroboration on that yet. But Lenny isn't exactly a genius. He didn't ask questions and didn't really care why he did what he did. He was in it for the money, doing whatever Chucky told him to do. Maybe he thought the goal was to scare Bex. But he wasn't told the real reason for the Piggly Wiggly assault."

Colby nodded. "Okay. I'm with you. But you're thinking the real reason wasn't to kidnap Bex either?"

"Look at who was hired for the job. Budding criminals, gang members who want to prove to other gang members that they're tough, who think they're way more badass than they really are. Too stupid to think through the odds and realize they probably wouldn't make it out of that store without being caught. They saw easy money, something fun and illegal to add to their résumés to make them look even cooler to the rest of the gang. Heck, maybe the three without gang tats were doing it to earn full gang membership."

"Yeah. So?"

"Then you've got Lenny. Younger than the rest, a new gang member. Not hardened yet. He's a weak link, a really weak link. As soon as we started questioning him and threatening him with the usual cop lies, he started singing, told us everything he knew—which wasn't much, but the end result could very well be exactly what whoever planned this whole thing wanted."

Blake leaned forward, resting his arms on the edge of Colby's desk. "The guy behind it wanted the gunmen to be caught?"

Colby frowned at him, then looked at Max. "Is that your theory?"

"Yes, but follow it through to its logical conclusion. The guy behind this wanted the whole incident to be public so everyone in town would hear about it. And he was counting on Lenny to squeal. His goal wasn't to capture Miss Kane. His goal was to force the police to look into the Bobby Caldwell case again."

Colby blinked in surprise. "Makes sense in a weird

kind of way. We always investigate the victim's past to see if there's a connection. That means looking at the old Caldwell case, too. You may be right. Pretty brilliant, in a sick kind of way. Which points the finger right back at Bobby Caldwell's father again. Robert Caldwell is bitter enough and rich enough to pull it off. And we already said he has nothing left to lose since he's terminally ill."

"What about the brother?" Blake asked.

"Deacon," Max said. "You think he might be behind this?"

"I think we should look into him, too, before jumping to any conclusions."

Colby narrowed his eyes. "Now look here, I'm not jumping to—"

"Stop," Max ordered. "You're both right. We need to focus on looking for a tangible link between any of the Caldwells and the gunmen. They had M16s. Those are military-issue. Deacon is ex-military. Maybe he's in on this and managed to get his hands on those guns. Has anyone traced the serial numbers yet?"

"Randy did that the first day," Colby said. "They're part of a shipment that was labeled as destroyed because they failed inspection. We're still following that angle to see how they ended up in those gangbangers' hands instead of being melted down for parts. Caldwell senior is ex-military, too, and a gun collector. Wouldn't surprise me if he's got some contacts who helped him get his hands on those rifles—assuming he's involved."

"It's all speculation for now but we need to follow the trail," Max said. "We're still right back to where we were. But having talked it all through, I feel like we're on the right track. We just have to hit them hard, help Donna dig up any information we can to piece together what the Caldwells and their hired hands were doing since Bex came to town. We need timelines, dates, places, witnesses.

Let's get some pictures together of everyone who works for the Caldwells and circulate those around, see if anyone can help us build those timelines. We can show those pictures to some of the rental car companies in Knoxville to see whether they recognize any of them, since I highly doubt the Caldwells or their men would use their own car when they hired those gangbangers. It's highly likely they rented one."

"That's good," Colby said. "I can follow up on the alibis and rental angles."

"I can help," Blake offered. "I can get the car companies in Knoxville to give us information without making us try to get a warrant, which we probably can't get right now."

"You're right," Colby agreed. "We probably couldn't get a warrant. Do it. That sounds good."

Blake jumped up and rolled his chair back to his desk. The sound of the keyboard clicking quickly followed.

"What about Marcia Knolls?" Colby said. "Are we not looking at her anymore?"

"I think we shouldn't rule anyone out yet. We'll work on a timeline for her as well, track her movements since Bex got into town. Who knows, maybe someone will remember seeing her talking to one of the Caldwells or their hired hands."

Colby stood and grabbed his jacket from the back of his chair.

"Where are you going?" Max asked.

"To the hospital. I'm going to see if I can't put the screws on Chucky and Lenny and get a make and model on that car."

"Sounds good." Max stood. "I'll go with you. We can play good cop, bad cop."

"Only if I get to be the bad cop this time," Colby teased.

"We'll toss a coin."

Colby laughed and they both rounded their desks.

Max stopped, staring at the double glass front doors of the squad room. One of the bodyguards he'd hired was opening the door. And behind him was Bex.

BEX'S DARK HAIR swirled around her. She clutched her jacket closed against the light wind that was a precursor to the storm that Mable Humphries had predicted days ago.

Beside Max, Colby said, "Wow. Never thought I'd see her voluntarily come here. You think maybe something else happened?"

That was exactly what Max was worried about. Bex's face was paler than he'd ever seen it. And he couldn't think of a single reason for her bodyguard to have brought her here unless something terrible had happened.

As soon as she saw Max, a look of relief seemed to pass over Bex's face and she hurried toward him.

"Max, thank goodness. Are you okay?" she asked, her eyes searching his.

Max frowned in confusion at the bodyguard standing next to her before looking at her again. "I'm fine. What happened? Did someone try to shoot you again?"

Her eyes widened. "No. No, nothing like that." She half turned and motioned toward the man beside her. "Mr. Granger, the picture please."

"What picture?" Max asked.

In answer, the bodyguard held up a manila envelope. Max noted he was wearing a latex glove, so he automatically grabbed one for himself out of the top drawer of the closest desk and yanked it on before taking the envelope.

The frightened look on Bex's face, and the way she kept glancing at the chief on the other side of the room still talking to Donna, told Max something was very wrong. The little hairs were standing up on the back of his neck. And he didn't like the determined glint in Bex's eyes, like she'd made some kind of important decision. Whatever had brought her here, he wished she'd spoken to him in private about it first.

"That was in my mailbox this morning," she explained. "The mail comes in the afternoon. But I forgot to check it yesterday. As soon as I saw what was inside, I had Mr. Granger drive me straight here."

Max pulled out the picture, then stared at it in surprise. Whatever he'd expected, it wasn't this—an eight by ten of himself walking into the police station.

Paint had been used to draw a red circle on his back. Special care had been taken to make the circle look like the crosshairs of a rifle. But that wasn't what worried him. What worried him were the words, also in red, painted across the bottom—CONFESS OR ELSE.

The meaning was clear. Whoever had sent this to Bex wanted her to confess or they would kill Max. It didn't take a genius to know what they wanted her to confess—that she'd killed Bobby Caldwell. He turned the envelope over.

"No stamp. No return address." He looked at the body-guard. "Were you on duty when the mail came?"

"No."

"It doesn't matter who was on duty," Bex said. "I wasn't home when the mail came. I was running errands."

"And the bodyguards are watching you, not your house," Max said.

"Exactly," she agreed.

Footsteps sounded off to Max's right. The chief was heading toward them.

Bex sighed. "That picture is karma I suppose, telling me it's time to face my past." She laughed nervously.

Max's gut clenched with dread. This was suddenly one conversation he did not want to have with a station full of cops listening.

"Miss Kane," the chief said as he stopped beside Max.

"Thank you for finally coming in. Let's go right to the interview room. We have a lot to discuss."

She swallowed and looked past him to the room at the front left corner of the station, a wide window clearly showing the table and chairs inside. "O-okay."

Thornton smiled like a Cheshire cat and crossed the room. He held the door to the interview room open and waved his other hand for Bex to join him.

She started toward him.

"No." Max stepped in front of her, blocking her way.

She frowned. "Max, it's okay. This is what I expected to happen. I can't hide from the past forever. I need to tell you what happened the night that—"

"Shut up, Bex."

Her eyes widened with surprise.

"Now listen here," Thornton half shouted from across the room. "Sounds like Miss Kane has important information pertinent to our investigation. You need to be very careful about what you're doing, son."

Max ignored his boss. He frowned down at Bex. "You need to go back home. Now."

She shook her head, apparently trying to be brave even though she was trembling. "I can't. You're in danger. Don't you see? And it's my fault. I have to tell you what I—"

"Not one more word." He grabbed her hand and hauled her toward the exit.

Chapter Fourteen

Bex stared through the windshield of Max's truck as he raced down a gravel road, far faster than she'd have dared but somehow managing to maintain complete control. The truck stayed smoothly on the road, without those scary slides toward the ditch that always happened when she went over thirty on one of these back roads.

"I don't understand," she said. "You've been trying to get me to go to the station for an interview and the moment I do, you practically kidnap me to shut me up. And then send my bodyguard away."

"I'm your bodyguard now. I'm protecting you from yourself."

He slowed the truck, then turned down another gravel road, this one even more narrow than the last. If they came across someone coming the other way, she had no idea how they'd pass each other.

"Max, where are we going?"

In answer, he slowed even more and waved his hand toward the windshield. The trees thinned out and gave way to a wide expanse of cleared land with only an occasional shade tree dotting the rolling hills. Winter grass was coming up new and thick, turning the dried brown summer grass into a gorgeous green swath of color. And on the top of the hill a football-field length away was an impressive looking log cabin. The front was dominated by a large glass A-frame in the middle and a covered porch that appeared to run all the way around the cabin. The roofline was irregular, pitched sharply in places, hinting at massive open spaces inside.

He pulled his truck up in front of the porch and killed the engine.

"Yours?" she asked.

"Yep. Let's get inside before this storm breaks."

She leaned forward, peering up at the dark clouds swirling overhead. Before she'd even managed to open her door, Max was lifting her out. She put her hands on his shoulders until he set her on her feet, then quickly stepped away, trying not to think about how good it had felt to be in his arms again.

"I could have gotten down by myself." She motioned toward the metal steps on the side of his truck.

"I know." He directed her up the porch steps and followed behind.

Feeling his gaze on her, her face flamed with heat and she found herself wishing she'd put on something nicer than a pair of jeans and a plain white blouse. And that, in turn, had her angry with herself for caring about her looks, and Max, when that was the last thing she should be thinking about right now.

She stopped at the glass door set into the wall of A-shaped glass that allowed her to see into the expansive two-story foyer and main room. The back wall was A-frame glass, too, with an even more breathtaking view of a gorgeous lake and the rolling hills beyond.

"What an incredible home. And the view is amazing."

He unlocked the door and shoved it open. "I like it."

"Like it? This is paradise." She hurried inside, drinking in the warm golden tones of the log walls, the soaring ceiling with its massive beams. The circular metal chandelier entwined with deer antlers, suspended from a heavy chain in the middle of the room. The furniture was dark brown leather with metal beading. Chunky wooden end tables and a massive coffee table took up the rest of the sitting space in the center, with lots of open floor surrounding them. The whole place was incredibly masculine, elegant in its simplicity, uncluttered.

As he took their jackets and hung them on hooks beside the door, she said, "This place suits you. It looks like you made all your dreams come true—working as a cop, having a gorgeous piece of land away from town. I'm happy for you."

He cocked his head, studying her. "What about you? Did your dreams come true?"

The only dream she'd ever had was to spend her life with him. She stepped away from him and stood looking out the back wall of glass at the water, beaten into small whitecaps by the wind.

The sound of clinking glass had her glancing over her shoulder. Max stood at one end of the room, pouring drinks at a bar built out of what appeared to be old barn wood, stained honey gold like the rest of the cabin.

He joined her by the windows and handed her a glass. "Something relaxing, like old times. Still like bourbon and Coke?"

She smiled and took it from him. "Still do. Even though I wasn't even legal drinking age back when we shared a few of these."

He leaned against the wood frame, facing her. "There were a lot of things we did that we shouldn't have back then. Our parents would have been furious if they knew."

She almost choked on her drink, coughed, then gave him a watery smile. "Don't you know it. My mama would have killed me if she realized half the nights I was supposed to be staying with a friend I was sneaking out to be with you."

His brows raised. "You really think your mom didn't suspect what was going on? I practically lived at your house, we spent so much time together. You don't think she figured out you were sneaking out to be with me the rest of the time?"

She shrugged. "She was a smart lady. I suppose she might have known and turned a blind eye. She loved you like the son she never had. You won her over just like you won…" She stopped and shook her head.

"Just like I won you over?" he said.

She nodded, seeing no point in denying it. How could she? She'd loved him since she was twelve or thirteen.

He sipped his drink, his gaze never leaving her face. He took both their drinks and set them aside on the brick hearth of the fireplace not far from the doors. Then, very slowly, he leaned down, giving her every chance to turn away, and he kissed her.

She closed her eyes, melting against him, her arms, as if of their own will, sliding up his chest to wrap around the back of his neck. He cupped her head, his other hand caressing her back, his thumb tracing little circles against her skin through the thin fabric of her blouse.

The kiss wasn't rushed or frantic as many of their kisses had been when they were teens. This kiss was more of an exploration, more of a question, hesitant but confident, if there was such a thing. It was as if he wanted her to give him the green light or tell him to stop. There was heat, but it was carefully banked. A fire ready to burn, but ruthlessly held back. All it did was frustrate her and leave her wanting more.

She broke the kiss and shoved out of his arms. She gave a nervous laugh and retrieved her glass from the hearth.

"Will you have to confess to one of your interns that you kissed me? I'd hate to get in the middle of a happy couple."

She downed the rest of the drink in one swallow, then had to swipe at her eyes when the burn had them watering.

"I wouldn't have kissed you if I was still dating someone else." His tone was clipped, his eyes cold.

She regretted her words as soon as she'd said them. Apparently Marcia's earlier gibe about Max and interns had struck deeper than Bex had realized. Not that it should matter. Max wasn't hers, could never be hers again. She needed to remember that.

She moved into the kitchen, separated from the living area by a black granite–topped island. After washing her glass out in the sink, she set it on the drain rack to dry.

"You didn't need to do that," he said, his voice quiet but the deep timbre carrying easily through the massive space.

She shrugged and crossed to one of the couches. Worried that he might sit beside her, she chose one of the recliners instead, kicking off her leather loafers and pulling her legs up. "You didn't need to bring me out here to talk, either. I could have done my talking at the station. All you did was delay the inevitable."

He set his glass down on the coffee table and sat on the end of the couch closest to her. "What's inevitable?"

She rubbed her hands up and down her arms, even though she wasn't cold. "The inevitable is that you'll just have to take me back to the station again."

"Why? So you can confess to something you didn't do, just because you think you're protecting me?"

She shook her head. "No, Max. I would confess to something that I *did* do, in order to protect you. I'm guilty. I killed Bobby Caldwell."

Chapter Fifteen

"I don't believe you," Max said.

Bex stared at him. He was calmly sitting on the couch, proclaiming his belief in her innocence.

"I thought you'd be shocked, or angry, or...something, when I finally confessed. I didn't expect you to refuse to believe the truth."

"Oh, I believe that you believe you killed him. That's something I suspected all along. It explains why you wouldn't see me when the chief threw you in jail. It explains why you left town the first chance you could. And it also explains why you stayed away so long. But do I think you could actually murder someone? Not a chance in hell."

Her fingers curled against the arm of the chair. "So, what, I hallucinated the whole thing? Some cop you are. The guilty party confesses and you ignore the confession."

He let out a deep sigh. "Bex, something awful happened to you after you left me that night. I think Bobby was probably stalking you again, maybe he lured you somewhere, or forced you to his cabin. He tried to rape you, maybe he did rape you—"

She shook her head. "No."

His jaw tightened and he nodded, a look of relief flashing across his features. "But he attacked you. And you fought back. If he died as a result of that, it was self-defense. Not murder."

Unable to sit still, she jumped to her feet and began pacing across the room. "It's not that simple." She rubbed her hands up and down her arms. "Yes, Bobby tricked me into going to his cabin that night. Yes, he attacked me, and I fought back. I may not have meant to kill him, but I did." She stopped pacing. "Self-defense?" She laughed bitterly. "Of course it was. But who would have believed me?"

"I would. I do. I would have helped you, if you'd given me a chance."

"All that would have done was destroy your dream to become a police officer. Thornton wouldn't have overlooked that you were siding with me. Trust me—he believes I'm a murderer, and he believed it back then, too."

"That's because you wouldn't talk. You refused to say anything in your defense."

"I couldn't. You know how things were. Bobby had been stalking me and making my life hell. But he was too clever to do it in front of others where I'd have proof. He manipulated everyone into thinking I was the crazy one making up stories about him. His father would have painted me out to have been the one to lure him to that cabin. And he would have said that I did that in order to kill him for making me look like a fool. He was rich enough, and blind enough when it came to Bobby, to make everyone believe him. I'd have gone to prison for the rest of my life. That's why I couldn't tell anyone. My only hope to avoid prison was to keep my mouth shut and hope that there wasn't enough evidence to prosecute me."

"Then why confess now?"

"You know why. Someone—probably Bobby's father— is trying to bring up the past, make me face what happened. If I don't—"

"They'll kill me? Good grief, Bex. I'm a police officer. I know how to take care of myself. I don't want you to be a sacrificial lamb on my behalf, especially when you're innocent."

She crossed her arms. "Am I innocent if I was glad he died? Because I am. That sounds terrible. And I've felt guilty for years over not feeling guilty about that, if that even makes sense. I know I shouldn't be relieved that someone lost their life. But Bobby was sick, evil. And I know that he would have killed me eventually if he hadn't died that night."

He stood and stepped in front of her to stop her pacing. Then he put his hands on her shoulders, making her face him.

"You have nothing to feel guilty about. Looking back, with my years of experience behind me, I've no doubt that you're right. He would have killed you eventually, or tried to. But I would have protected you, Bex. If you'd only let me."

She blinked away the moisture that was suddenly in her eyes. "I told you it's not that simple. It never was."

He tilted her chin up. "Because you wanted to protect me. Don't you realize it's my job to protect you, not the other way around?"

She shook her head. Because he was wrong. Bobby's friends had beaten up Max more than once in that terrible year when Bobby was harassing her. It was only a matter of time before something terrible happened to Max. And it was her fault, for somehow drawing the attention of someone like Bobby. She couldn't let Max pay the price for her failures.

"Bex," he said, his deep voice soft, but with a thread of steel underlying it that hadn't been there when they'd been teenagers. "There's absolutely nothing to gain at this point in bringing any of this up now. Leaving town like you did back then was like running away. It only made you look guilty in the eyes of most. And it makes claiming self-defense this many years later extremely hard to prove. Which is why you have to be quiet. No confessions."

She shook her head. "We both know I can't just go back to Knoxville and pretend none of this happened. As soon as I came to Destiny, I started something. And whether it's Mr. Caldwell, or someone else behind what's happening now, they aren't just going to stop."

"All right. Then there's only one thing we can do. We have to investigate Bobby Caldwell's death on our own and get the evidence we need to prove you're innocent. Then, and only then, we'll go to the chief and present our case." He dropped his hands from her shoulders. "Wait here. I'll be right back."

He left before she could argue again and headed through an opening at the far right side of the room, near the kitchen. His boots echoed on the hardwood floor. A few moments later he returned with what appeared to be the same thick manila folder he'd brought to her house last night. He also had a legal pad and pen.

He plopped the pad and pen on the end table beside him and put the folder on the coffee table. Sitting on the edge of the couch, he flipped the folder open and sorted through the various papers and pictures. He finally found whatever he was looking for, a page with a graph of dates and times with bulleted sentences next to each time. He tapped the page.

"I've got the official timeline surrounding Bobby's death right here, the record of what he did the entire day until a specific time, and then later when his body was discovered by Deacon and his father."

A chill passed through her at the thought of the father and son finding Bobby's body. That had to be a nightmare they'd never gotten past. And from the hate and bitterness she'd seen in the senior Caldwell at the lawyer's office, he'd definitely never moved past his son's death.

"I've read everything in this file dozens of times over the years. So I'll know if your story jibes with what we know or not."

She blinked again, surprised. "Why did you read it dozens of times?"

"The woman I loved ran away. What do you think?"

She shrank back from the bitterness in his tone. "I'm sorry, Max. I truly am."

"Meaning if you could do it over again, you wouldn't have told me no when I asked you to marry me that night?"

"I didn't say that."

"Exactly. Then you aren't truly sorry, are you?"

She winced. "If we're going to fight, maybe you should just take me back to the station and let me get my confession over with."

He closed his eyes briefly, then shook his head. "No fighting. I'm…sorry, Bex. Seeing you again after all these years has been a huge shock. Apparently I'm not taking it very well."

She swallowed hard and nodded. "Me either. I never know what to say around you without making you upset. That's why I didn't go to your mom and dad's when I got in town. I would have loved to say hi to your family. But I didn't want to risk upsetting you after the way I left things between us."

He stared at her incredulously. "You wanted to see my family, but, what, you were trying to run in and out of town purposely not trying to see me?"

"I'm doing it again. Everything I say comes out wrong. Can you please just drive me to town, Max? Neither of us is doing each other any favors here."

"Sit down, Bex."

The bite in his tone had her sitting before she even thought about it. Then she got so mad at herself for following his directions that she jumped up and started past him toward the front door.

He stood and grabbed her arm, stopping her. "Bex—"

"No." She shook her hand, but his fingers remained around her wrist, like an iron band. Tears burned at the backs of her eyes and her breath started coming in gasps. "Stop it, Max. You don't have the right to tell me what to do or keep me from leaving if I want to leave. Don't you get it? That's what he did. He'd corner me in some alcove at school, or surprise me in my own backyard when Mama wasn't home. And he'd scare me, use his superior strength to try to make me do what he wanted. He'd grab my arm, just like you're doing now."

His eyes widened and he immediately let her go. The blood drained from his face as she rubbed her wrist.

"Bex, my God, I'm so sorry. I wasn't thinking about... about what you went through." He held his hands up and took a step back. "I won't physically try to stop you from leaving. But please, please think about what you're doing. I want to help you." His eyes took on a tortured look. "I couldn't protect you back then, even though I tried. But I'm a grown man now. And I know what I'm doing. Let me protect you now. Let me keep you safe."

His phone buzzed. He frowned and checked the screen, then flipped a button on the side to silence it.

"Bex? What's it going to be? Will you let me help you?"

She couldn't bear to see the hurt in his eyes, hear the hurt in his voice, knowing she was the cause. No matter what she did, she always seemed to hurt him. Ever since he'd asked her to marry him and she'd turned him down. Her entire life had turned upside down after that. And now she was turning his upside down, too. What would have happened if she'd said yes?

No, she couldn't go down that road. She couldn't have said yes back then. No matter how much she loved him, she'd known that if she said yes, she was signing his death warrant. Because that was one of Bobby's many taunts to her—that if he couldn't have her, no one would. And she believed him. He would have killed Max if she'd agreed to marry him. And that was something she couldn't bear.

True to his word, Max wasn't trying to stop her by using his physical strength against her. Because he wasn't Bobby. Max was a good man, always had been. And it was wrong of her to ever compare the two.

"I'm sorry," she said. "I shouldn't have said that, about Bobby, and you…it was cruel. And a lie. Because I know you would never hurt me. You're nothing like him, Max. You never were, and never will be. You're the most decent man I've ever known."

He gave her a tight smile. "I don't know about that. But I do know I want to help you. Will you let me, Bex?"

She slowly nodded. "If I can. What do you want me to do?"

"I need you to tell me exactly what you did the day Bobby Caldwell died, from the moment you woke up until the cops knocked on your door around one in the morning." He grabbed the legal pad and pen and sat down on the couch, waiting.

"But…you know most of it. We were together until around nine thirty that night." She didn't meet his gaze. She couldn't. Because that was when he'd asked her to marry him. And she'd turned him down.

"All of it," he repeated, not missing a beat. "From your perspective, from the moment you woke up."

She let out a deep sigh and sat beside him, pulling her legs up on the couch to get more comfortable. At least, sitting here beside him, she didn't have to look into his eyes while she recounted the more intimate details.

"Mom woke me up, as she often did. I've never been much of an early riser. But it was my birthday, and a Saturday, and she knew I didn't want to miss a single minute. We had a lot of plans."

"We who?"

"We, Mom and me. And then...you and me." She cleared her throat. "We were supposed to meet later."

He hesitated for just a moment, then said, "Go on."

She described the day of shopping with her mom, going to a nail salon to get matching manicures and splurging on pedicures, too, at the last minute. Her mom was a retired schoolteacher, having had Bex late in life as a surprise baby. So she had a lot of free time, but not a lot of money. But she'd promised Bex an eighteenth birthday to remember and had saved all year for it. Nothing was too good for her Bexey.

She plucked at the fabric of her pants. "I'd forgotten that nickname until now."

He put his arm around her, pulling her close. "I'm so sorry about your mom."

She blinked back the moisture in her eyes. "Thank you. I'm glad you were there for her. She...spoke about you a lot. She loved you very much."

He squeezed her shoulders. "Do you need to take a break?"

"No." She wiped her eyes. "I want to get this over with." It took a minute to get her bearings. Then she began telling him about the rest of her day with her mom. Buying matching purses at one of the little stores in town that had handcrafted items Bex always thought were way better than anything she'd ever seen in any fashion magazines. Lunch at her favorite restaurant, a seafood chain the next town over.

"That was pretty much it. I spent my daylight hours with Mom. Oh, she also made homemade strawberry cheesecake and we stuffed ourselves with a piece of that when we got home. Then she gave me a kiss, we hugged, and she gave me her car keys so I could go see you."

"You left the house around what time?"

"Seven thirty, give or take. I drove straight to the barn at the edge of the Caldwell property, just a stone's throw from where your daddy's land began. You were already there."

His fingers idly rubbed her shoulder through her blouse, but he didn't say anything.

She sniffed, wiped her eyes again. "It was the most romantic evening we'd ever had. You thought of everything. You had fresh hay strewn all over the floor with soft blankets and pillows. Lanterns cast a soft glow."

He let out a puff of laughter. "We're lucky we didn't roast alive with all that flammable fuel. I don't know what I was thinking."

"You were thinking that you wanted my eighteenth birthday to be perfect. And it was. And so was your proposal. I'm so sorry that I ruined everything, Max."

His arm dropped from around her shoulders and he made a few notes on his pad, as if she hadn't just mentioned the moment when she'd destroyed their future. But she could tell from the lines of tension on his forehead that he wasn't as immune to the memories as he pretended.

"We left at the same time," he said. "You in your mom's car, me hoofing it across the field to go home. That was about nine thirty. I had to get up early the next day so my dad could help me rebuild the carburetor in the old junker we were restoring together. But you didn't go straight home, did you? You were seen later that evening in town. With Bobby."

She stiffened beside him. "I wasn't *with* Bobby. I was never willingly with Bobby. Ever."

He tilted her chin up. "You don't have to tell me that. I knew firsthand how obsessed he was with you, that he wouldn't leave you alone. I fought more than one fight with him and his father's hired hands out at the farm trying to get him to leave you alone. So don't get all upset like you think I'm implying something when I'm not. He was a sick stalker. Period. But because of the crappy laws, there wasn't anything Thornton could do until Bobby actually crossed the line and hurt you. It sucks, it really does. But that's how it was back then."

She blinked against the burn of unshed tears and let out a shaky breath. "I know. I'm sorry."

"Stop apologizing, Bex. Let's just try to stop doing things that hurt each other and get through this, okay?"

"Okay." She settled back against the couch. A burst of lightning lit up the darkening sky. The water behind the house was so choppy now that it reminded her of the rapids in the creek that ran behind the Caldwell property, gouging deep cliffs thirty feet and higher, hidden from the Caldwell mansion by a copse of thick trees. Cliffs she and Max and a group of other teens had climbed a dozen times on dares, until the farmhands that doubled as Robert Caldwell's security men had chased them off with guns one night.

They'd all been fools and were lucky to be alive. She had never understood why old man Caldwell felt he needed all those thugs around him. But maybe that kind of paranoia came with being wealthy. Then again, he did have a spate of vandalism one year, some neighborhood kids spray painting his barns with sexually explicit cartoons. It was funny until he produced footage from some hidden cameras on the property and was able to get those kids thrown into juvie for their crimes. So maybe he wasn't so paranoid after all. Maybe he was the smart one.

"Go on," Max encouraged. "You left the barn at nine thirty. Then what happened?"

"When I went into the house—"

"You went directly home?"

"Yes."

"What time was it when you got there?"

"I drove straight from the barn to the house, so that probably took about fifteen minutes. And I was only home a few minutes, like maybe ten. Mama was on the verge of one of her migraines. I think we overdid it—maybe she was dehydrated from drinking too many sodas while we were out, I don't know. Anyway, she was out of pills. I got back in the car and drove into town to the only twenty-four-hour convenience store, on Maple Street and Fifth."

"Smiths."

"Yes."

"I remember looking up at that huge clock above the door and it was 10:22."

"Ten twenty-two exactly?"

She nodded.

"How can you be so sure?" He scribbled down the time.

"I remember saying to myself that if something horrible happened to me that night, I needed to tell the police it happened at 10:22."

His gaze shot to hers. "Why would you think that?"

"Because that was when Bobby Caldwell walked into the store."

Chapter Sixteen

Bex twisted her hands together, the bad memories washing over her from that awful night ten years ago.

"He harassed me, as usual. Grabbed my arm, rubbed up against me."

Max's pen stopped, his knuckles whitening around his pen. "Was anyone else in the store?"

"The sales clerk. I don't know his name. Oh, and Marcia."

"Marcia Knolls?"

She nodded. "She was following Bobby around as usual. And he was ignoring her, bothering me instead. I told him to leave me alone and I hurried to the register to buy Mama's pills. After paying, I ran out to my car and left."

"Where were Bobby and Marcia at that time?"

"Marcia came out shortly after me, drove off in her car. I remember she ended up behind me at a stoplight and gave me the finger. I didn't see Bobby come out of the store. I'm not sure where he went right after that."

"You drove straight home?"

She shook her head. "No. I realized I was almost out of gas and was worried I wouldn't make it home, so I stopped and filled up." She told him which station she'd used.

"Did anyone see you?"

She waved toward the manila folder on the table. "If that's the case file, don't you know this part? I'm sure the chief had his men comb the town to create a timeline for his persons of interest. And with me as the number-one suspect, you probably know exactly how many gallons of gas I got and how I paid for it."

"I knew you were at the store and got gas. But I didn't have your side, that Bobby was harassing you. And I didn't know Marcia was at the store. I'm not trying to be cruel by taking you through every step. I'm just trying to ensure that we don't miss anything, okay?"

"Okay."

"You filled up, went inside to pay?"

"Had to. I didn't have Mama's credit card, didn't expect to need gas. She only gave me five bucks for the pills. Luckily I had some of my babysitting money in my purse. But, yeah, I had to go inside to pay. Mr. Alverson was the one working that night. That one's easy to remember. He's there all the time. Even now. I saw him there last week."

Max's mouth quirked in a half smile. "He runs that place like his own little fiefdom. How long were you inside?"

"Not long. Maybe five minutes. I drove home, gave Mama the pills, put her to bed. I was about to go to bed myself when I heard a soft knock on the door. But no one was there. That's when I saw the note. Someone had slid it under the door."

He stopped writing. "A note? Who was it from?"

"You."

His head jerked up. "Me? I didn't send you a note."

"I know that now, of course. The note was supposedly sent through one of your friends. It said your dad was mad at you for something and took your phone. But that you really needed to talk to me, that it couldn't wait. I figured you were still angry at me turning down your proposal, that maybe you were going to try to convince me to say yes. But I was also worried that something else had happened, that maybe you were in trouble. The note said to meet you at a cabin on the Caldwell property. It even had a little hand-drawn map."

"You didn't think that was odd? You didn't think to call me?"

"Why would I? I had no reason not to believe the note, that your dad had your phone. We'd met in that barn on the Caldwell property a dozen times. I figured the cabin was somewhere new you'd discovered, yet another building close to the border of your dad's property where we could meet without being caught. It really didn't seem any different than meeting you in our usual spot. And, well, after we'd left on such bad terms, I figured maybe you didn't want to meet at the barn. Karma and all that. I was anxious to try to smooth things over. I didn't want you to hate me."

A pained expression crossed his face. "I could never hate you, Bex. I assume that was the same cabin where Bobby's body was later found?"

She nodded.

"Please tell me you kept the note."

"I had it with me when I went to the cabin. But not when I left."

"I didn't see it listed in the police report of items found."

"All I know is that it was in my pocket when I got there. But not later. I assume Bobby took it."

He set his pen and notepad on the end table and turned to face her. "Tell me everything, Bex. Exactly as you remember it."

"As soon as I got there and went into the outbuilding, I knew I'd been tricked. You weren't there waiting for me. Since your house is so close by, there's no way I'd have gotten there before you. I turned around, and Bobby had just come inside. He was grinning like an idiot as he closed the door. But I was the idiot." She clenched her hands into fists.

"What did he do?"

She closed her eyes, wishing she could block out the memory of Bobby just as easily. "He threw me to the floor and…and lay on top of me. He held my face still and kissed me. When I tried to bite him, he squeezed my jaw until I cried out. I didn't try to bite him again. It was awful. He ripped my shirt, sending buttons flying all over the cabin. He had a knife. He cut my bra off. And then, then he…" She shook her head. She couldn't tell Max all the horrible things that Bobby had done to her, how he'd held the knife to her and put his mouth where Max's had so recently been. It was like he'd destroyed every beautiful touch she and Max had shared before he'd asked her to marry him, and then turned it into something ugly.

"Earlier, at your house when I first questioned you, you said he didn't rape you. Was that true?" His voice broke on the last word, and she realized this was just as hard for him as it was for her.

"No. No, he didn't…penetrate me. After he tore off my clothes and did his worst, he was about to…and I knew I couldn't live with myself if he did. I couldn't get my knees up to kick him, so I…" She shuddered. "I grabbed him… there…and squeezed as hard as I could. He screamed and fell off me. I scrambled to my feet and he was calling me ugly names and I'd just reached the door when he grabbed my hair. He yanked me back and I remember I flailed my hands out for something, anything to stop him. And I grabbed something off one of the shelves. Later, I realized it was an empty wine bottle. Probably from the last kids who'd snuck onto the farm and used that cabin. I swung it around in an arc. There was a horrible, sickening thud. And then he fell down on the floor. Dead."

Tears were flowing down her face now. "I gathered up my clothes, searched for the buttons, but I couldn't find the last one. I couldn't stay another minute, knowing he was dead. So I ran, got in the car. Drove home. And that's why my mama wouldn't let me talk to the police. She knew what I'd done the moment I got home in my torn clothes. She burned them in the fireplace. She vacuumed the car, scrubbed it down, just in case I'd brought any evidence back with me. And she burned the vacuum bag, the paper towels she used, everything. And she made me swear never, ever to say anything at all to the police."

She was crying hard now, and hated that she was crying. And suddenly Max was in front of her, kneeling on the floor. He'd scooted the table out of the way and was pulling her hands down from her face, looking up at her with some kind of emotion she couldn't even fathom.

"Are you absolutely sure you told me everything from that night? You didn't leave out any details?"

"The only details I left out were the vile things he did to my body before he tried to rape me. No, Max. There's nothing else to tell. I killed him. I didn't mean to, but I did. And Mama and I were both too afraid to say anything because I'd made so many complaints about Bobby. And his father always made the complaints go away. And everyone knew I hated him. There was no way they'd believe me over Bobby's father."

She drew a shaky breath. "I'm not a complete idiot. When I was in jail, after the chief locked me up, I had plenty of time to sit and think about what had happened. And I knew that Mama and I had made some really bad decisions. Maybe if we'd called the police right away and didn't burn my clothes, the clothes might have helped build my case of self-defense. It's possible, I suppose. But by then, we'd already destroyed evidence. Even at eighteen I knew that was wrong, illegal and only made me look guilty. I couldn't tell the chief what really happened at that point. He could have arrested my mom for helping me cover up what happened."

She could tell from the intensity of his gaze and the way he was looking at her with laser like focus that she wasn't going to like his next question.

"Bex, you said you wouldn't let me see you in jail, to protect me. Because you were worried that it could hurt my future career aspirations. While I might not agree with your decision, I can sort of understand it. At that age, as young as we both were, I get how things could look different. But when the chief didn't have enough evidence to press charges, you left town. And you stayed gone for ten years. Why, in all that time, did you never once call me?"

And there it was. The question she'd both expected and dreaded ever since she'd come back to Destiny. It was one of the primary reasons she'd hoped to avoid him. She twisted her hands in her lap, and said the only thing she could think of.

"You didn't call me, either."

His brows raised. "You made it painfully clear through Chief Thornton that you never wanted to see me again. I respected your wishes, even if I didn't understand them."

She looked away.

"Bex. Why?"

She squeezed her eyes shut, swallowing hard against the tightness in her throat before looking at him again. "Everything just sort of built on everything else. After what happened with Bobby that night, I knew that if I let you back into my life you would do everything you could to protect me. If I spoke to you, I knew I'd tell you exactly what I did, what my mom did to help me cover it up. That would make you complicit in destroying evidence and would ruin your future career. Whether you agree with my reasons or not, all I can say is that my life became a snowball that kept rolling downhill and getting bigger and bigger. I left town to let things die down, hoping Mr. Caldwell would quit lobbying for me to be arrested. Mama kept me updated on what was happening with the case and I knew it only got worse after I left. For a long, long time Mr. Caldwell pushed and pushed the chief to find and arrest me."

Max slowly nodded. "You're right. He was like a crazy man for the better part of a year before he stopped visiting the station every day, demanding your head on a silver platter."

"I know. And by then, I was building a life in Knoxville. I had the antique business going. And from there, it was easier if I didn't think of Destiny and what I'd run from."

"Including me?"

Her lip wobbled when she answered. "Yes. Including you. It hurt just to think about you. You were the reminder of everything that I'd lost. It was easier to push you to the back of my mind. To try to never think of you again."

He winced and looked toward the back wall of windows at the ever darkening stormy-looking sky. What had he expected her to say? That she loved him then, loved him still? She did, with her whole heart. But she'd lost everything the night Bobby Caldwell died, including Max. And the only way she could survive that loss was to start over.

A long time passed in silence. When Max finally turned back toward her, he was Detective Max again. All business and professional. With none of the earlier warmth he'd shown. He asked her more questions, and every time she heard his cold voice, her heart broke a little bit more.

Finally, after answering another one of his questions, she said, "This is such a nightmare."

His jaw tightened, and she knew he was probably thinking the same thing. Except that his nightmare was that he had agreed to help her. And that he was most likely regretting that decision now.

"Just tell me one more thing," he said. "Do you remember if Bobby wore his ring that night?"

"The chunky one with diamonds all over it, the one his

father gave him as some kind of heirloom? That he lorded over all of us at school? That ring?"

"Yes. That ring."

"Definitely. It got caught in my hair when he grabbed me. Ripped out some of my hair by the roots. Or, at least, it felt like it."

"Did you take the ring with you when you left?"

"No. I wish I'd thought to. It probably has my DNA all over it, from my scalp. Yet another reason not to cooperate with the police. Why? I'm guessing you found it and want me to give a DNA sample for comparison?"

He shook his head. "The ring was never found."

She frowned. "But that doesn't make sense. He was definitely wearing it."

"You said you hit him on the head with a wine bottle?"

"Yes. It was one of those blue ones. I don't remember the label."

"What did you do with the bottle?"

She frowned again. "Other than hit him? Nothing. I already told you what happened."

"Humor me. Please. Did you take the wine bottle?"

"No. I didn't take anything but the buttons from my shirt, the ones I found anyway. The note that was in my pocket was gone. All I can figure is when Bobby was... pawing me, that he yanked it out. Probably to make sure I couldn't show it to anyone to prove that he'd lured me there. I didn't think to look for it when I left, because I didn't know it was gone at the time."

"Did you clean the cabin?"

She gave him an incredulous look. "I just told you I didn't take anything or even stop to see if I still had the note."

"Bex. It's important. Did you clean the cabin?"

"No. No, I didn't clean the cabin. I was too messed up to even think about something like that. I grabbed the buttons that I saw, grabbed my clothes and just…ran, back through the trees to where I'd hidden my mom's car."

"Are you sure about these details? You've told me everything?"

"I've been seeing that same night play out in my nightmares for ten years. I'm sure."

"Bex, if you're telling me the truth—"

"I am. I swear."

"If you're sure you've told me everything, then I'm sure of something else. You absolutely did not kill Bobby Caldwell."

Chapter Seventeen

Bex stared at Max in disbelief. "Don't give me the usual cop platitudes of self-defense and yada yada yada. I'm telling you it doesn't matter. No one would believe me any more today than they would have back then. They're going to put me in prison, so I might as well get used to the idea."

"I'm not giving you platitudes. You didn't kill Bobby."

She frowned. "What are you talking about?"

"When you left the cabin, I promise you, Caldwell was very much alive."

"But…the police found his body a couple of hours later, when his father and brother went looking for him."

"Yes. But the most you did was knock him out for a few minutes. That wasn't what killed him. Bobby died from internal bleeding, a ruptured spleen."

"I don't…understand. How is that possible? When I hit him, he fell so hard that his spleen ruptured?"

He shook his head. "No. That wouldn't have done it. Someone beat him. They took a baseball bat or something like that and hit him across the lower back and abdomen. The coroner counted at least a dozen blows. They beat him, left him there to die. And then they took his ring. His father reported it as missing in the police report, said Bobby never went anywhere without it. That means that after you left, someone else went inside that cabin and killed him. There's no other explanation."

"I didn't kill him," she said, in wonder.

"No. You didn't." His smile faded. "But right now all we have is your word. And, unfortunately, if you tell anyone else what you just told me, it only corroborates that you were at the murder scene."

She blew out a frustrated breath. "No telling what physical evidence your boss has that ties me to that cabin. I imagine he found my missing button. There had to be hair, too, and fibers from my clothes that he tore."

"No. There isn't. That's one of the reasons that Thornton never could get a judge to sign a search warrant for your home. That cabin was pristine. Like someone had scrubbed it down top to bottom that night. There was no blue wine bottle. No button, no hair or fibers. And no note, either."

"Why? Why would someone do that? Do you think they saw me go into the cabin and wanted to…what, protect me from being blamed?"

"Possible. More likely whoever killed him just wanted to clean every inch of the place in case any trace evidence could be used against them. I think they took advantage of the fact that you'd knocked Bobby woozy and they decided to finish him off. Then cleaned up afterward so no one would know they were the one who'd killed him."

Her earlier elation faded. "So I did kill him after all. I left him there, semiconscious, unable to defend himself."

"Don't start feeling guilty over his death now. You said it yourself earlier. Bobby Caldwell was a bad person. He was the worst kind of scum, someone who preyed on women. The only person Bobby can blame for what happened is Bobby."

His words made sense. She'd accepted long ago that she'd killed him, and didn't feel guilty for that. But now, knowing that she'd left him injured, easy pickings for someone else to kill him, she did feel guilty. It was an

odd feeling, to finally have compassion for a man she'd
hated all of her adult life.

"What do we do now?" she asked.

"We go over your story again, from beginning to end."

"What? Why?"

"I need to know every single detail that you can remember. Someone out there, whether it's Bobby's father
or someone else, believes you killed him. And they're determined to get you to confess. If there's anything else that
you can remember about that night that I can use to help
your case, and put the true murderer away, then going over
and over your story will be worth the pain."

He grilled her about every single detail that day. He
even made her recount as much as she could remember
about the week leading up to Bobby's death, looking for
anything that might give them a clue about who else might
want Bobby dead. He took mercy on her well past the
lunch hour when her stomach started rumbling. But after
they wolfed down ham and cheese sandwiches and potato
chips, he was back at it.

"What about after Thornton released you from jail?"

Bex was lying on the couch now, her head propped on
a throw pillow and one arm thrown over her face. Mad
Max, as she was beginning to label him in her thoughts,
was currently perched on the edge of the coffee table beside her, pen scribbling after every question he asked her.

She wanted to grab that pen and snap it in two.

"What about when I got out of jail?" she asked wearily
without moving her arm.

"You were in town for two weeks, rumors swirling
around, people saying terrible things. And all the while,
Bobby's family was making things really difficult for you,
demanding the chief arrest you."

"No, not his whole family," she said. "Just his parents."
She lowered her arm and rolled her head on the pillow to

look at him. "I never did hear how the father ended up in a wheelchair. And I haven't seen Mrs. Caldwell in town since I got here. Were they in a car accident or something?"

"Worse. She died of breast cancer earlier this year. A few months later, he was diagnosed with late-stage bone cancer. His bones are so brittle he was walking down the sidewalk one day and his hip just snapped. That's why he's in the wheelchair. They say he doesn't have long to live, maybe a few months, best case." He straightened and frowned off into the distance.

"Max? Something wrong?"

He slowly shook his head. "No. I need to make a phone call. Hang on a sec." He grabbed his phone and punched in a number. A few moments later he said, "Hey, Colby, yeah, it's me. Mmm-hmm. Mmm-hmm. I figured he'd be ticked. That's why I ignored his earlier calls. Nothing I can do about that right now, but I'm still working the case. I need to ask you something. Remember when Mrs. Caldwell was being treated for cancer, where did she go for that? Uh-huh. And Mr. Caldwell, he's been going through chemo at the hospital. But I never asked which one. I just assumed Maryville. But where…" His gaze shot to Bex as he nodded. "Right. Got it. That's what I was thinking. Did Blake make any headway with his contacts? What about your interviews?"

Several minutes later, he hung up the phone.

"Well," she asked, "do I have to beg you to tell me what that was all about?"

He smiled. "That was Colby, one of the other SWAT guys who's also a detective like me."

"I know who Colby is."

"Right. Well, he reinterviewed two of the gunmen at the hospital. One of them, a guy named Lenny, finally admitted that he'd seen the guy who hired them to go after you. He worked with an artist to do a rendering of the guy."

"It can't be Robert Caldwell if he's in a wheelchair. He couldn't drive."

"It wasn't. But close."

"Deacon? He's such a nice guy."

"No, it wasn't Deacon. The picture is the spitting image of one of the security guys Caldwell senior keeps at his farm. Even more importantly, the new guy on our team, Blake, was able to link that car to that security guy. It sure looks like he was the one in Knoxville who hired those thugs to go after you. And it's not like he had that kind of money, or a motive. Only his employer had that. Even better, Mr. Caldwell—the father, not Deacon—was quite familiar with Knoxville, since he and his wife were both there most of this year for cancer treatments."

"Okay, sounds like he's probably the one behind going after me. At least now we know who it is."

His confidence seemed to take a tumble. "Well, I'm not sure about that. Yes, he's the one who hired the gunmen, through his personal security guy. We should be able to prove that after we get a warrant for his bank records and follow the money. But what's his motive? He believes you killed his son and he wants you to confess. He wants you to go to prison because he thinks you're a murderer. That's problematic."

"I really hate that I see where you're going with this," she grumbled. "Your point is that the current bad business between Mr. Caldwell and me makes it seem highly unlikely that he's also the one who killed his son. Because if he'd done that, he wouldn't dredge all of this back up right now and shine light onto it."

"Exactly. Now you're thinking like a cop."

"Lord help us all."

He laughed, but quickly sobered. "Who does that leave us, suspectwise? I'm thinking we're back to Marcia Knolls."

"Marcia? But she was in love with Bobby. She wouldn't want to kill him."

"He wasn't in love with her. He treated her like an insect he wanted to brush off his shoe. You said yourself that you saw her in the store that night with Bobby. Maybe she followed you and you didn't know it. And after you ran out of the cabin, holding your clothes, she thought you'd actually been his lover and were running home, maybe to make curfew. I can see her justifying it that way, and being angry and hurt and going into the cabin to confront Bobby. When she found him lying there, unconscious, assuming he was naked—"

"He was." Her voice was so tight she could barely speak.

"Okay. He was naked, and she thought he was cheating on her, at least in her mind. So she grabs whatever is handy. Cabin like that, on the edge of the woods, there's bound to be stuff in there, maybe in a closet. A bat or something like it. She could have hit him with it while he was still unconscious, so that even if he woke up while she was hitting him, he'd already be too hurt to put up much of a fight." He pulled out his phone. "The more I think about it, the more I'm convinced she's the only one who makes sense for Bobby's murder. I'll get Colby to bring her in for questioning."

A few minutes later, he hung up the call and pitched his phone onto the coffee table. "Okay, I put everything into motion that I could. Hopefully the guys will come through for us and get proof and wrap it all up."

She eyed him with dread as he picked up the legal pad and pen again. "I thought we just solved the case. Marcia killed Bobby. And Caldwell senior had one of his men hire the thugs to get me to confess. Why are you getting your torture devices out again?"

He rolled his eyes. "Because I still want to review the two weeks you were in town after Thornton let you go. I want to know who all you spoke to, and what they said. Who you might have seen skulking around. Until Colby tells me that he has Marcia's confession, I'm not letting down my guard. We need to see if anyone else around town did anything odd those two weeks that might make them rise to the top of my suspect list for having killed Bobby."

She groaned and collapsed back onto the pillow.

Chapter Eighteen

Max rubbed the back of his neck and looked out the wall of glass to his deck and the angry, broiling sky over the lake beyond. The sun had set long ago, but the frequent cracks of lightning illuminated the heavy clouds that had been threatening rain most of the day. He figured the storm would finally let loose its full fury and drench them with rain soon. But until then, it was doing its best to whip the last of the dry leaves from the trees, making winter look even closer than it was.

A snuffling sigh sounded behind him and he turned around to see that Bex had fallen asleep on the couch while he'd taken a few minutes to stretch his legs. He was tempted to smile at the adorable picture she presented. But he didn't really feel like smiling. It was hard to when the woman he'd loved had rejected him so soundly all those years ago, and then put him out of her thoughts for ten years. He sure as hell hadn't put her out of his.

In the beginning, he'd been pathetic, begging her mother to tell him where Bex had gone. Later, once he'd become a cop and knew how to find her, he'd tracked her down. He'd driven to Knoxville and planned on confronting her. By then, he was well past the blubbering love-struck fool phase. He'd lived in the anger phase for a good year or two. And he wanted to demand an explanation. But when he'd seen her, he couldn't do it. Couldn't go up to her and debase himself to ask her why she'd left. Ask her why she'd never called. He was too angry to even form a coherent sentence.

After that, he'd never gone to Knoxville again. And he'd almost convinced himself that he'd forgotten her until she'd shown up at that deli counter. And just like that, all his old feelings of anger, grief, resentment had risen to the surface and formed a crack in the heart he'd thought he no longer had. And in just a matter of days he'd brought her to his home and begged her to tell him why she'd never tried to see him, talk to him, after she left.

He was such a fool.

He strode to the couch and looked down at her. But the anger and resentment faded away, replaced by a pathetic longing that went deep in his soul. Bex. His Bex. She would always be his in his battered and bruised heart, even if not in reality. No matter how much he wished he didn't care about her.

Her exhaustion was evident in the dark circles under her eyes. She needed to sleep. But he still had some questions. And he imagined his boss would be parked at his doorstep early in the morning, demanding that he get his butt back to work and bring Bex with him.

On the outside, Thornton was a grumpy pit bull. But when it came to his team, he was often full of bluster. He considered the SWAT team his family, and because of that he'd forgive Max the sin of ignoring his orders and walking out of the station with Bex. But Max knew better than to push it a second day. That would cross the line. He'd be suspended at best, fired at worst. Being a cop was something he'd wanted for as long as he could remember.

But what he'd really wanted, more than anything else, was lying on his couch, a thin line of drool drying at the corner of her mouth.

God, she was beautiful. Maybe not in the classic way most men thought of beauty. She had short legs, her mouth was wide, her cheeks round—something that had always bothered her, especially in middle school when other kids had called her chipmunk cheeks. She'd practically starved herself in eighth grade trying to get the narrow, thin face she thought she should have until she'd made herself sick. She'd finally had to realize that no matter how thin she was, her face never would be. Max liked to think that maybe he'd helped her with that, by telling her how beautiful she was, over and over, until she started to believe it.

He hadn't been lying. He really did see the beauty others missed. It came from inside and shined through her bright, curious, intelligent eyes. The silky hair she despaired of never holding a curl was a wonder to him, soft as a rabbit. Those legs she thought were too short were perfectly proportioned to her body. She looked like one of those Disney fairies. All that was missing was a set of wings and a wand. She already possessed the magic, because she had utterly enchanted him.

She snuffled again, grumbling something in her sleep as she scrubbed at her mouth. Then she rolled over toward him. And opened her eyes.

He crouched down, almost at eye level. And his heart ached. "Hello, beautiful."

Her eyes blinked. "Don't call me that. I must look terrible." She covered her face with her hands.

He gently pulled them down and, despising his inability to resist her lure, pressed a soft kiss against her lips.

Instead of kissing him back, she shoved at his chest and hurriedly sat up, covering her mouth and mumbling something behind her hand.

She was so cute when she was half-asleep and still confused.

"Betghrm," she mumbled behind her hand again.

He tilted his head. "Hard to be sure, but I think you might be asking about the bathroom?"

She nodded enthusiastically.

He held out his hand. "Come on. I was going to question you some more, but I think I'll give you a reprieve. You're too far gone to make sense anyway. I'll show you the guest room."

She hesitated, then put her hand in his and let him pull her to standing. She let his hand go and stepped back, running her hands through her hair as if worried about her appearance.

"I'll just freshen up and then you can drive me home."

"I'd rather you stayed the night."

She frowned. "Why?"

"You mean other than the fact that the wind is whipping and dry lightning is cracking outside?"

Her gaze went to the windows. "I must really be tired. I hadn't even noticed."

"Even if it weren't storming, I'd strongly suggest that you consider staying. Whoever is after you knows about your mom's house. I can protect you here, if it comes to that."

She ran her hands up and down her arms and nodded. "Makes sense. Thanks. I appreciate it."

"No trouble at all. The guest room's the first one down the hall on the left. There are toothbrushes, shampoo, everything you need in there. Oh, except something to sleep in. My room is right next door. You're welcome to grab one of my T-shirts to sleep in if you want."

"Sounds good." She grabbed her purse from one of the end tables and started toward the hallway, then stopped. "Max?"

He'd just rounded the island going into the kitchen but waited and raised a questioning brow.

"Thank you," she said. "For everything. I know we haven't figured out how to clear my name yet. But for the first time in, well, forever, I feel like there's hope. So, thanks."

"You can always count on me, Bex. I'm always here for you. No matter what." Sappy, but true. No sense in denying it.

Her eyes widened, and then she whirled around and disappeared down the hall.

Max let out a deep breath and headed into the kitchen. They'd talked right through dinner and his stomach was rumbling. He grabbed a handful of grapes from the refrigerator and leaned against the counter, popping them into his mouth and chasing them with a bottle of water. When he finished his snack, he headed into the main room to kill the lights.

Was Bex asleep already? Probably. She'd seemed so worn out. He couldn't help smiling, thinking about her lying in the middle of the bed, wearing one of his T-shirts. He froze in the middle of the room, his smile fading. His T-shirts. He'd told her to grab one. He kept them in his top dresser drawer.

But that wasn't all he kept in that drawer.

He swore and flipped off the main light then hurried down the hallway. The light was on in the master bedroom, streaming into the hall. *Hurry. Stop her.* He bolted to the doorway then froze. Bex was standing in front of the dresser, her hair freshly brushed, but still wearing her jeans and blouse. One of his T-shirts dangled from her left hand. Maybe he'd caught her in time.

Her eyes slowly rose to his, and then she held up her other hand, the one holding a diamond solitaire ring.

BEX'S WHOLE BODY shook as she held the same ring that Max had offered her so long ago. There was no mistaking it. Every facet had been branded into her memory. It was definitely the same ring.

"Why?" she asked, her voice barely above a whisper. "Why did you keep it?"

His jaw tightened and he crossed the room to her, swiping the ring from her palm and grabbing the little black box from the drawer full of T-shirts. "No reason, just never got around to returning it." He shoved the ring back in its velvet bed and popped the lid shut.

"It had to have cost a small fortune. You probably made payments on it for years," she said. "You couldn't have forgotten it."

His expression was shuttered, remote, as he faced her. "I believe that you have everything you need in the guest room. Have a good night's sleep. I'll see you in the morning."

"Oh, Max. What have I done?" she whispered. Hot tears traced down her cheeks.

He let out an impatient breath and strode to the door, holding it open. "Good night, Bex."

Like two duelers at ten paces, they faced each other—her with his T-shirt clutched in her hand, him with the promise of forever in his. A promise he'd once offered out of love and she'd refused, also out of love. But he didn't understand that. She'd never explained any of that to him. And seeing the ring in his drawer had shocked her to the core, and made her realize for the first time that maybe she'd been wrong. She'd made a decision to protect him. But she'd also shut him out, never explained her reasons, and left him in a state of limbo, always wondering *why*.

This amazing man in front of her deserved so much better than that. She wasn't the girl she'd been back then. She was a grown woman. And it was high time she came clean about everything, not just the horrible events around Bobby's death. She needed to explain to Max why she'd told him no.

She slowly padded toward him in her bare feet and lifted his hand away from the door.

He frowned down at her, obviously not sure what she was doing. She smiled sadly and pushed the door closed.

A wary look came over him. "Bex, what are you—"

She pressed her fingers against his lips, startling him into silence. "I owe you an explanation, for this."

She tried to take the velvet box, but he pulled it back, a gentle tug-of-war.

"Please," she said. "I don't deserve your trust, but I'm asking for it. Trust me. I'll just put this back in the drawer."

Without a word, his back so stiff he could have been a soldier submitting to inspection, he relinquished his hold on the box.

Unable to resist another look, Bex opened the lid and turned it, watching the solitaire twinkle beneath the overhead light

"Bex—"

"I know, I know. Sorry. It's just so beautiful." She slowly closed the lid and replaced the box in the drawer. After tossing the T-shirt onto the king-size four-poster bed, she crossed to Max again and took his reluctant hand in hers. "Can we sit down, just for a few minutes? I need to tell you what I should have told you years ago."

The struggle inside him was evident in the expressions on his face. Unlike a lot of tough guys, Max didn't do stoic very well. He was tough, yet sensitive, always caring. It was one of the things she'd always admired about him, one of the reasons she'd known he'd be an excellent cop—because he cared.

Although the master bedroom was large, it was neat and sparse, like the rest of the house. There was only one chair, on the right side of the bed. So she tugged his hand, urging him toward the bed with her. She let his hand go and had to climb up on the blasted thing, it was so high. Then she turned around and patted the spot beside her.

He looked like he was trying not to laugh, and finally gave in to a grin. "You look like Tinker Bell climbing up on that bed."

She shook her head. "I never did understand your fascination with fairies."

"Not with fairies. Just you." His smile dimmed and he sat beside her. "Whatever you think you need to say, you don't. I don't have any expectations of us getting back together. There's no reason for you to feel uncomfortable or worry that I'm going to hit on you."

"You kissed me in the family room."

"Momentary insanity. I recovered. It won't happen again."

She looked down at her hands, trying not to let him see that his words had struck their target. Her heart. She braced herself and forced herself to look up, not to cower and not to run again when the going got tough.

"It's time I faced my past," she said. "I've already told you about the night of my birthday in regards to Bobby Caldwell. But I didn't tell you everything, not the part about us."

He swallowed, his Adam's apple bobbing in his throat. "You don't have to do this, Bex. It really doesn't matter anymore."

"It does matter. I hurt you, and that was never my intention, in spite of how it must have seemed. All I ask is that you listen. It won't take long. I just want to explain why I said no."

He shrugged as if he didn't care. But his gaze was riveted on her and he didn't protest anymore.

"You'd been hinting about that night for a while, talking about how special it would be, how important it was. It didn't take a genius to figure out you were probably going to propose. We'd certainly talked about the possibility of spending the rest of our lives together often enough. I think we both always assumed we'd end up together. I certainly thought I'd be your wife one day, that we'd build a life together, create our own little family."

His breathing hitched, but he didn't move, just kept watching her.

"I don't know if you remember, but Chief Thornton had come to the school earlier that week for one of his career day speeches. And just like every year before, you hung on his every word. And after it was over, you talked about your big dream, of being a police officer here in Destiny, of being a detective and working your way onto the SWAT team. It's the only dream you ever really wanted."

His jaw tightened, but again he said nothing.

She sighed. "Anyway, I knew how important that was to you. And I also knew that if that dream was ever taken away, it would utterly destroy you." She twisted her hands in her lap. "You'd already gotten in trouble fighting Bobby many times to try to protect me. That was okay while you were still a minor. But you turned eighteen two weeks before I did. If you fought Bobby again, you could have been charged as an adult. And that would have given you a criminal record. I couldn't let that happen."

He frowned. "Bex—"

"Wait. Let me finish. There's more to it than that. I was afraid for your life. The situation with Bobby kept getting worse, and I didn't know what was going to happen or what to do. All I knew for sure was that Bobby was winning the war. And he was evil and told me many times that if he couldn't have me no one would. If I had married you, Bobby would have killed you. I know it. I couldn't live knowing that I had caused your death."

He stared at her incredulously. "You told me no because you thought I couldn't protect myself?"

"What? No, I mean, yes. But you make it sound so simple. It wasn't. I truly thought Bobby would kill you if I didn't end things between us."

Tears splashed down her cheeks onto her hands. She impatiently wiped them away. "But even if I was wrong, if Bobby tried to hurt you and you ended up killing him instead, that would have destroyed you just as completely. Because it could have destroyed your dream of becoming a police officer. What if you were convicted of manslaughter or something like that? Thornton wouldn't have allowed you on the police force with a record. I couldn't let that happen. I couldn't live with myself knowing you'd grow to hate me a little bit every day we were together, realizing that I was the reason you'd given up what you truly loved."

His hand firmly tilted her chin up so she'd look at him. The anger that flashed in his eyes startled her.

"Are you saying you turned down my proposal to protect me? Either from Bobby or from myself?"

She tried to nod, but couldn't, so she whispered, "Yes."

He swore and stood up, his boots ringing against the floor as he paced in front of the bed like a caged tiger. "All this time, I thought maybe you'd played me. That you didn't really love me."

She blinked in shock. "I've always loved you."

"Funny way of showing it."

"I know. I'm so sorry. I never meant to hurt you."

He stopped pacing in front of her. "You may have loved me, but you sure as hell didn't know me."

"Excuse me?"

He braced his hands on the bed on either side of her. "Do you honestly think that being a cop was my biggest dream? That what I truly loved, more than anything else, was the idea of being a detective and a SWAT officer? Sure, I wanted to be a cop. And I wanted to stay in my hometown to do it. But a career wasn't the love of my life. You were. I'd have given everything I had for you and never regretted it for a single second. Ten years, Bex. For ten years I've been asking myself what I did wrong, what was there about me that made me unworthy of you. I couldn't figure it out. I thought, maybe, one day, if you ever came back, you'd tell me about this horrible thing that I'd done to you and it would make the lightbulb click in my mind. I'd be like, *oh, wow, that's what I did.* And then I'd apologize and do everything I could to make it right. But I didn't do anything wrong."

He thumped his chest. "I did everything I could for you, loved you with every ounce of my being. And you didn't love me enough to even have a freaking conversation over your fears so we could work through it. You know what, Bexley? If you'd just asked me what I wanted, I'd have told you that we could move away somewhere, start over in another town. I'd have gone anywhere, done anything and been happy, as long as I was with you. Instead, you didn't trust me, or love me enough to give me a chance. You didn't give me my dream by leaving me. You stole my dream, Bex. Because being a cop wasn't my dream. Being with you was."

He whirled around and strode out of the room, slamming the door behind him.

Chapter Nineteen

Bex's mouth fell open, Max's angry words repeating themselves in her mind as the sound of his boots rang through
the house. Wind suddenly howled outside the bedroom
door, followed by a metallic thump. He'd gone outside, in
the middle of a lightning storm. Because of her.

Oh, God, what had she done?

She shoved off the bed, hopping down to the floor just
as the lights flickered and went out. Letting her memory
of the house's layout guide her, she flung the door open
and ran down the hall into the main room. She froze at a
loud pinging sound against the glass.

"It's just the storm." Max's deep voice spoke from the
dark. "It's finally raining. The wind is driving it in sheets
against the back of the house."

She turned toward his voice, but the room was too dark
to make out anything but silhouettes. He was standing by
the fireplace, one of his booted feet resting on the raised
hearth, a hand braced against the mantel.

She turned, looking for one of the lamps she'd seen
earlier.

"Don't bother." He spoke from the gloom again, his
voice already drained of anger, sounding flat, emotion-
less. "The power just went out."

She started toward him, then let out a curse when her
shin banged the coffee table.

"Wait there," he said.

He bent down, but she couldn't tell what he was doing. Light flared, like from a long match. Then a small fire began to grow in the fireplace. He must have had it set up with kindling and logs, ready to go, because it quickly caught and grew into a roaring fire. The flames threw a flickering, eerie light across his features and through the room.

He turned his back on her. "Go to sleep, Bex. The house is sturdy. You don't need to be afraid of the storm."

The coward inside her, the one who'd never picked up the phone or tried to talk to him for all those years, urged her to do as he said. But coming back to Destiny had changed her irrevocably, had reawakened feelings long ago buried, had made her realize just how her actions had impacted those around her. Running away, going back home without making things right, wasn't something she could do now. She had to face what she'd done. All of it. And that meant facing Max one more time.

She circled the coffee table and crossed the room to stand directly behind him.

"Max, you didn't let me finish explaining why I told you no."

He sighed wearily. "I've heard enough."

"Maybe you have. But there's one more thing I have to tell you. It might not matter to you. But it matters to me. I realize how much I've hurt people by leaving when I did, by running away. And I'm trying to make it right the only way I know how, by telling the truth. There might not be any proof of what really happened that night with Bobby. But when this storm is over and the sun comes up, I'm going to call the chief and tell him to come get me so I can give a full statement. Because it's not just about me. It's about Bobby's father, and his brother. They deserve to know what I know. Someone killed their loved one that night, and they need to know my role in it, if nothing else, so they can expend their energy looking for the right killer."

He turned his head, hand braced on the mantel, boot still resting on the hearth. But at least he was listening.

"I already explained why I turned down your proposal," she continued. "But I didn't explain why I left. Bobby was dead. So there wasn't any worry by then that you'd get in trouble fighting or going after him."

He frowned. "I wondered at that, after I left the bedroom."

The fact that he was at least talking with her now gave her hope. She plodded forward. "I left because I thought I'd killed Bobby. I've thought that all this time, until you proved to me today that I didn't kill him. I left because I knew that if I stayed in town, you would do everything you could to help me. And I wouldn't be strong enough to resist you for very long. I talked it through with Mama and we both agreed, the only way to protect you was for me to leave."

He shook his head in disgust. "There you go talking about protecting me again. Don't you realize that's my job? To protect you?" He looked back toward the fireplace. "Or it would have been. If you'd stayed."

"Exactly."

He frowned and looked at her again.

"That's my point," she said. "You would have felt it was your duty to protect me, even after I'd turned you down. Because that's how you are, a wonderful, good, loyal, kind man who would protect the woman he loved even if she was a murderer. Even if it cost him his career."

He swore again. "We're right back where we started. Bex, you're way more important to me than any job. Don't you get that?"

"Actually, yeah, I do. Now. You've ignored your boss's

calls all day and risked everything to be here with me, to keep me from confessing back in town. You're doing exactly what I tried to prevent by running away in the first place."

He shook his head.

She stepped closer, placing her hand on his chest, feeling his muscles bunch beneath her fingertips. "But I'm not running this time. I'm not going anywhere. I love you, Max. And we're both adults now. I don't know if you can ever forgive me for not trusting you and giving you the chance to make your own decisions about your future all those years ago. But I'm hoping you can at least try."

His gaze dropped to her hand. "It's been a long time, Bex. A lot has happened since then. I don't know that I want to go down that same road, risk you crushing me like you did. It took me years to get over you. But I'm happy now. I like my life, enjoy my family, this house, the life I've built. I'm not sure you fit in anymore."

She smoothed her hand over his shirt, her hand shaking, sadness welling up inside her. "I'm not asking you to fit me back into your life. I'm asking you to work on trying to forgive me. And then maybe we'll see where we go from there."

Slowly, as if he wasn't sure what she'd do, he moved his left hand toward her face, then gently stroked her hair back, feathering his fingers through the strands.

"Still as silky as ever," he whispered.

"Still so handsome you can stop a girl's heart with one look," she whispered, smiling up at him.

His mouth twitched. "That handsome, huh? Sounds dangerous."

"You have no idea." She moved closer, until her breasts pressed against his ribs.

His lids lowered to half-mast. His hand shook as he

continued to stroke her hair. "I don't think this is a good idea, Bex. We haven't settled anything at all between us."

"You're right. Nothing's settled. But we've had an incredible run. And I can't think of a better way to say goodbye—if this is goodbye—than to share ourselves with each other one last time. It sure beats how we ended things last time. How *I* ended things. Let's write a better ending to our story than walking away from each other angry and bitter. We deserve that. Max and Bex deserve that. Don't you think?"

In answer he groaned and yanked her to him, his mouth slamming down on top of hers. Heat filled her, warming her from the inside out. She struggled to get closer to him, standing on her tiptoes. He lifted her with one hand beneath her bottom, setting her feet on the edge of the hearth, the roaring fire warming her back, Max warming everything else.

This kiss was nothing like the one he'd given her earlier. That one had been distant, questioning. He'd held back. He wasn't holding anything back this time. And even though she'd always thought they had something special between them, comparing everything before to this was like comparing a candle to an out-of-control wildfire.

Thunder boomed overhead. Lightning lit up the house like broad daylight. But it barely registered in her mind. There was only room in her thoughts for Max and how he made her feel. She twisted against him, her tongue tangling with his, her fingers sliding down between them, eagerly working at the buttons on his shirt.

Groaning deep in his throat, he lifted her again, striding across the room to the big leather couch. He gently lowered her back onto the cushions, following her down, down until his delicious weight pressed against her. Every inch of her body was plastered to his, and it felt so good she stretched, rubbing the side of her calf against his hip as they kissed and kissed and kissed. It was as if they were trying to catch up on every moment they'd lost in the years they'd been apart. And neither of them could bear to stop long enough to shed a single item of clothing.

Desperate for more, she reached between them and fumbled with his belt. She managed to get his jeans unzipped, and then she slid her eager fingers inside. His entire body shivered as she filled her hands with him. He broke their kiss, gasping for breath, already rock hard, his hips jerking against her.

Then he was sliding his own hands down her body, and they were like two frantic teenagers all over again, working at each other's jeans, only managing to get half-undressed before he was poised at her entrance, pushing against her.

He swore and pulled back.

She wrapped her knees around him, trying to pull him down again.

He laughed, his harsh breath rasping against her ears. "Hold it. Just give me a second, sweetheart."

The sound of foil tearing jolted her out of the haze of passion enveloping her. A condom. Had he kept it in his pocket? That thought had her remembering the interns he'd dated and she stiffened beneath him. But then he was pressing against her again and all her jealousies evaporated beneath the need to have him inside her, filling her. She'd wanted this for so long, with him, and nothing was going to spoil it.

And then he was inside her, and it was even more wonderful than she'd remembered. Her body knew Max's, yearned for his, as if they'd been made for each other. Every thrust was met with an answering arch of her hips, heightening her pleasure, making his heart gallop faster in his chest where it pressed against hers.

He braced his forearms on the cushions, keeping the full weight of him from crushing her as he made love to her.

And she took full advantage of the space between them, sliding her hands up beneath his shirt, relearning his contours, every muscle, every dip. She wanted to slide down his body, taste him, stroke him. But that would have to wait. The delicious things he was doing to her, his clever fingers caressing her as he thrust inside her, were bowing her body back against the couch.

Panting, she drew her knees up on either side of him, twisting, arching, her fingers curling on the leather couch as she strained with him to reach that pinnacle of pleasure she knew was waiting for her.

He leaned down and captured her mouth with his, his back arched, his hips bucking against hers. And then, with one clever stroke of his body and his hand, she came undone in his arms, crying out his name as she exploded in a shower of ecstasy around him.

His powerful body thrust into her several more times, wrenching every last bit of pleasure from her that he could, all while he worshipped her mouth with his. Then he stiffened, his body spasming inside hers as his own climax washed over him. His fingers tightened on her bottom, clinging to her as he spent himself. And then, ever so slowly, like embers from fireworks floating to the ground, he lowered himself to the couch, turning with her in his arms.

They lay there, holding on to each other tightly, their hearts racing, breath coming out in harsh pants until their bodies began to cool and they could once again breathe without rasping.

She kissed the base of his throat, and he whispered romantic words in her ear, making her hot all over again. A few minutes later, he left her long enough to clean up. She should have gotten up, too. But she felt like her bones had turned to water and couldn't bring herself to do more than pull up her panties and jeans and collapse back onto the couch.

Then he was there, fully clothed again, like her, pulling her into his arms as he cradled her against his chest on the couch.

"I'll carry you into the bedroom when I get my strength back," he promised. Seconds later, he was softly snoring.

She smiled, then closed her eyes and joined him.

THUNDER BOOMED OVERHEAD, startling Bex out of a deep sleep. She jerked upright in the dark, confusion clouding her mind as she tried to remember where she was. Lightning streaked across the sky, illuminating the family room for a brief second. She let out a breath of surprise. She was on the couch. But Max wasn't with her. Had he gone to bed and left her there? No, as soon as that thought occurred to her, she pushed it away. He was probably in the bathroom, or maybe in the kitchen getting a late-night snack.

She swung her legs over the side of the couch and stood, expecting to see him standing on the other side of the island, maybe grabbing a couple of beers out of the refrigerator.

"Max?" She squinted in the dark. "Where are you?"

He didn't answer.

"Max?"

She felt her way through the house, checking the three bedrooms, yanking blinds open so the moonlight and lightning would help her see. One of the bedrooms was set up like an office. But she didn't find any sign of him. Worry began to coil in her stomach. She tried a light switch, but the house remained dark. The power was still out. Maybe he was in the garage, checking the fuses. Yes, that made sense. That's what she'd do if the power was out.

She hurried through the family room to the left side of the house, which boasted a powder room, a laundry room and a three-car garage. Lightning flashing through the glass panes in the garage door showed her that he had a Jeep parked inside. But there was no Max to be seen. Where else could he be?

Real fear began to gnaw at her. She ran back into the family room, turning in a wide circle.

"Max, where are you? This isn't funny. Max?"

Again, nothing.

Had he gone outside in this wretched storm? She couldn't think of any reason for him to do that. But maybe he liked watching the rain. Her mom always had. Yes, that was it. There was an enormous wraparound porch on the front and sides of the house. She ran to the door and jerked it open. The front porch was empty, except for some man-size rocking chairs on either end.

"Max," she yelled out into the yard. "Where are you?" The wind seemed to capture her words and snatch them away.

His truck remained parked just a few feet from the steps. Empty.

Panic had her fairly flying through the house again, checking every room, every closet, even looking beneath beds. Finally she stopped in the middle of his bedroom. She had to acknowledge what she'd been trying to avoid all along. He was gone. Something must have happened to him.

She couldn't fathom what that might be. All she was sure of was that he must be in danger. And she needed help to find him. She ran back into the main room and grabbed her purse to get her phone. But her phone wasn't there. She frowned. Had she left her phone at her mother's house? She couldn't remember the last time she'd seen it.

A landline. There had to be a landline in the house somewhere. No, she hadn't seen any phones either time she'd run through the house. What was she supposed to do now? Lightning lit up the back wall of windows again, illuminating the back deck. Could he be out there? It was the only place she hadn't looked.

She ran to the sliding door. The storm was getting worse, blowing rain in great sheets. She peered out at the darkness.

Thunder boomed overhead, and a brilliant flash of lightning lit up the deck before plunging everything into darkness. Wait, something was off. What had she seen? She leaned forward, peering in the moonlight. Part of the deck seemed charred. From the lightning? It flashed again, and she let out a startled scream. There was a large handprint on the glass. And it was covered in blood.

Chapter Twenty

Rain whipped at Max's face like dozens of icy-cold needles pricking his flesh. The ground was turning to mud, making the field treacherous and hard going. Lightning flashed overhead. He instinctively ducked down, not that it would have done him much good if the lightning had been close enough to hit him.

"Stop stalling. The cabin's straight ahead. Move."

He looked over his shoulder. The long bore of the rifle pointed steadily at him, but too far away for him to have any chance of knocking it down.

"Move," Marcia repeated, shouting to be heard above the storm.

"Drop the gun," he called out to her. "You haven't shot anyone yet. You can still get off without much jail time, maybe only probation."

She laughed bitterly. "I'm not going to jail. And if you want your girlfriend to live, you'd better get moving."

He clenched his fists but started forward again. Just ahead, the silhouette of a familiar cabin loomed in the dark. The same cabin he'd seen in dozens of crime-scene photographs, the one at the edge of the Caldwell property where it joined his father's, and now his, as well. The cabin where Bobby Caldwell had been killed ten years ago.

And now Max knew who'd killed him.

He stopped at the door and glanced back. "Now what?"

Marcia motioned with her rifle. "Go inside and shut the door behind you."

Something metallic flashed in the moonlight just over Marcia's shoulder. She stiffened, then very slowly raised her hands in the air. The person behind her yanked the rifle away and shoved her toward Max. Lightning flashed again, illuminating the man behind her.

Deacon Caldwell, holding a wicked-looking knife.

He shoved the knife into the top of his boot and straightened, the rifle pointed at Marcia now.

"You okay, Detective?" he called out.

Max looked at Marcia, who was glaring at Deacon.

"I'm fine," Max yelled back. "Thanks to you. Follow me back to my house and I can handcuff her and check on Bex." He grabbed Marcia's arm and yanked her toward Deacon.

When they reached him, Deacon was shaking his head. "Too far. This lightning's getting too dangerous to be outside. My house is much closer, and I've got a generator. We can call the police from there."

Another bolt of lightning struck close by, the thunder boom almost right on top of it. Sparks showered down from a nearby tree.

Max swore, the hairs on his arms standing up from the electricity in the air. "That was close. Where's your house? I thought you lived with your father?"

He motioned toward the trees on the other side of the cabin. "Straight through there. I had it built for when I got out of the military. Close enough to help my dad when he needs me but not so close that I give in to the urge to strangle him." He grinned. "You know how families can be." He waved at the cabin. "The roof's gone on that, no shelter there. My house is the only place that makes sense. Let's go."

He headed past Max, going at a fast clip toward the trees.

Max hesitated, looking up the hill that would lead him back to his house. He hated leaving Bex alone. If she woke up and saw the charred wood on the deck and his bloody handprint on the glass—both courtesy of Marcia's sick plan—she'd think the worst. What would she do then? Especially since Marcia had forced Max to take his and Bex's cell phones and toss them into the lake?

"He's waving at us," Marcia grumbled beside him, tugging at her arm to get him to let her go.

He tightened his grip. "Come on." He hurried after Deacon, pulling Marcia with him.

As soon as they rounded the copse, the lights from a two-story house came into view. Deacon was right, his house was much closer. He was standing on the porch already, waiting for them.

Max bounded up the steps, pulling Marcia with him. When he reached the top, he shook his head. "It's a monsoon. Can't believe we were out there in that."

Lightning flashed again, thunder cracking overhead.

"It'll play itself out soon if you believe the weatherman. Come on in. The mudroom's on the right. We can dry off there."

The three of them sloughed off the rain with a handful of towels as best they could, then they headed into the main room of the house.

Max directed Marcia to a chair beside the couch. "Sit down. Don't make me chase you. I'm mad as hell at you and won't take kindly to having to run out in that storm after you again."

She rolled her eyes and plopped down, crossing her arms and promptly ignoring both of them.

"Mad as a hatter," Deacon said.

Marcia glared at him, then turned away.

Max shook his head. "I don't think Marcia's insane. I think she knows exactly what she's doing. She must have planned this from the moment she saw Bex and me in town."

"What exactly did she do?" Deacon asked.

"Set my back deck on fire, for starters. I saw flames flickering outside and ran out to see what was going on, thinking lightning might have hit something close by. She was waiting right outside the sliding glass doors with her rifle. The rain put the flames out pretty quick and she poured a bottle of blood onto my hand and made me press it against the glass. Bex is going to think the worst if she wakes up and sees that."

"It was possum blood. But your girlfriend won't know that. She'll think you got hit by lightning and you're done for. It'll be nice for her to be scared for a change, for her to see how it feels to have someone you love die," Marcia said.

"That was your plan?" Max asked. "To kill me in that cabin? Like you killed Bobby?"

Her eyes widened. "I didn't kill Bobby. Bex did."

Was Deacon right? Had Marcia lost her sanity and convinced herself she hadn't done what was now obvious? He studied her carefully as he said, "Bex didn't kill Bobby."

"Oh, please. Everyone knows she did."

"I'm afraid that's my fault," Deacon said, sounding regretful. "I allowed everyone to think that for so long that after a while it seemed more like fact than conjecture."

Max grew very still and turned toward Deacon. "What are you talking about?"

The rifle in Deacon's hand lifted, pointing straight at Max's gut. "I think it will be better if I show you. Marcia, be a dear and get the DVD out from beneath the TV over there, the one on the bottom in the red case." He shrugged. "Red seemed only fitting. Makes it easy to find, too."

Marcia hesitated, looking confused.

The rifle swung toward her. "Hurry up," Deacon ordered. "Knowing dear old Dad, he'll make one of his men bring him over here to check on me in this storm. Not because he gives a damn but because the chosen one is long dead and I'm the only heir he has left." His mouth twisted in a sneer. "I'd rather have all of this over with before he does. It will be easier that way."

"What will be easier?" Max asked, taking a step toward the other man.

"Don't," Deacon said, aiming the rifle at him again. "I don't want to hurt anyone. Don't force my hand. All I want you to do is watch a movie. Marcia, if you please."

She pressed a button, and a black-and-white picture displayed on the TV. Max recognized it immediately.

"That's the interior of the cabin where your brother was killed."

"Yes, it is. Father is a bit obsessive about security. He has cameras all over the place. Imagine my surprise when I discovered he had one at the cabin. Thank goodness I was smart enough to look for it. This is the recording from that day. Oh, I have to warn you. Parts of it might be hard for you to watch, Max. And the end, Marcia, I guarantee you won't appreciate that part. But I'm looking forward to our little movie night. I've been wanting to set the record straight for some time now."

The door opened on the screen.

"Ah, here we go," Deacon said. "Too bad we don't have popcorn. Ah, well. It's not like I planned this for tonight. When I saw Marcia out skulking around the property, I had to act fast. But I'm rather good at making the best of a bad situation. You'll see."

Max clenched his fists at his sides as, on the screen, Bex entered the cabin. There was no sound. But he could see the puzzlement on her face as she looked around. And he could clearly read her lips as she apparently called out, "Max?"

"Isn't that sweet?" Deacon said. "She's looking for her lover, for Max. Marcia, you'll want to pay particularly close attention to this next part. You've convinced yourself that Bobby loved you, that he wasn't using you for sex every time he went after his primary target and failed. I mean, come on, Marcia. Did you really think Bex wanted Bobby? He was a slimeball. He stalked her for months. And every time someone saved her from his clutches, he'd run to you so he could pound out his frustration inside your body. That wasn't love, my dear. That was abuse. The man was sick."

Marcia stood off to the side, her face pale from both Deacon's words and the tableau playing out on the screen.

Max wasn't doing much better himself. He was sick to his stomach seeing Bobby surprise Bex in the cabin, then throw her to the floor, pawing at her and forcing her to suffer his groping hands all over her body. If Bobby Caldwell had been alive today, Max would be hard-pressed not to kill him himself.

"Turn it off," Max ordered.

"And miss the best part? I think not." He winced. "Oh, that had to hurt."

On the screen, Bex had just smashed a wine bottle against the side of Bobby's head. He dropped to the floor like a stone.

Marcia keened an animallike cry between her clenched teeth.

"Oh, good grief," Deacon said. "Even after seeing her supposed boyfriend trying to rape another woman, she's still upset over him getting hurt. You really need professional help, Marcia, love."

Max had a pretty good idea that Deacon was the one who needed professional help. All these years he'd thought

Bobby was the only crazy one. Apparently the crazy gene ran in the family.

As Bex ran out of the cabin on the TV, Max inched his way toward Deacon, very slowly so as not to draw his attention.

Deacon stared at the screen, his eyes lit with a half-mad light. "And now, folks. We've finally reached the good part."

Max looked at the screen. A man wearing a dark jacket with a hood over his head entered the cabin and bent over Bobby. He slapped Bobby's face several times. Bobby winced, then his eyes fluttered open.

"Ah, there, you see?" Deacon said. "Bex didn't kill my brother after all. That's what I wanted you both to know. Now watch very closely."

It didn't take long. The man in the cabin, with his back to the screen, was apparently arguing with Bobby. Bobby shoved him out of his way and headed for the door. The bat seemed to come out of nowhere, swinging right for the middle of Bobby's back. His body slammed against the door and plopped down onto his back on the floor, a trickle of blood dribbling out from the corner of his mouth. The bat slammed down again, this time on Bobby's stomach. Again and again it came down. Bobby raised his hands to protect himself and rolled over, trying to push himself up. The bat came down once more, twice, and then Bobby was still.

Max stared in horror at the screen. Marcia had covered her mouth with her hands. And then the hooded man turned around, looked directly up at the camera, and smiled.

The same smile Deacon Caldwell was giving Max.

"Now you know," he said, sounding as if they were discussing the best crops to plant next spring, his voice relaxed and upbeat.

They were in big trouble.

Max glanced at Marcia, then toward the French door

behind her. She gave him a subtle nod, letting him know she understood.

He took a step toward Deacon as the movie went to black-and-white snow before replaying on a loop. "Why did you keep that recording all these years? And why play it now?" He intentionally positioned himself to give Marcia the most cover, moving another step forward to hold Deacon's attention.

The rifle pointed straight at him. Deacon held it at hip level, both hands keeping it steady. "Not another step, Max. I just did you a favor. I saved your life out there."

"You did. And for that I'm grateful. But I'm not so sure you intend for me to live out the rest of this evening. Otherwise you wouldn't have played that movie."

"Well, yes. There is that. I might have lied just a bit about not wanting to hurt either of you," he conceded in a companionable voice. "It's been so hard keeping that secret all these years when all I ever wanted to do was brag to anyone who would listen that I'd finally erased that scumbag from the Earth. He was sick. I could tell you stories for days about the things he did. But it didn't matter. Not to our father. He knew how evil Bobby was. But he was the firstborn, the heir. So Daddy dearest did nothing, turned the other way. The only concession to Bobby's sick tendencies was that Dad hired all those security thugs to keep an eye on him. Not that they did much good. Bobby had his hands in Daddy's money already and he used it to grease the palms of the guys who worked for our father. Soon they were his cohorts, covering his tracks instead of stopping him. You know that better than anyone, Max. They must have beaten you up half a dozen times while you were trying to get Bobby to back off from Bex. You should be thanking me for killing him."

"I repeat, why save the recording?" Max asked.

"For Bex, of course. I like Bex. She was always good to

me back in school, even in middle school when I got teased and picked on so much, before I grew bigger and taller than the bullies and they became afraid of me. Before all that, Bex would take up for me, tell the bullies to leave me alone. Don't you remember the early years of middle school when the girls were taller than us, before we sprouted up? I do. Bex saved me from a lot of beatings back in the day. And I always regretted that I couldn't do more for her. Until Bobby. When I finally realized what he was doing, I vowed to figure out how to stop him once and for all. So I did. I saved Bex. And I cleaned up all the evidence of her having been there so your boss couldn't prosecute."

Max took another step toward Deacon, then stopped when the rifle raised to chest level. He put his hands in the air and wondered if Marcia was close enough to the door yet to make a run for it. "Easy, Deacon. I'm just trying to understand here. You saved Bex by killing Bobby, but then you let everyone think she was the one who killed him. Why?"

Deacon winced. "I hated that part Of course, I didn't want to go to prison. But I would have, if I had to. I saved that recording, and all of the evidence I took from the cabin, to use one day if I absolutely had to in order to keep her from being convicted. I would have sacrificed myself for her if it was necessary. You have to believe that. It's the only reason I saved such damning evidence."

He didn't know what to believe. But he played along. Why hadn't Marcia gone outside yet?

"I believe you," Max lied. "You were a good friend to Bex."

"Yes. I was."

"So what happens now?"

Deacon sighed. "Sadly, you and Marcia have to die. Neither of you will let Bobby's murder go. Ever since Bex came back to town, you've started digging, digging, digging. That has to stop. With you and Marcia gone, and my dad dying soon from the cancer, there won't be anyone left who cares enough to push for answers about Bobby's death."

Deacon's finger moved from the frame of the rifle to the trigger.

Max tried to stall him a little longer, inching closer. "Wait. I don't understand why you hired those gunmen— to grab Bex at the Piggly Wiggly? Or to scare her?"

Deacon shook his head. "Don't ask me. That was all dear old Dad's doing. Say a quick prayer, Max. Renounce your sins. Because you're about to meet your maker."

"What about the blood?" Max rushed to ask him, holding his hands in the air. "If killing me is supposed to make the investigation into Bobby's death go away, won't my blood all over your living room just start a new investigation and put you right back in the same situation?"

"Well, I do plan on cleaning up the mess," Deacon reasoned.

"You can't clean up blood completely, not good enough so that a CSI guy can't find traces of it. You need to kill me outside, in the rain."

Deacon moved his finger back to the frame of the gun. "I know you're just stalling for time. But you do have a point. I wasn't too worried about blood when Bobby died, since it was all his anyway. But you're right. Explaining your DNA in my home might prove to be a problem. Move." He motioned with the rifle toward the front door.

The French door behind Max finally swung open, slamming back against the wall in a burst of wind and rain.

Deacon's eyes widened and he stepped to the right, swinging the rifle toward the door.

Max lunged toward him, praying he was close enough to reach him as Deacon swung the rifle back toward him.

Bam!

Chapter Twenty-One

Bex froze, her sneakers squishing in the mud just outside the cabin that had haunted her nightmares for over a decade. She raised the butcher knife that she'd grabbed from Max's kitchen and turned in a full circle. Was that a gunshot she'd heard? Or had the lightning hit one of the trees close by?

Rain pelted her from above, no longer blowing in stinging sheets. The storm was easing, but she was still soaked and cringing every time lightning flashed across the sky. She started forward again, using the flashlight she'd discovered in a kitchen drawer. Too bad Max hadn't had a gun in the kitchen drawer, too. She could have searched his house for one. But she'd been too worried the rain would obliterate his trail and she wouldn't be able to find him if she waited any longer.

Twenty minutes later, her pathetic tracking skills that she'd learned as a Girl Scout too many years ago to count had brought her to this cabin. She shined the flashlight all around, hoping to see some sign of Max. She'd called his name over and over when she'd first started looking for him. But her voice was so hoarse now she didn't think she could scream if her life depended on it.

After testing the cabin's doorknob and finding it unlocked, she pushed it open, shining the light inside and holding her knife at the ready. But the one-room structure was obviously empty, and drenched and dirty from rain pelting through a hole in the roof. She whirled around and headed back to where she'd last seen a shoe print in the mud. Rain had already filled the print and was distorting its edges. She ran the light along the ground, weaving back and forth, searching for the next print. Nothing. Rain was running along the ground like a stream past the cabin, obliterating everything in its path.

She ran behind the cabin, shining her light all around. And then she saw it—another shoe print, heading toward the woods. Was it Max's? It seemed large enough to be but it was hard to tell. Not seeing any other prints nearby, and completely out of options, she started toward the trees.

MAX SLAMMED HIS FIST against Deacon's jaw. Deacon grunted in pain and rolled to the side. Max scrambled across the hardwood floor, reaching for the rifle that he'd knocked out of Deacon's hand earlier. Fingers circled around his ankle and yanked him backward.

He kicked his legs, slamming his boot into the side of Deacon's shoulder. Deacon let out a howl of pain and immediately let him go.

Max pushed himself up on his hands and knees and lunged for the rifle. He grabbed it, twisting around and bringing it up toward Deacon.

Except that Deacon was gone.

The sound of boots clomping across the porch outside the open French door had Max shoving to his feet and racing for the opening.

BEX HAD LOST the trail twenty feet from the cabin. But then she'd spotted a new trail, a recent trail. The pounding rain had distorted the prints so badly she could barely tell they were made by a human. But since any humans out in this storm had to either be Max or someone who could hopefully lead her to Max, she took off in pursuit. Jogging, head down, flashlight pointed at the ground so she wouldn't miss any of the rapidly disappearing prints, she hurried up an incline, faster and faster.

Wait. Incline? Weren't there cliffs around this area? She lifted her head and sucked in a breath at the black maw opening just ahead. She scrambled to stop her forward momentum, dropping to her knees in the mud at the cliff's edge. The knife flew out of her hands and disappeared over the side. Her feet slid in the muck, her momentum continuing to carry her toward the drop-off.

"Bex!"

She glanced over her shoulder to see Max running toward her. Her heart soared with relief that he was okay even as it swelled with panic as she slid toward the edge.

"Max!" She clawed desperately at the squishy ground.

He dived like a baseball player trying to steal first base, his hands outstretched. Her fingertips brushed against his, and then she fell into open air.

"BEX, NO!" MAX yelled her name, horrified, as her frightened, pale face disappeared over the cliff. He shoved to his knees, trying to find purchase in the slick mud. Digging his fingers around some tree roots embedded in the mire, he pulled himself just over the drop-off and looked down. "Bex? Bex?"

"I'm here."

Her voice sounded impossibly hoarse, but it was definitely her. He inched another half foot forward, and then he saw her, clinging to the side of the hill, the fingers of her left hand wrapped around tree roots protruding from the slick dirt.

"Hang on," he called down. "Don't let go."

"I'm slipping."

"Try to find a better handhold. There are roots all over the place. You might have to dig."

She punched at the dirt with her right hand. "I've got another root!"

"Good. Hold on. I'm coming to get you." How, he had no idea. But going over the edge wasn't an option. He'd pull the whole slick hillside down on top of both of them. He needed to go back down the hill and come up from beneath her, below the cliff face.

He half slid, half ran down the hill to circle around beneath the cliff. A shadow moved off to his right. He jerked his head around just as Deacon Caldwell slammed into him from the cover of trees.

Bex's LEFT FOOT slid off her foothold and cartwheeled her sideways. She let out a squeal of alarm and scrabbled for a new foothold. The root she was holding in her right hand started to move. It was pulling loose. Where was Max?

A muffled grunt was her answer. The sound of cursing, a shout. Max was in trouble. Whoever was after him must have found him again. What in the world was happening?

"Bexley, look up."

She did, and was shocked to see Marcia Knolls's face pale in the moonlight, looking over the edge at her. Bex was even more surprised to see a rope being lowered. The rope stopped at her waist. All she had to do was grab it. In theory. But this was Marcia, the same woman who'd hated Bex all her life. The same woman who'd shot a bullet through her car window just a few days ago.

"Grab it," Marcia yelled. "What are you, stupid? You're going to fall."

The root suddenly pulled free, and Bex automatically grabbed for the rope. To her relief, it held. She looked up at Marcia, who had both hands wrapped around the rope above.

"It's tied around my waist," she said. "I'm a lot bigger than you, and stronger. But you're still going to have to help. Try to climb up while I pull."

Bex slammed the toe of her sneaker against the wall of dirt until she made a deep enough gap to get a toehold. She tried to think of it like climbing a rock wall for exercise, only without the steep drop to almost-certain death below. Inch by inch, working as a team, she and Marcia managed to pull her all the way to the edge.

But Marcia didn't move to help her climb up.

"Marcia," Bex gasped. "Move back. I can't climb up with you right in front of me."

A slow, feral smile curved Marcia's lips. "I know. And the end of the rope isn't tied around my waist, either. All that's keeping you from falling to your death are two loops of rope around my wrist. Kind of makes you wish you were nicer to me in high school, doesn't it? Or that you'd kept your hands off my freaking boyfriend."

Bex stared at her in horror, seeing her own death mirrored in the other woman's black eyes.

MAX GRAPPLED IN the mud with Deacon, both of them fighting for control of the rifle. Sirens sounded in the distance, drawing ever closer.

Deacon's mouth contorted with rage. "Damn my father. He must have heard the gunshot and called the cops."

"Just let the gun go," Max gasped, straining against the man who outweighed him by a good thirty pounds, most of it muscle. "No one else has to get hurt." He wrenched one hand free and slammed it under Deacon's jaw.

Deacon fell back against the ground, cursing. Both men lost their grip on the gun. It went flying over their heads, landing somewhere near the tree line. Deacon got to his feet first, shoving himself toward the woods. Max punched him in the middle of his spine. A bloodcurdling scream filled the air and Deacon flipped onto his back, arching off the ground and whimpering like a dog that had been kicked in the ribs.

Max whirled around and sprinted toward the cliff to find Bex. His stomach clenched with dread when he saw Marcia on her knees at the edge, a rope wrapped around her left hand. Just beyond her, Bex clutched the other end of the rope with one hand, while clawing at the dirt with her other hand, desperately seeking a handhold.

The sirens stopped somewhere down the hill, back toward the cabin. But Max couldn't wait for backup. He slipped and slid on the muddy ground, using both his hands and his feet to make his way toward Marcia and Bex. Then moonlight reflected off what was lying on the ground beside Marcia.

A machete.

Shouts sounded from farther down the incline. Blue and red lights flashed. Deacon was coming after him. But Max couldn't waste even a second to turn around.

He half ran, half slid the last few yards toward Bex, watching with horror as Marcia raised the machete.

"No!" Max dived forward in a rolling slide, grabbing Bex's arms. He swung her up and over the cliff toward solid ground as the machete arced through the air.

Wind rushed beside Max and Bex as the wicked blade narrowly missed both of them. But without something to block her forward momentum, Marcia couldn't stop herself. She screamed as she plummeted over the side of the cliff. Then her scream was abruptly cut off.

Bex cried out in horror. "No, Marcia!"

They both carefully looked over the edge. Bex cried out again and closed her eyes.

Max pulled her to him, rocking her against his chest. "There was nothing we could do."

A guttural shout of rage sounded from down the hill.

Max jerked his head around just as near the tree line Deacon brought up his rifle, swinging it toward them.

Max shoved Bex to the ground, covering her body with his as the rifle boomed.

Everything went silent.

Even the thunder had stopped, and the rain had slowed to a gentle mist.

Max slowly lifted his head.

Deacon Caldwell lay in the mud twenty feet away, his sightless eyes staring up at the moon overhead. And behind him, standing with the aid of a cane, was his father. Holding a pistol. He stared a long moment at Max and Bex. Then his shoulders slumped and he slowly lowered the gun. Without a word, he dropped it in the mud and started hobbling back down the slope.

Bex pushed herself up on her elbows, her eyes wide and frightened. "What just happened?"

"Deacon's father saved our lives. I have no idea why."

She blinked as if she couldn't comprehend what he was saying. And then she covered her face with her hands and collapsed against him, great gasping sobs making her entire body shake.

"Ah, honey." Max scooped her up in his arms and rocked her against him.

The hillside erupted into chaos. Max's SWAT team descended upon them, securing the scene. Thornton started barking out orders. And soon a team of EMTs was racing up the hill.

Max didn't wait for them. He ran with his precious burden to a waiting ambulance.

Chapter Twenty-Two

Two months later...

Bex stood at the wall of glass, watching the season's first snowfall drift down onto Max's deck. This was her first day back in Destiny since she'd nearly fallen to her death off a cliff and Max was almost killed by the one Caldwell who'd ever shown Bex a kernel of kindness. She was still trying to come to terms with everything that had happened. But it was going to take a while.

Strong, warm arms wrapped around her waist and pulled her back against a solid, familiar chest. She wrapped her arms over Max's and sighed.

"I love you," she said.

"I know. You don't have to keep telling me that. I'm convinced."

"And?"

"And I love you, too." His voice was husky and deep with emotion.

She sighed again, happier than she'd ever thought she could be.

He kissed the side of her neck and gently swayed with her in his arms as they watched fall turn into winter right before their eyes.

"I never heard what happened to the cashier who helped that gang at the Piggly Wiggly," she said. "Reggie, right?"

"Thornton argued for her to be sent to a minimum security facility instead of doing hard time. She's finally getting the counseling she needs. Maybe without her ex-con father's influence, she'll turn her life around and not end up like him."

"That was awfully nice of your boss."

"He's not the ogre you think he is."

She shrugged, not quite ready to forgive. Although she was pretty sure she would one day soon.

"Is everything finally settled with Robert Caldwell Senior?" she asked.

"Mmm-hmm. He confessed to hiring the gunmen. He was convinced you'd killed his son. But after hearing the gunshot the night we were on the cliff, and driving out to his son's house and seeing that recording, he couldn't fool himself any longer. I guess we owe our lives to the fact that Deacon kept that recording. If his father hadn't seen it before tracking us, he might not have chosen to shoot Deacon. He'd probably have shot us."

She shivered, the memories of that night still capable of giving her nightmares. "What happens to Mr. Caldwell now?"

"Nothing. He's under hospice care. He probably won't live out the week. And I don't know about you, but I think he's suffered enough for his sins. Losing two sons, one by his own hand, has to be devastating."

"You feel sorry for him?"

"I suppose I do."

She squeezed his arms. "I'm not surprised. You're a good man. You care about people, whether they deserve it or not."

"If that's yet another way of apologizing or saying you aren't worthy of my love, knock it off."

He knew her so well. She turned her head to the side and rubbed her cheek against his chest. He rested his head on top of hers and they stood there a long time, content just to hold each other.

Finally, he said, "How did your assistant, Allison, take the news that you're taking an extended leave of absence from the antique shop to spend some time with me?"

She stiffened in his arms. "That's not exactly what I told her."

He stepped back and turned her around to face him. His brows were a dark slash of worry. "You've changed your mind?"

"I guess you could say that. I sold my store to her."

He couldn't have looked more surprised. "But I thought you loved restoring and selling antiques."

"I do. But I can do that anywhere. Like, say, in Destiny."

He grew very still, his eyes blazing at her with an intensity that had her whole body flushing hot.

"What are you saying, Bex?"

She slid her arms around his waist and tilted her head back to look at him. "I'm saying that with Bobby Caldwell's case finally closed, and nothing else hanging over my head, it's time that I rectified a terrible decision I made many years ago."

His throat worked, but no sound came out.

She cleared her own throat, already getting tight with emotion. "Max, I love you so much. I was wondering…"

"Yes?" he rasped.

"I was wondering if I could wear one of your T-shirts."

He blinked, then threw his head back and laughed, a great booming sound that filled her heart with joy. He grinned and scooped her up in his arms, then jogged through the house to his bedroom. He didn't stop until he was in front of the chest of drawers. Then he settled her against him, holding her with one arm as he yanked the top drawer open.

"Any particular T-shirt you prefer, Bexley Kane?"

She dipped her hand into the drawer and pulled out the black velvet box. "This one will do nicely."

He turned serious, cradling her against him as if he'd never let her go. His eyes darkened with more love than seemed possible for one person to hold in his heart for another. More love than Bex could ever hope to deserve. But she would happily spend the rest of her life trying, and loving him back even more.

"And I prefer to be called Mrs. Remington from this day forward, if you don't mind."

His mouth slowly lowered to hers, stopping inches away as he carried her toward the bed. "I don't mind, Mrs. Remington. I don't mind at all." And then he kissed her.

* * * * *

Look for more books in award-winning author
Lena Diaz's series
TENNESSEE SWAT, *coming soon.*

You'll find them wherever
Mills & Boon Intrigue books are sold!

MILLS & BOON®

INTRIGUE
Romantic Suspense

A SEDUCTIVE COMBINATION OF DANGER AND DESIRE

A sneak peek at next month's titles...

In stores from 9th March 2017:

- **Drury** – Delores Fossen *and*
  Sheik's Rule – Ryshia Kennie
- **Operation Nanny** – Paula Graves *and*
  Locked, Loaded and SEALed – Carol Ericson
- **Mountain Blizzard** – Cassie Miles *and*
  The Last McCullen – Rita Herron

Romantic Suspense

- **Colton Undercover** – Marie Ferrarella
- **Covert Kisses** – Jane Godman

Just can't wait?
Buy our books online before they hit the shops!
www.millsandboon.co.uk

Also available as eBooks.

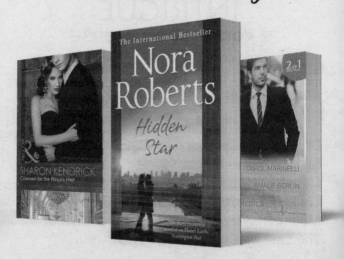

Join Britain's BIGGEST Romance Book Club

50% OFF your first parcel

- **EXCLUSIVE offers every month**
- **FREE delivery direct to your door**
- **NEVER MISS a title**
- **EARN Bonus Book points**

Call Customer Services
0844 844 1358*

or visit
...illsandboon.co.uk/subscriptions